Ted VerPlanck adored this nocturnal inventory. It was a ritual that calmed the millionaire art collector. No matter how harsh the world had become, a few square inches could always be contained in a gilded frame. Tonight, especially, Ted needed that comfort.

He walked to the wall niche and reached for the spotlight on the Sardonyx Cup but stopped, aghast.

The Sardonyx Cup was gone! The alcove was empty, and the pedestal was bare!

THE STOLEN CHALICE

"A roller-coaster ride of suspense, adventure, action, and glamour, speeding the reader to the most romantic spots in the world, full of fascinating facts, ingenious plots, and satisfying conclusions."

—Nancy Thayer, author of *Summer Breeze*

"Entertaining escapist fare."

—*Kirkus Reviews*

"Full of suspense and action . . . a fascinating read."

—*Night Owl Reviews*

"Let your minds drift in an adventure that will have you thinking."

—*The Reading Cafe*

THE EXPLORER'S CODE

"Masterful . . . sure to appeal to fans of Iris Johansen and Sandra Brown."

—*Booklist*

"Discovery, exploration, and real scientists . . . a merry chase through some of the most glamorous and sophisticated places in the world. I couldn't put it down."

—Paula Zahn, television host, *On the Case*, Investigation Discovery

"A whirlwind hunt from one exotic locale to the next . . . a storybook romance, odious and loathsome villains, Hollywood settings—it all works, providing a heady and highly engaging mix."

—*Publishers Weekly*

"What a page-turner! Kitty Pilgrim has turned her journalistic skills and keen understanding of the world to pen an exciting novel. . . . A wild ride to exotic places filled with greed, intrigue, suspense, and colorful characters—rich, beautiful people and villains worth hating."

—Miles O'Brien, science correspondent, *PBS NewsHour*

"Captivating characters, scientific intrigue, polar exploration, and romantic tension . . . a vivid and unforgettable novel."

—Christine Romans, CNN host and author of *Smart Is the New Rich*

ALSO BY KITTY PILGRIM

The Explorer's Code

KITTY PILGRIM

The Stolen Chalice

POCKET BOOKS

New York   London   Toronto   Sydney   New Delhi

Pocket Books
A Division of Simon & Schuster, Inc.
1230 Avenue of the Americas
New York, NY 10020

This book is a work of fiction. Any references to historical events, real people, or real places are used fictitiously. Other names, characters, places, and events are products of the author's imagination, and any resemblance to actual events or places or persons, living or dead, is entirely coincidental.

Copyright © 2012 by Kitty Pilgrim

All rights reserved, including the right to reproduce this book or portions thereof in any form whatsoever. For information, address Scribner Subsidiary Rights Department, 1230 Avenue of the Americas, New York, NY 10020.

First Pocket Books paperback edition July 2013

POCKET and colophon are registered trademarks of Simon & Schuster, Inc.

For information about special discounts for bulk purchases, please contact Simon & Schuster Special Sales at 1-866-506-1949 or business@simonandschuster.com.

The Simon & Schuster Speakers Bureau can bring authors to your live event. For more information or to book an event, contact the Simon & Schuster Speakers Bureau at 1-866-248-3049 or visit our website at www.simonspeakers.com.

Manufactured in the United States of America

10 9 8 7 6 5 4 3 2 1

ISBN 978-1-4391-9730-1
ISBN 978-1-4391-9740-0 (ebook)

To my mother, Nan

All men dream: but not equally. Those who dream by night in the dusty recesses of their minds wake in the day to find that it was vanity: but the dreamers of the day are dangerous men, for they may act their dream with open eyes, to make it possible.

—T. E. Lawrence, *Seven Pillars of Wisdom*

When the plague visits Egypt, it is generally in the spring; and the disease is most severe in the period of the Khamsin.

—Edward William Lane,
   An Account of the Manners and Customs of the Modern Egyptians, 1860

East Seventy-Seventh Street, New York

T HE BLACK MERCEDES CLS 550 stopped in front of the Mark Hotel on East Seventy-Seventh Street and the doorman rushed out to open the passenger door. In the fraction of a second it took John Sinclair to step out of the limousine, time collapsed. It had been five years since he last stood in this exact spot, but it seemed like yesterday, with one important difference—life had vastly improved, thanks to Cordelia Stapleton.

He turned to help Cordelia from the car, lacing his fingers through hers, as she surveyed the quiet Upper East Side neighborhood. The canopy of the Mark Hotel was before her, and golden, fan-shaped ginkgo leaves whirled down in the autumn breeze.

"I can't believe we're actually here!" she said, her green eyes lighting up with excitement.

"I know I put up some resistance about coming to this gala," Sinclair admitted, "but now I'm actually looking forward to it."

The Ancient Civilizations Ball was the most glamorous event of the fall social season. International celebrities and New York society people mingled with the elite of the art and antiquities world. Sinclair's attendance was sure to generate a buzz. He was a celebrated archaeologist and had discovered more ancient sites than anyone since Howard Carter, the legendary explorer who found King Tut's tomb.

As Sinclair entered the hotel, the desk manager looked up.

"Welcome back, Mr. Sinclair! So nice to see you again."

"How are you, Bernie? It's been entirely too long. I'd like you to meet Cordelia Stapleton."

"Miss Stapleton, delighted! No need to register, I have your information. What time would you like the hotel car to pick you up this evening?"

"Seven-thirty would be fine," Sinclair said, checking his watch.

The manager walked with them to the elevator, reached in, and punched the button for the tenth floor. As it ascended, Sinclair watched the lights—3, 4, 5—and then turned to Cordelia.

"I'm so glad you're here with me, Delia," he said, using her childhood nickname.

She gave him a look that lingered for another two floors. Then he moved decisively, pulling her toward him. She melted into his chest, pressing her cheek against his white shirt. He bent down and kissed her until the chime of the elevator registered in his brain and she pulled away.

"I'll get the bags settled and then we can continue our . . . conversation," Sinclair said as he followed the uniformed bellman into the bedroom of the suite.

Cordelia watched his broad shoulders retreat down the hall and turned to survey the living room—tastefully decorated in shades of pale gold. On the bar, an ice bucket held Veuve Clicquot and Badoit mineral water. Out the window, skyscrapers glowed silver against the evening sky.

"John, you should look at this view!" she called.

All was silent, only the air conditioner was whirring.

"John?"

No answer. She entered the bedroom and found Sinclair asleep, fully clothed. He was a gorgeous sight, stretched out in his elegant Savile Row suit. There was a formal stateliness to his position—flat on his back, arms at his sides—as if he were an ancient pharaoh lying on a bier. His face was still deeply tanned from the expedition to Egypt, a contrast to the white pillowcase. Sinclair had strong features, classically handsome, but with a rugged appearance that spoke of sun and sand, and a life spent outdoors.

Careful not to disturb him, Cordelia tiptoed over to her suitcase. The zipper made a tearing sound and he stirred.

"I drifted off," he said sleepily.

"Sorry, I need to hang up my dress."

Sinclair rolled on his side and propped his head up.

"Care to join me?" He patted the bed next to him. "I know a great cure for jet lag. You'll feel like a new woman."

His eyes were dancing, and a smile played around his lips.

"I'm so tired, I might not get up again," she demurred.

"What's that over there on the desk?" he asked.

Cordelia hung up her gown and then walked over to a huge vase of white lilies wrapped in glistening cellophane. She pulled off the card and read it aloud.

"Dear Delia, Have a great time at the gala. Love, Jim Gardiner."

"He really *does* spoil you," Sinclair observed.

"He always did," she agreed, walking toward the bathroom. "I think there's time for a nice soak before we go out."

The bath was palatial—a large, footed tub and his-and-her marble sinks.

"Ohhh . . . they have my favorite ginseng bubble bath!" she called back to him, seizing the Molton Brown bottle.

"Is that tub big enough for two?" she heard him ask from the bedroom.

"Of course."

She turned on the tap, undressed, pinned up her hair, and slipped in, feeling the warm water slide over her limbs. Sinclair appeared in the doorway, holding the bottle of champagne and two flute glasses. His tie was pulled loose and his shoes were off.

"May I join you?"

Long Island City, Queens, New York

THE WORKING-CLASS NEIGHBORHOOD was a few miles away from the gleaming luxury of Manhattan. Decades ago this had been a respectable place to live. Now the family row houses were dilapidated and streaked with grime, and vacant lots were interspersed with industrial warehouses.

Vojtech threw his cigarette to the curb, picked up his bag, and walked over to the dented steel door of Fantastic Fetes.

"You're late!" the catering manager yelled at him. "You were supposed to be in the van five minutes ago!"

The manager's florid neck undulated with rage.

Vojtech felt the cold metal grip of his pistol in his canvas coat. As he pulled the weapon out, it caught on the pocket. He tugged the barrel free and pointed it at the catering manager.

His hand shook a bit. But the boss didn't see that—his eyes were on the gun, bulging with fear.

Vojtech squeezed the trigger. The recoil was as satisfying as sexual release. The bullet entered the man's open mouth at an angle, severing the carotid artery. A pinkish mist flecked the wall where the bullet had passed through his throat. Then blood spurted out, spraying sticky red.

Vojtech watched fascinated at the way the blood pooled on the steel counter and ran off in rivulets to the floor. Bright red. A faint copper scent permeated the room.

"Didn't you hear me?" the man shouted at him again. "Don't just stand there staring at me. Get going . . ."

Vojtech quelled his fantasy. The pistol was not in his hand or pocket. It was still in his duffel bag on the floor.

"Sorry." Vojtech ducked his head.

"Cut the bullshit! Find your jacket and get your ass into the truck. They're waiting for you."

Vojtech shuffled out, carrying his nylon bag. He went to the laundry room and selected a medium-size waiter's jacket and a white shirt encased in dry cleaner's plastic. Fantastic Fetes always insisted on sartorial perfection. The only items Vojtech had to supply were dark pants and black shoes. He carried them in his duffel along with the pistol.

He picked up his bag and went out to the parking lot to join the other waiters, sitting down between Juan and Jose. On the opposite bench were Vlad, Chongli, and Miguel. They all glared at him. Jumpy as cats—none of them were legal.

The truck took off as soon as he climbed in. He checked his watch. In forty-five minutes they'd be standing in the catering kitchen at the Metropolitan Museum, and everything would be in place for the attack.

1010 Fifth Avenue, New York

I N HIS PENTHOUSE apartment, Theodore Stuart Ver-
Planck parted the drapes and looked across the street at
the Metropolitan Museum of Art. The neoclassical facade
was lit up, the pale columns glowing against the darkening
sky. A red carpet flowed down the broad steps. Huge silk
banners rippled in the wind for tonight's gala: ANCIENT
CIVILIZATIONS—ART—WAR—CULTURE.

He watched a convoy of television satellite trucks and
news vans pull up to the curb. The entrance to the museum would soon be cluttered with camera crews preparing to report on "the event of the season." As co-chairman
of the gala, VerPlanck had spent considerable time and
energy making sure tonight would be a success.

The First Lady of the United States was the guest of
honor. But the tabloids were more interested in Lady Xandra Sommerset, or Lady X, as they called her—a British
royal and an international party girl.

"Is there anything else, sir?"

VerPlanck dropped the heavy damask curtain back
into place and turned to see his butler hovering in the
doorway.

"No, thank you. I'll be leaving shortly."

"Very good, sir. I've already locked the doors to the
terrace."

"Have a pleasant evening, Clark."

The butler noiselessly shut the library door. VerPlanck looked out the window again. A long line of black limos had formed on Fifth Avenue, discharging passengers in front of the Met. The gala was starting.

VerPlanck's wife, Tipper, had promised to be back by seven, but she was still at a cocktail party downtown. Apparently Tribeca was her new Mecca—she spent all her time there.

He adjusted his cufflinks and glanced down at subtly etched initials—TSV—Theodore Stuart VerPlanck. The Dutch VerPlancks were one of the oldest families in America, setting foot on American soil in 1632. But Tipper had turned the family name into a public joke.

She was a tabloid disaster, constantly in the gossip pages. It had taken years for Ted to admit that his wife was addicted to drugs and alcohol. He had done everything he could, even accompanying her to a fancy rehabilitation clinic.

Six months ago, with bloodshot eyes, she had promised him she was finished with drugs. She would live a more respectable life. And now she was late for the most important gala of the season.

15 Desbrosses Street, Tribeca, New York

TIPPER VERPLANCK TOOK a sip of her San Pellegrino and looked around the cocktail party celebrating Conrad's movie release. The überstylish loft took up the entire floor of an old factory building. The apartment had been decorated with a simplicity that telegraphed enormous expense—black leather couches, a slate floor strewn with colorful antique kilim rugs.

Conrad was slouching against the enormous picture window, holding a cigarette away from his body as if to avoid the fumes. Tipper watched him take a drag, barely inhaling. It was totally preposterous to smoke like that—as if you didn't like it.

Several admirers were grouped around him talking about *Samurai Princess,* his directorial triumph. Conrad, clad in black jeans and red suede skateboard shoes, played the sensitive artist well.

This was the place to be tonight, and not that dreary gala uptown at the Met. But she couldn't stay. Tipper walked over and slid her hand around his waist. Conrad put his lips to her ear and spoke seductively.

"Don't go, Tipper."

She could feel his breath on her skin.

"Connie, I have to."

"Nobody will miss you."

He looked at her with a smoldering gaze.

"*My husband* would miss me. We're seated with the First Lady, and I promised I'd be on time."

Brooklyn Museum of Art, Brooklyn

IN THE CONSERVATION wing of the museum, the large worktables were covered with muslin to protect the artifacts that were undergoing repair. This evening, most of the museum staff had already left. Only the corner office was brightly lit.

Carter Wallace paused in Dr. Hollis Graham's doorway to observe her. The electronic glow of the computer screen highlighted her blond hair. It was so late! Shouldn't she be home, getting dressed for the Met gala?

"Holly, what are you doing still sitting here?"

Startled, she looked up at him.

"Oh, Carter, come on in and take a look at this."

He ambled in and leaned over her shoulder.

The black-and-white image on the computer screen was clearly a human form. To a layman, it would appear to be a medical X-ray. But an Egyptologist would know this was a computer-aided tomography (CAT) scan of a mummy. Every bone of the desiccated corpse was visible.

"What's this dark patch?" Carter asked, pointing to a shadowy area on the skull.

"It's *clearly* a fissure," Holly noted. "Except look here, the opening is larger at the top."

"So what do you figure happened?"

"I don't know, but I'd hate to think someone *killed* him."

She leaned back in her chair and pulled out the

number pencil she had wound into her chignon. Her hair tumbled in gorgeous disarray. Carter's breath caught in his throat. She had absolutely no idea of the effect she had on him.

"Anything else you want to show me?" Carter asked, forcing himself to look back at the computer screen.

Holly advanced to an image of the casket. The stucco casing of the coffin was painted deep red, with gold details. This was a rare "red shroud" mummy. His bandages had been infused with a lead-based red pigment, favored by people of high rank during the Roman occupation of Egypt.

"Roman period?" Carter asked.

It was an easy guess. The exterior of the coffin had a portrait of the deceased attached to it, typical of that period.

"Yes, Fayoum region. Isn't he beautiful?"

Holly moved the mouse, and the arrow traveled across the encaustic painted face, zooming in on the eyes of the young man. He was ruggedly handsome, with a head of black curls and a gold-leaf laurel crown on his head.

"Artemidorus," Carter read the Greek lettering, painted in gold across the stucco casing of the coffin.

"He's on loan from the British Museum."

"Yeah, I figured. I never saw him downstairs."

Carter knew every mummy in the climate-controlled vault. Their coffins were aligned in rows, like patients in hospital beds, painted eyes staring up at the ceiling. A real cross section of Egyptian-Roman society—young men, matrons, officials, and even children.

"Do the Brits know the skull is damaged?" Carter asked.

"No. We just found out. I *hate* to tell them. I feel . . . like it's somehow my fault."

Carter laughed.

"No need to go all maternal on us. His skull was cracked a couple of *centuries* ago."

Carter looked at his watch.

"Say, aren't you going to the Met gala tonight?"

She turned and looked out the darkened window. The streetlights were on.

"Oh, my gosh!"

"You'd better get a move on," he said, starting toward the door. "I'll see you there. I think our table is thirty-five."

"I hope I get there in time. Traffic is going to be a nightmare with the First Lady coming."

The Mark Hotel, East Seventy-Seventh Street, New York

JOHN SINCLAIR KNOTTED his black silk necktie and smoothed it down under his collar. Most of the time he wore his clothes with casual indifference, but tonight, with Cordelia on his arm, he had made a special effort.

For the black-tie gala, he was breaking tradition by *not* wearing a conventional tuxedo and bow tie but, rather, a black velvet dinner jacket. Sinclair, with his lean, six-foot-four-inch physique, carried it off with the confidence that comes to a man who spends his time in the natural elements.

Sinclair had rejected the traditional patent-leather shoes that were normally worn with a tuxedo. Again, he went with something simple—black calfskin slip-ons made by Adriano Stefanelli, the same cobbler who supplied the Holy See with red shoes for the pope.

As a last touch, he fastened on the black crocodile band of a 24k dress watch. The wafer-thin timepiece was a legacy from his father, the founder of the global financial firm Sinclair International. That watch was the only thing of value Sinclair had ever accepted from his family. It served to remind him of how precious time was, and how important it was to live his *own* life.

Sinclair checked the length of his cuffs in the mirror.

Tonight was going to be interesting. He hadn't gone to one of these New York social events in quite some time. Life had been rough over the last fifteen years—first the death of his wife, then his estrangement from his parents and the move to Europe. Hopefully by now the New York crowd had forgotten the past. *He* was ready for the future.

Cordelia came to him in the mirror.

"John Sinclair," she said with a smile. "I do believe you were preening just now."

He turned to face her.

"Of course I was. I need to look my best if I am going to escort the prettiest girl to the ball. Shall we go?"

Metropolitan Museum of Art, New York

T HE METROPOLITAN MUSEUM chief of security couldn't take his eyes off a wall of monitors. After a thirty-year career as an NYPD cop, he *knew* when something was wrong—like tonight.

But nothing turned up on the scans. A collection of fifty video screens rotated live pictures of all the rooms in the museum. He could also see heat-sensor silhouettes of the guards doing a last-minute security sweep.

During the evening, some galleries would be monitored only electronically. To hell with the Picassos! All manpower would be needed for protecting the First Lady. And she'd be moving among a crowd of a thousand people.

The Feds were supposed to help. All week the Secret Service and Immigration and Customs Enforcement had been collecting the Social Security numbers of the museum staff, checking for any criminal convictions. They had turned up a museum guard who had overstayed a visa from twenty years ago. Ridiculous! With all the *real* terrorist threats in this city, why were they wasting their time on some perfectly respectable Polish guy with three kids?

There was only one obvious flaw in the whole security setup for this evening. For the price of a thousand bucks, a terrorist could gain access to the First Lady simply by *buying* a ticket to the gala.

Vojtech tried to delay getting out of the van as long as possible. The other waiters pushed past him, trailing their plastic-covered jackets. He finally stepped out and followed them as they made their way to the side entrance of the museum.

As he trudged along, Vojtech looked up at the imposing facade of the Met—a bastion of wealth and privilege. Even the traffic on Fifth Avenue appeared to be slowing down to pay respects.

He started to sweat, thinking about their plan. It was like acting in a play, and the performance was about to begin. The organization Common Dream had been planning to do something like this for months, yet nothing had happened. Their leader, Moustaffa, kept urging patience. But Vojtech had decided to take things into his own hands.

Why should they wait? Tonight he and two others would go ahead. It was important to prove that they were not passive. They were warriors.

Vojtech stood nervously at the side entrance of the museum for an identity check. In front of him, a line of waiters and waitresses snaked out to the sidewalk as a uniformed museum security officer marked off names on a clipboard. With the cocktail hour approaching, everyone needed to get in quickly.

Here at the service door there was no dog to detect anything in Vojtech's duffel bag. The police had posted their K-9 unit—dogs trained to detect explosives or ammunition—at the main entrance. The door also didn't have an X-ray machine to check bags. Everyone entering here had been preregistered. This was going to be only a quick, perfunctory verification of ID.

A week ago, each caterer, florist, and service provider had given the authorities the names, Social Security numbers, addresses, and descriptions of their workers. Vojtech's employer, Fantastic Fetes, had exhausted the ranks of its own family members in providing ID data for all its illegal workers.

"Name and last four digits of your Social?" the guard said to Juan.

"Salvio Manucci, 8256."

"Next?" the security guard said to Vojtech.

Vojtech pointed to the name he had been assigned—Mario Manucci.

"7761," he said.

The guard marked off his name without looking up.

Carlyle Hotel, New York

GAZING OUT THE window in her suite, Lady Xandra Sommerset noticed that traffic on Madison Avenue was at a standstill. It was much too early to leave; her wristwatch showed only 7:30 p.m.

She was planning to pull up to the curb several minutes *after* the other arrivals. That way, the TV crews could record her grand entrance—solo and dressed to kill.

Restless, Xandra slunk back across the suite and sank into an armchair. She untied the sash of her emerald green robe, allowing it to fall open. Underneath she was naked. Since childhood, her favorite outfit had been her birthday suit. The feel of fabric on her skin had always been irritating. Moustaffa once remarked that making her wear clothes was like dressing up a wild animal.

Xandra punched a button on her cell phone and someone immediately answered on the other end.

"Are you ready?" she asked.

"Good. Wait until activity is at its busiest, then go in," she instructed.

She stayed on the line for a moment more.

"Very well, good luck."

She pressed the disconnect button and began to pace, her silk robe billowing behind. Her eyes fell on the pale green box of Ladurée macarons on the sideboard. The French confections were her favorites, delivered that afternoon from the shop on Madison Avenue. Xandra pulled off the lid, selected a pale green pistachio meringue, and bit into the crust, releasing ganache onto her tongue. It was heaven! She dropped the rest of it into her mouth and chewed, looking at her reflection in the mirror.

A large pair of topaz gold eyes gazed back at her, heavy-lidded and tilted up slightly at the corners—the eyes of a lion. At least, that's what her lovers always told her. When people noticed her eyes, she would lower her lids and blink at them slowly. Men would just stare, mouths agape. It was her favorite seduction trick.

Lady Xandra ran her hands through her dark hair, holding the strands this way and that. Was it too late to call the hotel salon and have someone come and arrange it in an elegant upsweep? She should have thought of that sooner. But there had been other things to plan.

She walked to the closet and took out a gown that resembled a *kalasiris*—the long, formfitting ankle-length dress worn by women in ancient Egypt. In most tomb depictions, the garments were white. Her modern version was red pleated silk, with rows of gold beading around the neckline. Nobody else would have anything like it.

Tonight, she would also flaunt the stuffy conventions of the Fifth Avenue crowd in another way. Underneath the dress, she would not wear anything.

Half an hour later, Lady Xandra Sommerset picked up her evening bag—inside were a comb, lipstick, cell phone, and small pocket mirror. She couldn't risk taking the pistol with her. They'd be screening purses at the door.

Just as she was about to leave, the phone rang.

She opened the bag and looked at the number. It was Moustaffa.

"Xandra, there's a problem."

"No. Everything's all set."

"Listen to me! They are going ahead with an attack plan of their own, instead of waiting for the one we have in place for Egypt."

"Who would do that?"

"It's Vojtech and two others," Moustaffa said. "I've seen veiled references to it on the Internet."

"That's just talk. They ramble on like that all the time."

"Well, it's drawing attention."

"They'd never dare act on their own. Besides, everyone in the organization knows Egypt is in three weeks."

"But a reliable source told me they are planning something *tonight,* to prove themselves."

Xandra paused to think, smoothing her eyebrow in the mirror.

"Vojtech always was a little wild," she agreed. "But I don't think he would have the nerve to preempt your plan."

"I hope you're right. If they take things into their own hands, they'll screw everything up."

"What can I do?"

"Keep your eyes open. If anything happens, just remember to get out quickly."

"Moustaffa, once we have the art, I'm gone."

"Good. Just put in an appearance, and then get out of there as fast as you can."

Metropolitan Museum of Art

HOLLYWOOD-STYLE KLIEG LIGHTS scanned the night sky, and a red carpet ran up the steps to the columned portals of the museum. Several couples were making their way up as camera flashes went off all around them.

Cordelia and Sinclair got out of their limo and paused on the sidewalk.

"Can you believe this?" Cordelia asked, staring up at the billowing white-and-gold banners. "It's incredible!"

Sinclair reached over and took her hand, his grasp warm and strong. He looked wonderful tonight, certainly as debonair as when she met him last year in Monaco. Cordelia hoped she was carrying off her floor-length strapless chiffon gown with equal style.

"Do I look all right?"

He turned to look at her, his expression astonished.

"What do you mean? You're *beautiful*!"

"Well, I just spent the last four months in Egypt, roughing it. I feel like there's still sand in my hair."

Sinclair's eyes traveled down her form, surveyed the deep red gown.

"You look like a goddess."

She smiled. Typically, comparisons to Greek and Roman deities were his highest compliments.

"Shall we?" Sinclair started to ascend the steps. A

wall of flashbulbs erupted. Reporters and photographers started shouting.

"*Look this way!*"

"*Over here, miss . . . over here!*"

A bright flash lit up the night, blinding Cordelia. There was a solid wall of lenses all the way up to the door.

"I can't believe how many reporters there are," she said, hesitating on the first step.

"Just look straight ahead and smile," Sinclair coached. "And don't stop until you hit the top."

Sinclair slowed his pace to accommodate Cordelia's high heels. Her nervousness was apparent from the tight grip on his hand. The press were at it again, snapping away over on the other side of the black velvet cordon. It had been almost a year since he had faced their lenses in Europe.

Of course, that romance with Shari was an embarrassment now—but who could resist a gorgeous supermodel? They had been photographed constantly. The affair had ended in disaster. It was over, and he'd broken up with Shari, blaming the whole thing on high testosterone and bad judgment.

He had met Cordelia on the rebound. Who knew what fates had thrown her into his path, but it was the best thing that had ever happened to him. And he was eternally grateful to be here tonight, holding her hand as they climbed the steps of the Met.

He turned and looked at her. That flimsy gown she was wearing was beyond sexy. The pure silk chiffon flowed down the lines of her willowy body and billowed out behind her in the breeze. As he went up the stairs, he pictured the two of them later this evening, when they returned to the hotel, and that put a spring in his step.

Dr. Holly Graham took a sip of her champagne and surveyed the fashionable crowd in the Greek and Roman Gallery. The Met invitation asked that women limit their choice of color to "Roman Legion red" or "Classical Greek white." Everyone seemed to have gone for shades of crimson, but she wore white.

"Holly!"

She turned and saw Carter Wallace over the heads of the guests. Was it only an hour and a half ago that they had pored over the CAT scans of a mummy in her office? This was not the shaggy young Egyptologist she knew. His evening clothes were a vast improvement over that wooly Harris tweed blazer.

Objectively, most people might think Carter was handsome. He had broad shoulders and the strength of a former college football star. Usually that type didn't appeal to her, but tonight he was transformed.

"Carter, I barely recognized you," she teased.

"You look pretty glamorous yourself. . . . And as beautiful as ever."

Nice compliment, but he couldn't possibly mean it. Holly was too old for him by at least a decade. She didn't kid herself. Her looks were fading. Fine lines were appearing around her eyes and her hair was turning darker.

In one way, maturity was good. Her appearance had

often been a distraction to the men around her, especially when she was trying to establish her bona fides as a serious scholar.

She glanced around and her spirits rallied. Carter wasn't exactly her idea of a hot date, but an evening like this didn't come along very often—the champagne was flowing like water.

"Kind of a snazzy crowd, don't you think?" she observed.

"It's definitely above my pay grade," he agreed, taking a flute from a passing tray. He smiled at her as he raised it.

"Cheers!"

Dr. Carter Wallace watched Holly over the rim of his champagne glass. My God, she looked like a movie star tonight. He had suffered a raging crush on her for five years now. Although he dated other people, Holly was definitely his main fantasy.

That cool sophistication was irresistible. His pulse quickened whenever she was around. His feelings were not reciprocated, however. She had always relegated him to the status of junior colleague.

It was clear that she was conscious of their age difference. The tone of voice she used to address him could be condescending *and* infuriating.

It didn't dissuade him, however. Most afternoons, he'd find an excuse to drop by her office. Sometimes he'd catch her eating her sandwich at her desk, a pencil stuck through her chignon, glasses halfway down her nose. He'd ask her questions to prolong the visit, and no matter how obscure the query was she always had a detailed and flawless answer. Inevitably, as she talked, his mind would drift, and he would start thinking about what it would be like to take her glasses off and lean over and kiss her.

Holly had a mind like a computer . . . and the full figure of a Greek goddess, especially tonight in that white dress. The graceful folds of the fabric had the simplicity of the classical statues all around her. The red lipstick was a nice touch. He had never seen her dressed up before. She really camouflaged her body in those cable-knit cardigans and slacks, but if she didn't half the leches in the museum would be after her.

Including him. Not that *he* was a lech. His intentions were honorable. He just wanted . . . well, a respectable dinner date for a start. Not much to ask, was it?

Carter looked around. The gala was so crowded the waiters could barely navigate with their trays. He'd play it cool during cocktails and wait until dinner to lay on the charm. Then, during the dancing, he was planning on sweeping her off her feet.

Vojtech passed through the Roman Gallery with a tray of stuffed grape leaves. He was invisible. As a waiter, he was merely an hors d'oeuvre opportunity for the guests.

He had an enormous sense of calm after speaking to the others and reviewing the timetable. Two other waiters were going to join him during the dessert course. And together the three of them would execute the plan.

The Metropolitan gala was on the main floor, but the galleries upstairs were closed to the public. Charlie Hannifin climbed the empty service stairs to the American Painting section. The room was empty.

He pulled on a pair of latex gloves and took a strobe out of his pocket. He needed to land the puck-size device squarely in the center of the gallery to trigger the alarm. If he overshot, he couldn't retrieve it or he would show up on the heat/motion sensors.

This called for a gentle lob. He took two steps back in the stairwell to give the toss some momentum, swung underhand, and then let it go. The spherical strobe arced through the air, landed, and rolled as slowly as a golf ball on the last green of the Masters Tournament. Right in the middle. Perfect. In ten minutes the alarm would go off.

Charlie peeled off the latex gloves and stuck them in the pocket of his tuxedo—he'd flush them down the toilet later. Right now he needed to get out of here. He quickly bolted down the interior stairwell and stepped out to the main lobby.

Two guards approached. Charlie flashed his gold-and-red security chit, but the board of directors lapel pin gave him the right to be anywhere on the premises.

"Everything all right, sir?" one of them asked.

"The elevator was busy, I had to take the stairs," Charlie explained.

"It's filled with cops," the museum guard informed him.

"I'd rather have *you* guarding the paintings," Charlie told them.

"Why's that?"

"Those Nineteenth Precinct boys wouldn't know a Pissarro from a pepperoni pizza."

The guards smirked.

"Have a good night," Charlie said. "Keep up the good work."

"Yes, sir."

1010 Fifth Avenue

TED VERPLANCK WALKED through his penthouse securing window fastenings and testing the brass handles on the French doors. It was better to keep the alarm system turned off. In all likelihood, Tipper would rush in to get dressed and would trigger it by accident. Then he'd have to spend half the night on the phone. Why was it that she could never get the hang of the security code?

As he walked through the living room, all the paintings glowed. Later this evening he would indulge in his cherished nocturnal ritual of enjoying each masterpiece as he shut off the lights.

His most prized possession, the famous Sardonyx Cup, was in a small alcove in the living room. He paused briefly to look at it. The cup had been carved from a single piece of the mineral sardonyx. Of all the precious stones, rust-colored sardonyx was the most prized in ancient Egypt—even more valuable than gold or silver; it was believed to have mystical powers that could eliminate evil forces.

Fragile and carved to a thinness that made it nearly transparent, the Sardonyx Cup had started as an Egyptian drinking vessel. Later, in medieval France, it had been turned into a gold chalice.

Over the ages, the Sardonyx Cup had generated a cult-like following. Both princes and popes had held it in their hands. A mere sip of communion wine from the cup at Mass was said to cure any disease.

A legend began. Most early Egyptian artifacts seemed to have curses attached to them. But this cup was considered a talisman, and bestowed great blessing on its owners.

That was why Ted VerPlanck cherished it. If the cup stayed right here in its niche in the living room, he believed nothing bad would ever happen to him.

Metropolitan Museum of Art

THE STEPS LEADING up to the museum were empty. All the cameramen were inside their TV vans, hunkered over their Subway sandwiches. It was time to chow down and kick back until the gala was over.

The reporter for *Extravaganza Tonight* was still on the sidewalk, rolling up his microphone cord. Disappointing. It looked like Lady X was a no-show, but this wasn't the first time that the rumor of her attendance had proved to be false.

Out of the corner of his eye, he saw a lone figure sprinting across Fifth Avenue. It was the billionaire art collector Theodore Stuart VerPlanck. The famous mogul was late. VerPlanck hit the top step without a pause. Damn, that guy kept himself fit! At fifty-two, he had the spring of a twenty-year-old.

So where was the lovely *Mrs.* VerPlanck? Tipper was a lush and a pill popper. Ted defended his wife, insisting that her stint in Betty Ford had cleared up all that. But this reporter wasn't buying it. He'd bet his press badge that Tipper had fallen off the wagon again.

Ted VerPlanck disappeared into the museum. That was probably the last arrival for the evening. Around midnight the camera crews would reassemble on the steps to catch the people leaving. What a dog's life. Just once he'd like to drink the bubbly with the swells.

Another black sedan turned the corner onto Fifth and slowly pulled up to the curb. It wasn't a hired town car but, rather, a chauffeur-driven sedan—a Maybach. This was *someone*.

"Tony, get this one on tape, pronto!" The videographer lifted the camera to his shoulder as he went.

Sure enough, a long, tanned leg emerged from the car, wearing a high-heeled gold sandal. Then a beautiful mane of hair appeared, followed by a bloodred dress. The reporter gasped in amazement when he realized who was getting out.

"Holy shit! It's Lady X!"

This was the money shot—and brother, did she look like a million bucks tonight.

Lady X was fascinating. Her beauty came from her Egyptian mother. Her vast fortune came from her father—a British businessman who had the Midas touch with fish and chips. The Chippy's logo, a jolly walrus, was an instantly recognizable road sign all over the United Kingdom, Australia, and New Zealand. But in every fancy school she attended, Xandra had been made well aware that *nothing* was more common than fish and chips.

Then, in a social coup, Xandra had married Lord Sommerset, a cousin to the queen. His first wife had died while producing an heir. With the succession assured, the elderly Lord Sommerset was free to marry whomever he chose.

Xandra became his adored second wife. They were a surprisingly happy couple. British aristocracy was forced to turn a blind eye to what they considered to be Xandra's mongrel pedigree. Secure in her position in society, Lady X was free to flaunt the conventions of the upper classes. She did so with a vengeance.

The tabloids loved her. She became their bankable celebrity. Every newspaper sold out if they put Xandra on the cover. Tonight, if rumors were correct, Xandra would be seated across from the First Lady of the United States.

"Lady X, this way please," the reporter called.

She turned to look and slowly blinked her enormous amber eyes.

At the south side of the museum, two uniformed NYPD officers walked up to the employees' entrance. They were each carrying New York deli cups and paper bags with bagels. They flashed their badges through the window and the guard buzzed them in.

"Thanks a lot. We went out for coffee."

"Yeah, I packed a sandwich," said the security guard. "This thing won't be over until midnight."

"Well, hang in there."

The four Secret Service agents didn't deign to join in the chatter. Their eyes were glued to the glass-paneled door, as if waiting for an ambush.

The two cops drifted away, not speaking until they were out of earshot.

"Well, that was easy."

"The more hectic things are, the easier it is."

"How so?"

"On a night like this, nobody looks at two cops in plain sight. We're part of the scenery."

Security Chief Tom McCarthy stared at the monitor. It was eight-thirty and the fire alarm was going off in the Portrait Gallery of the American Wing.

"Come with me," he said to his computer guy. Yanni was not much backup, but nobody else was available.

McCarthy walked rapidly through the grand lobby and heaved his bulk up the grand staircase to the European and American Painting galleries. This area was off-limits and surveillance was by electronic camera only.

Sprinting through the labyrinth of corridors, McCarthy knew every hallway, every exhibit. He barreled into Room 14. The silent red bulbs of the fire alarm were flashing, tingeing the priceless paintings with a rosy tone.

But nothing was amiss. All the canvases on the walls were intact: the stately colonial portraits by Gilbert Stuart, the somber James McNeill Whistler figures, and the tender mother and child studies by Mary Cassatt.

· At the far end was John Singer Sargent's majestic life-size *Portrait of Madame X,* posed with her head angled away in profile. The artist had managed to capture her aristocratic hauteur. Only now her posture suggested she was irritated by the disruption in the gallery.

McCarthy stopped in astonishment. There was a light strobe on the floor, which must have set off the alarm. At the slightest sign of an increase in temperature, the sprinklers were supposed to come on. But they hadn't. So clearly someone had wanted to trigger the alarm *without* damaging the paintings.

He lifted his radio to call the security control room.

"Turn off circuit six alarm, please."

Yanni looked concerned.

"I wouldn't do that, sir. That camera circuit covers five of the rooms along this corridor."

"I am *aware* of that," McCarthy said as he brushed him off. "This is a diversion, designed to get us worked up about something here while they hit another part of the museum."

"I understand, sir, but it would leave you without *any* security in this section."

Yanni stood there shaking his head at him for emphasis. His eyes were intensified by thick glasses and he looked like a bobble-head doll.

"They wouldn't call attention to this gallery if they were going to steal something here. They would strike somewhere else," he explained again.

"Oh, I see. That makes sense. You're probably right," Yanni agreed hastily.

"Of *course* I'm right. I didn't spend thirty years in the department for nothing."

"Yes, sir."

"Now, get back downstairs. The First Lady is arriving in twenty minutes."

1010 Fifth Avenue

Mrs. Ted VerPlanck stood in front of her dressing-room mirror. Her evening gown was a crimson Carolina Herrera in heavy dupioni silk. The Harry Winston necklace was made of rubies and diamonds. She was back from the rehab clinic, and this town had better watch out!

A phrase ran through her head, advice her father had always given her.

"Never, *never* let anyone give you guff," he would say.

Tipper's father had been a brilliant businessman and the center of her universe. He was the one who came up with her nickname—Tipper.

When she was a toddler, her father used to sing "It's a Long Way to Tipperary" over and over as they drove the snowy roads to their ski house in New Hampshire or to Lake Winnipesaukee in the summer.

"Sing Tipper again," she would lisp as soon as he finished. He'd keep it up until she fell asleep. Then, at the end of the journey, he'd bundle her up in his arms and say, "Come on, Tipper, we're here."

The nickname stuck. He was still calling her that as he packed the little blue Alfa Romeo she drove to college.

"Bye, Tipper," he had said, standing there, gaunt and riddled with cancer. She could still see him in her mind, waving as she drove away to Massachusetts. The memory still brought tears to her eyes.

That's when she started drinking. It helped with the loneliness and pain, and had become a habit. Now, thirty years later, it was such a problem, the tabloids had re-christened her Tipsy. The ups and downs of Ted and Tipsy VerPlanck were fodder for the masses. Tipper sighed. They were always ready to dump on the billionaires in this town.

But tonight she'd show them. As her father said, she wasn't going to take guff from anybody. And she was definitely staying off the booze.

Metropolitan Museum of Art

M ET BOARD OF Directors member Charlie Hannifin was waiting by the circular information desk,
dwarfed by a gigantic red flower arrangement. He made
an unimposing figure—tuxedo jacket drooping off his
shoulders, pant legs puddling into his shoes.

He saw Security Director Tom McCarthy walking
through the lobby at a fast clip with his assistant, Yanni,
trailing along after him. They bolted up the main staircase
in the direction of the American Painting Gallery. The
strobe light diversion was going as planned.

All around the entrance hall, large noisy groups of
people were making their way to the Greek and Roman
Gallery for predinner cocktails. Charlie stayed at the main
desk—the perfect position for viewing incoming guests as
they stopped to pick up their entrance cards.

Long tables had been set up for check-in; a gaggle
of committee ladies were in charge. There was nothing
better than a flock of sharp-eyed New York doyennes
to screen the guests. You couldn't *buy* that kind of security.

The museum had set up a ticketing system that was
simple and effective. At check-in, each guest was quickly
photographed and given a gold-and-red security card with
a bar code. There were checkpoints all over the museum
where the card had to be re-scanned. Without a card there

was no way to enter the cocktail reception or the dinner. This system was as close to foolproof as they could get. Almost.

Hannifin's operatives had already slipped through the employee entrance. Two ersatz police officers were making their way to the Egyptian Gallery to steal a king's ransom of artifacts.

Charlie caught sight of the man he had been trying to intercept—Ted VerPlanck—arriving late. But where was his wife, Tipper? That was the person he *really* wanted to talk to.

"Charlie, nice to see you," VerPlanck called out with a quick wave.

Charlie fell into step beside him.

"Ted, how have you been? It's been ages."

"Long time. Can't even remember."

"I think it was last summer at the Vineyard?" suggested Charlie.

"Oh yes, that reading at the Chilmark Book Festival," Ted said and kept moving.

"Is Tipper doing well?" asked Charlie.

"Sure, never better. She's back at the apartment, still dressing. You know these gals. It takes forever."

"I'm looking forward to seeing her," Charlie said heartily and disappeared into the crowd.

Cordelia sipped her champagne and looked around the Greek and Roman Gallery. New York society women were greeting one another with air kisses. Everyone seemed to know each other!

There was a waiter standing just over Sinclair's left

shoulder. He hadn't moved in at least ten minutes as he held his tray aloft, entirely in another world. His eyes were strange, with a glassy thousand-yard stare.

The waiter turned and caught Cordelia observing him. His eyes flashed with animosity. She removed her gaze quickly. When she glanced back, he was still boring a hole through her, eyes narrowed. Cordelia looked over at Sinclair, but he hadn't noticed. He was studying the architecture.

"Quite an event," Sinclair said as he flagged a passing waiter. He speared an hors d'oeuvre with a toothpick and ate it whole. The fancy caterer had got it right—the rice blended nicely with the slightly bitter grape leaves. These *dolmades* could have been straight from Greece.

"They're good, Delia, try one," Sinclair urged.

"OK," she said, taking a toothpick. "Do you see anyone you know?"

"No, thank goodness. But I fully expect some moldering old geezer to come up any moment and tell me how wonderful my father was."

"Oh, come on. It can't be all that bad."

"Yes, it can. Sinclair père was quite a piece of work. I'm glad you never had the torture of meeting him."

They lapsed into silence. After a few moments Sinclair glanced over at Cordelia and noticed she was a little subdued, quietly watching everyone. Time to lighten things up.

There was a marble statue next to him, a Greek goddess, carved to life-size proportions. He pretended to notice it with a quick, comic double take.

"*Hold* on! I think I met this lady in a rooftop tavern in Santorini," he clowned.

She laughed at him, shaking her head.

" 'Aphrodite, Roman Period, first or second century BC,' " he said, reading the plaque out loud. " 'The goddess wears an ungirt chiton of thin clinging material that reveals the curve of her body.' "

Sinclair put his hands up to Cordelia's eyes as if to shield them.

"My goodness. *That* Aphrodite. I *told* her to girt her chiton, but she never listens."

Cordelia laughed, and he continued to read the sign.

" 'Her pose was developed by Polycleitus in the mid-fifth century, and the figure probably held an apple in her left hand.' "

Sinclair leaned over and checked Cordelia's left hand.

"No apple, that's a relief."

"Why?"

"I don't want to chase you. At least not here."

"You will *never* have to chase me, John."

"How about chasing *me*? They just rang the gong for dinner, and I'm starving."

"I don't see any of the conservation staff," Carter remarked to Holly as he looked around the Greek and Roman Gallery.

"It looks like the Fifth Avenue crowd to me."

"Well, since I can't introduce you to anyone, I guess you're stuck talking to me."

"Why don't I show you one of my favorite sculptures?" she suggested.

"Sure, I'd love that."

Holly threaded her way through the large atrium, and Carter followed.

"Here we are."

It was a carved marble bust. Carter circled around, taking in details.

"Quite a guy. Who is it?"

"Hadrian," Holly answered. "The Roman emperor."

The marble head was thrown boldly back, the face strong, exuding an aura of power.

"He must have been fairly young when this was done," observed Carter.

"He was about your age. Do you see he has a beard?"

"Yes."

"Romans usually shaved when they reached maturity. But Hadrian was the first emperor to keep his beard, and all the generals copied him."

"Why?" Carter asked.

"He had a great love of Greece, where a beard signified wisdom and maturity."

"Wisdom and maturity, hmmm . . . maybe I should . . ." Carter said, fingering his chin. "How do you know so much about this?"

"My doctoral thesis was on the period after 30 BC, when the Roman Empire annexed the Ptolemaic kingdom of Egypt."

Carter wasn't looking at the marble bust. All he saw was Holly, and the beautiful line of her temple where her blond hair was swept back.

"There's a personal story about this bust," she added.

"I'm all ears."

"When I first came to New York more than twenty years ago, my mother always wanted to know if I had a boyfriend."

Carter nodded, looking at her over the rim of his champagne glass.

"So finally I just told her I had met someone at the Met named Hadrian."

"Oh, that's too much!" Carter laughed.

"I meant it as a joke, but she didn't understand and would always ask 'How's Adrien?' "

"Did she ever find out?"

"No, I didn't have the heart to tell her. You do funny things when you're young."

"Yes, you do," Carter agreed.

Holly paused to listen. A waiter was walking through the gallery, striking chimes with a padded mallet.

"I guess it's time for dinner," Carter said. "After all this champagne, I really could use some food."

"I'm famished," Holly admitted. "All I had for lunch was an apple."

"Well, then, let's go!"

Carter took the empty champagne glass from her and set it down on a passing waiter's tray.

Vojtech stood immobile in the Greek and Roman Gallery, his gaze fixed straight ahead. He kept his arm steady as people deposited their empty champagne flutes on his tray.

Right in front of him was a statue of a Greek athlete.

The marble was sculpted with muscles and sinews—as lifelike as living flesh. It was beautiful, except, over the centuries, the ancient figure had lost a hand.

Vojtech looked around at the other marble statues. They were all broken in some way. Some were missing fingers, others arms. Many were decapitated. The bust of the Roman general in front of him was missing his nose.

Suddenly, it looked like there was blood pouring from the broken nostrils, coursing over the marble lips, and dripping off the chin. Vojtech looked around at the other statues. Rivulets of red spurted from the missing limbs, flowing down the draperies of the stone goddesses.

All around, blood ran off the statuary. The white marble corridor was slippery and covered with red. Tonight, women in their long silken dresses walked right through it, their hems trailing.

None of these people had any idea that soon *their* blood would be on the floor. This evening would end in a massacre. Vojtech stood there planning everything. No one noticed him. The guests laughed and drank their champagne.

The two policemen ambled along the corridor checking the passageway. This was where the guests would walk to go in to dinner, through the Egyptian wing, past the various galleries—the Old Kingdom, Middle Kingdom, Ptolemaic period—right up to the archaeological splendor of the Temple of Dendur.

A velvet rope blocked a closed gallery.

"What's in there?" asked one cop.

"It's the Tut exhibit on the New Kingdom, Eighteenth Dynasty," a museum security guard replied.

"Anybody in there?"

"No need. Everyone is supposed to walk straight through."

"Undo the rope. I want one last sweep before they start coming this way."

The guard unhooked the cordon without hesitation.

Cordelia walked down the corridor of the Egyptian wing with Sinclair.

"This is all very romantic, wouldn't you say?" he asked, looking down at her.

"Absolutely."

She had an intense flashback to when she met him almost a year ago. It had been an evening like this in Monaco. He had cut an impressive figure, every inch the handsome explorer. Their whirlwind romance had been filled with danger and adventure, and a lot of heartache too.

Because of their rocky start, they had spent time apart and then tried a long-distance romance, but in the end they had decided they couldn't be without each other. Sinclair had moved to London five months ago to be with Cordelia. And then they had left to go on expedition in Egypt. His excitement about ancient culture was contagious.

"I can't believe how great Dendur looks!" Sinclair said, pausing at the threshold of the gallery.

Cordelia came up to stand next to him. It was an

unbelievable sight—an ancient Egyptian temple in the middle of Manhattan! The enormous glass wing of the museum was still fairly empty, the lights dimmed. The massive sandstone edifice was elevated above a shallow reflecting pool designed to mimic the Nile River.

"Ohhh, it's beautiful!" Cordelia gasped.

"Stunning is the word."

"How old is it?" she asked, knowing Sinclair would have the facts at his command.

"Commissioned in 15 BC by the Roman emperor Augustus for Egypt. The Met moved it here in the 1960s, or it would have been flooded when the Aswan Dam was built."

"I'm glad we have it to ourselves for a moment."

Fifty empty tables were placed around the temple, draped with red tablecloths, set with crystal and china. Small candles glowed—shimmering points of light, like a votive rack in a dim cathedral.

Sinclair walked through the dining area, found their places, and held out her chair. As she sat down, several other people arrived, still carrying their champagne flutes. This was going to be a gorgeous evening!

Tipper VerPlanck swept into the museum, her stiletto heels echoing in the empty lobby, the train of her satin dress dusting the marble floor. A young woman with a clipboard came rushing up and handed her a plastic card.

"Mrs. VerPlanck, delighted you could make it. I'll escort you to the table."

"What's this?" Tipper asked, confused about the plastic security chit.

"Your entrance card. If you would please follow me."

Tipper tucked it into her purse and glided after the young woman. The museum guards eyed her as she walked through the Egyptian Gallery. Standing in the entrance to the atrium, she could see the dinner had started. Waiters were threading their way through the tables, trays held high.

The murmur of conversation filled the large space. The Egyptian temple stood floodlit and exotic, flanked by soaring columns of red and white flowers. The grandeur of the setting was impressive—New York at its very best.

"You are at table two," the young woman said.

Tipper paused on the verge of entering. It was going to take a lot of nerve to appear in front of this crowd again. She had endured such a string of public humiliations lately, albeit self-inflicted.

She steeled herself for the plunge, then swooped into the room, head held high. As she approached table 2, she saw Ted engrossed in conversation with the curator of the Greco-Roman collection.

Tipper's chair was empty, and the wineglass was turned over as a signal to the waiter not to serve the place setting. But, inexplicably, next to her empty seat was that little wretch of a man, Charlie Hannifin! Why on *earth* was she sitting next to *him*?

Ted stood up as he saw her approaching, a smile stitched into place.

"Delighted you made it," he said.

His tone was disapproving. But something in his eyes asked for reassurance.

"Traffic was horrific. You have *no* idea."

"I'm sure it was. The police lines have been set up outside the museum for hours."

"Is she here?" Tipper asked, looking around the hall.

"Who?"

"The First Lady."

"Yes. She's here."

Tipper looked around.

"Why isn't she at *our* table?"

Ted pressed his lips together in resolute silence, clearly not wanting to discuss it publicly. He stepped over and held her chair with great formality before taking his place again. Tipper sat down, fussing with the arrangement of her skirts.

"So, where *is* she?" she finally asked sotto voce.

Ted moved his eyes toward the next table. The First Lady was directly across from them, her back turned.

Tipper's spirits plunged. A wave of disappointment washed over her. *Ted* was co-chairman of the gala! As his wife, she had the right to sit at the head table.

She took a deep breath and felt the hate rise in her heart. Ted was a dunce. A dull, plodding dummy. He had traded away the best social card of all!

"We should be there," Tipper hissed. *"You're* the co-chairman of the gala."

"The committee was concerned about putting us at the table."

"Why!"

"You were in the clinic at the time, and I didn't know if you would be able to attend."

"I can't believe you let them do this to me!"

Ted's eyes filled with pity. And that's when she really lost her temper. How *dare* he look at her like that! She was not some pathetic creature! She was Tipper Ver-Planck, one of the most important women in this entire city!

She straightened her spine. She wasn't going to take guff from anyone. Including her husband.

"*Why*, Ted?" she said, her voice pure ice.

"I'm sorry, Tipper, this is your first event since you were away. I thought it was for the best."

"You thought wrong."

"I wouldn't want you to be embarrassed."

Tipper clamped her mouth shut in a firm line. She *hated* this horrible dinner.

"*Embarrassed?* I'll show you embarrassed!"

"Tipper, what . . . ?"

She shot him a scathing look, picked up her inverted wineglass, and held it high.

"Waiter!" she called, and wiggled the glass.

The waiter nodded and came over with a wine bottle. He started to pour. Tipper watched the liquid fill the goblet.

"Leave it," Tipper told him, looking Ted in the eye. "Leave the bottle."

Two cops walked along the hallway, intent on following their instructions. The plan was to steal seven objects from case number 98—funerary statues, about six inches high. Small, yet incredibly rare and valuable.

The thieves had exactly six minutes until the security camera would flash an image of the gallery back to the control room. But there was little chance of discovery if all went according to schedule. Charlie Hannifin had set up five diversionary strobes to confuse and distract the Met chief of security. It was causing havoc. Museum guards and federal security teams had been rushing about all evening.

"It's this way," said one of the faux policemen. "Straight ahead to case number 98."

"This it?"

"Yes. See, every piece has an exhibition number. We need case 98—items 121, 122, 123, 124, 125, 126, and 127."

"This stuff is small, so why not grab a couple more? You know, for us."

"No, let's stick to the plan. We don't have time."

"OK, I was just saying . . . we're here already, why not grab a couple extra?"

"Shut up and give me the circuit cutter."

The man unbuttoned his voluminous shirt and took out a canvas roll fitted with small implements. Within seconds they had hooked up the electrical loop that would keep the current intact. They carefully cut the glass and removed the items. As they worked they could hear people talking and laughing out in the corridor.

Each figurine was wrapped and secured to the men's bodies with surgical tape. When they buttoned their shirts, they had gained thirty pounds.

"You're suddenly looking kinda fat," his partner said, surveying him.

"Yeah, I know. When I put on weight, you know who I blame?"

"Who?"

"My mummy."

They both laughed as they walked out of the gallery.

John Sinclair passed two portly NYPD officers in the hall-way. The security was pretty tight this evening. He even had to show his pass to go to the men's room!

As he reentered the hall, the beauty of the temple struck him all over again. The red roses and white Casa-blanca lilies had released their scent, and now the whole room smelled like an August afternoon.

Sinclair wound his way through the gilt ballroom chairs to his table. Passage was difficult. The gala commit-tee had sold so many tickets it was almost impossible to walk between the tables. A big-band orchestra was start-ing to play, and everyone was getting up—some to dance, others to table-hop.

Charlie Hannifin leaned over to speak to Tipper. She was helping herself to more wine, clinking the bottle hard against the glass. Charlie took it from her and poured.

"I have an art deal to talk to you about."

"Art? You know I don't give a *damn* about art."

People at the next table looked over at her. She put down her goblet. It was time to stop drinking. Dessert had been served—a dark chocolate tartufo in the shape of a sphinx, decorated with gold leaf.

She speared the confection with a fork. The frozen chocolate shell shattered and shards of dark chocolate shot out all over the tablecloth. Tipper picked up a fragment and popped it into her mouth, licking her fingers clean.

Charlie was looking at her in consternation.

"You may not care about art in general, but you will care about *this* kind of art."

"What makes you think so?"

Tipper scouted around for another piece of chocolate and found one near the centerpiece of roses.

"I hear you are divorcing Ted."

Tipper turned and stared at Charlie. "Who the hell told you that?"

"It was on the gossip page—Page Six in the *New York Post*, last Tuesday."

She shrugged and picked up another piece near Charlie's plate. "So what does the divorce have to do with anything?"

"Ted's collection is worth a fortune. It could mean a lot to you."

"Nope. Art is outside any settlement. It's all spelled out in the prenup."

"*You have a prenuptial agreement?*" Charlie asked in shock.

"Sure do."

"I thought you and Ted got married right after college. Who had a prenup back then?"

"We broke up about five years ago. During reconciliation Ted wanted a midlife prenup."

"You mean when you ran off to Reykjavík with that bandleader?" Charlie asked unpleasantly.

"He isn't a bandleader. He is a *rock star*. And it wasn't Reykjavík, it was Glastonbury."

"What's the difference?"

"Glastonbury is in *England*. It's perfectly respectable. Even *Ted* goes to England."

"Yeah, but not for rock festivals."

"Jesus, Charlie. Blades is one of the most successful commercial entertainment groups in the world."

"I stand corrected," Charlie said, smirking.

"What does all this have to do with art?"

"What would you say if I told you that you could get ten percent of the value of some of Ted's art?" Charlie said.

"How would that work?"

Tipper took another shard of dark chocolate off the table.

"Art can be stolen."

"You are going to *steal* Ted's art?" she whispered, turning to stare at him.

"No, but there are people who would pay big money to know when and where Ted's art collection could be"—Charlie paused to search for a word—"accessible."

She looked at him in disbelief.

"Why should I tell people how to steal from Ted?"

"Because they would pay you millions in commission."

Tipper let the chocolate dissolve in her mouth as she thought about it. Last year there had been rumors that Charlie Hannifin had lost his fortune in a stock swindle. Well, apparently they were true; Charlie Hannifin was so broke he was thinking about stealing art from his friends.

Sinclair came up to the table and saw Cordelia talking animatedly to the guest across from her. She pushed her dark hair back, exposing her beautiful shoulders. Tan from the expedition in Egypt, she looked fit and athletic.

Without question, Cordelia was one of the most beautiful women in the room. And that strapless dress was magnificent. Sinclair leaned over and spoke in her ear.

"You look so beautiful. I can't wait for this party to be over."

She smiled up at him, radiant.

"John, you've flown more than five thousand miles to come here, and now you want to *leave*? We could have stayed in Egypt."

"We could have," he admitted. "But I wouldn't have the pleasure of seeing you with the Temple of Dendur behind you."

"It's so beautiful," Cordelia said with a sigh. "It almost looks like a movie set—except it's *real*!"

He sat down and held her hand as they watched people dancing.

"You know, Delia . . . I've been thinking . . ." Sinclair started. But just then one of the other dinner guests leaned across the table and spoke.

"Pardon me, Miss Stapleton, but may I have this dance?"

Cordelia looked up, startled. She clearly didn't want to leave, but she smiled graciously.

"Yes, of course," she acquiesced. "Excuse me, John. I'll be right back."

Carter Wallace patiently bided his time through five dinner courses: squash soup with walnuts, seafood pâté, chicken breast stuffed with pomegranate and figs,

Belgian endive salad with goat cheese. Finally, the waiters came around with dark chocolate tartufo and coffee. Holly was nibbling on a piece of crystallized ginger when he decided to speak up.

He felt his face grow flush and a trickle of sweat creep down his back. She could laugh or refuse. He went for it.

"If you don't mind, I'd like to ask you to dance."

She looked at him, seeming to take his measure.

"Carter, I would be *delighted*."

Her tone was cheerfully condescending, as if she were indulging the six-year-old ring bearer at a wedding. As she rose, he gallantly offered her his arm, but it was so crowded he had to abandon ceremony, and they threaded their way single file through the tables.

The orchestra was set up right in front of the temple—a stunning backdrop to the dance floor. When he reached the middle, they fell into step.

Wow! Dancing with Holly Graham! He never thought he would see the day. She seemed quite cool about it all, looking off over his shoulder, so he gazed out the glass wall at the beautiful night sky above Central Park. They kept silent for quite some time until he decided to venture a comment.

"I haven't stepped on your toes yet."

She smiled up at him. "No, you haven't. In fact, you're a very good dancer."

John Sinclair sipped his wine and watched Cordelia's progress on the dance floor. She was in the arms of a particularly short fellow who looked completely enthralled.

As he was observing, another couple moved in front of Cordelia, eclipsing his view—a stocky young man and a blond woman. The man said something, smiling down, completely smitten.

His heart stopped. *It couldn't be her, could it?*

He stared at the lovely back and knew that if she would just turn a fraction he would know for sure. She was wearing a white Grecian-style dress. Fantastic figure—her curves were deeply voluptuous yet graceful. Suddenly, the woman turned. *It was Holly Graham!*

Sinclair felt as if he had been hit with an electric shock. It made sense that she would be here—Holly was one of the top people at the Brooklyn Museum.

On impulse, Sinclair headed to the dance floor, launched up the three stone steps, and wove through the crowd. When he got nearer, he circled around behind and tapped her escort on the shoulder.

"Sorry to cut in, but this lady is an old friend."

Carter Wallace turned and stared at Sinclair.

"John!" Holly exclaimed. "How nice to see you!"

The young fellow stood like a dolt, scowling at him and still clinging to Holly's hand. Sinclair smiled pleasantly at him.

"I'll bring her back, I promise."

"Carter, excuse me for a moment," she said gently. "John is an old friend."

The fellow crumbled visibly, finally letting go.

"Of course," he mumbled.

Sinclair deftly steered Holly to the middle of the dance floor, then took her in his arms.

Holly Graham. *Imagine!* He held her a bit closer than

he needed to, but it seemed perfectly appropriate. They had history together.

Physically, they didn't match; she was nearly a foot shorter than he was, her head barely up to his shoulder. Holly was so small, so delicate, but that only added to her allure. He danced silently for a while, falling into a dreamy reminiscence.

How long had it been since they first met at Wadi Rum? He remembered the day well. It had been beastly hot—110 degrees. But she had looked very fresh standing there in her white shirt and khaki shorts—a little blond doll—impossibly perfect. Her skin had been flawless, not a drop of sweat or a stain on her clothes despite the long journey by Land Rover to the middle of nowhere.

Someone had introduced her as Dr. Graham. Holly had shaken his hand politely, but under the shade of a broad-brimmed Tilley hat her blue eyes had been dismissive. I've seen plenty of guys like you, her look had said. I'm not easily impressed.

Of course, that aloofness had made her immediately irresistible. Sinclair had vowed on the spot to trump her professionally and *then* seduce her, in that order. An arrogant assumption, except it didn't work out that way.

Holly was absolutely brilliant. She ran rings around him in the field. And when it came to seduction she reeled him in like a hooked trout.

During that archaeological season in Jordan, he had fallen completely under her spell. The more he lusted, the more she put on the ice-princess hauteur. At the dig during the day, his pulse would rapid-fire whenever she approached. And at night, as he lay on his cot, she became the woman of his fevered dreams.

Finally, she had spoken to him, asking him to come to her tent when the others were sleeping. He nearly fell to his knees in gratitude.

But making love to Holly had been like entering into a pact with the powers of darkness. He didn't have a coherent thought during the entire time of their affair.

It had been nearly a decade since she left him sitting in a bar in Aqaba, nursing a gin and tonic and a broken heart. And to this day he could still picture that farewell drink.

He never forgot her. Over the years, he had a recurring fantasy of bumping into her. Sometimes he pictured an exotic dig, or perhaps a far-flung airport in a remote country. But dancing at the Temple of Dendur!

"Hello, Hols," he finally said, his voice gruff with suppressed emotion. "How've you been?"

She looked up at him and smiled.

Vojtech pushed his dessert cart, laden with little chocolate sphinxes filled with vanilla ice cream. Tartufo, they called it. They looked like little toy zoo animals, staring at him impassively. Most of the tables had been served already, and the other waiters had returned to the kitchen. These were the last cartloads, for the people at the back of the room.

He stood in the prep area, hidden behind a temporary screen. On the other side of the partition, a thousand people were laughing, talking, and dancing. The atrium was filled with excited voices. In another moment there would be screams.

Vojtech removed the black nylon bag from underneath the white drape of the rolling cart. The duffel had been under there all evening. But who bothers to lift a tablecloth when a thousand melting ice-cream desserts had to be served?

Now, standing behind the screen, he started to sweat. This was the moment of action. Vojtech heard the elevator doors open behind him. Two other gunmen rolled their carts in. They were stone-faced and determined.

Vojtech stuck his head around the partition.

"Now!" he said.

Instantly they pulled out their automatic weapons and crouched down, ready to storm the dining room. Vojtech grabbed his bag, fumbled with the zipper, and pulled out his gun. His hands were shaking. A drop of sweat dripped off his nose and made a dark mark on the nylon bag. It was time to move!

Behind him, he heard the service elevator doors open again.

"Hey, you! What are you doing there?"

Vojtech kept going.

"Freeze! Secret Service! Everybody put your hands in the air!"

Vojtech ignored the command and began to raise his weapon. Again a voice behind him was telling him to halt. He looked over and saw that the two other gunmen were obeying—lying on the floor in submission, their assault weapons cast aside.

But Vojtech lurched forward. He was not going to give up so easily! Three more steps and he would be in the main dining room.

An instant later he heard the zing of a silencer and he was hit in the knee. As he fell, he glanced underneath the bottom of the screen and saw the majestic temple and all the partygoers dancing in front of it. That was his last second of life. A Secret Service agent blew his head off from behind.

Cordelia drifted back to the table to find it littered with abandoned plates of melted ice cream. Sinclair had disappeared and everyone was dancing, so she picked up her wineglass and looked around the room, catching an arresting face or a beautiful dress. So many interesting people!

A distinguished man with a beard was winding his way through the tables, greeting everyone. She idly followed his progress through the room. He looked very elegant and carried himself with great formality.

As she watched him, she gradually became aware of a disturbance near the entrance of the gallery. There were small pops, like the sound of champagne corks. Three men in dark suits hastily approached the First Lady and surrounded her chair. The president's wife stood up, picked up her evening bag, and walked briskly to the side door.

Cordelia watched her go, perplexed. Surely the guest of honor wasn't leaving so soon? Just then there was the crackle of the intercom and a male voice spoke carefully and with authority.

"Ladies and gentlemen, we have encountered a security breach. There is no cause for alarm. But we must evacuate

the room. Please collect your belongings and exit through the rear door."

There was a collective "Ahh" from the room and the people around her started to mutter in disappointment.

Cordelia looked around to find Sinclair.

"You should go outside quickly," a voice right next to her said. She turned and saw the tall bearded man she had noticed earlier.

"I've lost my partner . . . he seems to be gone . . ." she said as her voice faded.

"You won't be able to find him with this crowd. Come with me."

"But I don't know you. . . ."

"I'm Ted VerPlanck. I'm the co-chair of the gala."

Cordelia recognized the name instantly. He was one of the most famous antiquities collectors in the world and a client of her legal adviser, Jim Gardiner. Still, she hesitated.

The room was starting to get very disorganized. People were jostling in the narrow spaces between the tables. The music had stopped, and the glass-enclosed museum gallery rang with the shrill calls of people trying to locate each other.

"Everyone exit the museum," a booming voice announced through a megaphone.

The man extended his hand to her.

"I'll show you the way. Follow me."

He guided her along as they moved through the tables. They made their way to the rear of the atrium and around to the back of the temple. There, hidden from view, was a set of double doors.

"Only a few people know about this exit," he explained.

They stepped through and the heavy doors shut behind them. Then there was only a deep silence.

"Thank you, Mr. VerPlanck."

"Think nothing of it. I would like to go out into the lobby if you don't mind," he said.

Cordelia nodded, allowing him to take the lead, following his tuxedoed back through a labyrinth of empty galleries until he finally halted in a large two-story-high hall.

"I'll just stop here for a moment," he said, pulling out a handkerchief and wiping his forehead.

His jacket fell open and Cordelia could see that his pleated tuxedo shirt was sticking to his torso, damp with sweat.

"Are you OK?" she asked.

"Yes," he assured her, rebuttoning his jacket. "I'm a bit flustered, that's all. The evening has just turned into a public relations disaster."

"Do you think anyone was hurt?"

"I don't know," he said.

"I'd better get outside," Cordelia replied anxiously. "I need to find my escort."

John Sinclair pushed his way against the flow of people, to the table where Cordelia had been sitting. *She was gone!* All around, people were pressing past him.

"Cordelia!" Sinclair called out.

"John!"

He heard his name being shouted and whirled around.

It was Holly, standing where he had left her a moment ago, her white dress a beacon in the crowd. Sinclair had told her to wait, but now she was being buffeted by masses of people.

"Holly, I'll come get you!" he called and made his way back to her.

Suddenly the room was filled with the sound of a bull-horn.

"Move away from the main entrance. Go to the back of the room and exit behind the temple."

The announcement seemed to redirect the crowd. People moved quickly, purposefully. Policemen were channeling the guests toward the exits. One officer stepped up to Sinclair and Holly, his radio squawking.

"Move along, sir," he said firmly. "Follow instructions to exit the museum."

"Officer, my girlfriend is missing," Sinclair argued.

The policeman looked at Holly holding on to Sinclair's arm.

"Please move on, sir."

"She probably left already," Holly assured him.

They joined the large phalanx of guests—hundreds in an endless stream—now oddly silent as they hurried through the winding galleries. Finally they reached the main foyer.

The cavernous space was filled with a huge crowd. Many people were milling about, searching for their friends. Others were standing around speculating about what had happened.

"I thought I heard five or six gunshots," a man was saying. "At least, that's what I thought they sounded like."

"No, you must be mistaken. If there had been gunfire, we would know about it."

"I think something went wrong with the alarm system. That's what I heard some guards talking about."

"I was sitting near the First Lady," an elderly woman said. "Her security detail got her out right away."

NYPD officers were walking through the main hall, urging people to go home. The gala was over, they explained. The security breach had been detected and stopped. Everyone was safe.

Sinclair pushed through the crowd. There must be several hundred people in the lobby. Even with his towering height, it was impossible to find Cordelia. Almost every woman in the place was wearing the same color, and the entrance hall had turned into a sea of red gowns!

He elbowed his way gently, Holly hanging on to him. Finally, he turned to her.

"I can't manage this if we stay together. Do you mind if I leave you here?"

Holly looked down and seemed to realize that she was still holding his arm. She released it hastily.

"Yes, go ahead. I'll be OK."

"Are you sure you'll be all right on your own?"

"John darling, I'm *fine*. You should go look for your date."

"No need," a voice said behind him. "His *date* is here."

Sinclair whirled around and stood face-to-face with Cordelia.

Ted VerPlanck strained through the crowd, trying to locate Tipper. There was a slim possibility she had gone outside or had even gone home. As he walked out on the steps, the autumn air was suddenly refreshing. He looked across Fifth Avenue at his apartment, but the oblong windows of the living room were still dark. No one was there.

Ted VerPlanck lingered a moment to observe the scene on the street. Police cars were parked at angles up on the sidewalk. Fifth Avenue echoed with wailing sirens. Photographers and reporters were running up and down the red-carpeted steps, snapping pictures. The camera crews had turned on their floodlights and were beaming live video back to their studios via satellite trucks.

VerPlanck sighed and turned to see the Met chief of security standing behind him.

"Mr. VerPlanck, I've been asked to locate you. The FBI would like a word."

Carter Wallace stood outside, waiting for Holly to emerge. There was no use looking for her in that mob. It would be better to intercept her out here as she passed by.

When they started to evacuate the hall, he had been swept up in the center of the crowd and pushed out onto the steps. There he had witnessed the First Lady's dash to the waiting motorcade, with crimson skirts flying, looking like some exotic bird of prey surrounded by a flock of black crows. Except the crows were carrying automatic weapons.

The motorcade tore away, sirens shrieking at pedestrians to get out of the way. Now Fifth Avenue was eerily devoid of moving traffic, and the side streets had been cleared.

He lit a cigarette, shakily. It wasn't a regular habit, but he always kept a couple of Dunhills in a silver case for the occasional jitters. To his mind, this evening definitely qualified as a legitimate time to light up.

The last time he saw Holly, she had been dancing with John Sinclair in front of the Temple of Dendur. *He* should have been dancing with her, instead of that damned interloper.

Of course, he knew who Sinclair was—the archaeologist was a legend, a titan in the field. The man had discovered more artifacts than any person alive. And now, rumor had it, he had located Pharos, the ancient lighthouse of Alexandria.

While Sinclair's professional reputation was stellar, his *personal* reputation was notorious. He was a playboy, a real lady-killer. And if you listened to the excavation gossip, he had legions of ex-girlfriends from Khartoum to Kazakhstan. It was *incredible* that Holly had greeted him in such an intimate tone.

As Carter stood there, a woman exited the museum. With her pitch-black hair, golden skin, and high cheekbones, she could have been an Egyptian deity fleeing the scene of destruction. He noticed that she was attired in what looked like a modern version of an Egyptian *kalasiris*. Carter had never seen a dress like that, except perhaps carved on the wall of a tomb.

The woman carried high-heeled gold sandals in her hand and ran down the red-carpeted steps in her bare feet, lifting the hem of her dress as she moved. Carter could see she was not wearing stockings; her legs were tan and bare.

Several news reporters noticed her and the camera crews turned on their lights. The crimson silk of the *kalasiris* became as transparent as gauze.

"Will you look at *that*!" Carter said to himself in surprise.

He blinked, half wondering if he was hallucinating. She was wearing *nothing* underneath that dress!

"I'll be *damned*," he said.

There were two policemen at the bottom of the steps, both portly, one short and the other tall. She stopped and spoke to them for several minutes.

Then the woman did something odd—she leaned heavily on the arm of one policeman to retain her balance as she fastened the straps of her evening sandals. The policeman didn't seem to mind. He just kept talking to her. When she had finished putting on her shoes, the woman and the policemen started off together down Fifth Avenue. Carter had a final glimpse of the trio as they wove in and out of the parked patrol cars—an Egyptian goddess escorted by the two uniformed officers.

Ted's search for Tipper was futile. The marble hall was packed with hundreds of people walking around aimlessly. Police officers were now urging people to move outside. Suddenly Tipper stood before him, ghastly, white-faced, weaving.

"Ted," she demanded. "Take me *home*."

His heart sank. Drunk again. Would it never end? Her first trip out into society and she gave in to the bottle.

He held her arm and escorted her out of the building. The stairs were going to be a challenge. Tipper kept her head down to monitor her voluminous skirts. Just as she navigated her way past the camera crew, she tripped and nearly fell. Ted caught her in time. Then she managed to wobble down the remaining twenty-eight steps without incident.

The doorman at 1010 Fifth Avenue was standing outside, gawking at the mayhem. When he saw the VerPlancks, he recovered himself and swung open the heavy iron doors.

"Good evening, sir."

VerPlanck gave him a nod as Tipper sailed straight past him.

Inside the lobby, it was as cool and silent as a tomb. There were several large vases of calla lilies, which reinforced the impression of a sepulcher. Ted escorted his wife to the elevator. But it wasn't until the doors closed that he finally spoke.

"Tipper, you're drunk."

Tipper pulled her arm away from him with irritation and stood in silence. As the elevator door opened, she stepped directly into the foyer of their penthouse, but ruined her haughty exit by tripping on the Persian carpet.

Ted leaped forward to steady her, but she waved him off and plowed straight on toward the bedroom, shedding her shoes and handbag as she went. Ted had often witnessed Tipper's late-night drunken trail of clothing and walked behind, collecting things as she dropped them.

As he bent for the bejeweled pump in the middle of the living room, he marveled at its small size. The tiny evening slipper looked fit for a child. That's what she was, Ted mused, a child who had never grown up.

He straightened up and started turning off the lights: the twin antique Chinese porcelain table lamps on the sideboard, the overhead lights for the paintings. As he turned off each one, his eyes caressed his cherished possessions: the stately Sargent portrait in the dining room, the Monet in the breakfast room, the majestic Bradford Arctic landscape in the library.

He adored this nocturnal inventory. It was a ritual that calmed him. No matter how harsh the world had become, a few square inches of beauty could always be preserved within a gilded frame. Tonight, especially, he needed that comfort.

He walked to the wall niche and reached for the spotlight on the Sardonyx Cup but stopped, aghast.

The Sardonyx Cup was gone! The alcove was empty, and the pedestal was bare! He felt a jolt of horror.

Had it fallen off its column? He looked frantically on the floor and all around the base. Even as he searched, intuitively he knew the answer. *It had been stolen!*

Holly Graham stood on the top step of the Met getting her bearings.

"May I get you a cab?"

She turned at the sound of Carter's voice. He looked a little disheveled, the jacket of his tuxedo hanging crookedly.

"*Carter,* are you all right?"

"I'm fine. I've been looking for *you.*"

There was a hint of accusation in his voice. Inexplicably, his annoyance seemed to be directed at her.

"I just got out here a moment ago," she said.

Carter said nothing and took a pull on his cigarette, his hand shaking.

"Are you *smoking*?" she said, aghast. "I never knew you smoked!"

He flashed her a look and crushed the remainder of his cigarette underfoot.

"I don't. I just carry a few around to prove to myself that I don't need them. Last time I had one was two years ago."

"Well, you shouldn't smoke, *ever,*" she scolded.

"I'll get a cab to take you home now," Carter said. "If you want me to. Maybe you have other plans."

Their eyes met. Carter's mood was shockingly bitter. Was it because she had agreed to dance with John Sinclair? She hadn't meant to hurt Carter's feelings. In retrospect, leaving him like that was probably a little bit cavalier.

Holly dropped her gaze in embarrassment and suddenly noticed her gown had a large tear. She picked up the white chiffon skirt and showed it to him.

"Oh, *no*! I must have caught it on something."

"Maybe it can be fixed?" he suggested, barely looking at it.

Holly examined the gown further. It was shredded in several places, clearly beyond repair. For some reason the destruction of her new gown, along with Carter's sudden hostility, put her over the edge. The entire evening was ruined. Inexplicably, she started to cry.

"Holly, what's wrong?" he said with a gasp.

He took a step toward her. She moved away to hide her face, but he grasped her hand. His grip was strong.

"I'm sorry," Carter apologized. "I was being rude to you. Please don't be upset."

She started to draw back but, surprisingly, found she didn't want to resist. Suddenly, she was in his arms. She felt like a fool, letting him embrace her in public like this, but it was comforting. Her lips were trembling and a tear escaped and rolled down her cheek.

"Holly, don't be upset," he said, his voice low and consoling. "Your dress can be fixed. It's all right."

He was such a big bear. She pressed her cheek against his jacket and let out a long, shaky breath. After giving herself a moment to recover, she stepped back. He released her gently.

"I'm so sorry, Carter."

"Are you OK?"

"Yes, I just seem to have . . . lost it. I'll be all right."

"What can I do?" he asked, standing with his hands hanging down.

Holly turned away, taking a tissue out of her bag. She faced out toward the street, blotting her eyes.

Why was she feeling so emotional? She *never* cried. Then she realized the problem. There were three things that had caused her to weep: the ruined dress, the spoiled evening, and the fact that she was still in love with John Sinclair.

Carlyle Hotel

LADY XANDRA SOMMERSET marched into the lobby of the hotel trailed by two New York City police officers.

"There's been an incident at the museum," she told the desk clerk.

"I *know.* We've been watching the TV in the bar."

"Well, don't concern yourself. Nobody was injured." She lowered her voice in a conspiratorial whisper. *"I have to have a police escort to my room. . . ."*

The clerk flushed. "Oh . . . of course . . ."

The two policemen nodded brusquely to the hotel clerk and then walked with her through the lobby. Even in the elevator, they kept up their stone-faced composure, protectively flanking her in full sight of the security cameras. But once inside the door of her suite, they immediately lost their formality and sprang into action.

"Quickly. Do it fast," she instructed.

They unbuttoned their shirts and stripped off the felt packing, laying the stolen artifacts on the bed. Shirts were rebuttoned and they were out the door in less than thirty seconds. Back in the hallway, the policemen had lost several inches off their waistlines.

As they left the Carlyle Hotel, they gave a departing nod to the desk clerk, who was in the doorway of the bar, listening to the CNN report on TV.

Metropolitan Museum of Art

CORDELIA STOOD ON the top of the Met steps, her hair blowing, her eyes narrowed, and her lips pressed into a firm line. She looked absolutely furious.

"Cordelia, what's wrong?" Sinclair asked.

"I don't like it that you went off with that woman and left me alone!"

"I *didn't* leave you on your own. I was dancing."

"*Exactly*. I leave you for thirty seconds and you run off with some blonde!"

Sinclair stared at her. She was jealous! It was incredible how irrational she could become.

"Her name is Hollis Graham. She's an old friend."

"Is that why she called you *'darling'*?"

"Figure of speech," said Sinclair, waving the word away in the air. "She's like that. It means nothing."

"How do you know her?"

"She is one of the top Egyptologists in the country. I've known her for years. Why are you so upset?"

"I was worried! Weren't you?"

"Yes, of course I was. I was looking for you."

Cordelia ignored his reply and picked up her skirts in a huff and flounced down the red carpet. He followed along resignedly.

Delia was a complicated woman and didn't always sort out her emotions quickly. Most times she reacted first, and then thought things through later. It didn't take long for her to calm down. By the time she reached the sidewalk, she was out of steam and turned back to him.

"Should we walk back to the hotel? The limo's gone," she said with a certain degree of contrition.

"I'd carry you in my arms if you'd let me," he replied, and meant every word.

"I was so afraid that you were going to get hurt," she said, her lips trembling. "I thought I heard gunshots, and you weren't around."

So that was it! The horror of her parents' accident still haunted her. Losing both her mother and father at the age of twelve had been a terrible shock, and even now she had a deep fear of being abandoned.

"Surely you know that I would never leave you, Cordelia," he said.

"John, I hate it when one of your old girlfriends pops up. It happens all the time."

"Holly is *not* one—"

"She isn't?"

"No, she isn't. You're the only woman in my life," he replied and held out his arms to her. Mercifully, she came to him.

"Delia, how can you even *think*—"

"John, I never want to lose you."

"You won't," Sinclair said, pulling her closer. "You're *trembling!*"

"No, I'm just cold. I left my wrap inside."

"Well, too late to look for it now," he said, peeling off his jacket and putting it around her shoulders. "Let's get back to the hotel."

Madison Avenue and Eighty-Second Street, New York

CARTER WALLACE WATCHED the yellow cab move away and thread its way through traffic. He wished Holly would turn around and wave. She didn't. The cab took a right and headed down a side street. Suddenly, his life was empty again.

The beautiful Holly Graham. After tonight, his crush was worse than ever. The whole time she was with Sinclair on the dance floor, he had been miserable. And then he had made a total ass of himself by acting jealous and hostile.

But somehow everything had worked in his favor. Upset by the turn of events, she had clung to him. That counted for something, didn't it?

He closed his eyes, remembering the feel of her body in that brief moment of contact—her hand on his lapel, her hair brushing his face. It took every ounce of self-control not to kiss her on the spot.

"In your dreams, pal," he said aloud, and laughed.

God, what a beautiful night! The air had cooled off. It was almost chilly now as he started to walk. Up in the sky, the moon was a comma between the buildings.

He should go home. But why not take one more look at the museum before getting a cab? It was gawking, of course, but how many times had he been in the middle of something like that? And he was still curious—nobody had explained exactly what had happened.

As he approached, he could see the dome lights of the police cars alternating blue and red, painting the facade of the Met. East Eighty-Second Street was silent, most of the brownstones shuttered for the night. There were dark pools of shadow under the trees.

Suddenly, on the far sidewalk, he saw two workmen carrying a crate between them—treating it as gently as if it were an egg carton. They approached a white van parked at the curb and lowered the box onto the sidewalk. The taller of the two men took keys out of his pocket and unlocked the back door. Then they lifted the crate into the van, bracing it so it would not move during transit.

Working silently, neither man noticed Carter walking by. The vehicle had New York plates—76823N.

Funny, two guys loading a crate like that in the middle of the night. Carter's job was to transport rare artifacts for the museum. That crate was state-of-the-art.

Carter reached Fifth Avenue and stopped to watch the activity. The police vehicles were still there, radios squawking, but there was not much to see, so he doubled back to find a cab.

"Sheridan Square," he told the driver, and fished in his pocket for a pen and notepaper to jot down the license plate number.

Those movers certainly didn't look legitimate to him. Who loads a van in the middle of the night with a custom-made crate? Tomorrow he'd report it. He tucked the note in his pocket.

Then he sat back and relaxed for the twenty-minute ride downtown—plenty of time to indulge in his alpha-male fantasies about Holly. Too bad his imagination was the only thing he'd be taking home to bed.

1010 Fifth Avenue

Ted VerPlanck sat in the darkened living room and swirled a brandy. His eyes were focused on the crystal snifter because he couldn't bear to look at the empty wall niche.

It had been a brazen act to steal the Sardonyx Cup tonight. Half of the NYPD had been just across the street protecting the First Lady. Or *not* protecting her, as it turned out.

Ted could still hear the police activity outside his windows. He had closed the drapes, unwilling to watch the ruins of the evening in the street below. Since he was a director of the museum and co-chairman of the gala, the security chief had notified him about the thwarted attack. FBI agents had also requested that he keep any knowledge of the attempted attack to himself. Federal authorities, not local police, would spearhead the investigation.

No one at the gala had been allowed to view the attacker's body. It was behind the catering screen. The fast-thinking security detail had explained away the gunshots as exploding champagne corks. Museum officials were instructed to say the security breach had been minor.

Ted couldn't believe how close they had all been to disaster. Just a few more minutes would have been fatal! With this kind of incident, his missing Sardonyx Cup was a minor problem. There was no point in calling the police tonight.

Suddenly the phone rang, blasting his nerves to shreds. He stared at it. Who was calling him at this hour? Ted checked his watch. Two a.m.

"Hello?"

"Ted, are you still up? It's Andy Thompson. I am sorry to call, but I just heard about the theft."

Ted froze, and the silence lengthened. Anderson Thompson cleared his throat.

"I'm sorry. I guess you hadn't heard yet. I just assumed."

"No, no," Ted said. "I'm afraid . . . I have no idea . . ."

"At the gala tonight. Quite a lot of art was stolen."

"*Stolen?*"

"Yes, the Egyptian Gallery was robbed. The glass case was cut and they got away with some valuable objects."

"Oh, my gosh, that is terrible," Ted replied cautiously. "What did they take?"

"Let me see . . . I have the list right here," he replied, reading off a list of valuable Egyptian funerary figurines.

"That's quite a loss. I just can't *believe* it."

"I can't either. Listen, I know it is late, but I wanted to give you the word in advance. It will be all over the papers. They may be calling you for a quote."

"All right, I'll be prepared. Much appreciated," said VerPlanck. "Take care."

Ted put down the phone. Art theft? The museum had been hit and so had he! That meant lots of publicity. Not something he wanted right now with Tipper on a bender.

On second thought, he wouldn't report his missing

cup to the police or to the insurers. Private investigators were the way to go. That way he'd keep his affairs to himself.

He picked up his phone and called his lawyer, Jim Gardiner, in London. There was no answer, so on voice mail he laid out his tale of the theft, along with instructions to find someone to help track the cup privately. Then Ted sat back on the sofa and drained his brandy snifter and stared at the empty pedestal.

The Mark Hotel

JOHN SINCLAIR POURED himself a dram of Macallan and tossed it back. Hell of a night! It was hard to believe they had arrived in New York only ten hours ago. The hotel had seemed so peaceful then. Now the evening was in ruins, tainted with fear and recrimination—not quite the romantic ending he had envisioned.

Steam was coming out of the bathroom. Cordelia had retreated to the shower. After fleeing the gala she had been chilled to the bone, her teeth chattering all the way back to the hotel. Even his dinner jacket hadn't helped.

Sinclair walked over to the bed and pulled back the duvet. The sooner he could get her to sleep, the better. The door opened and Cordelia came out wrapped in a large terry-cloth robe.

"Hop in, darling girl. I'll join you in a minute."

"We both need a good night's rest," she agreed as she slid between the sheets.

"I had room service send up something warm."

Sinclair poured Belgian cocoa from the pot and handed her a cup.

"Oh, John, thank you. . . ."

He sat on the edge of the bed, while she sipped the hot chocolate.

"I feel much better," she said with a smile, settling down.

Sinclair took the empty cup and carried it over to the table.

"Try to get some rest," he said as he put the saucer down. When he turned around, Cordelia was fast asleep.

Mayfair, London, England

IT WAS NINE a.m. when Jim Gardiner went into the kitchen to make coffee. It had been a long night. Sleep had been elusive, but he had finally managed to get three scant hours.

The insomnia wasn't because of his age. Pain kept him up at night. The result of a near-fatal accident nine months earlier. He had been poisoned by a toxic nerve agent and was suffering serious physical damage.

He had survived—just barely—but now the specialists were telling him he might have chronic pain for the rest of his life. Not exactly a cheerful thought!

Reaching for the canister of coffee, he saw the message light beeping on his mobile phone. Gardiner unplugged it from the charger and hit the retrieve button. The timing, this early in the morning, suggested the call was from the States.

Ted VerPlanck had left a brief, desperate voice mail. He had been robbed of a *very* valuable piece! And he wanted to recover the object through a private inquiry.

Poor Ted. Add this to the litany of calamities that had befallen him. First, his wife ran away with a rock star. Then she became addicted to drugs and alcohol. VerPlanck was old school—a real gentleman who stood by his wife.

Gardiner saved the message and leaned back against

the kitchen counter to think. Legally, it was a delicate matter. Keeping the insurers in the dark wasn't a very good idea.

He pulled the belt of his robe tighter and turned to his immediate task—making breakfast. As he began to measure out the coffee, he realized who might be able to help. One man had done more to recover lost artifacts than anyone else he knew—John Sinclair.

Carlyle Hotel

LADY XANDRA SLIPPED on her sheer peignoir and carried a latte to the window. The pedestrians on Madison Avenue were going about their normal weekday—city buses stopping for mothers with schoolchildren, people hurrying to the office.

Xandra watched the activity as she sipped her coffee and bit into her croissant, slathered with sweet butter and strawberry confiture.

Last night had gone well, despite the thwarted attack. She had played her part to perfection: vamping for the TV cameras, charming the First Lady with amusing anecdotes, chatting up the museum patrons. Meanwhile, throughout the city her men had been stealing treasures that had been carefully selected for their high market value. The stolen figurines from the Met were still there in her hotel room, lying on the dresser.

The other goods were stashed on her yacht—a two-hundred-foot Feadship, *The Khamsin,* docked at the base of Manhattan in North Cove Marina. Two special compartments had been built in the ship's cabinetry to facilitate smuggling. The boat crew had instructions to sit and guard the yacht all night.

Xandra calculated the time difference in Cairo and dialed Moustaffa. He answered from 5,600 miles away.

"It's Xandra. Everything is fine. I have it all."

"What's going on there!" he snarled in a foul temper.

"You were right about an attack, but it didn't succeed."

"Who was responsible?"

"I don't know. I got out. But don't worry. We have everything."

"I *knew* they were planning something . . ." he fumed. "But *you* said no . . . they wouldn't dare . . ."

"I only said I didn't *know* about it."

"So what *happened*?" Moustaffa demanded.

"Someone started shooting in the museum and everyone evacuated the building. Luckily I got out before it was mobbed with police."

"Was the gunman killed?" he asked.

"I didn't stick around to find out."

"Well, I hope it wasn't one of our men."

"What difference does it make?" Xandra consoled him. "The Manucci family hired them to cater the event. We're out of it."

"You're right. It's *their* problem."

"I think the attack helped a little. It's a diversion. The reporters will be busy uptown. Nobody is going to notice when I leave this morning."

"Good," said Moustaffa, softening his tone. "You're right. Fly, my little bird. Catch the desert wind and fly."

Balthazar Restaurant, SoHo, New York

TIPPER VERPLANCK SAT in the booth and sipped a Bloody Mary very slowly. The crowded downtown bistro was filled with the usual mix of fashionable artists, designers, and filmmakers. Conrad sat across from her, his expression supercilious as he surveyed the menu. Before his movie success he had cheerfully lived on a low-rent diet of hot dogs and pizza, but now that he was a recognized director nothing was ever good enough.

She didn't want to talk to Conrad right now. There was too much on her mind, after what had happened that morning at breakfast.

She had eaten her morning meal with Ted at their apartment on Fifth Avenue. Her husband had consumed his habitual three-minute egg, half a grapefruit, and one slice of brown toast with English marmalade. Initially, he had acted as if nothing had happened. But then, in the most chilling tone, he had asked her to please come with him to the living room. She had gathered up the folds of her cashmere robe and followed him down the hallway.

VerPlanck sat on the couch and patted the seat cushion for her to join him. She had no idea what he was doing. Sitting side by side, they looked mutely out at the room. After a long pause, he spoke.

"Do you notice anything amiss, Tipper?"

She looked around. Not one item was out of place.

The antique furniture was polished to a gorgeous patina and books were perfectly placed on the coffee table. Wood for the fireplace was laid in a chevron pattern on the hearth. Even the orchids were in full bloom. The living room could have been photographed for a decorating magazine.

"No," she said.

He closed his eyes in a display of patience, exhaled slowly, and turned to her.

"Try *harder*."

"Stop playing games, Ted. What do you want me to *say*?" she snapped. Her head was throbbing.

"My cup is gone."

"*O-K*. You don't have to carry on. If you want Consuela to bring you another coffee, I'll ring for it."

He looked at her as if she were insane.

"No, not my *coffee* cup. My *Sardonyx Cup*," he said, pointing across the room.

She looked at the wall niche. The pedestal was empty.

"I see," she said.

There was silence. What did he want *her* to do about it? Then she suddenly remembered Charlie Hannifin's little proposal about stealing Ted's art. She flushed bright red. *Could Charlie have stolen it?*

"I'm . . . so sorry . . ." she stammered.

He took her distress for sympathy.

"I know, it's awful," he said confidentially. "Listen to me, Tipper, we can't tell *anyone*."

"If you say so," she said, not really comprehending.

"I'm going to make private inquiries. I don't want the police involved."

She nodded, relieved that he seemed to require no real response from her.

"That is all," he said.

She got up to leave.

"Tipper," he said gravely. "I am doing this for you. To protect you. If we have one more disaster, the press will use it as an excuse to start hounding you again. They'd never leave you alone."

Her heart lurched. She didn't dare answer. The guilt was overwhelming. *He was protecting her.*

"Thank you, Ted," she managed to say, chastened.

Across from her Conrad was talking to the waiter about his order. She took another sip of the Bloody Mary and felt the vodka kick in. Oh yes, that was much better. To hell with Ted and his stupid cup!

Tipper smiled at Conrad, slid her hand under the table, and squeezed his knee. He was such a handsome man, especially with that silk shirt half-opened on his chest. It wasn't going to be such a bad day after all.

Time Warner Center, One Columbus Circle, New York

SINCLAIR AND CORDELIA walked into Ted VerPlanck's glass-walled office. His shipping firm was global in scope, one of the top freight-moving operations in Asia and Europe. His offices reflected enormous wealth, the decor very stylish, with chrome and black leather Italian-designed furniture—clearly the private fiefdom of a powerful man.

"How good of you to come so quickly," VerPlanck said as he shook Sinclair's hand.

"How are you, Ted?" Sinclair greeted him. "Jim Gardiner said you needed to meet right away."

"Yes, it's urgent." VerPlanck stared distractedly at Cordelia.

"May I present Cordelia Stapleton?" Sinclair said.

VerPlanck looked closely at her, hesitating.

"Aren't you the young woman I met last night?"

"Yes, and thank you again for everything."

"It was my pleasure." VerPlanck smiled. "I had no idea you were looking for my old friend John Sinclair."

"I guess I never mentioned his name."

Cordelia turned to Sinclair to explain. "Mr. VerPlanck was kind enough to escort me out of the museum when they evacuated it last night."

"Oh, thank you. I'm afraid I got separated from Delia."

"Have you heard anything further about what happened?" Cordelia asked.

"Nothing concrete," VerPlanck answered. "The investigation is not complete. Please, please have a seat."

Cordelia took her place in one of the modern leather chairs, but her attention was drawn to the scene below—an unimpeded vista of Columbus Circle from the fifth-floor window. Yellow taxis swirled around the traffic circle like bees. A statue of Christopher Columbus stood atop a column, his head cocked to the side, a hand on his hip. Beyond the intersection were eight hundred acres of green trees.

"What an incredible view of Central Park!" Cordelia exclaimed.

"Yes, one forgets how big it is until you see it from above," VerPlanck remarked.

"Is that the Metropolitan Museum over there on the far side?" Sinclair asked.

"Yes, you can see the roofline of my apartment, right there," VerPlanck pointed out. "It's the one with three chimneys."

"Jim Gardiner told me about the theft. I still can't believe someone robbed you," Sinclair said, taking a seat across from VerPlanck.

"It hardly seems real, even today," VerPlanck said. "I was hoping you could help me."

"Certainly, but why me?" Sinclair asked.

"I'm sure Jim Gardiner told you; I don't want the police involved."

"Why not?" Cordelia chimed in.

"The publicity."

"Certainly the press would be sympathetic," Sinclair insisted.

"I don't want to draw attention to my art holdings. I prefer to recover the cup through private means."

Ted VerPlanck leaned back, his long frame draped over his chair. "Do you think you can help?"

"Certainly, I can try," Sinclair replied. "But I need more information."

"Such as?"

"I'd like to see the layout of the apartment so I can get an idea of what happened. Was it an amateur job or professional? That sort of thing might help me pinpoint what kind of people we are dealing with."

"That's easily arranged," VerPlanck said.

He pressed the intercom button on his desk. "Margaret, have Gavin bring the car around please?"

VerPlanck checked his watch.

"It's noon already," he said. "We'll head over to the East Side. I do hope you can stay to lunch."

Conservation Labs,
Brooklyn Museum

IT WAS NOON when Holly Graham juggled coffee and newspapers onto her desk. Luckily, she didn't have to be there earlier. Her head was aching from too much champagne and lack of sleep!

Beautiful sunlight flooded through the window. Her office was situated where the north light was best—essential for the detailed repair work she did on the museum collections. The office was so bright she could grow a ficus tree in the corner and a couple of African violets on the windowsill.

There wasn't much time to relax this morning before heading out. Her team had been preparing a CAT scan over at North Shore Hospital. The mummy they were working on today required a climate-controlled truck, 70 degrees temperature, and constant humidity of 40–60 percent.

It was a lot of work. They had to place the cartouche in custom-cut foam and then in a wooden crate. Carter always insisted that the mummy's eyes be painted on the top of the outer box, as a courtesy. He said the deceased needed to see where they were going.

Thinking of Carter brought back the memories of

last night. *Had she really let him hold her in his arms?* The thought of it made her smile. He probably didn't have a clue why she was so upset. She'd look for him later to thank him for his concern.

But first things first. Caffeine! She wasn't going to budge before finishing her coffee. Holly sat down at her desk and pried the lid off the paper cup. The steam smelled glorious.

The first sip helped wake her up; then she turned to the newspaper headlines:

SECURITY SCARE AT THE GALA!
FIRST LADY FLEES FANCY FETE!

The images were dramatic. People leaving, police cars on the sidewalk. Holly was startled to read a headline on page two.

Rome Gala Robbed—Rare Artifacts Stolen!

Was the evacuation related to the burglary? As she started to read the details, her phone rang. The sound startled her and the coffee sloshed all over the desk. Mopping up the mess with a napkin, she grabbed the receiver on the fifth ring.

The voice that greeted her was the one she had been hearing in her mind all night.

"Good morning, Holly. How are you?" Sinclair's deep tones sounded confident, in control. "I'm calling to make sure you're all right."

"Hello, John. I'm fine. No ill effects," she managed to say, sounding surprisingly normal.

"I half expected to get your voice mail."

"I needed to come in. It's a busy day."

"I hope you don't mind me calling."

"Not at all. It's very thoughtful."

Holly shut her eyes; the formality of the exchange was excruciating.

Sinclair's voice shifted to a brisker tone. "Actually, Hols, I wanted to ask a favor."

"What's that?"

A surge of excitement went through her. Was he going to ask to see her again?

"I've given your name and contact number to an art collector who had a rare antiquity stolen last night. His name is Ted VerPlanck."

"Oh, I see."

"He wants to put out some feelers. If you don't mind, he may get in touch with you."

"Sure, John," she said, trying not to sound deflated. "I'll be happy to help if I can."

Sinclair seemed to notice something in her tone, so he went on to explain.

"I hope it's not an imposition, but I remembered that art security is something you know a lot about."

She fought to keep her voice dispassionate.

"Yes. I've been consulting with the FBI fairly regularly about stolen art, so I'd be happy to talk to him."

"Great. His attorney, Jim Gardiner, may call you directly."

There was in imperceptible pause as Sinclair's voice switched to a heartier register.

"So . . . it was nice seeing you again, Holly."

"You too, John," she said as her heart flopped over. Would he ask her out after all? But her hopes were dashed instantly.

"Take care," Sinclair said and rang off.

Holly put down the phone and exhaled. How was it he could rattle her after all these years? She twisted her hair back up into a chignon and secured it with a pencil. It was time to get over the man. But since they parted company there had been no one even remotely as exciting as Sinclair. In fact, these days her social life was pathetic. The only confirmed date she had was with a two-thousand-year-old mummy.

She glanced at her watch. Almost time to leave for the CAT scan. The appointment at the hospital was for one p.m.

As she started to gather her things, her supervisor poked his head in. Holly's greeting died on her lips. He looked absolutely distraught.

"Holly, how late were you here last night?"

She searched her mind quickly.

"About six o'clock . . . I guess. I remember I was running late for the gala."

"Did you go to the storeroom at all yesterday?"

"No, I was working with the CT images on my computer. I found something unusual with Artemidorus. He—"

"He's gone," the director said, cutting her off.

An awful lurch of fear stirred deep down inside her.

"Maybe someone—"

"No."

She stared at him in silence.

"He was stolen," he said. "I need to call the police."

"Oh, my *God!* Are you *sure*?"

"Yes, I am *very* sure. I may need you later, to answer some questions."

"Absolutely. If anyone wants me I'll be at North Shore Hospital doing a scan."

W HEN CARTER WALLACE walked up to the counter, the cop at the desk didn't look up.

"Excuse me, I have something to report about the gala last night."

"At the *Met*?" the cop asked with sudden interest, putting his pen down. That was a good sign. Carter didn't want to spend his entire day convincing some jaded officer that he had something serious to report.

"I saw some very suspicious activity last night," Carter explained. "Two guys loading a van. I wrote down the license plate number." He pulled the scrap of paper out of his jacket and offered it.

"Hold on to that for a moment. I need you to fill out some forms."

"Sure." Carter tucked the number back into his pocket.

The officer slid a sheet of paper onto a clipboard.

"Name, address, and phone number. Somebody will be along to take your statement."

Carter walked over to the scarred wooden benches along the wall. In his mind he clearly saw the white van and the two men loading the crate. He sat down and began to write.

Brooklyn Museum

A T NOON CARTER Wallace poked his head into Holly Graham's office. Nobody was there. No brown bag lunch in the usual spot.

Disappointed, he headed back down to his little cubby in the basement. The subterranean passage was empty, but he could hear the phone ringing on his desk. He speeded up and grabbed the receiver just in time.

"Carter here," he said, hoping like hell it was Holly. Instead it was the nasal whine of the director of the antiquities department.

"Carter, I need you to check something out for me."

"OK. No problem."

"It's stolen art. Egyptian artifacts. I know that Holly usually does this sort of thing, but she's doing a scan today over at the hospital and then she's leaving for London. Can you look into it?"

Carter felt his spirits sink. She was going to London and didn't even *tell* him? He must be pretty low on her radar for her to go out of the country without saying good-bye.

"Sure. Just tell me where to go."

He wrote down an address, tore off the sheet, and stuck it in his pocket. He'd leave right away. With Holly gone, there was no use hanging around.

North Cove Marina, New York

THE DOCK AT the base of Manhattan's Financial District was empty except for Lady Xandra Sommerset's megayacht, *The Khamsin*. No private boats remained in New York this late in the season. Most people had already headed down to Florida or the Caribbean for the winter. But the nautical charts on *The Khamsin* were for another destination—a transatlantic crossing.

Xandra walked up the gangplank and glanced out over the harbor. It was a beautiful sunny day. Across the glinting water the Statue of Liberty had her arm lifted, as if in a cheerful wave. Ferries were churning by, taking commuters to New Jersey and Staten Island.

The boat's engines were already idling and the twenty-four-man crew was standing by, ready to cast off. She gave an affirmative nod to the captain as she boarded, and the men immediately set about clearing the lines. In the main salon one of the stewards was waiting.

"Would you like some tea, madame?" he inquired.

"Please." Xandra tossed her camel-hair coat on the nearest chair.

The interior decor of the yacht was tasteful, with a subtle palette of cream and beige. She stopped to survey the Orientalist painting above the couch—a portrait of a naked young woman entitled *Femme Nue,* by Jean-Léon Gérôme. Moustaffa had said it reminded him of Xandra.

The classic odalisque depicted a young woman with pearly flesh bathing in a Turkish hammam.

The steward returned with a pot of freshly brewed Egyptian chamomile tea. She kicked off her shoes and tucked her feet up on the couch. This was her favorite place on earth. Unencumbered by any man-made laws, Lady X ruled this universe of twenty-odd people. She alone dictated the schedule of daily life and could go wherever the wind and sea permitted.

Xandra had named her boat after the hot Sahara wind—a seasonal gale that blew in April. The *khamsin* had raised choking, blinding dust against Napoleon's army in Egypt and caused Allied and German troops to halt their battles during World War Two.

Today, *The Khamsin* motoryacht would not raise any attention. It would cruise quietly out of New York Harbor past the Statue of Liberty, under the Verrazano Bridge to Ambrose Channel, and out into the Atlantic Ocean.

From there, they'd follow the coastline of the Eastern Seaboard, along the Great Circle Route—the shortest geographic distance between two points on earth. They'd travel steadily at fifteen knots for ten days until they reached the coast of France, where she would meet Moustaffa.

1010 Fifth Avenue

A T A QUARTER to one, Sinclair, Cordelia, and Ted entered the VerPlancks' penthouse. The formal entrance hall had a black-and-white marble floor, a crystal chandelier hanging from the ceiling, and a white-jacketed butler standing at attention.

"Thank you," Cordelia said, handing him her trench coat.

Ted VerPlanck lived the life of a Gilded Age tycoon— his penthouse was every bit as grand as the nineteenth-century showplaces of the Carnegies, Vanderbilts, and Astors.

"Where did you keep the cup?" Sinclair asked, looking around.

"In the living room. I'll take you in there in a minute, but first I want to show you the atrium."

"Is that where they broke in?" Sinclair asked.

"Yes. As you can see, the apartment is designed so all the rooms open into an enclosed courtyard. This is the same construction as a *peristylum* in ancient Roman architecture."

As he spoke, they entered an enormous interior garden with palm trees and tropical plants. The air was filled with the lush scent of foliage and flowers. It was a private, exotic jungle, right in the middle of the apartment!

"Of course, this is not *really* a Roman courtyard,

because the roof has to be enclosed," VerPlanck explained, almost as if apologizing for its deficiency.

Cordelia walked around, staring in astonishment. The atrium had a tranquil feel. Filtered sunlight came down through a vaulted glass ceiling. A large birdcage held tiny colorful South American parakeets. There was an oblong reflecting pool with a small jet of water burbling gently and lily pads floating on the surface, their waxy leaves accented with spiky pink flowers.

"Oh, how *beautiful*!" Cordelia said with a gasp.

"It was designed by the famous architect Rosario Candela in 1910."

"It's incredible," Sinclair remarked, looking around.

"I'll give you a little bit of the layout." VerPlanck swept his arm toward the front of the building. "On this side of the atrium we have a reception room, the living room, dining room, and library."

"The entertaining spaces?" Cordelia asked.

"Exactly. The bedrooms and other private rooms are on the other side."

"So where did the intruders break in?" asked Sinclair.

"Astonishingly, they came in through there," VerPlanck said, and pointed up at the glass ceiling.

"That must be twenty feet high," Sinclair observed.

"They lowered themselves down on ropes," VerPlanck said. "On the way to bed last night, I noticed shards of glass all over the floor."

Cordelia examined the entry point with interest.

"But the glass isn't broken," she observed.

"I had it replaced this morning. We keep extra panels in the basement."

"They didn't touch any of this art?" Sinclair asked, examining the canvases on the walls. "I'm assuming that these are not copies."

"No, they are originals," VerPlanck assured him.

Cordelia walked over to a canvas of pastel swirls.

"Haven't I seen this one before?"

"Yes. It is one of the many water lily studies by Monet," VerPlanck explained. "And over here is a jungle scene by Henri Rousseau. And there, a Peruvian landscape by Frederic Church."

"Priceless," Sinclair observed. "Yet they didn't touch anything."

"No, it appears they were after only one item."

"The cup," Sinclair said.

"Exactly. Come this way," VerPlanck encouraged. "I'll show you where it . . . was."

The living room was at least sixty feet long. Six enormous windows swathed in rose silk moiré faced Fifth Avenue. The Metropolitan Museum was directly across the street.

"After you left the apartment, no one was home?" Sinclair asked.

"Tipper came in after I left. She was running late. But the butler and housekeeper were both off for the evening. And the cook and cleaning staff come in only during the daytime."

He walked the length of the living room and stopped at a curved niche in the wall. Inside was a freestanding marble Ionian column—obviously a pedestal for an art object.

No explanation was necessary. This was where the cup

had been displayed. They looked at the empty space in silence. VerPlanck sighed.

"I just can't believe it's gone."

There was no mention of the Sardonyx Cup during lunch. Ted VerPlanck spoke of art, archaeology, and his extensive travels. Only after the plates had been cleared of cucumber salad and salmon, and they had finished their lemon tarts, did he broach the subject of the cup.

"John, what do you think about the possibility of recovering it?" VerPlanck asked. "And please be honest. I don't want to have any false hopes."

"I can't offer any guarantees, but I would be happy to make some calls and see if it is on the international black market . . ."

"That's exactly what I had in mind."

Sinclair waited in silence. The butler poured the demitasse and left before he continued.

"The problem is most of my contacts in the black market are overseas. I often deal with criminal gangs to try to recover artifacts that were stolen directly from archaeological digs."

"How do you get them back?"

"Cash. Pure and simple. Things can usually be bought back for a fraction of what they are worth."

"That sounds fine to me," VerPlanck said.

"Except in New York it's different. Things surface in the art market through vendors. You need local connections to art dealers and auction houses."

"I understand, but surely you have those kinds of networks also?"

"Some," Sinclair assured him, "but I'm based in London. To pursue this properly, you would need someone who lives here in New York."

"Is there anyone you can suggest?"

There was a long silence. Sinclair gave a calculating glance at Cordelia.

"Yes, there *is* someone," he finally said. "The person I am thinking of is often called in to verify ancient artifacts before they are put up for sale—to see if they are authentic."

"They sound perfect."

"It would take someone with a Rolodex built up over decades to quietly start the type of inquiry you are looking for."

Ted took a note card out of his jacket pocket to jot down the name. His pen was poised above the paper.

"I don't have the *private* phone number, you understand," Sinclair explained. "But I can tell you how to get in touch with her at work."

"Please . . ." said VerPlanck.

He looked up, sensing Sinclair's reticence.

"Dr. Hollis Graham," Sinclair finally said, not looking at Cordelia. "She works at the Brooklyn Museum. I've already spoken to her. She expects your call."

North Shore University Hospital, Manhasset, Long Island

THE NORTH SHORE Hospital was known for its state-of-the-art cardiac imaging. Today, the middle-aged man on the scanning bed was beyond any lifesaving measures—he had been dead for two thousand years.

Standing around the gurney were museum conservators wearing masks and gowns. The protective clothing was to prevent them from ingesting any toxic particles that would be released when they moved the mummy. It was a difficult maneuver they were attempting—trying to slide the human remains out of a wooden container and onto the bed of the CT machine.

"Everyone, get ready," Holly instructed. "When I say 'three' . . ."

They usually didn't have to lift the body out. The machine could penetrate anything organic, including a coffin, and most mummies could be scanned intact. But this mummy lay in a wooden crate that was too big to scan. Worse still, the body had been unwrapped and was now fully exposed, held together by strips of linen.

When the conservators at the Brooklyn Museum first saw the mummy's condition, they were appalled. An unwrapped mummy was a throwback to the gruesome practices of the Victorian age. Back then, unraveling was a form of entertainment. Members of high society would sometimes host "unwrapping parties," followed by champagne and a midnight supper!

On one ghoulish evening in 1825, Dr. Augustus Granville stood before the Royal Society of London to "scientifically autopsy" an embalmed Egyptian woman. He added a theatrical touch—candlelight, with tapers made from the same kind of wax used to preserve the deceased. The British archaeologist Flinders Petrie set a new course in 1898 by using an X-ray machine.

Holly looked down at the desiccated cadaver before her.

Usually, lifting a mummy was like moving a person in a sleeping bag. Roman-era mummies often had wooden planks aligned along the spine under the wrappings to keep them rigid. But this one was no longer tightly bound.

Holly adjusted the surgical mask over her nose and took hold of her corner of the sling. They had improvised with a bed sheet, threading it under the bones to use like a hammock and swing the body up onto the table.

"Now it's going to shift around a lot," Holly warned. "You have to be ready."

The three assistants picked up their ends of the sheet.

"One, two, three . . . *Lift!*"

They gently cantilevered the sling and lowered it onto the scanning bed. After they were done, Holly bent over and reexamined the ancient figure.

The linen was degrading a bit, but there was no real damage to the bones. Almost like clockwork, a young assistant's stomach began to heave. He started tearing at his surgical mask.

"Excuse me!" He coughed and rushed out.

As the door swung shut they could hear him retching loudly in the next room.

Opening up a mummy case always resulted in an utterly unique eye-watering aroma of ancient resin, embalming spices, and organic decomposition. Carter had once described the smell as "two-thousand-year-old potpourri mixed with the odor of a ripe garbage can."

Holly looked down at the slim body. The phrase "ashes to ashes, dust to dust" popped into her head. Fragile wrappings clung to the rib cage—the torso was festooned with strips of linen the color of dried coffee. The leg bones were all rickety knees and delicate shins. Only the feet were intact, with parchment-like skin stretched over them.

The cadaver still looked very human and appeared to be grimacing in pain, its teeth protruding. The head was tilted at an angle that, if it had been alive, could only have been interpreted as agony. The scalp was covered with patches of russet hair, and the skin on the mummy's face was remarkably smooth, the texture of glove leather.

"OK, go on . . . all of you . . ." Holly sighed, pulling off her mask and making shooing motions to dismiss her assistants. They scrambled out gratefully.

After everyone left, the room was silent.

"This will take just a moment," she quietly instructed the figure on the slab. "We need to know more about you. Then we'll let you rest. I promise."

Holly usually talked to her mummies. Some people questioned her about it, wondering if she was a little batty.

But she explained that it was a gesture of respect. These former human beings had gone to considerable expense and effort to ensure that their afterlife would be comfortable and dignified. Who was *she* to thwart their final wishes?

The radiologist was waiting behind the glass window to begin the scan. She joined him in the adjacent room, which served as a control booth.

"This is one patient who won't be squirming around," the young radiologist said with a grin.

"I can guarantee this one's not budging."

He pushed the button and they watched the ancient figure slide into the machine.

"It'll take about twenty minutes. Mind if I step out for a sandwich?"

"Sure, no problem," Holly agreed. "Why don't you set the timer for a few minutes longer. Because he's dead, we can get a lot more detail without risk of overexposure."

"I'll set the clock at forty-five minutes. The body will come out automatically. But I should be back."

"OK, don't rush."

Holly sat down on a chair and watched the monitor. Every angle of the figure—both internal and external—would be scanned. They would image the body at 2-millimeter thicknesses at 1.5-millimeter intervals. New techniques in the medical field were helping Egyptologists every day: radiography, computer tomography, endoscopy scanning, electron microscopy, and even DNA testing. Looking at the high-resolution images, they would be able to determine what the man died of and any medical conditions that he suffered from while still alive.

But all that would come later. Right now, there was really nothing to observe. She tipped her head back and closed her eyes to rest.

Holly woke up with a start, surprised to find herself in the hospital imaging room. She had been dreaming about the gala. Her body was stiff from being immobile, and she was again aware of the fatigue from the late night. The lab was empty. She looked through the window and saw that the mummy was still inside the machine.

The door behind her opened. But it wasn't the lab worker. There was a handsome man standing there. Tall, possibly in his early fifties, dressed in a blue blazer and gray slacks.

"Sorry to disturb. The attendant said I could come in."

"How can I help you?"

"I'm looking for a Dr. Hollis Graham."

His voice was soft, and he gave a slight smile. Holly sat up, adjusting her white coat.

"I'm Dr. Graham."

"I'm Ted VerPlanck. I believe your friend John Sinclair told you I would be in contact."

"*Mr. VerPlanck,* nice to meet you! I was expecting to hear from you, but not in person."

"I called the museum and was told you could be reached here. I was wondering if we might talk after you are finished?"

"This scan will take a few more minutes, so I have time now."

"Excellent."

"Won't you sit down?"

She offered him the only other seat in the room, a rolling stool. He perched there and started explaining how a rare Egyptian sardonyx cup had been stolen from his home. Did she think it could be recovered?

Halfway through his account Holly realized that he was talking about *the* Sardonyx Cup—the famous artifact that had been fashioned from an Egyptian drinking vessel, carved from a single block of sardonyx. Holly had always assumed the chalice was in a museum in Europe, not a private collection!

"What did the police say when they looked at the crime scene?" Holly asked.

"I didn't call them."

"Why not?"

"There can be absolutely *no* publicity," he replied brusquely.

"I assume you have photos of the object."

"Yes, for the insurance records."

Holly considered that for a moment. He didn't look like someone who was involved in insurance fraud. But she had her reputation to consider.

"I must admit, I'm not comfortable with this."

"Why?"

"The theft at the Met. You are telling me the two events occurred the same evening?"

"Yes."

"If so, the police may already be involved in this case. It's not a matter for private investigation."

"I am very convinced the events are not related."

"Well, there is always the FBI Art Crime Division if you want to investigate quietly. Why not go to them?"

"I can't do that."

"You haven't done anything wrong, have you?"

He flushed, clearly embarrassed by the question.

"*Certainly* not!"

The timer on the control panel began to beep. The scanning process for the mummy was nearly complete.

"I'm sorry, but I have to take care of this."

"Of course."

He followed her into the other room, as if waiting for an answer. The digital display was counting down the last ten seconds. Holly looked around. Still no sign of the technician.

"So you'll help me find it?" VerPlanck pressed.

Completely absorbed, she didn't answer.

"Dr. Graham?"

"Look, I don't mean to be dismissive," she said, glancing up at him. "But no. I don't think I'll be able to help you."

"You *won't*?"

"Not unless you tell me the whole story."

"But—"

"I'm sorry, Mr. VerPlanck. But the way I see it, you should go to the police."

The machine beeped, and the mummy began to appear. The skull, with its horrible grimace, slid out first. VerPlanck recoiled and stared at the bundle of rags and bones. As the body emerged, the stench increased. VerPlanck stumbled backward toward the door, holding his handkerchief to his nose.

"I'm sorry to have disturbed you, Dr. Graham. Thank you for your time."

15 Desbrosses Street

A CELL PHONE woke Tipper VerPlanck. She opened her eyes and realized she was still in Conrad's bed. A clock on the night table said three p.m. She and Conrad had been naked since they finished lunch. He was snoring gently, exhausted from their strenuous activities. She pushed his heavy arm off and felt around the floor for her phone.

Her ring tone was the hit song "Society Girl"—written for her by the lead singer of the band the Blades. Tipper's fingertips made contact, and she slid the cell phone out from under the bed.

"Hello," she croaked.

"It's Charlie."

Who the hell was Charlie? She thought about it for a long, fuzzy moment.

"Charlie *Hannifin.*"

"What do you want?"

"Is now a good time to talk?"

"Actually, no." She groped for the bedsheet, pulling it around her. Then she suddenly remembered.

"*Wait!*" She asked, "Do you know anything about the Sardonyx Cup?"

"That's what I'm calling about."

Conrad stirred next to her and mumbled something unintelligible. She turned away and whispered, "Charlie, did you *steal* it?"

There was a long pause.

"Not personally, no."

Tipper gasped.

"I never agreed to *anything*! We were just talking."

"Is there a way we could meet?" he asked.

Tipper looked over at Conrad. His face was crammed into the pillow and he was snoring with his mouth open.

"Sure, I'll meet you at the Red Parrot."

There was a long pause.

"Where's that?" asked Charlie.

"Tribeca."

"You're kidding!" Charlie said in disbelief. "Are you still seeing that rock star?"

"Oh, for Pete's sake, Charlie, just meet me at the Red Parrot in an hour."

Red Parrot Bar,
Vestry Street, New York

WHEN TIPPER WALKED into the Red Parrot, the bartender called out his usual greeting. He was a longtime acquaintance—but not of her uptown world. A gold earring dangled from one earlobe and he wore a red bandanna knotted over his bald cranium.

"Simon, get me something for this hangover."

He looked at her critically and moved his head side to side with pursed lips. His eyes were calculating.

"Was it hard liquor or wine?"

"What?"

"Last night. What'd ya drink?"

"Both," she said woefully.

He slid his hand across the bar and patted hers sympathetically. There was a small plastic ziplock bag hidden under his palm. He slipped it to her and then moved away to pick up the vodka bottle.

"Vodka? Or something more exotic?" he asked innocently, holding up a bottle.

Tipper sat very still, her palm covering the drugs.

"Simon, I just got out of the clinic."

"Hey, no pressure. I'm going to make you a fabulous cocktail and you just sit there."

He turned his back and began to shuffle bottles.

Tipper felt the small plastic bag burning a hole through her palm.

She tried to clear her mind. She had been foolish to drink so heavily at the gala. It had started her on another bender. As far as drugs went, it would be very stupid to begin that all over again.

But her life was horrible. Her Upper East Side friends didn't call anymore, and Conrad's downtown friends treated her like a fossil from Madame Tussauds. No, actually she felt like a mummy: wrinkled outside, dead inside.

Tipper slid off the bar stool and headed to the ladies' room. Simon turned around and glanced at the space where her hand had been. The bar was empty.

"Back in a moment, Simon," she called over her shoulder. "If someone comes in asking for me, tell him to wait."

"You got it, honey."

The ladies' room was at the back of the large space, marked with a Queen of Hearts playing card tacked to the door. She entered cautiously, making a lot of noise. You never knew *what* was going on in there.

Charlie walked by the Red Parrot twice, thinking he had gotten the address wrong. Then he realized her genius. Who would find them in a dump like this?

"May I help you?" The bartender eyed him speculatively.

"I'm meeting someone. I guess she hasn't arrived yet."

"Is it Tipper VerPlanck? She's inside. Can I get you anything?"

Just then Tipper appeared looking very bright and cheerful. Surprisingly normal.

"Hello, Charlie. Glad you found me."

He was relieved. At least he wasn't going to have to sit in here alone.

"Can we get a table?"

"Sure."

Even though the place was empty, she walked to the back booth and sat down. Charlie sat on a banquette with his back to the wall.

In a moment, Simon appeared holding a small round tray with two drinks. He swooped it down with a flourish.

"Here you are. Drink slowly. These are *strong*."

The liquid was light apricot in color, served in martini glasses.

"What's this, Simon?"

"I'm calling it the Park Avenue Peach." He winked at her and walked away.

Charlie looked at his glass with distaste. Tipper picked hers up and took a big, long sip.

"*Damn,* that's good! You should try it."

Charlie said nothing.

"Did you have anything to do with the theft at the Met?" Tipper asked in a whisper.

"Absolutely not."

"What about Ted's Sardonyx Cup?"

"Not personally. I knew about it."

"Charlie, I want no part of this scheme of yours!"

Tipper was angry, her voice starting to rise. Charlie said nothing and just slid an envelope across the table.

"What's that?"

"It's yours. Keep it. When we talked, the cup had already been stolen."

She opened the envelope and gasped.

"It's a check for fifty thousand dollars!"

"That's right."

"I never agreed. And here you go and *steal* the damn thing from my apartment."

"Well, not technically. It was done by professionals."

"I don't want any part of this, Charlie."

"OK, keep the check or don't. But if you tear it up the money will just go to waste."

Tipper opened the envelope and looked at the check again.

"It's signed by Marco International. Who's that?"

"A shell company in Italy."

"I can't even cash this! I'll get caught. The money will show up in my bank balance."

"Open an account in Gibraltar."

"I don't know how to *do* that, Charlie."

Charlie stuck his index finger in the drink and tasted it. He made a face.

"Tipper, *everybody* knows how to do that."

"Well, *I* don't, and I can't see myself actually asking Ted to show me how."

Suddenly that struck them both as funny, and they laughed a little too loudly about it. It broke the tension.

"OK. Look, I can show you. No reason to let this money go to waste, Tipper."

Suddenly, she was on her guard.

"What, exactly, do you want me to do? Leave the kitchen service entrance open for your friends?"

"Not really." Charlie leaned in close. "Forget about Ted. You know a lot about art, right?"

"Yes, my college degree was in fine arts."

"And you know a lot of people in this town. They *all* have important art."

"Yes, everybody has fabulous paintings. But I don't want to get involved in stealing art."

"You don't have to get involved. We just have a casual conversation from time to time. The same kind we always have."

"What do you mean?"

"I say, 'How's Ted?' And you say, 'He's in France until the end of the month.' Bingo. Done. That's it."

"That's *it*?" said Tipper. "And you *pay* me?"

She held up the check and scrutinized it as if it might be counterfeit.

"It's good money, Tipper. You could earn enough to get away from Ted for the rest of your life."

Tipper drained her glass and reached for his. He hadn't really touched it.

"So you want me to spy on my friends?"

"*Are* they your friends? *Really?*"

His tone was sympathetic. She didn't answer.

"*Seriously,*" he said. "Nina Barker told Ted that you were cheating on him. I heard your co-op board had a meeting about asking you to leave because you were dealing drugs."

"I *never* dealt drugs!"

"I *know* you didn't," he assured her, patting her hand.

"So what's your point?"

"My point is, who in hell has been nice to you lately?"

Tipper looked at him with narrowed eyes.

"You know a lot, don't you, Charlie."

Tipper folded up the check and put it back in the envelope. It lay there on the table as she eyed it. "Maybe I'll keep this. I'll call you."

She picked up his drink and drained it, squinting at him over the rim. Then she put down the empty glass and licked her lips.

"Why are you doing this?" she asked. "You don't need the money."

"Actually, I do. I lost a ton in that pharmaceutical scam last year."

"Ted always thought that was a fishy investment. I guess a lot of people got burned."

"Yes, well, I need the money."

"Sorry to hear that, Charlie."

"Thank you, I appreciate that," he said, leaning over and touching her arm confidentially. "But so do you. Need the money, I mean."

"Why do you say that? I have plenty."

"You're used to living very well. What are you going to do after you and Ted are divorced? It won't be quite the same, now, will it?"

"I'm not divorcing Ted."

"No. But I hear he is divorcing *you*."

Tipper glared at him. "You aren't just saying that, are you?"

"No, I'm not. He's filing papers. You're going to be left high and dry."

Tipper put the envelope into her purse and snapped the clasp shut.

"Don't be ridiculous. I don't know about high, but I'll never, *ever* be dry."

The Khamsin Motoryacht,
Off the Coast of Maine

LADY SOMMERSET WHIRLED the mahogany Indian clubs in elaborate circles on the top deck of the yacht. The wind whipped around her, stinging her skin with salt spray. Gradually increasing the size of the bowling pin–shaped weights, she followed her daily routine, flexing her knees to keep her stance.

The captain suddenly appeared on deck. "Lady Sommerset, we have removed the cargo from the storage compartment."

"Thank you."

"What should we do with it?"

"Put everything in the salon."

"Very well, madame."

The captain descended to the lower level. She stopped to breathe in the fresh air. What a glorious, exhilarating day! She gave the ocean a final glance, noting the three-foot swells, then turned and climbed down the ladder to the lower deck.

A large object filled the entire leather banquette in the salon. At first glance, it looked like a person covered in a red quilt. But the trompe l'oeil effect lasted only a second. It was the mummy Artemidorus, his crimson coffin sculpted into the vague shape of a body.

Lady X sat and looked at the magnificent object in triumph. The gold-leaf filigree on the exterior depicted the story of the afterlife. Below the encaustic portrait panel was a falcon collar and a series of traditional Egyptian scenes. The god Anubis was flanked by the goddess Isis. There was a short Greek inscription across the breast of the bier that read "Farewell Artemidorus."

A lot of planning had gone into stealing the massive twelve-foot-long mummy case. She had been obsessed with Artemidorus for the last decade, ever since she had seen the lovely young man, immortalized in death, at the British Museum. He had a face to fall in love with.

In the portrait panel, his beautiful black curls were crowned with a laurel of gold leaf, an indication of his high birth. He was a prince—a ruler in ancient Egypt— and by every right he should be buried in his native soil.

She would take care of him now. They would not keep him imprisoned in a museum, probing, X-raying, and scanning him with their medical machines.

A steward came in with a medium-size wooden crate and placed it on the low table in front of her. Another steward entered with a champagne bucket. He opened a bottle of Louis Roederer Cristal and inserted it into the shaved ice.

"Is there anything else, madame?"

"No, thank you."

The steward left and shut the door. Xandra lifted the lid of the wooden box and there, encased in the custom-cut foam, was the Sardonyx Cup. It glowed with the splendor of burnished gold as she carefully lifted it out and put it down on the low table. Then, taking the bottle out of the ice bucket, she poured champagne into the ancient vessel. Carefully, reverently, she grasped the Sardonyx Cup by the base and raised it in a silent toast to Artemidorus.

Central Park, New York

CHARLIE HANNIFIN SAT on a bench in Central Park and looked at the stone obelisk known as Cleopatra's Needle. It was much older than the Egyptian queen. The pharaoh Thutmose III had built it in 1450 BC in the city of Heliopolis.

The monument now stood in Central Park, right behind the Metropolitan Museum, having traveled to New York in the 1880s, when Egyptian mania was sweeping through American society. Financed by some wealthy enthusiasts, the granite pillar had been brought from Alexandria, Egypt, to New York Harbor by barge. It took thirty-two horses to drag it up the banks of the Hudson River to its current location. On Sunday afternoons, during the Gilded Age, people from all walks of life would drive by in their carriages to view it.

These days the ancient pillar stood on Central Park Drive, in the middle of the modern city. Joggers now used the obelisk as a mile marker as they ran their laps around the park. Gasoline fumes and decades of pollution had pitted the hieroglyphics, and the carvings were rapidly becoming indecipherable.

Charlie had come to appreciate Cleopatra's Needle for reasons other than historic ones. It was his favorite rendezvous spot, located directly behind the Met. The benches nearby were always empty—a perfect place for a clandestine cell phone call.

Charlie dialed a number that connected to a satellite phone somewhere in the Atlantic Ocean.

"Lady Sommerset, please. Tell her Charlie Hannifin is on the line."

There was a long pause. Charlie studied the inscriptions, added to the pillar by Ramses II to commemorate his military victories. A brass plaque below gave the translation:

> The golden Horus, content with victory,
> Who smiteth the rulers of nations
> Hundreds of thousands
> In as much as father Ra
> Hath ordered unto him
> Victory against every land.

There was a crackle on the line.

"Hold for Lady Sommerset, please," a male voice said.

"Charlie, how are you?"

"Just fine. We are sending that last art shipment out to Italy in two days."

"Where is it going after that?"

"China."

"Beijing or Shanghai?"

"The art scene in Beijing is still pretty provincial. But we are getting a lot of interest in Shanghai and Hong Kong."

"They *are* the ones with the money, aren't they?" Lady Sommerset laughed.

"Tons of it. This one will net fifty million."

"Pounds or dollars?"

"Renminbi."

There was silence on the other end.

"I'm *joking*," Charlie continued. "Euros."

"Very funny. I'll let Moustaffa know."

"Please give him my regards."

"I will," Xandra replied. "I certainly will."

Cairo, Egypt

MOUSTAFFA FILED HIS daily blog, closed down his computer, and shut off the light. Hundreds of his acolytes had already commented on the post "The Triumph of the Common Man"—his call to topple the Anglo-American oppressor who ruled their "democracies" with lies and deceit.

Moustaffa's apocalyptic vision was almost complete. He would be meeting Lady Xandra Sommerset off the coast of France. Together they would begin a carefully orchestrated attack to topple half the governments of the industrialized world.

Moustaffa closed the apartment door and walked out onto the landing of the building. The smell of spicy food wafted up the stairwell as he clomped down three flights and out the front door. Two young teenagers lounged on the steps in dirty T-shirts with the logos of Nike and Puma. They eyed him and slunk away into the crowd.

Brooklyn Museum

HOLLY GRAHAM CLOSED down her office computer. She had finished up the CAT scan at the hospital and filed all the paperwork. The poor unwrapped mummy from Thebes was on his way to a more dignified end. The conservation staff would sew him up and award him a place of honor in the museum galleries.

It had been a brutally long day, starting with the discovery of the theft of Artemidorus. Now it seemed part of the blame would be placed on her. The online tabloids noted she had been "in charge" of Artemidorus, implying she had been negligent!

A snapshot of Holly leaving the hospital earlier in the afternoon was posted next to the article "The Case of the Missing Mummy." She was identified as "the Marilyn Monroe of the mummy world."

The FBI had been more respectful. After talking to the Art Recovery Division on the phone for almost an hour, she had confidence they would find Artemidorus. After all, a twelve-foot cartouche would be pretty hard to transport without someone noticing.

The museum was sending her to London tomorrow, to talk to her colleagues at the British Museum. The theft of their precious artifact called for face-to-face diplomacy, and she was the ambassador.

Holly closed up her office and stepped outside for

the brief walk to the number 2/3 train station on Eastern Parkway. After being cooped up all day, it was nice to be outdoors. The fresh air helped her lingering fatigue.

What a lovely time of year! The temperature was nippy and there was the scent of wet leaves and damp earth. Streetlights were casting a golden light on the sidewalk in front of the museum.

Suddenly she heard footsteps running behind her and turned, half expecting to see Carter. But it was Ted VerPlanck!

"Dr. Graham! Terribly sorry, I didn't mean to startle you."

"Oh, I thought you were someone else."

Again she was struck by the handsome man—distinguished in a "senior diplomat" sort of way. He wore a cashmere topcoat and carried a pair of shearling gloves.

"I wanted to talk to you, if it is not too much to ask."

"Certainly."

"I am ready to tell you why I can't go to the police."

"All right."

"It's my wife—she is not well. She is . . . went through rehab just recently."

"I don't understand."

"My wife and I were at the gala last night."

"So was I."

"Well, then, you saw the press lining the steps."

"Yes . . . ?"

"My wife was not in good . . . well . . . she had been drinking."

Holly felt sorry for him. Despite the cool night, his forehead was beaded with fine drops of perspiration. He shifted from foot to foot in anxiety.

"If news of this theft goes public, they'll dig up those pictures and she'll be subjected to another trial-by-tabloid about her so-called relapse."

"Well . . . I'm sure—"

"She had only a couple of glasses of wine, you understand," Ted cut in, "but I think Tipper's system is very delicate and it hit her hard."

Holly nodded, uncertain what to say.

"Can I drop you somewhere?" VerPlanck asked. "We could talk further in the car."

"I'm just going home on the subway."

"Please let me give you a ride."

Before she could answer, he punched a number on his cell phone.

"Gavin, would you please bring the car to the front of the museum?"

Within a moment, a dark blue Bentley Mulsanne pulled up and the driver came around to open the rear door. There really was no choice. Holly got in.

British Air, First-Class Lounge, Kennedy Airport, New York

"L ET'S EAT HERE SO we can sleep on the flight," Sinclair suggested to Cordelia.

She silently perused the menu, so he went ahead and ordered. "I'll have the sole, and a green salad to start."

"The same, please," Cordelia said, handing the menu back to the waiter. When he walked away, she turned to Sinclair.

"John, *darling,* I was very surprised you want Holly Graham to help you find the Sardonyx Cup."

The "darling" made it clear she was annoyed. Sinclair shifted and took a sip of his drink.

"She often consults with the FBI Stolen Art Bureau to identify missing objects," he replied.

"So her name just *sprang* to mind?"

"Look, I almost didn't mention her. But then I assumed you couldn't possibly be *that* petty."

"You think I'm being petty?" she asked.

"Holly and I won't be working *together.*"

"Oh, really?"

"I'll be in London. And she'll be based here in New York."

"So you think it's silly of me to be making a fuss?"

Cordelia accepted her Perrier, and Sinclair kept quiet

until the waiter walked away. Then he leaned forward and spoke to her quietly.

"Look, Delia, Holly and I were very serious—once upon a time. But it's been over for years."

"Mmmhmmmm . . ." she said, pulling the paper end off her straw and taking a sip of Perrier.

"Delia! I can't believe you are carrying on about something that ended years ago!"

"You're so defensive, John. Why *is* that?"

"Because you are being *ridiculous*! When I tell you it's over, it's really over."

"Not for *her*."

"What makes you think *that*?"

Cordelia gave him the look she always used for proving her points. "The night of the gala, she was absolutely *clinging* to your arm."

Flight A 31 overnight to London was ready for takeoff. Sinclair turned off his reading light and looked over at Cordelia. She was curled up, her hand tucked under her cheek.

A painful thump squeezed his heart. Thank God she had not been hurt at the gala.

It would be good to get home to London and settle into a normal life. There had been too much change, and Cordelia was emotionally fragile.

The nonsense about Holly being in love with him was a prime example. Cordelia was imagining things. A few days of a predictable schedule, lots of free time, and some TLC on his part would do her a world of good. He made a vow to let her know just how much he loved her. Then he closed his eyes and went to sleep.

Brooklyn, New York

HOLLY GRAHAM SET her briefcase down on the back-seat of the Bentley and tried to appear relaxed. Ted VerPlanck leaned forward to give directions to the driver and then sat back in the leather seat.

She looked out her side window as they drove toward Brooklyn Heights. Traffic passed by on Atlantic Avenue in a soundless panorama. It didn't take long for VerPlanck to bring up the Sardonyx Cup again.

"I don't know what else to say to persuade you to help me."

"I don't think there is anything *to* say. I'm sorry."

She kept her eyes turned toward the window. What more did the man *need* to realize she wasn't interested in helping him?

"It's not like you'd be working alone. You'd be consulting closely with John Sinclair."

Holly's heart skipped a beat, but she stayed composed. Funny, Sinclair never mentioned they'd be working *together*.

"I know him well," she admitted. "He has a lot of important connections in the antiquities world."

"He says the same about you."

Why did Sinclair want to work with her again? Maybe this cup business was a ruse to get back together.

"I'm tempted," she conceded. "Sinclair and I have often worked on projects in the past."

"Do you want to think it over for a few days?"

Holly looked at VerPlanck. He really had no idea what he was asking. This was a huge job. It could take months, even years. The cup could be anywhere, floating in the underground market for purloined art. But if Sinclair was convinced the cup could be found, it would be wonderful to try to find it.

"Well, I can't really decide on the spur of the moment. And, in any case, I'm heading out to . . . London, for a meeting."

"How long will you be there?"

"A few days. I've been consulting with the British Museum about some of their Egyptian collection. The Met wasn't the only museum that was hit last night. We lost a Roman-era mummy."

"Oh, I'm sorry. So it seems you'll be busy for a while, then?"

"Yes, I'm afraid my work is even more complicated, under the present circumstances."

"Listen, speaking of mummies. I'm sorry I rushed off at the hospital earlier today. I'm afraid I don't have the . . . talent to deal with that sort of thing."

"It does take some getting used to," Holly said, smiling.

There was a moment of silence, and then VerPlanck spoke.

"Forgive me if you think this is out of line—and you can refuse if it makes you feel uncomfortable—but I was planning to fly to London tonight. Why not come with me tonight to meet my lawyer, Jim Gardiner?"

"Why?"

"You might be more comfortable about all of this if you talk to him."

Holly looked at him in surprise.

"My flight is tomorrow."

"I could fly you there tonight."

"You have a *plane*!" said Holly.

"Yes, I keep it at Teterboro Airport, in New Jersey. We could be in London by morning. You could meet with Jim Gardiner and still make your appointment at the British Museum the next day."

"I'm . . . I'm not packed."

"I can wait."

She was booked on the overnight flight in an economy seat. The last-minute booking had put her in the worst row on the plane, opposite the restroom. If she accepted VerPlanck's offer, it certainly would be more comfortable. And it might be better to get away from the newspaper reporters. The last thing she wanted to do was have them calling her all day tomorrow.

"We are here, sir," the chauffeur announced.

Holly looked out the window at her apartment building and made an impulsive decision.

"I would need about a half hour."

"That's fine. I'll wait for you in the car."

The driver came around and was opening the door for her.

"I won't be long," she assured him as she got out.

"Take your time."

Holly looked back. There was something forlorn in VerPlanck's expression.

"You can come up if you prefer."

"Yes, I'd like that."

Her apartment was on the top floor of an old 1901 brown-stone. The daily slog up the five-floor walk-up had become so routine she barely noticed it. Now, with Ted VerPlanck on her heels, she realized how strenuous it was. But as they ascended he was easily keeping pace with her.

"It's just one more floor."

"Good way to get your exercise."

"I took the top floor for the view," she said, not mentioning that it was also much cheaper.

Her apartment had always seemed large in the past, but with a billionaire standing behind her it suddenly appeared small. There were just three rooms: a large square living room with an enormous bay window alcove, a dining room, and a bedroom.

The view across the water to Manhattan was gorgeous. The kitchen was the kind New Yorkers favor—just large enough to open the Chinese food containers. Her bedroom was at the rear of the apartment, but there was no way he was seeing *that*.

"What a lovely view," he said, glancing out the window.

"I find it very soothing after a long day."

"Like today?"

"Exactly. Please make yourself comfortable. I'll only be a moment."

Ted VerPlanck stared out the window at the treetops and the promenade. He waited until he heard Holly go into the bedroom, then he turned and surveyed the apartment.

It was a beautiful space, with polished oak floors and a slightly nautical feel: blue-and-white-striped couches, cream wool area carpet, lovely old blue-and-white Chinese jardinieres. A traditional Nantucket basket held knitting. A classic nineteenth-century sea chest served as a coffee table. He looked at the nautical charts on the wall—the Elizabeth Islands off the coast of Cape Cod, Massachusetts, and a series of excellent oil paintings of the ocean, a fishing port, a lighthouse—the brushwork all by the same hand.

Holly reappeared wearing a pair of black slacks, short black boots, and a tan cable sweater. Her wavy blond hair was freshly brushed and pulled into a chignon. She looked absolutely smashing.

"I'm admiring your paintings. I see they are signed H. Graham. Did you do them?"

"No, actually, my mother—Helen Graham."

"I gather from her work, she spent a lot of time around the sea."

"Yes, my father ran the ferry from Cuttyhunk Island to the mainland."

"I know the area well. I have a sailboat. The ocean is a great solace for me."

"I'm afraid I don't get much chance to go there these days," she admitted, looking at a beachscape on the far wall. Her expression was wistful.

"Are you ready to go?"

"Yes, all set."

"Let me carry your case." Ted reached for the small rolling bag she had packed. He glanced at his watch. "If there is not much traffic on the way to the airport, we'll be in London by seven a.m."

Grosvenor Street, London

JOHN SINCLAIR TOSSED the two suitcases into the entrance hall of Cordelia's town house and fended off the slobbering advances of his dog with both hands. Kyrie was a Norwegian elkhound, a former stray. Years ago, during an excavation in Turkey, the puppy had attached itself to Sinclair. He had been skinny and near starvation, and Sinclair had nursed him back to health. They were now inseparable.

"Kyrie, down."

He had named the puppy Kyrie—short for the Valkyries in Wagner's opera. Sinclair had been listening to the CD the night he brought the animal home with him.

"Come here," Cordelia said gently.

Kyrie dropped down on all fours and padded over to her.

"Look at that! You have everyone in the whole household trained."

"Hardly," she said with a laugh. "This place is filled with wild creatures."

"*Wild* creatures?" he said, pulling her into his arms. "Is that what you think I am? We'll see about *that*!"

Teterboro Airport, New Jersey

TED VERPLANCK'S JET was at quarter throttle and began to taxi onto the runway. Holly was sitting knee to knee with him, looking out at the tarmac. She'd never fly again without thinking of this private jet. Or she'd never take a yellow cab to the airport without thinking of the Bentley. His treatment of her had been positively royal!

She never even *saw* her luggage; the bag was loaded immediately from the trunk of the car into the Gulfstream G650. The crew greeted her by name and served her a glass of wine and a platter of water biscuits, fruit, and cheese. And there was no waiting—the moment she buckled in, they prepared to take off.

"We're first in line, sir," said a steward. "It should be only a few more minutes until we are cleared."

Just then Ted's cell phone rang with a discreet chime. He took the phone out of his inside jacket pocket and answered. Holly could hear someone talking rapidly on the other end. Ted cut in.

"Yes, Tipper. I told you earlier. I'll be out of town for a few days. London."

He listened with a resigned expression on his face and looked out the window.

"Sure, why not. Jackson Hole sounds like a good idea. Give my best to Jane and Arthur. OK. Good-bye."

Ted hung up the phone without looking at Holly. The aircraft lifted off smoothly, and they climbed until the lights of the buildings turned into yellow pinpricks and then faded entirely. Clouds drifted over the wing in a mist. Finally, total whiteness engulfed the plane and there was nothing more to see.

Holly turned her attention to her host. He looked very withdrawn as he gazed out the window. After they reached cruising altitude, the hostess came into the cabin.

"Dr. Graham, Mr. VerPlanck. May I offer you some dinner?"

"What do we have tonight, Angela?"

"There's lobster bisque to start, lamb chops with wild rice and steamed snow peas. Raspberry trifle for dessert."

"Does that sound OK? We preorder everything from a very good restaurant in New York."

"That sounds *wonderful*," Holly said.

Holly awoke to the gentle tap on the partition of her berth and realized she was still on Ted VerPlanck's Gulfstream G650. She had slept soundly, almost as if she had been in her own bed.

"Dr. Graham, we'll be landing in forty-five minutes," the stewardess announced. "I'll have breakfast for you when you are ready."

"Thank you."

Ah, what luxury! She stretched languorously underneath the covers and then reached over and slid up the window flap. There were big, fluffy clouds outside.

As tempting as it was to just lie there, Holly got up and went to the adjacent lavatory to change. Last night, the stewardess had given her a set of Egyptian cotton pajamas and told her that her clothes for today would be steam-pressed as she slept.

She was also informed that ventilation would be boosted inside her berth during the night. In the Gulf-stream, the interior air was not recycled, as it was on commercial flights. In VerPlanck's plane, new air was pumped through every ninety seconds, diminishing the ill effects of jet lag.

This morning, in the harsh light of the vanity, Holly noticed her complexion was as fresh as if she had woken up at home. She rubbed on cleanser, splashed cold water on her face, brushed her teeth, and applied tinted moisturizer and lipstick. As promised, her newly pressed blue suit hung on the door. Finally, dressed and ready, she walked out into the main cabin.

It was empty. There was no sign of activity from VerPlanck's sleeping berth in the forward part of the plane. All she could sense was the soft whir of the air jets on the ceiling and the tantalizing scent of fresh-brewed coffee.

Again, she was struck by the elegance of it all—the cream leather chairs, the flowers on the burled-walnut table, fresh croissants, muffins, and fruit laid out on the counter with an assortment of English jams. A hostess appeared from the back with a cup of coffee on a tray.

"Dr. Graham, we will be landing in about twenty minutes. If you would like to take a seat, I can get you your breakfast."

"Oh, thank you very much."

Holly accepted the coffee and added cream and sugar.

She helped herself to a bran muffin, butter, and jam and turned to look out the small window at the outskirts of London.

Just then Ted VerPlanck stepped into the cabin. He was transformed into an English gentleman by a tailored, chalk-stripe suit. His shirt collar had a distinctive British width, and the rep tie was maroon and hunter green. Even his shoes were proper English wing tips.

"Good morning. I hope you slept well."

"Yes. Wonderfully, thank you."

She finished her coffee and replaced the cup on the tray held by the hostess. Ted waved off breakfast and the stewardess disappeared. VerPlanck seemed in a much better mood this morning.

"I really love London. I would base my company here if I could."

"I have to admit, I don't come here often," Holly told him. "And when I do, I'm always in the basement of the British Museum."

VerPlanck checked overnight e-mails as they landed while she watched him surreptitiously. Today he seemed so distinguished and solid, not as emotionally fragile. There was a new confidence about him. As they touched down, he turned to her and smiled.

"Welcome to London. Shall we go?"

They collected their coats and went to the aft door, where the flight crew was lowering the automatic steps. Ted put on his raincoat, ducking under the frame of the cabin. He carried an umbrella for her and led the way across the tarmac. After a perfunctory customs check, they found the car waiting for them at the security gate.

"Here we are, Dr. Graham," Ted said, gesturing for her to step in first.

Holly realized that VerPlanck had made that same gesture twelve hours before. At that time, she was accepting a ride home. And now they were standing on another continent!

London

TRAFFIC WAS MOVING at a glacial pace. Holly marveled at a world where these kinds of delays were inconsequential. Ted VerPlanck never needed to rush—planes took off when he was ready, meals were served when he was hungry, and meetings started when he arrived.

They drove past the verdant swath of Regent's Park, and the limo pulled up to the solid-looking brick offices of Bristol and Overton. VerPlanck reached for the door handle but turned back to Holly.

"I forgot to tell you. I just got an e-mail from Jim Gardiner. We're in luck. Sinclair is back home in London and will be at this meeting. He flew in last night."

"Really?" said Holly, feeling the flush creep into her face.

"Actually, it's quite a coincidence that Sinclair knows my lawyer, Jim Gardiner. They were introduced through Cordelia Stapleton."

"I met Cordelia briefly the night of the gala in New York," Holly said.

"Yes, I met her that evening also. And we all had lunch yesterday at my apartment," VerPlanck said as he stepped out of the car onto the sidewalk.

"So she lives in New York?"

"No. Apparently Sinclair and Cordelia have been living here in London for the past few months."

"Oh, I had no idea they were *together*."

Holly managed to sound casual, but her mind was in turmoil. *Sinclair was taken!* She had entirely misread his intentions. If he and Cordelia were living together, Sinclair *couldn't* have any romantic designs on her.

That changed everything! The only reason she had agreed to help VerPlanck was to reconnect with Sinclair. Now all she wanted to do was climb back into the car and get as far away from this meeting as possible. What a disaster! How could she bail out of this without hurting VerPlanck's feelings?

Holly flashed a look of concern at Ted VerPlanck. Poor man. He was walking ahead, dodging puddles, and swinging his British umbrella jauntily. He finally looked cheerful now that he thought he was going to get his Sardonyx Cup back. How could she tell him she wanted out?

Manchester Street, London

JIM GARDINER SAT in the wood-paneled office of Bristol and Overton with John Sinclair, waiting for the others to arrive. This project made him nervous. Contacting people in the netherworld of stolen art was not legal. They'd have to bargain with all kinds of international criminals.

Having Sinclair here was a great comfort—the man had such calm assurance. And he was the only person who would even *know* how to begin. His previous successes in recovering stolen artifacts were legendary in archaeological circles.

Sinclair looked unconcerned as he lounged in the high-backed leather chair. He was more focused on Gardiner's health.

"I hope you don't mind me asking, but how are you feeling?"

"I'm coming along pretty well," Gardiner assured him. "A couple more weeks of physical therapy and I'll be able to walk better."

Of course, that was absolute *bunk*! Gardiner knew he was a physical wreck. It had been almost a year since he had ingested lethal poison in his coffee. The Russian agent had intended to kill him but failed. Even so, the single sip had left him struggling for his life.

Gardiner turned his wheelchair around to pick up a file. On good days he could walk almost normally, but on bad ones he needed the motorized chair. Today was a bad day.

"Paul says I will be 'fit to tango in a fortnight,'" he joked.

Sinclair smiled a rare smile. Gardiner's domestic partner was his doctor, Paul Oakley. Gardiner and Oakley had met at the London hospital as Gardiner convalesced.

"How *is* Paul?"

"Great. He is up in Edinburgh doing some research on bubonic plague, if you can believe it."

"The *plague*! Why not study the common cold or something simple?"

"You know Paul. He's not happy unless he is tracking down an exotic contagion," Gardiner said with a laugh.

"Do you mean the *black* plague?"

"Apparently there were several strains. He just helped sequence the DNA of the original Black Death."

"That must have been fun," Sinclair joked. "What does all that have to do with Edinburgh?"

"Paul's been looking at the old bubonic plague sites that are still underground. Apparently a couple hundred years ago, in Edinburgh, they cleared the people out, boarded up the houses, and built a new city right on top of the old one. All the original streets are still down there."

"How *fascinating*!"

"The only problem is, I can't reach him most of the time. His cell phone doesn't work underground."

"When you get hold of him, please give him my best."

Gardiner's intercom buzzed, and he picked up the phone.

"Please show them in," he said, and turned back to

Sinclair. "We're in luck. VerPlanck has managed to persuade your friend Holly Graham to join our meeting."

"*Holly is here!* I thought she was back in New York."

"She just flew in. Is something wrong?"

"Oh no, nothing. I just wasn't expecting her to come
to London."

"Apparently VerPlanck's brought her on his plane,"
Gardiner said. "Personally, I think it's better if we all talk
together."

Holly stood in the ladies' room at Bristol and Overton, ap-
plying lipstick in the mirror. She figured a little cosmetic
help was probably advisable before meeting John Sinclair.
She snapped her purse shut and walked out into the hallway with a flutter of apprehension.

How could she have misinterpreted Sinclair when he
asked her to help find the Sardonyx Cup? He had been
perfectly straightforward. The misunderstanding was *her*
fault! One chance meeting and her common sense had
vanished. Did Sinclair really still have that kind of power
over her? Apparently so.

She had *always* been attracted to him. But it was
more than physical. Sinclair's intellectual detachment
had always intrigued her. He lived most of the time inside his own head and seemed quite oblivious of everyone else. Sometimes he was so aloof he seemed almost
indifferent to women. But the cerebral manner served
only to mask his intense sexuality. When he decided to
turn his attention on you, it was like opening the door of
a blast furnace.

Of course, half the archaeological world was in love

with him. Every season, countless of her colleagues nursed hopeless crushes. Even she had finally succumbed, despite her best efforts to resist.

They had become lovers in Jordan all those years ago. At first, she had rationalized their affair by telling herself there would be no lasting emotional attachment. But then, of course, there was.

Sinclair was impossible to forget—the expression in his eyes, the way he spoke, and the way he conducted himself. But he was a very dangerous liaison. All his other women had been, quite literally, left in the dust.

For that reason Holly vowed to be smarter than the rest. *She* would be the first to leave the relationship and not linger with him. And when they broke up it had been *her* little farewell speech that *he* had to endure, and not the other way around. So why did she find herself regretting her decision?

Holly turned the corner and caught sight of Sinclair standing and chatting easily with VerPlanck, looking very elegant in a dark gray suit and crimson paisley tie. Their eyes connected, and he immediately crossed the room to give her a quick kiss on each cheek.

"Holly. Nice to see you again so soon," he said quietly.

As he stepped back she caught a drift of that glorious aftershave he wore. It brought back a flood of memories of those sweltering digs in Jordan with him working beside her. That herbal scent would mingle with the aroma of dust and sweat.

"I hadn't planned to come to London, but an emergency meeting turned up at the British Museum."

Her little excuse was feeble, defensive. Even to her

own ears it sounded as if she were overexplaining. Sinclair smiled enigmatically.

"I know I need not introduce you two," Ted interjected. "But, Holly, may I present Jim Gardiner?"

A heavyset man in a wheelchair maneuvered over.

"Pleased to meet you, Dr. Graham," he said, shaking Holly's hand from his chair. "I didn't think we would be so lucky as to have your schedule accommodate our meeting."

"Nice to meet you also, Mr. Gardiner. It turns out the timing was perfect."

"Excellent," said Jim Gardiner, wheeling himself briskly to the head of the conference table. "Shall we begin?"

The Khamsin Motoryacht,
North Atlantic, N 44°38', W 43°56'

LADY XANDRA SOMMERSET stood in the wheelhouse of *The Khamsin* looking out at the stormy sea. The yacht was pitching steeply in eight-foot swells coming from west to east, and the captain looked like he was doing the polka as he gripped the wheel.

The method for measuring storms at sea—the Beaufort scale—was at a Force 6, which meant strong winds of twenty knots or more. The weather didn't bother Xandra; she never suffered from mal de mer, and had actually come to love the constant motion of the waves.

Xandra checked the GPS. They were 1,785 nautical miles from Southampton, England, about 500 miles off the coast of Newfoundland. It would be a long trip—nine days if the storm subsided.

The Khamsin was built for transatlantic crossings. This time of year the seas weren't really rough. Iceberg season began in March in this part of the world, so there was almost no chance of hitting ice.

Xandra walked into the salon, threw her black anorak on an upholstered chair, removed a tortoiseshell clip, and shook out her long hair. A steward came in and poured her some Egyptian chamomile tea. She sank onto the couch and sipped it, looking around the room.

The salon was very stark tonight, stripped of anything that could fly around, all the "hatches battened down," all movable objects stowed. The Sardonyx Cup was safe in her stateroom.

Xandra glanced over at her other precious cargo. Artemidorus was strapped to the banquette with padded bungee cords. Bound up like that, he looked as if he were being kidnapped.

Meadow Lane,
Southampton, Long Island

TED VERPLANCK'S BEACH house was empty except for one exhausted security guard, who was trying to stay awake. The property was a large waterfront estate on Meadow Lane owned by generations of "old money" Ver-Plancks—in contrast to "new money" Wall Street hedge-fund houses built in the 1980s.

Old money, new money, the guard didn't care just as long as Mr. VerPlanck continued to tip him four or five Benjamins at the end of the season. It was a great gig. They paid him twenty-five dollars an hour, and half the time he was asleep on the living room couch.

The Hamptons summer season was over. Almost everyone was gone. The housekeeper had already put white sheets on the furniture, and the insurance people were coming tomorrow to take the paintings back to the city.

The guard lifted the protective cover off the couch and lay down, carefully kicking off his shoes. The Cézanne was visible from this position.

A couple of mil. That's what it was worth. A lot of coin for a few dabs of paint. But any fool could see this canvas was primo. It was a bunch of apples and pears and other stuff on a table. A "still life," they called it.

The yellows and oranges on the fruit were really cool on the nights he was stoned. Once, he and his friends drank a bottle of red wine and played their guitars right here on the carpet. Who else could say they partied in the same room with a genuine masterpiece?

Tonight was going to be tough. Last night, his band had played the late set at the Captain's Table in Bridge-hampton. Now he could feel his eyelids burning and slowly shutting. He'd take a quick nap. If anyone tried to steal the painting, they'd have to lean right over him.

He drifted off the second his head hit the couch. In what seemed like a minute later, a pounding noise startled him awake. What time was it, anyway? Two a.m.! He checked the painting. It was fine.

The guard leaped up so fast his head spun. Struggling to jam his feet into his shoes, he hobbled out to the kitchen. Two large policemen were standing outside, pounding on the door. A flashlight shone through the glass, blinding him.

"Open up, we have an emergency," a voice said.

"What is going on?" he asked as he punched in the security code.

"Disturbance on the grounds. We think someone broke into the house. We need to get in, now."

He disabled the alarm and pulled the door wide.

"I didn't hear anything. I've been here all night."

"We saw someone go through an upstairs window. Anybody else home?"

"It's just me. The family is gone for the winter."

They smiled at him. He suddenly realized they didn't look like any cops he knew. Certainly not the out-of-shape patrol officers from Southampton. These guys looked like they were on steroids.

"I've never seen you before."

There was no point in mentioning that he knew the local constabulary from a teenage DUI conviction.

"We're new. Backup."

"Backup for what?"

"Special detail for this weekend."

"What's going on *this* weekend? Oh, yeah. Is it that rap star Rob Dinero?"

"Yes."

"Where is the living room?" one of the officers asked.

"Right in here. I'm supposed to be watching this painting. The insurance guys are coming to get it tomorrow."

The three of them walked into the living room. Even in the semidarkness, the orange and yellow glowed. It was beautiful.

"That's it, there?" asked one of the policemen, standing in front of the painting.

"Yup. It's worth 1.4 million smackeroos."

Suddenly, he felt his arms being wrenched behind him and the cold steel of handcuffs snapped around his wrists.

"What are you . . . ?"

"Shut up, kid," said the cop.

"Am I under arrest?"

They didn't answer.

"What is going on? Am I under arrest?"

"You're not under arrest. We need the painting."

"You can't steal *that,* I'm guarding it."

"Yeah, well, you shouldn't have let us in."

The two men lifted the Cézanne off the wall, set it

down, and knocked the canvas out of its wooden frame. One of them rolled up the canvas while the other leaned the wooden slats against an upholstered chair.

"We won't hurt you if you tell the police you didn't see us clearly," one thief said.

"I didn't see you. They don't pay me enough to get hurt."

Flight UA 6534,
Denver to Jackson Hole, Wyoming

TIPPER VERPLANCK FELT the stress drop away as the United Airbus A320 headed west. It was actually a relief to fly commercial. Ted had taken the family jet to England, but it felt good to set off on her own just like a normal person. The anonymity of boarding the connecting flight in Denver with 124 other passengers was refreshing.

Just as she was landing in Jackson Hole, her cell phone rang. She checked the number. It was Charlie Hannifin. The only reason to take the call was that he had promised her a $100,000 commission for stealing the Cézanne.

"Hello, Charlie."

"Hi, Tipper. How is your trip to Wyoming?"

"I just landed. I'm staying at Jane and Arthur Monroe's ranch."

"Give them my best," Charlie said. "I just got back from the Hamptons."

"Nobody's out there this time of year."

"Yeah, you're right."

"Did you have a nice time?"

"Yes. The weather was *picture perfect.*"

Tipper rolled her eyes. He probably thought he was being clever.

"Well, it's great talking to you, Charlie, but I have to go."

"Take care, Tipper. Thanks. You're a real friend."

Tipper shuddered as she hung up the phone. Charlie Hannifin was *not* her friend.

She looked out the plane window as they taxied to the terminal. It was a beautiful clear day. The ragged peaks were already frosted with the first high-altitude snowfall of the season.

Jackson Hole was located in a small valley tucked into the Grand Teton Mountains. This was where the super-wealthy went to pretend they were simple folk. Jane and Arthur Monroe owned one of the most lavish ranches around.

They were old friends. Jane was the kind of woman who would sit up all night and gossip. Arthur's main interests were a cold beer and whatever sport was in season. Over the years, Tipper habitually found refuge with them whenever she was feeling low. Jane understood the demons of addiction; she herself had become hooked on painkillers after her face-lift a few years ago.

Grateful for their friendship, Tipper lavished presents on them—invitations to New York or the ski house in Klosters. Last year for Christmas she had given them carbon offsets for their jet. This holiday season, she was planning to invite them to her Oscar party; Conrad was certain to be nominated.

Tipper drove to Buffalo Ranch in her rented SUV. As she approached, the beauty of the place struck her, as it always did. The Grand Teton Mountains provided a backdrop for the sprawling wood-framed house. It had been constructed to resemble a rustic log cabin, except its size was enormous—twenty thousand square feet! Flanking the ranch house on either side were traditional Wyoming jack fences, which set off acres of meadows where horses grazed.

Jane must have been watching from the window, because as Tipper pulled up she came out to the car, wearing a fuzzy green mohair shawl.

"Oh, sweetie, it's so good to see you!"

She pulled Tipper into a big warm hug.

"I missed you too," Tipper said, a lump forming in her throat. "I don't know why I didn't come sooner."

"Well, all that counts is you are here *now*."

She looped an arm around Tipper and started back toward the house. Jane looked fabulous—her hair was shorter and blond, her skin clear and healthy.

"What's this I'm hearing about you and a new *amour*?" she asked.

"Oh, you mean Conrad. I'm so glad we can talk about him. I can't breathe a word in New York because of Ted."

"Well, nobody's here to spoil our fun except Arthur. And he won't mind, so long as you are happy."

As if on cue, a portly man stepped out onto the veranda.

"Jane, get the hell on in here and stop yammering out in the yard!"

Tipper broke into her first genuine smile in weeks. It really was good to be here!

Inside, Tipper looked around the house with admiration. Decorated in "western deluxe style," with leather furniture, fur throws, and Native American rugs, the great room had a cathedral ceiling and a stone fireplace large enough to stand in. A broad glass window looked out across the valley. How many evenings had she spent here sitting around the fire, drinking wine and laughing?

For Tipper, the serene beauty of Jackson Hole had always been restorative. Her father had been one of the early investors in the area, and she had spent her summers here when she was young.

The western lifestyle suited her—active days of riding and hiking, followed by a full night's rest in a downy bed. The food was hearty. At the ranch there were huge breakfasts of sourdough pancakes with butter and syrup, and elk, bison, and buffalo for dinner. The livestock was grass-fed and pesticide-free—a much healthier diet than she had in New York, where she fueled herself on arugula and caffeine.

"You know," she said impulsively, turning to Jane, "I've just decided. I'm coming back to Jackson to live after my divorce from Ted."

"*You are?*" she asked, delighted.

"Yes, I'm leaving New York. To hell with them all!"

Bristol and Overton Solicitors, Manchester Street, London

TED VERPLANCK SAT at the head of a conference table surrounded by three people who were willing to scour the criminal underworld to find the Sardonyx Cup. It was a small cabal—Jim Gardiner, John Sinclair, and Holly Graham.

Ted was filling them in about the provenance of the object, projected on a laptop. Even in a two-dimensional format, the cup was magnificent.

"What is the estimated worth?" Gardiner asked.

"That would be nearly impossible to determine," Ver-Planck answered. "It's one of the most valuable pieces of art to survive the Middle Ages."

"Middle Ages? I thought it was ancient Egyptian?" Gardiner interjected.

Ted indicated the bowl of the chalice.

"The cup itself is originally from Alexandria, Egypt. Ptolemaic period in the second to first century BC. Hand-carved sardonyx."

"What *is* sardonyx, exactly?" Gardiner asked

"The stone belongs to a class of semiprecious minerals—like onyx, carnelian, turquoise, malachite, or lapis lazuli," VerPlanck explained.

"What's the difference between onyx and sardonyx?"

"Onyx has bands of black and white. As you can see, this cup alternates white with a russet color, which was known as sard."

"Oh, I understand—sard-onyx," Gardiner exclaimed.

"Exactly. The original bowl was brought to France by itinerant peddlers from the Middle East and purchased by the French Benedictine monk Abbot Suger."

"That's where the gold base was added?" Sinclair asked.

"Yes, in 1137 AD the cup was made into a chalice studded with pearls and cabochon-cut gems."

"The design is absolutely *amazing*," Holly said.

"Just think," VerPlanck said. "A pagan Egyptian drinking vessel being used at High Mass in the royal court of France."

"It was used by a king?" Gardiner asked, impressed.

"Eleanor of Aquitaine and Louis VII drank Communion wine from it at their marriage ceremony."

"I can't believe you *own* it!" Holly gasped.

"*Owned* it," said VerPlanck ruefully. "But let me continue. . . . During the French Revolution, it was hidden in an underground vault in Paris."

"How did it get to the United States?" Sinclair asked.

"The cup was stolen from Paris in 1804 and surfaced with a London collector, Charles Towneley, who then sold it to someone else. It changed hands a few more times until it ended up with Joseph Widener, the scion of a major American industrial family in Philadelphia."

"How did *you* get it?" asked Gardiner.

"My father bought it in 1942 and promptly locked it up in his vault in New York."

"Why would he do that?" Sinclair asked.

"For safekeeping. Legend has it the cup brings its owner long life and prosperity."

"And *does* it?" Gardiner asked, fascinated.

"Apparently so. My father lived to the age of ninety-eight and made a fortune in the stock market."

"And you?" Gardiner asked VerPlanck. "Do you believe it's a good luck charm?"

"The cup has certain powers," VerPlanck said quietly.

A thoughtful silence settled over the room as everyone looked at the screen.

"Any idea on how to recover it?" Jim Gardiner asked Sinclair.

"I'm sure Holly will agree that time is often the enemy of art recovery."

"John is right. The trail goes cold quickly. If we have any chance of getting this back, we have to do it now, while the cup is on the move."

Jim Gardiner leaned forward. "Ted, I have to caution you—these are master criminals, not small-time operators."

"I always *assumed* they were professional."

"International art theft runs some six billion dollars a year. These days, when criminal gangs can't make deals with drugs and weapons they often try to fence stolen art."

"So you are saying it's too risky to contact whoever stole it?"

"It's a consideration."

"I'll pose as a buyer," Holly said, jumping in. "I can put out feelers for the cup *and* my missing mummy."

"No, Holly!" Sinclair burst out. "It's too dangerous."

Jim Gardiner held up his hand like a crossing guard.

"Dr. Graham, I would advise against it. You could be prosecuted."

"As long as money doesn't change hands, it wouldn't be a criminal act, would it?" she asked.

"That's beside the point! You have your job at the museum to consider," argued Sinclair.

"I wouldn't have to tell them."

"You can't risk your career," Sinclair insisted. "*I'll* do it."

"I really don't understand why you are being so protective! It's *my* decision," she said testily.

"First things first," Jim Gardiner said, cutting off the discussion. "Before we decide on a plan of action, we should each go home, draw up our lists of contacts."

"Agreed," said Ted VerPlanck. "Shall we meet here again at the same time tomorrow?"

"That's fine," Sinclair agreed.

"What about you, Dr. Graham?" Gardiner asked. "Does that suit your schedule?"

Holly looked over at Sinclair.

"Yes," she said. "I can make it."

Grosvenor Street, London

IT WAS ONE o'clock in the morning when John Sinclair picked up his distressed leather jacket and motorcycle boots and walked quietly down the carpeted stairs, past the living room, and through the empty kitchen. The garage lights blinked on harshly. There, in the large space, were two vehicles: his Aston Martin DBS and a Triumph Speed Triple. He wheeled the motorcycle out onto the street before starting it up. No use waking Cordelia.

Night riding was Sinclair's secret vice. He'd done it often while working in Turkey. The winding roads were deserted after midnight, and he would take his BMW R 1200 GS Adventure out to roam the vast countryside. Ever since then, the habit had stayed with him.

Even in London, he'd get on his motorcycle whenever he had to work out a problem. A couple of fast miles usually got the cobwebs out and focused his mind. Sometimes he'd come to a solution of what was bothering him. Tonight his chief preoccupation was a five-foot-five-inch blonde—Holly Graham.

Sinclair turned on the ignition and pressed the start button, and the headlight shot a beam into the dark street. He depressed the clutch lever, put it into first gear with the foot pedal, let out the clutch, and shot forward.

The engine reverberated down the row of town houses.

He lapped Grosvenor Square like a racetrack and headed out onto Park Lane, taking random turns, searching for straightaways where he could open it up.

The night was cool. The joy of flying through the dark was intoxicating; he rode mindlessly, the beautiful machine responding to his every whim. After a while he allowed himself to think about her.

Holly was haunting him a lot these days. Was this new obsession a bruised ego or something more? Whatever was causing it, the whole thing was inappropriate. His life was happy, settled. And Cordelia was the beautiful, brilliant partner he had always been looking for.

In figuring this out, he decided to focus on the positive—list all the things he liked about Cordelia. She was smart enough to keep him interested, strong enough to handle his past, and a real soul mate. Their relationship was still young, but already it was solid.

Why did Holly have to appear right now? He should tell her plainly that he was not interested. But the look in her eyes was clear. Holly wanted something more, and he didn't.

But if it was *that* simple, why was he out here riding in the dark?

Cordelia Stapleton woke up after a few hours of deep sleep, rolled over, and glanced at her alarm clock. It was three a.m. She reached for Sinclair, but the bed was empty, the sheets cold. He must be on one of his nocturnal rambles in the kitchen or the library, or out on that motorcycle. The man needed so little sleep!

She threw off the duvet and slipped on her satin robe.

In the hallway she could see a light farther down the staircase, and music was floating up from the floor below. Cordelia tiptoed down the spiral steps and peeped into the book-lined room. Sinclair was fully dressed, seated at his map table, writing.

"John?" she said.

He looked up, startled.

"Delia, sorry if I woke you," he said, standing up and moving toward her.

"What on earth are you doing in the middle of the night?"

"Working up a list of potential dealers in stolen art. I am determined to get that cup back for VerPlanck."

"Oh."

Was it her imagination or was he trying to hide something?

"We also have to get back something for the Brooklyn Museum," he added.

"What?"

"A mummy. It was stolen the night of the gala. I am helping to recover it."

"The *Brooklyn* Museum?" Cordelia asked.

"Yes."

"Where your friend Holly is?"

"Yes."

"Are you also working with her on recovering the mummy?"

"No. Not *directly*." Sinclair folded up his notes and yawned copiously. "Let's get back to bed."

"We'd better. I have a morning meeting at the Royal Geographical Society."

Cairo, Egypt

M OUSTAFFA SENT AN e-mail from the Bodega Café:

> Xandra. Charlie Hannifin tells me that Mrs. VerPlanck
> is at Buffalo Ranch in Jackson Hole Wyoming with
> Jane and Arthur Monroe. Have our men collect her
> for ransom and await further instructions. M.

Jackson Hole, Wyoming

IT WAS A crisp fall afternoon as Tipper stood and watched the ranch hands saddle up a handsome pinto. The brown-and-white horse was prancing in anticipation of freedom.

The open range, where she could ride hundreds of miles without encountering a single human being, was also calling to her. Just what she needed to get her mind off everything.

Neither Jane nor Arthur ever had any interest in riding with her. Arthur spent his time bouncing through the sagebrush in a beat-up pickup truck, western music blasting on the radio. Jane preferred reading trashy novels and knitting.

Today, Jane and Arthur were driving into town to do a little shopping and have an early dinner at the Snake River Grill. Tipper had decided to stay here, saying she wanted some time alone to think. They totally understood.

As the ranch hands cinched the western saddle, Tipper held the lead and stroked the horse's nose. Sweet hay-scented breath blew out of its nostrils.

She heard the chime of her cell phone, switched the reins to the other hand, and fished the phone out of her jeans. The area code was 212—New York. She took the call.

"Mrs. VerPlanck, this is Global Industries Insurance Company. We cover your art collection."

Tipper's heart began to beat faster.

"Yes?"

"We are calling about the Cézanne painting in South-ampton. Our agents went out there to pick it up, but they found the house closed for the season."

Tipper searched for something credible to say.

"Oh, I don't really handle the art collection. My husband must have made other arrangements."

She kept her tone brisk and businesslike.

"Mr. VerPlanck hasn't notified us, and we haven't been able to reach him," the insurance agent replied.

"He had to fly to London unexpectedly."

"I see. Well, all this is very unorthodox."

"I realize that. My husband's assistant will be in touch."

"When would that be?"

"I don't know. I'm afraid I can't help you. I'm in Wyoming."

The horse whinnied, as if backing up her story. Tipper ended the call as politely as possible without raising any suspicion. If Ted asked her about the painting, she would deny all knowledge. How could she know anything about a theft if she was almost two thousand miles away?

Out on the trail it was warm in the sun, but there was enough breeze to make the day comfortable. The thin oxygen of the high altitude was a welcome change after the dense smog of Manhattan. Tipper scanned the three distinct elevations of the Tetons—the jagged snow-frosted peaks above the timberline, lower slopes still glowing with fall foliage, and verdant grasslands down below.

She planned on riding most of the afternoon. Her

mount, an Indian paint horse, was surefooted on the narrow track. The animal's pungent scent wafted up as it climbed the ridgeline.

Tipper reined in and looked out over the high plateau. Beyond stretched the vast wilderness of Grand Teton National Park. This area was a private land reserve, zoned to keep real estate developers from chopping up the valley. By law, all horses and riders had pass-through rights.

Suddenly, her mount spooked. Tipper automatically clamped her legs to its sides and gathered the reins, looking around as she calmed the skittish animal. What was wrong?

Straight ahead, she saw two men step out of the brush carrying pistols—not the usual rifles used by elk and deer hunters.

For the briefest second, Tipper had the urge to kick her horse and bolt. If she acted fast, she could put a lot of distance between herself and these men. But something in their manner told her they would shoot to kill.

"Get off," one gunman ordered, leveling the weapon directly at her forehead.

"What *do* you want? If it's money, I'm not carrying any."

"You, lady. We came for you."

"Me?" Tipper said, incredulous. "What *for*?"

They didn't answer. That's when she knew she was in *very* serious trouble.

Alone in a small abandoned building at the edge of the woods, Tipper was barefoot, her hands and feet bound with leather rawhide ties. Her ostrich-skin boots were lying in the dust next to her. She looked around her rustic prison, trying to figure out what to do. The building appeared to be an old cowshed, and there was not much in there—a feeding trough in one corner, an old tractor tire, and a rusty pitchfork.

She settled back against the wall and looked through the dust-streaked window. The sun was setting. Her captors had left her here without explanation.

She hoped Arthur and Jane would alert the police when they got home. But that might take hours and this place would be hard to find. She and her captors had ridden about ten miles into Grand Teton National Park.

How could anyone know where she was? The men had released her horse to find its way home. Perhaps someone would follow the trail the animal had left.

The physical discomfort was intense. The rawhide bonds bit into her skin, her wrists and ankles were bleeding, and she desperately wanted to pee.

As bad as this was, the situation was about to get a lot worse. It would get very cold tonight. Fall weather in the Tetons sometimes dropped below freezing. But her biggest problem would be one of those withdrawal headaches. Tipper had no little pick-me-up pills to rely on.

She didn't have any water either, and she was already thirsty. A gin and tonic would do nicely right about now—a tall one, with ice.

Jane and Arthur would call Ted, and he would make sure someone would come and find her. No expense spared, even if it meant hiring a posse of a hundred men. Ted was a decent man. He'd do his best, no matter what his feelings. He could always be counted on in a crisis. And God knows she had created a lot of them.

This abduction was clearly related to the art theft. One of the gunmen had said something about getting a ton of money for her ransom because Ted was rich enough to own a Cézanne. It had been stupid to get mixed up in this—these people were *criminals*.

Sitting in the little shed, Tipper had a fully sober moment of reflection. When it came right down to it, her husband was the best man she knew. So why on *earth* had she been suckered into helping steal his art?

And Charlie Hannifin was a sneak and a liar. He had manipulated her into helping him. But she couldn't blame him entirely. *She* had also screwed up.

For the first time in years, Tipper realized that she didn't really hate Ted at all. She hated herself.

The two gunmen rode across the ridge to Coyote Corral and dismounted. The dude ranch was on the outskirts of Grand Teton National Park, a few miles from where they had left Tipper.

The proprietor, a tired-looking man, unhitched their horses from the fence posts.

"Nice ride?" he asked, not really listening to their replies.

"It was great."

"Real pretty."

Both men headed back to the guest lodge to clean up for dinner. Just as they reached the porch, a cell phone rang. The taller man pulled it out of his jeans pocket and listened intently.

"So what do you want us to do with her?" he asked.

"OK, fine."

He hung up and turned to his partner.

"Lady X says we should get outta here as soon as we can."

"What's the deal?"

"The Feds found the warehouse in Queens. We have to pull the plug on this whole thing."

"Oh, *shit*! Did they get anybody?"

"No. They raided the place earlier today—no one was there. Somebody ID'd the plates on the van the other night."

"*Son of a bitch*. What about the VerPlanck woman? I thought we were going to call for ransom."

"Can't. Plans changed. Just leave her."

"Leave her *there*?"

"Yeah, they'll find her soon enough. We can't be anywhere nearby."

"Can we eat first? That steak we had last night was delicious."

"I don't see why not. It would look suspicious if we just took off."

"I was hoping you would say that. I'm starving."

The lights of the Mercedes SUV swept across the windows of the house at Buffalo Ranch. A few minutes later, Jane and Arthur Monroe came in, laughing.

"I can't believe he said that," Arthur said with a chuckle.

"Oh, that's not the only thing—" Jane stopped short when she saw the look on the housekeeper's face.

"What's wrong?" Jane asked.

The woman stared at her, speechless.

"*What's going on? Where's Tipper?*" Jane demanded sharply.

"She never came back from her ride. We found her horse, wandering."

"Did you call anyone?" Jane gasped.

"No, I thought it was better to wait until you got home."

"How long has it been?" asked Arthur, looking at his watch.

"She went out about one o'clock this afternoon."

"That's nine hours!" Arthur said, grabbing the phone. "How on earth are we going to find her now?"

"Oh, my God!" Jane said. *"A search party needs to get out there, now!"*

Bristol and Overton Solicitors, Manchester Street, London

Sɪɴᴄʟᴀɪʀ ᴡᴀs ʀᴇᴀᴅɪɴɢ aloud a list of potential contacts for buying black market art. VerPlanck and Gardiner were listening intently. Only Holly was distracted. Something must be wrong with Sinclair—he hadn't even glanced in her direction all morning.

"There are at least four dealers I know in London who could quietly look for the Sardonyx Cup," he was saying.

Just then, a soft electronic melody sounded. VerPlanck began feeling his jacket pocket, found his phone, looked at the number, and sighed.

"Jackson Hole. My wife is there," he apologized. "I have to take it."

He punched the button.

"Hello?"

There was a long pause as he listened for a moment. Holly saw his face change. He stared straight ahead, then mumbled a few words and hung up.

"What's wrong?" asked Sinclair.

"That was my friend Arthur Monroe from Wyoming," VerPlanck said. "He says my wife is missing. I'm afraid I'll have to go back to the hotel to make some calls."

Ritz Hotel, London

TED VERPLANCK SAT anxiously in his suite, staring at the phone. A few moments ago, a waiter had brought in a tea tray and put it on the table in front of the couch. Ted poured himself a half cup of Earl Grey, added milk and sugar, and looked over the plates of scones and short-breads. He took a cucumber sandwich and nibbled on it as he gazed up at the crystal chandelier, thinking. After he finished, he checked his tie for nonexistent crumbs and took a sip of hot sweet tea.

He was deeply worried. There had been a flurry of conversations with local authorities in Wyoming. The law-enforcement people had pieced together a story about what might have happened.

The horse had returned without a rider, that much they knew. There were several possibilities. She could have fallen off, been kidnapped, or sent the animal back on its own. The local ranchers were organizing a scouting party to start out in the morning. There was not much else they could do in the dark.

A Missing Persons Report *could* be filed—but only after twenty-four hours. That's because people had a habit of turning up a few hours after the alarm had been raised.

The law-enforcement people were skeptical about Tip-per's disappearance. The local Jackson Hole sheriff had put in a call to the Feds, but they were holding back on a full search operation, saying they needed more information.

VerPlanck couldn't really blame the sheriff for not dashing out right away. Jane and Arthur had been obliged to tell him that Tipper had gone missing once or twice before, usually with a virile young man in tow.

Considering the circumstances, it was probably better to wait until morning. It would be embarrassing if they came across Tipper in flagrante delicto in some little cabin in the woods with a local cowboy. Knowing Tipper, she'd probably turn up by tomorrow morning with a smirk on her face and some tall tale about being rescued by a handsome stranger.

Everyone assured Ted they would keep him informed. There was no point in him flying back home if there was nothing for him to do. At the very earliest, he'd head back to the States tomorrow.

Grosvenor Street, London

JOHN SINCLAIR SAT in his favorite leather chair, his feet propped up on an ottoman, working his way down a list of contacts. It was four in the afternoon. As usual, the tea tray was on the map table, laden with a sterling silver teapot and a plate of stem-ginger biscuits. Sinclair was just putting a cup of steaming Lapsang souchong to his lips when he heard Cordelia's voice in the hallway downstairs.

"Hellooooo!" she called.

"Up here, Delia."

She sauntered in and dropped her coat and handbag on a chair.

"I'm surprised you're home," she said. "Didn't you have a meeting with Jim Gardiner?"

"We ended early. Something turned up concerning VerPlanck's wife, so I've been working here."

Cordelia walked over and looked at his notes. As she stood next to his chair, the scent of her new French perfume enveloped him. He looked up.

She was absolutely lovely this afternoon. That outfit was terribly fetching in a ladylike way—the little tweed formfitting skirt and jacket paired with very high heels. Her legs were encased in shimmery stockings.

"What kind of assignation requires an outfit like that? If I may inquire."

"Nothing illicit," she replied. "I've been over at

Kensington Gore . . . a luncheon for female members of the Royal Geographical Society. I told you about it last night."

"But why so late? It's after four."

"It was a lecture also. A retrospective on Isabelle Bird."

She sat on the arm of his chair and leaned over his shoulder.

"What are you up to?" she asked.

"Looking for a lead on the Sardonyx Cup," he replied, checking off a name and turning the page.

"Who are these people?"

"Nobody *you* know. They're all pretty shady characters."

He put his teacup and legal pad on the floor and reached around to pull her into his lap. Her skirt rode up and he could see her stocking tops were fastened with frilly garters. He ran his hand along the silky nylon band and unfastened one of them.

"John . . ." She giggled, delighted.

He trailed a hand up her thigh. She was absolutely luscious this afternoon. He started kissing her neck, nibbling his way up to her ear. Her skin was warm and soft.

"John. What are you *doing*?"

"Kissing you. Any objections?"

"I didn't say that . . ."

She turned her face toward him and pressed her mouth to his. Her lips were pliable. The first kiss turned into another. His hunger mounted. He shifted her weight against him and fumbled with the buttons of her jacket.

"John, don't start something you can't finish," she warned. Her mouth sketched a line of kisses along his jaw.

"Who says I'm not going to finish," he said, unbuttoning the silky little blouse beneath her jacket. She was wearing some wisp of lace underneath.

"Don't you have work to do right now?" she asked.

"Yes, as a matter of fact I do," he answered, pulling her to her feet. "I have a meeting upstairs, with you."

Grand Teton National Park, Jackson Hole

It was Tipper's second night in the abandoned cabin, and nobody had come for her. It was getting a *lot* colder. All she was wearing was a thin shirt, a suede riding jacket, and jeans. As the sun went down and the temperature dropped, her body was racked with deep waves of uncontrollable shaking.

She heard something scurrying around in the far corner of the shed—probably mice. *Dear God, don't let it be a snake!* In the shadows, something was moving. For that reason alone, it was important to stay awake. She was convinced that if her eyes closed, she might die. Sleep finally came, and the shivering stopped.

Tipper dreamed of a warm place, and Ted was there. They were sailing on *The MoonSonnet,* and the ocean spray was cool on her face. They were happy.

She woke to the sound of dripping water. The ceiling was leaking and her clothes were wet. She could hear rainwater pounding on the tin roof. There hadn't been anything to drink for more than twenty-four hours, and she was mad with thirst. Tipper bent her head and licked the rainwater off her hand. Then she sucked some out of the sleeve of her leather jacket. It tasted like dust.

Another full day had come and gone. It was nearly dawn. Tipper's hands and feet were getting numb, but she didn't care. Life was slipping away. There was no longer hunger or cold.

She lay on the floor and looked up at the ceiling. The timbers of the shed were turning blue-gray in the early dawn and pale patches of sky were visible through chinks in the roof.

How did she end up here? Tears coursed down her face to the dirt floor. Was this some kind of divine justice? How could she have stolen from her own husband? And to take his favorite cup was unforgivable!

Ted didn't deserve that. Sure, he was dull and predictable. But she had known that when she married him. Over the years, she had wanted more excitement and had strayed. Then it got out of control. Too many men, too much booze, and, ultimately, the drugs.

The years had become a blur. There had been only a few moments of real enjoyment to remember. And when she really thought about it, the good times were in the early days—when she and Ted still loved each other.

With each outrage on her part, Ted's polite manner had become more rigid and unforgiving. With each passing year, she had done more and more to try to provoke him, until there was nothing left between them but animosity.

And that was the saddest thing of all. She would never again have the chance to tell him that she truly loved him. It was too late. She was going to die in this shed in the middle of the wilderness.

Tipper heard something moving in the corner. A long *shhhhhhh* sound, as if something were dragging along the dirt. The noise would stop and then start again.

Exhaustion and thirst had sapped her strength, and all kinds of terrors seized hold of her. Off and on, all through the night, she had imagined a snake. But then she told herself it was a figment of her fevered imagination.

With the first light of dawn her fears were realized—*it was a rattler!* She could see its eyes clearly—glimmering in the growing light; the scales had an oily sheen. It undulated sideways a few feet to the left or right, but seemed in no hurry to approach.

She watched the snake constantly, aware of its menace. During her childhood in Jackson Hole, she had picked up encyclopedic knowledge of rattlesnakes. The reptile would never approach a human thinking it was food. But if antagonized the snake could be deadly, striking and paralyzing her with a dose of its myotoxic venom. Death would come within hours.

"Get out of here!"

She shouted in the hope of scaring the reptile into retreat. Every time she yelled, it would coil and hiss but gave up no turf. Apparently this abandoned shed was its home, and Tipper was the intruder.

Horrified, she realized that her body was completely immobile. Drained of all strength, she could neither struggle nor move. Her hands and feet were still bound with leather restraints. After two full days of extreme temperatures, she was suffering from exposure.

Heavy rain had come through the roof in the evening, soaking her to the skin but not giving her much in terms of hydration. Nighttime temperatures had been close to freezing. And then there was the other extreme—heat. During the day, the high-altitude sun broiled the tin roof so that inside the shed it easily reached ninety degrees. The air filled with dust particles.

Tipper had not been able to drink water for two and a half days except the few drops of rain she could suck out of her clothes. Dehydration was robbing her of any will or ability to escape. A person could survive only a few days like this. Her head pounded from lack of fluid.

Thankfully, every time she shut her eyes it brought relief. Finally, unable to keep the snake in sight any longer, she closed her eyes and willed herself to let go.

It was seven o'clock in the morning and the sheriff was standing on a ridge, surveying the spot where Tipper had probably disappeared. They could only guess by figuring out her direction from the house and drawing possible routes through the wilderness.

There was no way to track anything up here. The high ground was unprotected from the wind. It had rained heavily last night, and most of the water had run off into the gullies. Now the earth was bone-dry again. The sagebrush was no help—the resilient groundcover sprang back instantaneously after the horses trod on it.

"You figure it was about here?" the sheriff asked Arthur. The heavyset man nodded slowly. "Tipper said she was going to ride out this way."

"About what time?"

"Just before noon. For a couple of hours."

"Alone?"

"Yes, Jane and I drove into town. We did some shopping and then stayed for dinner."

"That's kinda odd, to go into town when you have a houseguest." The sheriff squinted at the man with suspicion.

"Not really. Tipper was raised here. Her daddy was one of the early land developers in Jackson. She's a good rider and loved to go out on her own. Did it all the time."

The two men looked out over the expanse of the valley. There were hundreds of acres of private ranches and national parkland, all the way up to the Montana border.

"Well, my deputy and I'd better get going. We have a lot of trail to cover today if we are going to find her. The search party went north yesterday and didn't turn up so much as a broken twig."

"We better find her soon," Arthur worried aloud. "It's been two and a half days."

Late in the afternoon, the Jackson Hole sheriff rode up the trail that skirted the edge of the Grand Teton National Forest. He saw an old shed at the edge of the woods—an abandoned outbuilding for horses or cattle. It clearly hadn't been used in decades.

Thousands of these old structures were scattered throughout the national parkland. Many were log cabins and shacks from the 1860s—vestiges of the early settlers. Traces of the early inhabitants of the West were everywhere, preserved in the arid climate. As people rode through the park, they often came across old Conestoga wagon wheels lying in the high grass.

The sheriff pointed out the abandoned homestead to

his deputy. He couldn't check every building or they'd be out here for a month. They had nearly eighty acres to ride.

Still, it would be better to look. With a guy as rich as Mr. VerPlanck, the sheriff didn't want anybody saying his investigation wasn't thorough—even if finding VerPlanck's wife out here was like looking for a needle in a haystack.

The assignment wasn't bad. Nothing to complain about so far. Two days, beautiful and clear, fall foliage glowing in the hills. Even the horses seemed to enjoy the afternoon, walking with energy along the steep trails. Wildlife galore: yellow-bellied marmots, deer, elk, and antelope, and lots of little ground squirrels known as chizzlers. But, so far, no trace of any human presence.

The sheriff climbed down off his horse and strode toward the ramshackle building. He couldn't see through the dust-streaked windows.

He tried the latch on the door and found it locked, so he took out his folding knife and jimmied the rusting keyhole. When he pushed the door open, the hinges creaked heavily. It took a few seconds for his eyes to become accustomed to the light.

Then he saw her. In the middle of the dirt floor—a life-size rag doll with soiled clothes and dull eyes in a sightless stare, looking at the ceiling.

"Jiminy Cricket," he said to himself softly.

This was the lady they had been looking for, all right. There was no question. He could see that the boots next to her were top-of-the-line Lucchese, sold by the most expensive shop in town. And the fringed suede coat was too fashionable to be worn by anyone local. Her hands and her feet had been bound with leather restraints. She was quite dead. Coiled next to her was one of the biggest rattlers he had ever seen. His hand strayed to his gun as he stared at it.

"Curt, you better get over here! I think we found her," he called out. "And bring your Colt. We're gonna need it."

Long Island City

CARTER WALLACE PARKED his Prius next to the exterior of Fantastic Fetes catering company. The old warehouse looked derelict; the brick was worn, and there was no commercial sign on the dented steel door. Carter knew this was the right place because of the yellow crime-scene tape cordoning off the sidewalk.

He ducked under the tape and entered the building. The first room was a large kitchen equipped with stainless-steel counters, enormous Vulcan stoves, and half a dozen floor-to-ceiling refrigerators. The gleaming surfaces were spotless, but the scent of vanilla cake still hung in the air.

Sounds were coming from the back of the building, so he followed the noise and found a door ajar. Attached to the industrial kitchens were huge warehouses with garage doors that opened out into a parking lot. Sunlight flooded in. More than thirty shipping containers were stacked floor to ceiling.

"Sir, you can't come in here," an officer said, turning when he heard Carter's footsteps.

"I'm from the Brooklyn Museum," he said. "I'm supposed to meet Detective Polistrino here."

"Can I see some identification?"

"Sure."

Carter pulled his museum badge from his pocket and put the lanyard around his neck.

"OK, you can take a look around."

The shipping containers were all different colors. Carter instantly knew exactly where each box was from. Every museum had its own special crates with a distinctive color, so they could be identified in the airport cargo bays. The Met used bright blue, the Museum of Modern Art a paler blue, the Frick Collection black, and the Guggenheim yellow.

Some crates were taped shut, and others were open and partially unpacked. Carter walked over to the Met's containers. They had been crammed willy-nilly with a variety of objects: paintings, statuary, sculpture, stone and metal artifacts. As he looked at the jumble, he couldn't help but feel a flash of professional irritation. Whoever packed this had no idea what they were doing. These were not museum shipments at all. The thieves had used colored crates to mask their illegal activities.

Clearly, amateurs had packed this art. The warehouse floor was strewn with material known as excelsior, a type of straw made from the shavings of aspen trees. Art shipping companies had stopped using wood straw decades ago because it left traces of resin on anything it touched. Even the Chinese had moved away from it.

A few of the crates were jammed with Styrofoam peanuts. That was another tip-off. No museums *ever* used peanuts—they held a static charge and small pieces always broke off and stuck to the artifacts.

A real museum packing case would utilize the crate-within-a-crate system—custom-cut, four-inch-thick polyurethane Ester foam. It was PH-neutral, nonstatic, and shock-absorbent.

At the far end of the warehouse, a drop cloth was arrayed with several dozen Egyptian artifacts. Five policemen were standing around discussing what they had found.

"OK, Dr. Wallace," said the senior officer, reading the name on Carter's badge. "Take a look at these trinkets and tell me if they're from the Met."

Carter pulled on a pair of HyFlex gloves, bent down, and picked up an alabaster canopic jar.

"Try to avoid touching anything with your bare hands," he cautioned the officers. "Your fingers leave oil and acid residue."

"We got gloves," the senior officer said, showing him cotton gloves with rubber gripping dots on the fingers.

"No, don't use those!" Carter admonished. "The rubber comes off and leaves invisible marks."

"Really?" the cop asked, looking at the offending items.

"About twenty years ago, those gloves were popular because they were thought to have a better grip," Carter explained. "But now half the masterpieces in the world have traces of polka dots all over their frames."

"We didn't know."

"I'll have the museum send over some other gloves," Carter told him.

"OK, professor. Anything you say." The officer tossed his gloves into the trash.

As Carter began examining the objects, a heavyset policeman approached. "So whad'ya think? Museum gift shop crap or the real deal?"

"These seem to be genuine," Carter said without

glancing up. "I would need further tests to be a hundred percent sure, but these artifacts certainly don't appear to be copies."

"You wouldn't happen to know anything about paintings, would you?" another officer asked, pointing to a huge canvas lying on the tarp.

Carter looked over at the painting—a glorious array of yellow and orange fruit on a yellow tablecloth. The combination was stunning.

"What do you think of that thing?" the officer asked derisively.

"I'm no expert on paintings," admitted Carter, standing up and walking over to examine the still life.

"Well, *I* am," came a voice from behind him. Carter turned and saw the director of European paintings from the Met. He was a puny, nondescript little man who always wore a bright red bow tie when he appeared on cable TV shows.

"*That*," the man said, dramatically pointing at the painting, "is a Cézanne belonging to Ted VerPlanck. I would know it anywhere."

Brooklyn Museum

CARTER WALLACE WALKED through the modern glass entrance to the lobby of the Brooklyn Museum and made his way past the bustle of schoolchildren and teachers. A white marble sculpture of the archangel Michael battling a snarling demon was drawing the attention of the children; the little boys were making faces at Satan and squealing with laughter.

Carter smiled as he headed toward the bank of elevators. Wouldn't it be great if life were that simple? Just make ugly faces and evil would go away.

On the second floor, the executive offices were silent. This new wing was all soaring architecture and glass walls—a far cry from his little cave in the basement of the original building. He was so lowly he didn't even rate a window.

Carter walked down a corridor and knocked on an open door. Dr. Edward Bezel, a round little gnome if there ever was one, was hunched over his desk. The director of Egyptian, classical, and ancient Near Eastern art always had a bemused smile on his face.

"Hello, Carter." Bezel stared at him through oversized glasses. "I've been meaning to talk to you. What's all this about a warehouse of stolen antiquities?"

"I was called in to take a look at it because Holly is in London."

"Any sign of our mummy?"

"I'm afraid not," Carter said. "I was there until two in the morning, helping inventory everything. But no Artemidorus."

"A shame, really it is," Bezel said, losing his smile for a full minute.

"How long will Holly be gone?" Carter asked.

"She won't be back for another week," Dr. Bezel confirmed. "She had to go break the bad news to the Brits."

"I just don't understand why. After all, Holly's in the conservation department. Why didn't one of the curators go to London?"

"Holly is the person who arranged for the loan in the first place. But if you ask me, the press did a number on her," the director hissed in a sibilant whisper. "Have you seen the papers?"

"No, I haven't. I've been busy."

"Don't bother. They're practically blaming her for the theft."

Carter felt his face grow flush with anger. How *dare* they make Holly the public scapegoat? He wanted to throttle someone.

"Is there any way I can get in touch with her?" Carter asked.

"Oh, sure," Bezel said, smiling again.

Carter couldn't tell if Bezel was amused that he was asking for Holly's private phone number or if he was just being his jolly self.

Bezel clicked through a few screens on his computer

and came up with the number. He jotted it down on a fluorescent pink Post-it.

"I am sure she won't mind you calling," he said, extending the sticky notepaper toward Carter on his index finger. Then he winked.

London

VERPLANCK PACED AROUND the suite at the Ritz. Still no word about Tipper. Waiting like this was agony. With London five hours ahead of the United States, it was not likely he'd get a call from the States tonight.

He walked over to the tea cart and poured out some Earl Grey. It had gone cold, and all the sandwiches and pastries looked stale. He needed to eat something substantial.

But first he had to apologize to Holly. It had been rude to leave Jim Gardiner's office this morning and not offer any explanation. Holly had been so kind to come to London a day early, and now he had walked out on her. At the very least he owed Holly a dinner.

VerPlanck picked up the hotel phone and asked the operator to connect him to Dr. Hollis Graham. She was staying at the Ritz also, at his insistence. Holly answered on the third ring, her voice surprisingly sultry.

"I am sorry to disturb you," Ted began, "but I was wondering if I could persuade you to join me for an early supper?"

He could hear the moment of hesitation, but then came the smooth response. "Oh . . . yes. That would be lovely."

"I know a little restaurant nearby on Jermyn Street."

"Sounds good. When shall I meet you?"

"How about in the lobby at, say, six-thirty? Would that suit you? Or do you need more time?"

"That's perfect, I'll see you downstairs," she agreed, and rang off.

Ted VerPlanck put down the phone and smiled to himself. What on earth was he thinking? His life was in chaos. His most precious piece of art had been stolen. His wife was missing. And yet he distinctly felt his spirits rise at the thought of dining à deux with Dr. Holly Graham.

Holly found Wiltons to be exactly the kind of restaurant that would appeal to Ted VerPlanck—the epitome of Edwardian elegance, with white linen tablecloths, polished mahogany woodwork, and charming paintings of English landscapes. VerPlanck explained the restaurant had been famous for catering to an aristocratic clientele since 1742. There was a lovely main dining room, but VerPlanck had requested they be seated in one of the booths separated by etched glass so no one could hear what they were saying.

The restaurant specialized in fish—the raw-oyster bar was famous. But Wiltons was also known for classic English fare: game and meat dishes and traditional puddings. After Holly and VerPlanck ordered, the waiter came to place her fish fork and spoon. They'd be having *all* the courses.

Holly leaned forward to smell the single old English rose in a silver bud vase.

"Beautiful scent," she said. "I love the color."

"Pink," he answered, as if it were the answer to a game show question.

He had changed out of business attire and looked very natty in an English blue blazer and dark gray slacks. His smoke-blue pocket square matched his eyes.

The waiter served the soup course. Holly started in on a thick split pea as Ted spooned up the restaurant's celebrated beef consommé. VerPlanck had also suggested a fish course. Holly enjoyed the Scottish salmon, savoring the buttery texture as she watched Ted pick at his potted shrimp and toast points.

Throughout the meal, VerPlanck seemed preoccupied. Conversation lagged. Holly decided to keep her remarks to a minimum. The poor man. First the stolen cup. Now, with his wife missing, no wonder he looked so distracted.

Of course, it would be rude to question him. But she did wonder how a man could sit in a London restaurant enjoying his dinner while his wife was missing.

The waiter rolled the serving trolley up to the table for the main course. A lift of the silver dome revealed that Holly's lamb cutlets had been cooked to perfection—charred black on the outside, pink in the middle. At the sight of his Yorkshire grouse, VerPlanck finally brightened up.

"What will you be doing at the British Museum?" Ted asked, his tongue loosened by a second glass of claret.

"I have to talk to the museum directors about the mummy; they lent it to us. He was my responsibility."

"You have to wonder who would steal a *mummy*," VerPlanck remarked with distaste, obviously recalling his encounter with Holly's specimen at the hospital.

"A lot of people might. You have no idea the kind of mania that mummies generate," Holly explained.

"Like what?" he asked, slicing his game with the precision of a surgeon.

"Not to be too graphic while we are eating, but in the Victorian age, there were some *unspeakable* practices. The Pre-Raphaelite painters actually mixed up a paint color known as mummy brown."

"You can't be serious!"

"Totally. It was a blend of pitch and myrrh. The *exotic* ingredient was the ground-up remains of Egyptian mummies!"

"That is absolutely incredible!"

"Oh, it gets worse. Some Victorian medications actually contained mummy dust."

"How *appalling*!"

"You can see why I would believe anything when it comes to mummies. Stealing one seems fairly tame."

"Was your mummy very rare?"

"It was one of the most beautiful Fayoum mummies in existence," Holly said sadly.

"Fayoum? That would date from the Roman occupation of Egypt, wouldn't it?" asked Ted.

"Yes," Holly said, impressed with his knowledge.

Ted finished his entrée and wiped his lips with a linen napkin.

"Are you finished?"

"Yes, it was delicious."

He signaled for the waiter to clear the table.

"I actually owned one, once," VerPlanck continued. "The portrait, not the mummy. When I bought it, I found out there are only a thousand or so Fayoum portraits in the entire world. During the early years of Egyptian exploration, people took them as souvenirs. So quite a few survived."

"You *owned* one? How incredible!"

"Yes, I gave it to the Met a few years ago," he said, picking up the decanter and pouring her more wine.

"Well, next time you want to give away a Fayoum portrait, give it to the Brooklyn Museum," she joked. "I promise we won't let anyone steal it."

He laughed heartily, finally looking like he was enjoying himself. The waiter arrived with their dessert—traditional bread pudding for her and sherry trifle for VerPlanck.

Just then Holly noticed a buzzing sound near her feet, and her purse started vibrating on the floor. It was her cell phone! She bent down to retrieve it and saw the main number of the Brooklyn Museum. It was late in New York! Something must be wrong.

"Excuse me," she apologized. "I have to take this. It's work."

"Certainly."

"Holly Graham," she answered briskly.

"Hi, Holly, sorry to bother you."

Carter, of all people! He didn't waste time on pleasantries but wanted to know how soon she would be coming back to New York.

"Holly, I need your help. I've been working with the FBI Art Recovery Division to identify stolen objects. They just found a warehouse full of art in Queens. Many of the artifacts are Egyptian."

"Do you think they are the pieces from the Met?"

"Yes, some were taken during the gala."

"How did they find all that so fast?" Holly exclaimed.

"Well, they had a tip that led them to the warehouse."

"What kind of tip?"

There was a long pause on the other line. Holly thought for a moment she might have lost the call, but then Carter's voice came through again.

"My tip. After I left you that night, I noticed a suspicious van, wrote down the license plate, and went to the police the next day."

"Carter, that is wonderful!"

Carter brushed her comment aside. "The FBI found the warehouse, not me."

"Any chance there was a cup? A sort of chalice?"

"No, nothing like that. Mostly funerary objects. Artemidorus is *not* there, I'm sorry to say."

Ted was sipping his wine, looking around the restaurant, waiting for her to finish her conversation. Carter's long-windedness was getting embarrassing. The headwaiter had already glanced over at her several times, clearly perturbed she was talking on a cell phone in such a decorous establishment.

"Carter . . . listen, I'm at dinner right now—"

"It's not just ancient artifacts in the warehouse," Carter continued excitedly. "There's all kinds of stuff. There was a huge painting—a Cézanne that belongs to that famous collector Ted VerPlanck."

Holly's eyes flew over to her dinner companion. *How odd Carter would mention VerPlanck!*

"Who told you it was Mr. VerPlanck's?" she questioned.

Ted had been eating, but his eyes now scanned her face anxiously.

"*Did someone find the cup?*" he whispered.

She shook her head no and held her hand up for him to wait.

"The police told me it was Ted VerPlanck's Cézanne," Carter was saying. "I saw it with my own eyes."

"Well, it's good you helped recover those things," she said noncommittally.

"You know, Holly, I tried to see you the day after the gala." Carter was gushing. "But by the time I got back from the police station in Manhattan you had left."

Holly cringed at the sudden shift to a more personal tone. She looked over at VerPlanck. He was sitting across from her, eating his sherry trifle with studied concentration. Could he hear what Carter was saying?

"I had to go to London. There was no choice," she said briskly.

"When are you coming back?" Carter asked, his voice wistful.

"Next week. I'll be back . . . at *work* next week."

"You're staying that long?"

She couldn't elaborate on what she was doing because of her promise to protect VerPlanck's secret.

"Yes, I have to. Let's hope Artemidorus turns up," she said.

"I'll keep looking. Don't worry, I'll find him."

Silly boy. As if it were up to him to recover the mummy. She said good-bye and disconnected the call.

"Sorry," Holly apologized to VerPlanck. "I know that was rude, but I *had* to take the call."

"Not at all. It sounded important," said Ted, sipping his coffee. He seemed to be waiting for her to volunteer information.

"Good news!" she said. "They recovered the stolen artifacts from the Met."

"And the Sardonyx Cup?"

"I'm afraid not, but they found your Cézanne."

"My *Cézanne*?"

"Yes, it's in a warehouse in Queens."

He stared at her, his demitasse cup suspended.

"My Cézanne is in *Queens*?" he said. "I had no idea it was missing!"

Grosvenor Street, London

A T FIVE P.M., there were no lights on in the town house except in the master bedroom. Cordelia was wrapped in the sheet, her hair mussed, her lips without any trace of lipstick.

"John, please come to dinner with me and Jim Gardiner," she wheedled.

Sinclair pulled her to him, holding her in his arms. Her long body was warm and strong as it lay next to his. Her hair smelled glorious, and he took a dark lock and wound it around his finger.

"I just spent the entire morning with Gardiner. We had a meeting about the Sardonyx Cup, remember?"

"Yes, but it would be fun for all three of us to go out. There's a new Thai place in South Kensington I want to try."

"Sweetheart, you know I don't like Asian food. I'm always starving afterward. Why don't you two catch up on old times without me?"

"But I *want* you to come."

"I would think there are things you would like to talk about by yourselves."

"Don't be silly," Cordelia chided. "Jim *loves* you."

"I know, but you had such a long relationship with him *before* you met me. He's practically your father. I think sometimes I should just bow out," Sinclair explained.

"If you feel that way, I understand," Cordelia

acquiesced. "But you are just setting yourself up to be gossiped about all evening."

"There's a scary thought." Sinclair laughed, throwing off the duvet.

Hopefully Gardiner wouldn't tell Cordelia that Holly Graham was in town. Delia had absolutely no idea, and Sinclair wanted it kept that way. This dinner tonight was a gamble. But there was no way to dissuade Delia from going without raising suspicion.

Tonight, the best thing to do was avoid Gardiner entirely. If he came to dinner, Holly's name might come up in conversation. But if Cordelia and Gardiner were eating alone they'd probably talk about old times.

Sinclair walked to the bureau and took out a pair of his monogrammed pajama bottoms, custom-made for him in Paris out of navy blue *Gossypium barbadense* cotton from the Nile Delta.

"You and Jim enjoy yourselves. I'm sure you want a walk down memory lane," Sinclair said, pulling on his pajama trousers.

"Well, I won't be out late. Jim still tires easily."

"No rush," Sinclair said, rummaging in the closet for his paisley silk robe. "I'll just read and relax."

As if he *could* relax. Halfway through the day it had suddenly dawned on him that Holly Graham was going to the British Museum tomorrow at eleven o'clock for an appointment. He and Cordelia were scheduled to meet the same curator an hour earlier!

Suddenly, London was getting too small to keep both women apart.

With two such tightly scheduled meetings, Cordelia

and Holly were sure to run into each other! And if they met in the hallway he'd never get out of there alive!

There was no other way to fix this mess except to tell a whopping lie and pray Cordelia believed him. Sinclair tied the sash of his Charvet dressing gown tighter, took a deep breath, and turned back into the room.

"What time is our meeting at the British Museum tomorrow?"

He was not a great dissembler but managed to keep his tone offhand.

"Ten o'clock," Cordelia said, concentrating on tying the bow of a white satin bed jacket. Luckily, she didn't look up.

"Oh, I was hoping it was in the afternoon," he said casually.

Her head snapped up. Now he had her attention.

"Why? Do you have a conflict?"

"Actually, I do," he said, and spread his hands in a helpless gesture.

"John, this is important! We're meeting for the Alexandria Harbor project."

"I know, Cordelia. I'm sorry. I can't help it. Can you reschedule it for another day?"

She propped herself up on the pillows to watch him, suddenly suspicious.

"We've been talking about this for weeks! How could you *forget*?"

"I'm sorry."

"It's too late to change the appointment now," Cordelia complained. "It would be rude. Can't you reschedule your other meeting?"

"Well, I promised to meet with Ted VerPlanck

tomorrow morning," Sinclair insisted. "And he's been going through a lot. I hate to disappoint him."

Cordelia sighed. "Ted VerPlanck has all the time in the world. I'm sure he could move his meeting for you."

"He can't, Cordelia. He may have to go back to the States at any moment."

Sinclair nearly bit his tongue. Don't give too much information. That was the hallmark of a bad fibber.

Cordelia glared at him and slumped back against the pillows in a fit of pique. He started gathering up her discarded skirt and blouse from the floor.

"Why are you fussing with my clothes?"

He walked over.

"I'm sorry. I *would* come to the meeting if I could."

"Well, I'll go to the museum alone," Cordelia replied, playing with the silk tassel on the belt of his robe. "I'll just tell you about it later."

"Delia, I don't know why you can't just change the appointment. It seems pretty simple."

An agitated note slipped into his voice. Cordelia eyed him and then stretched luxuriously and settled back against the pillows.

"Don't be silly, John. I can certainly handle a meeting *without* you."

Ritz Hotel

HOLLY GRAHAM WAS reclining on the canopied bed in her room. The coverlet was silk brocade and the canopy hangings were richly tasseled, in a pale blue color that soothed the eye. All around her was luxury: from the silk moiré wallpaper and the damask settee flanked by two bergère chairs to the white marble mantelpiece adorned with Sèvres porcelain vases.

Feeling utterly decadent after the sumptuous dinner at Wiltons, she had helped herself to the drinks cabinet and was enjoying a Rémy Martin accompanied by a few squares of dark chocolate from Fortnum & Mason. Could life get any better?

Dinner with Ted VerPlanck had been civilized and tranquil. There was a lot to be said for a grown-up dinner with a slightly depressed billionaire. Not as bad as it sounded at first.

All through the meal Ted had been genuinely impressed by her work and career. He asked informed questions and gave thoughtful answers. By the time they were finished, Holly found herself liking him very much. When they had reached the hotel they were both in a wonderful mood, and his old-world courtesy was in full force as he said his good-bye for the evening. The arrangements were made to meet tomorrow for another consultation at Jim Gardiner's office.

Holly, now wrapped in the thick cream-colored terry hotel robe, was relaxed, bathed, and perfumed. She was reviewing some insurance documents regarding Artemidorus for her meeting at the British Museum tomorrow.

This certainly was a fine mess. There were no contingencies for theft! It seemed that no one thought a twelve-foot cartouche weighing two hundred pounds could disappear from a museum gallery.

Her phone rang. It was after nine p.m. Who would be calling her this late? Holly picked up the receiver and then nearly dropped it in surprise at the sound of Sinclair's voice.

"Hi, Holly, sorry to call you so late."

"No problem, John. I just came in from dinner."

"Listen, I hate to ask you, but could you reschedule your appointment tomorrow at the British Museum? It's important."

She hesitated. How could he ask that? He knew that the main reason she came to London was for that meeting.

"Why?" she asked. "What's turned up?"

"Well, it's hard to explain. I just need you to do it."

"Okkkkkaayyyy . . ." she said uncertainly. "Anything you want to tell me?"

"Well, yes, but I'd like to explain in person. Can you meet me at the Connaught?"

"Right *now*?"

She looked around her gorgeous suite, reluctant to go back out again. It was pouring rain, and getting dressed and meeting him seemed like a lot of effort. But if Sinclair wanted to get together it could only mean one thing: he was still interested.

"Sure," she replied. "I'd love to."

"OK. See you at nine-thirty?"

"You're on."

Queens, New York

CARTER WALLACE WAS kneeling on the tarpaulin, putting dates on the artifacts. They had inventoried almost half the stolen articles at the Fantastic Fetes catering company.

"Hey, professor!" the detective called over. "Take a look at this, will ya? This paperwork is strange. Everything's being shipped to the Freilager Zone in Zurich."

Carter poked his head up.

"Did you say Freilager Zone?"

"Yeah. What's that? Some kind of art depot?"

"It's a transshipment point for high-value cargos, metals, gold, that sort of thing."

The detective came over to him.

"What's a transshipment point?"

"Anything that comes into the Freilager Zone can be repackaged and reshipped anywhere in the world with anonymity," Carter explained.

"Seems to me that would be a perfect place for stolen art," said the detective.

"It could be," Carter acknowledged. "But most companies use the zone legitimately, to repackage and ship goods."

"Well, all these crates are headed there," said the detective. "The paperwork is signed by a Charles Hannifin."

"Charles *Hannifin*?" Carter stood up and dusted off his hands. "There must be some mistake. He is one of the directors of the Met."

Upper East Side, New York

CHARLIE HANNIFIN WAS sitting in the library at his town house on East Ninety-Third Street. The phone was silent, but it wouldn't be for long. The FBI had called him yesterday at his office to say they had found the stolen goods in Queens. They hadn't realized that he was also one of the *thieves*?

They'd know in a day or so—his name was all over the shipping documents. If he didn't get out of town soon, it would be prison for the rest of his life.

With seventy-five million dollars stashed away, he could afford to set himself up with a new identity anywhere in the world. But where should he go?

Italy was out. The syndicate would certainly demand retribution. And, with this mob, payback could be anything from a fortune to a finger or worse.

Malta might be a good choice. Or Gibraltar. That was where Russian gangsters and other international money launderers went, now that Cyprus had cleaned up its act.

Charlie swung open a painting on the wall to reveal a safe and punched in the access code—10021, the status zip code of Manhattan's Upper East Side. He grabbed his passport and several rare Egyptian funerary objects, all hotter than the sands of the Sahara.

From the side drawer of his desk he took bubble wrap, plastic tape, a can of spray glitter, and price stickers.

Charlie wrote $12, $14.95. $9.95, $30, and $25 on different stickers and stuck a label on each object. A final spritz of sparkle made them look cheap.

Now all he needed to do was blend them with real junk to get them through customs. He rooted around in the closet for a plastic bag filled with typical tourist trash—a small brass Statue of Liberty, a coffee mug with I LOVE NEW YORK on it, a Hard Rock Café T-shirt. All of it went into his black nylon duffel.

Suddenly, he heard the doorbell ring downstairs. *The police wouldn't be here already, would they?* The window was open and the fire escape was visible. Without hesitation, he stepped out onto the metal scaffolding.

It took only a minute to climb down the three stories. He stood on the back terrace, surrounded by wrought-iron patio furniture. The kitchen door was open and he could hear Benita singing and banging around with her pots.

"Beautiful day," he said to her as he walked through.

"Oh, Mr. Hannifin, I had no idea you were in the garden. You gave me quite a start!"

"I'm off to London. If anyone wants me, I'll be back the day after tomorrow."

"Have a good trip, sir."

Charlie poked his head out of the ground-floor door. At this hour, the neighborhood was quiet. Kids in school, dads at the office, moms taking yoga classes. He walked quickly outside and hailed an empty taxi.

"JFK Airport, please. And hurry, I'm late."

The driver grunted and never turned around.

Charlie had been booked on a noon plane to London.

He was supposed to meet with one of the directors of the British Museum tomorrow morning at ten. That appointment had been scheduled for the past few weeks.

He should act as if everything were normal. If he abruptly stopped taking calls or started canceling meetings, he'd only tip off the police that he was planning to flee. And he needed another day to plan.

By going overseas he would gain time. The FBI wouldn't realize he was gone. Even if they came looking for him today, they wouldn't be able to notify British authorities until tomorrow—the United Kingdom was five hours ahead.

Charlie dialed his assistant at the office. "Hello, Joan. Anyone call this morning?"

"Only someone from the Brooklyn Museum. A Mr. Carter Wallace. I said you were flying to London for your meeting."

"If anyone else calls, tell them I'll be back Thursday."

"Yes, Mr. Hannifin. Have a good flight."

Her choice of words made him smile. He'd make sure it was a very good flight indeed.

The Khamsin Motoryacht,
N 47°14', W 27°29'

Lady Sommerset dialed the satellite phone and listened to the distant ring. Moustaffa finally picked up.

"It's X."

"Anything new?" he asked.

"Yes, it looks like Charlie Hannifin is going to make a run for it. I just called his office."

"So the operation in Queens is blown? You're telling me we got nothing?" Moustaffa demanded.

"I'm not sure how, but the police found the warehouse," Xandra explained. "We had to cut our losses."

"What about the VerPlanck woman?"

"She's dead, but they'll never find her body out in Wyoming. She'll probably be eaten by coyotes."

"So where's Hannifin?" Moustaffa's volcanic temper was simmering.

"He's on his way to London. His secretary said he has a meeting at the British Museum tomorrow. Ten o'clock."

"Get Hannifin. And bring him to the boat. I'm going to hang him on the wall like a bad painting."

"You mean . . . ?"

"Yes, but keep him alive until I get there. I want to talk to him."

"All right, darling," Lady X purred.

Queens

CARTER WALLACE STOOD in the empty kitchen of Fantastic Fetes and listened to Holly's phone ring into voice mail. He spoke urgently.

"Holly, it's Carter. This is important. Are you meeting with Charlie Hannifin in London by any chance? I called the Met and his office told me that he was on his way to the British Museum."

Carter dropped his voice into a lower tone.

"*Stay away from him!* Hannifin signed for all the stolen art to go to Zurich. *He's one of the thieves!*"

He cleared his throat and continued.

"If you get this message, please give me a call back. *And stay away from Hannifin!*"

Carter hung up the phone and walked out to join the detectives. The contents of the warehouse were scattered all over the cement floor—paintings, statues, and antiquities. The investigators had to stop unpacking the crates because they were running out of floor space. Everything had to be identified, sorted, and returned to the museums.

The FBI agents told him it was the work of a major crime syndicate—a global operation. Carter knew he shouldn't talk about the case to anyone, but he was worried. Hannifin and Holly were heading to the same place tomorrow. Carter didn't like it one bit. *Why wasn't Holly picking up her phone?*

London

SINCLAIR WALKED INTO the Connaught Hotel and folded his umbrella. He had selected the hotel's Coburg Bar because of two advantages: it was nearby, and Holly could find the hotel easily.

He looked around. The stylish bar was decorated in rich, muted shades of persimmon, cinnamon, and amethyst. Large wing chairs surrounded each cocktail table. Holly was the only person in the room, sitting in the corner, her blond hair glowing in the soft light. She was leaning back in her chair, watching the flotilla of umbrellas pass by the window.

Sinclair had a moment of deep doubt. Tonight the place was too quiet. Meeting solo seemed so *clandestine*. When he called Holly, he had anticipated a room crowded with other people, but the downpour had apparently discouraged social drinking.

"Hi, Hols."

He slid into the seat across from her, avoiding the social smooch. He purposely positioned his profile away from the street.

"Hi, John. I'm afraid I didn't wait for you. I already started."

He looked at the glass. Vodka martini, dirty. Her usual.

"I'll have a Cragganmore on the rocks," he told the waiter.

It wasn't his standard choice, but he often ordered different whiskeys, just to savor the subtle distinctions. One of Sinclair's friends had joked that his promiscuous reputation was well deserved—he sampled widely, sometimes with women but *always* with scotch.

"Nice to see you," Holly said, and saluted him with her stemmed glass.

He watched her lips on the rim. She was still beautiful, almost unchanged. The blond hair fell in waves to her shoulders. Her figure had always been alluring, but over the past few years she had ripened. Beautifully. It was a body to dream about—spin a thousand fantasies.

He forced his eyes back up to her face. She was lounging in the wing chair, her head tilted back, eyes half closed. The expression was calculating.

The waiter came and put down his drink and a dish of olives and walked away.

"I think the two of us should talk," Sinclair said, reaching for his glass.

"Oh, *please*, what's there to say? I know why you asked me here."

Sinclair's head shot up. Her gaze was smoldering, her expression rife with dangerous innuendo.

"This is not about *us*," he replied levelly. "Is that what you think?"

"Well, if it isn't about us, then I'm at a loss why you wanted me to come here," she replied coolly. "Especially at *this* hour."

He sat staring at her over the rim of his glass, unable to look away. She met his gaze, clearly telegraphing that she was open to any overture. There was no mistaking it.

"I don't know how you got that impression," he said, shaking his head.

"I can't believe you! Didn't you feel the attraction in New York?"

"No, I don't know what you mean."

"Can you honestly tell me that you felt *nothing*?"

"No, I . . . well, seeing you again was . . . surprising."

"Surprising. I see."

She bent down and straightened the cocktail napkin on the table, lining it up exactly square with the corner. As she leaned over, her blouse gaped, partially revealing deep cleavage. He remembered clearly what it was like to touch her there; the pale skin had always been so delicate and soft. Holly glanced up and caught him looking.

"Holly . . . I . . ."

"What *do* you want, John?"

He cautiously looked around the room. The bartender was over in the corner reading a tabloid with Prince Harry on the cover. Sinclair took a deep breath.

"It's something else entirely. But first of all I should tell you that I consider it over between us, Hols."

"Who are you trying to convince, me or you?"

"Both, I guess."

"Well, thanks for clearing that up. I'm glad you invited me here to tell me I no longer have a place in your life."

He didn't reply. In any other circumstance, his natural inclination would be to soften the rejection. But tonight that would be a mistake.

"*Fine,*" she threw out. "If we're honest, it never was all that great anyway. . . ."

She shot him a quick look to gauge his reaction. It was

a classic sympathy ploy, and it worked. He felt regret over the furrow of disappointment between her eyebrows.

"It was plenty good, Hols, don't kid yourself," he amended.

"It was?"

"It was. But it's *over.*"

"So, then, what do you want to talk about?"

He didn't reply. How in hell was he going to explain sitting here like this?

She sighed heavily and looked around the room, then began a new topic. "John, how well do you know Ted VerPlanck?"

"Why?"

"Just curious. I'm *working* for him," she said, and dramatically rolled her eyes as if he were being dense.

For some reason her sarcastic little gesture triggered his suspicion. His radar went up. Why was she asking about VerPlanck? Was she interested? He hadn't come here so she could pump him for information.

"Curious about VerPlanck as your *employer*?"

"Correct."

"Didn't you find out about him when you were flying in on his *private* jet?" he asked, reaching for an olive. He chewed it slowly while she came up with an answer.

"We didn't talk much."

"I don't know, Hols. You two looked pretty cozy when you came into the meeting together. You sure nothing is going on?"

"John, I can't believe you! The man is *married.*"

"I noticed," Sinclair said. "Did you?"

"You're being ridiculous. *Stop!*"

"No, you're the one who's being ridiculous!" he snapped.

The flash of irritation coursed through him. She had pretty much put him through a full range of emotions—lust, regret, sympathy, and anger—and he had been with her for only two minutes. Typical. No woman could get under his skin like Holly. He sat there watching the ice melt in his glass, trying to compose himself.

"You asked me to change my appointment at the museum," she said. "The least you could do is explain why."

"I just needed you to go on a different day. It's no big deal."

"You sounded pretty upset on the phone."

"I'm fine."

"You don't *look* fine."

"Whatever it is, it's not your concern."

"It has something to do with Cordelia, doesn't it?"

"No."

"Second thoughts about her?"

"No, Holly, I'm in *love*."

"Really?"

"Yes, *really*."

Holly coyly took a sip of her martini.

"So why are you here with me?"

"Hols, listen. The reason why I asked you to change your appointment tomorrow is because I wanted to protect Cordelia."

"You're going to have to explain that."

"I'm *trying* to explain. Delia had an appointment for us to go to the British Museum tomorrow an hour before you were supposed to show up."

She threw her head back and laughed on a triumphant note.

"*Now* I get it. Worried about awkward moments in the hall, are we?"

"Well . . ." he demurred.

"Well, s*o what* if we run into each other? We're all adults."

"She doesn't know you are in town," Sinclair admitted. "I didn't tell her."

"Uh-huh . . . So you wanted me to change my appointment so she won't find out."

"Delia was upset when she saw us together in New York. She sensed something between us."

"Well, no worries. There's *nothing* between us. You just said so."

"Holly, *please.*"

"Don't worry, John. I won't spoil things for you. I'll keep out of the picture. Relax, I'm here only until the end of the week."

"Good. We should be able to wrap up these meetings with VerPlanck quickly."

"Right."

Sinclair could see she wasn't happy. He looked at her with regret. "I'm sorry, Hols. I don't mean to make this difficult."

"Me neither," she said. "I hate to admit it, darling, but you still get to me."

"The way I act?" He laughed, draining his glass. "I can't think why."

"Well, don't worry, I'll stay out of your way," she repeated unnecessarily.

He immediately signaled for the check. "Now that we've cleared the air a bit, I'd better get out of here."

"Right. It's late." She picked up her purse and smiled ironically. "*Too* late."

Holly stood with Sinclair under the Connaught Hotel canopy while the doorman flagged a cab. Torrents of cold English rain were drumming on the canvas awning overhead, making quite a din.

She stood close to him. In the cool night she could feel his body heat. He hadn't worn a raincoat, just a blazer. His shirt collar was open. She could see the pulse throbbing in his neck. His skin was tan and smooth, and she remembered how it felt under her fingertips.

"Thanks for everything, Hols. I mean it."

She looked up at him. His eyes were deep blue. The lines of his face so familiar, the lips she had kissed a hundred times. To reach for him would seem perfectly normal. She stopped herself.

"Hey, I'm glad we had the opportunity to get on each other's nerves again," she managed. "Just like old times."

"Exactly." Sinclair laughed. Their eyes met, and the moment extended for an agonizing second.

Holly almost didn't realize what she was doing as she leaned into him. But suddenly she was in his arms. He let her come to him, pulling her to his chest. He seemed to expect it. She clung to him and breathed in his scent, linking her arms around him. His body was leaner than she remembered but still as muscular. It felt so right.

And then she felt herself released, a kiss planted on top of her head. He stepped back.

"So, take care of yourself," he said gruffly.

She nodded, flustered. Tried to collect her emotions. She hadn't felt this way in years. Tears began to sting and she looked down.

It was then she noticed the flashing message light on her cell phone in the outside pocket of her purse.

"Excuse me while I check this, will you?"

"Sure," he said, looking off into the dark street.

She took the phone out of her bag. Grateful for the diversion, she focused on the recorded message. The call log had come from the Brooklyn Museum. It was Carter Wallace. His voice was so strange. He was whispering, talking about some director of the Met. She punched voice mail and listened twice, just to make sure.

The whole story sounded crazy to her: a director of the Met involved in art theft? That didn't seem plausible. Besides, Carter had his information wrong. She wasn't meeting Charlie Hannifin tomorrow. She had never even *heard* of him.

By now, the hotel doorman had managed to get a cab and was waiting for them. Sinclair took her arm and walked her to the taxi.

"Anything wrong?" he asked, noticing her expression.

"Just a call from work. Nothing important. Good night, John. See you tomorrow."

As she got into the taxi, she kissed him on the cheek.

In the town house on Grosvenor Street, the sun was streaming through the curtains and the grandfather clock was striking eight a.m. Cordelia woke up alone and stretched. Sinclair must be downstairs having breakfast already. He'd been sound asleep last night when she came in.

Before she got out of bed, she took a moment to think over dinner with Jim Gardiner. As he had sat across from her in the restaurant last night, leaning over a dish of Thai chicken, she found herself thinking it was a miracle he was alive! *Food* was his salvation. Jim's passion for gourmet cooking was helping with his mobility much more than any therapy could.

It had been almost a year since the accident, and he really was improving. Paul Oakley was such a godsend. Paul had started as Jim's doctor and was now his domestic partner. They were inseparable—an amazing couple.

Cordelia looked over at the bedside alarm. She'd better get dressed quickly! The meeting at the British Museum was at ten o'clock. She leaped out of bed and pulled open the door of her walk-in closet.

After the long summer months of scuba diving in Egypt, it took a real effort to dress like a London girl-about-town. She slid the hangers and selected a tailored suit. It was rather plain, but accessories would spice it up a bit.

On the bureau was a jewelry box, a beautiful red Moroccan case from Asprey. Everything in it was a gift from Sinclair, and her collection of expensive baubles was growing rapidly.

Cordelia's hand went to her dress watch and then hesitated. Without really thinking about it, she picked up her diver's watch. Bulky, with a luminescent dial and a digital GPS, this was the most familiar piece of jewelry she owned. She looked at it, holding it against her wrist, remembering what it was like to be on an expedition.

Who *was* she really? She paused, looking at herself in the mirror—was she a chic young woman or a marine explorer? Tall, slender, with green eyes, her face a pale oval framed by long, dark hair, she still *looked* the same. Yet there had been so many changes: the inheritance, Sinclair's whirlwind courtship, the decision to move to London.

She looked away from the mirror and fastened the black nylon watch strap into place, then turned over her wrist to check the dial. It was so *late!*

She was meeting Dr. Trentwell, a director she knew from previous visits. But the other person was someone from the board of the Metropolitan Museum in New York—Mr. Charles Hannifin.

John Sinclair sat in the backseat of the taxi and watched the bumper-to-bumper traffic. Central London was awash with rain, and the drive to Bristol and Overton Solicitors was taking twice as long as usual. That was good. He needed time to think.

This morning at breakfast, Cordelia had come in bright and happy. He'd had an awful moment of panic, remembering last night's drink with Holly. Such god-awful guilt—but late-night cocktails with blondes will do that to you.

To compensate for his perfidy, Sinclair had made an effort to discuss the Alexandria Harbor project with Cordelia. As he talked, she had sipped her coffee, her eyes trusting over the rim of the Minton china cup. Cordelia had absolutely no idea that Holly was in London.

Apparently Jim Gardiner didn't mention it. Now, *that* was pure luck!

Sinclair told himself that last night was necessary. He *needed* to work things out with Holly. His intentions had been pure, and he had neither the talent nor inclination for infidelity.

Sinclair pulled up to the stately offices of Bristol and Overton a half hour late. VerPlanck and Holly were outside waiting for him on the steps.

"Sorry," he said, slamming the taxi door. "Traffic was beastly."

He glanced over and checked Holly's expression. For some reason, he half expected her to look as guilty as he felt. She didn't—she looked worried instead.

"He's gone," Holly said.

"Who's gone?" Sinclair asked.

"Jim Gardiner," VerPlanck clarified. "He left early this morning, for Scotland. Edinburgh. An emergency."

"That's odd."

"What's odder still," Holly said, "he left an urgent message for us to meet him there."

British Museum, London

JUST AS THE cab stopped on Great Russell Street, the skies opened up in a torrential downpour. Cordelia had to dash through the puddles, cold water seeping into her shoes.

She stopped under the columned portico to shake her umbrella and fold it. Ten minutes late! If she remembered correctly, the administrative offices were on the right. She found them easily and the assistant looked up as she came in.

"Can I help you?"

"Yes, I have a meeting with Dr. Trentwell."

"Are you his ten o'clock?"

"I believe so."

The girl squinted at the electronic calendar.

"Some woman called this morning to cancel, but the temp took the message. Now I can't figure out who it was."

"It wasn't me."

"You're the lady to see him about the Egyptian . . "

"Yes," said Cordelia. "Sorry, but I'm a little late because of the traffic. Would you please tell Dr. Trentwell I've arrived?"

"He's already down in the Enlightenment Gallery with a Mr. Charles Hannifin. I can't reach him."

"How do I get there?"

"Down the corridor. Then a sharp left. Why don't you leave your umbrella and raincoat on the rack."

"Oh, thank you," Cordelia said, hanging up her coat. She turned on her heel and quickly went out.

Cordelia had always loved the Enlightenment Gallery. The three-hundred-foot room had the appearance of a great private library, wood-paneled with towering book-cases. The collections were a celebration of the great Age of Discovery, from 1680 to 1820. During that time, there had been groundbreaking accomplishments in every field: the birth of archaeology, the deciphering of ancient manuscripts, the development of a botanical classification system.

In the rush past the glass display cases, she caught a tantalizing glimpse of all kinds of exhibits, including journals from the great voyages of Captain James Cook, Alexander von Humboldt, and Charles Darwin.

At the far end, Cordelia saw Dr. Trentwell walking slowly, gesturing emphatically, accompanied by a funny-looking little man in a rumpled raincoat. On this inclement morning, there were no other museum visitors.

"Ah, Miss Stapleton," the director said, turning at the sound of her footsteps. "You've arrived."

"Sorry. Traffic was terrible."

"No worries. My eleven o'clock appointment canceled. May I present Charlie Hannifin. Charlie, Cordelia Stapleton is the chief diver on the marine archaeology project in Alexandria Harbor."

"A pleasure to meet you," Hannifin said with little enthusiasm.

He offered a limp, sweaty hand as his eyes darted around the room.

"Is there somewhere . . . we can talk?" Hannifin asked the director.

"Certainly, but first I want to show you artifacts from Cook's voyage around the world in 1768 on HMB *Endeavour*."

"How interesting!" Cordelia exclaimed, leaning over the case.

"I haven't much time," Hannifin said, walking away.

"Oh, certainly," the director said. "Why don't we go to my office?"

They started toward the administrative offices in the modern part of the building. As they walked along the corridor, Cordelia noticed a young man at the far end—he appeared lost, glancing furtively around. He was rough, unshaved, and seemed entirely out of place. Dr. Trentwell approached him.

"I'm terribly sorry, sir, but this section of the museum is off-limits to visitors."

The man turned and scrutinized Dr. Trentwell.

"Charlie Hannifin?" he asked.

Hannifin began backing away, and the man turned to stare at him. "*You're* Hannifin."

"No. I'm not."

"Yes, you are," the young man said, turning to Dr. Trentwell and Cordelia. "I've come for *him*. If you two get out of here, I won't make trouble for you."

"What do you mean, 'make *trouble*'?" the director demanded.

That mere comment unleashed a cyclone of violence. The intruder whirled and slammed Dr. Trentwell violently into the wall, knocking him to the floor.

"Guard!" Trentwell shouted as he went down. The man came after him, pumping three rapid punches to his stomach. The director curled up in agony.

"Stop it!" Cordelia cried out.

She had no effect. In a sudden, swift movement, the assailant aimed a martial-arts kick at the fallen curator, and there was a sickening crunch as Dr. Trentwell's femur buckled. Then the intruder smashed him with the butt of a pistol. Dr. Trentwell slumped unconscious to the floor, his leg twisted at a horrific angle.

The assailant, ignoring Cordelia, swung the dark muzzle back toward Hannifin.

"Don't," Hannifin pleaded. "I didn't . . . It's not my fault. . . ." He cowered, his mouth working nervously, his small eyes darting around looking for a way to escape. The gunman walked up to him and put the tip of the weapon against his forehead. The muzzle dented the flesh between his eyebrows.

"No!" Hannifin said, panicked.

The gunman pushed hard, forcing Hannifin's head against the wall.

"They told me to come after you."

Was the man going to shoot Hannifin? A wave of dizziness hit Cordelia and her legs began to shake; her heart was beating violently. She looked at the exit a few steps away and decided to sprint toward it.

"Hold it right there!"

She saw the weapon now pointed directly at her!

"Please, I don't have anything to do with this," she begged.

"Too bad, lady. Wrong place. Wrong time."

Cordelia opened her mouth to argue and thought better of it. She was fully aware her life hung in the balance. There was an agonizing moment when she thought he would shoot her. But finally he slipped the pistol into his pocket and angled the muzzle toward Hannifin. With the tip of his head, he indicated which way they should walk.

"We're going out the main entrance, nice and casual. If you pull anything, you're dead."

Cordelia walked stiffly through the museum courtyard, the gunman following closely behind. From time to time, she could feel the steel weapon poking her back. Charlie Hannifin was directly beside her, moving toward the street. Cordelia's eyes scanned the area, looking for escape.

The flagstone plaza was more crowded now. The rain had stopped and the sun was starting to break through the clouds. A few people were gathered in groups at the entrance to the museum: a couple of students, a trio of elderly ladies. There was no one she could signal to for help. They were all absorbed in their own activities.

Cordelia's mouth was dry, her pulse racing. Her best chance for escape was now, in the open. That much she knew.

As she walked across the plaza, she surveyed the possibilities. There weren't many. An ornate wrought-iron fence surrounded the enclosed courtyard. There was no way to get out except for a single, narrow gateway that led to the sidewalk.

She scanned the bystanders again. No police officers. No young men who could give this man a good fight. Only schoolkids, moms, elderly couples.

Suddenly, she noticed a group of Japanese tourists gathering near the gate. About thirty people were huddled close together to hear their guide. If she could get into the middle of the crowd, she might have some protection. The gunman would never risk firing into a cluster of innocent tourists. With any luck he'd just take Hannifin and leave her behind.

She walked slowly by the group, then pivoted and darted into the middle. It was more difficult than she thought. They were packed closely together, listening intently. Cordelia shoved frantically, pushing against their wet raincoats to work her way into the center of the group.

A young Japanese woman cried out, shocked at Cordelia's behavior. But then, with a short bow, she stepped aside to let Cordelia through. Almost on cue, the entire group parted, waiting for her to pass by.

Cordelia looked about in dismay. They had made a clear path right through the center. The gunman was on the other side, waiting for her. The outline of the muzzle protruded through the fabric of his pocket.

"Don't get funny now, or people will get hurt."

He laughed and shrugged at the tourists, as if it were a joke. They smiled back, unaware.

A wave of disappointment and frustration washed over Cordelia. There was really no choice but to fall back in step beside Charlie Hannifin. Together they resumed their forced march to the gate.

She looked over at Hannifin. He was sweating, breathing through his open mouth, staring straight ahead. He gave no indication he had even noticed what had just happened. His eyes were fixated on something across the street. She followed his gaze.

That's when she noticed the van. Motor running, lone driver. As they approached, an automatic panel door slid open.

Her opportunities for escape were dwindling. Now they were outside the courtyard, on the sidewalk. Pedestrians were walking by, businessmen on their way to appointments. Surely someone could help her! Should she risk calling out?

As if he had read her thoughts, the gunman prodded her back. She'd be dead before the word "help" left her lips. They crossed the street and Charlie Hannifin began to climb in the van.

"Wait," Cordelia pleaded, turning toward her captor. "Please, you don't want—"

"Get in!" the gunman said, pressing the weapon into her ribs. There was determination in his eyes. She closed her mouth and followed Charlie Hannifin.

Biggin Hill Airport, London

TED VERPLANCK'S GULFSTREAM G650 was waiting on the tarmac, wingtips elegantly curved upward as if it were alive and ready to take flight. Jim Gardiner had told them to come to Edinburgh as quickly as possible. The trip from London would take less than an hour in the private jet. Holly climbed the steps and the stewardess greeted her warmly.

"Welcome back, Dr. Graham. Why don't you take your usual seat."

Sinclair, bending his long frame to fit through the door, heard the remark and lifted his eyebrows in surprise. He started to make a crack but held back. VerPlanck was directly behind him. All three of them immediately sat down and buckled their seat belts, and the plane began to move.

Everyone seemed pensive during the flight. VerPlanck sipped ice water and steadily worked his way through a folder of documents, and Sinclair barricaded himself behind the salmon-colored pages of the *Financial Times,* drinking tomato juice with a wedge of lemon. Holly nursed her coffee, wondering how on earth she could have gotten mixed up in all of this!

Both men were quiet, thinking their own private thoughts. She'd have liked to talk about it further, but she was stuck with not *one* but *two* strong silent types.

In what seemed like twenty minutes, they were

landing at a private airport outside Edinburgh. A stretch limo, sent by Jim Gardiner, started moving toward the plane as soon as they landed.

Once seated inside the car, Holly summoned up the nerve to broach the topic.

"I can't even *guess* what this is all about," she ventured as a conversation opener.

"Jim called me late last night and left a message for me," Sinclair revealed.

"Really!" VerPlanck said. "Did you call him back?"

"No, I was asleep and got the voice mail only this morning. The message said something important had turned up and I should go directly to his office to meet you and Holly."

"He left me a handwritten message at the hotel desk," VerPlanck explained. "I received it when I came down this morning. But there wasn't much information. Holly's seen it already."

He reached into his coat pocket and pulled out the cream-colored Ritz Hotel stationery, unfolded it, and handed it over. Sinclair's blue eyes scanned it worriedly:

Dear Ted,

New developments. Very serious. Please come to Edinburgh as soon as possible. Sinclair and Dr. Graham should come with you. I will be at the Balmoral Hotel in the Walter Scott Suite.

—J. Gardiner

"I can't help wondering why Edinburgh. What an *unusual* place to meet," Holly remarked.

"It is," VerPlanck agreed. "Why Scotland?"

At that remark, Holly looked out the window and got her first glimpse of the countryside—rolling green fields dotted with sheep. Miles and miles of similar landscape went by unchanged until, suddenly, she saw the gray battlements of the old city.

In the distance, Edinburgh's castle towers jutted up, massive and solid, the church spires puncturing the clouds. The rain had stopped and the sun was trying to break through. Rays shone down like a benediction from above.

"Just *look* at that El Greco sky," VerPlanck remarked, lightly touching her sleeve.

The gesture was friendly, almost familiar. He looked out the window and then settled back, a fraction closer to her. Their arms touched.

Holly felt Sinclair shift in his seat as he watched their interaction. His discomfort was obvious. Maybe Sinclair's suspicions were right; VerPlanck certainly *seemed* interested. How awkward! She decided to ignore the gesture.

"It is a *beautiful* city," she commented. "The overcast sky gives everything such an air of mystery."

"Yes, this is typical," VerPlanck explained. "A century ago, they used to refer to Edinburgh as Auld Reekie—'reekie' is the Scottish word for smoke."

"From the coal fires?"

"Exactly. The temperature inversion from the hills beyond creates these conditions. The weather seldom clears."

Holly was entranced as they drove into the center of the city. There were broad avenues, paved in the mid-nineteenth century, but also small alleyways and cobblestoned streets.

Because the old city had been built hundreds of years ago, most passageways were wide enough to accommodate only the breadth of a horse carriage. Some of the ancient byways were mere pedestrian footpaths that ended in steep flights of stairs leading to the next level above.

"This section is very quaint," she remarked.

"And some say haunted," VerPlanck added. "Supposedly one of the most active paranormal sites in all of Europe. If you believe in that sort of thing."

A snort of derision came from Sinclair's side of the car. Holly glared at him. Hunkered in the corner, Sinclair had his arms folded across his chest; his eyes were focused on the middle distance above her head. Sinclair was telegraphing his disapproval of VerPlanck's inappropriate friendliness. *How dare he sit there in judgment like that!*

Holly decided to gall him further by feigning great interest in what VerPlanck was saying about the paranormal.

"*Haunted,* you say? *How interesting!* I generally don't look for ghosts. And I'll tell you why."

"Why?"

"Because I work with *mummies,*" she quipped. "Ghosts would be a conflict of interest."

They chuckled together at her little joke, as Sinclair sat in stony silence.

"So, have you been to Edinburgh before?" VerPlanck asked.

"No."

"We're in the historic district. The hotel where Jim Gardiner asked us to meet him is right up there."

The car pulled up to the entrance of the Balmoral Hotel, where a doorman, dressed in a kilt and sporran, greeted them. Holly stepped out onto the wet cobblestones and shivered. The Scottish day was damp and raw. Thank goodness she had brought a raincoat and a cardigan with her this morning.

The massive Balmoral Hotel—a huge, ornate structure crowned with multiple towers and peaked turrets—loomed before her. The clock tower resembled London's Big Ben and was striking the half hour as Sinclair and VerPlanck joined her in front of the hotel.

"Good day to you, sir. Will there be any luggage?"

"No luggage," VerPlanck began. "We're here for a brief meeting."

"*VerPlanck! Sinclair!*" a voice shouted from the hotel steps.

They all turned at once. Jim Gardiner was struggling toward the car, leaning heavily on his walking stick. He looked distraught.

"Thank God you're all here!" Gardiner exclaimed, limping up to them. He was looking directly at VerPlanck.

"What is it?" Ted asked.

"Ted, I'm sorry to say I have terrible news."

"Go on," VerPlanck said with great apprehension.

"I'm afraid it's your wife."

"She's . . . ?"

VerPlanck scanned Gardiner's face and there was a long moment of pained silence.

"Yes. I'm very sorry, Ted, but Tipper's body has been found in the woods of Wyoming. She's dead."

"*No!*" Ted VerPlanck cried out. He put out a hand as if he were about to fall, buckled, weaved, and nearly went down. Sinclair stepped forward quickly to offer support.

VerPlanck stood with a glazed expression, clinging to Sinclair's arm.

"I'm terribly sorry," Holly murmured.

VerPlanck turned at the sound of her voice. His eyes were filled with pain. Then, with stoic effort, he let go of Sinclair and managed to stand erect. He took a few breaths, attempting to recover, and then addressed Gardiner.

"Thank you, Jim, for telling me."

In that awful moment, Holly looked at the men surrounding her. VerPlanck's face was as pale as marble under the trimmed beard; Jim Gardiner was gaunt with distress. Only Sinclair seemed composed and strong. Nobody said a word. Then, unexpectedly, Gardiner spoke up again.

"I'm afraid there's also been some news about Cordelia. . . ."

"What about Delia?" Sinclair demanded.

Gardiner's eyes were terrified as he looked at him.

"Cordelia has been kidnapped!"

Balmoral Hotel, Edinburgh, Scotland

HOLLY, SINCLAIR, VERPLANCK, and Jim Gardiner were seated around a long table in a conference room on the fifth floor of the hotel. They were in lockdown. Two plainclothes policemen guarded the door, staring straight ahead.

Holly took everything in without speaking. Ted VerPlanck was crumpled in a chair, his hands flat on the polished wood as if clinging to a life raft. After a while he glanced over at her, as if suddenly remembering she was there. For a single moment, his eyes held hers. Holly quietly returned his gaze, mustering up the most reassuring look she could manage.

Sinclair's appearance was absolutely ghastly. He sat ramrod straight, staring at nothing. He was clearly in shock, a sheen of perspiration was on his forehead and his breathing was shallow.

It hurt her to see him like that; she would do *anything* to take that pained look off his face. Until now she had no idea of her role in this affair, but now she was certain. What she needed to do was help Sinclair get Cordelia back.

They had learned very little about what had happened to Cordelia. Sinclair had reacted to Gardiner's news with outrage.

"What do you mean she was kidnapped? Why are we here?" he had burst out wildly.

Gardiner had put a hand on Sinclair's arm and had urged calm.

"We're meeting with Peter Scripps of the London Metropolitan Police—Counter Terrorism Command, SO15."

"Counter*terrorism*!" Sinclair's eyes had been frantic as he searched Gardiner's face.

"That's a general term. They handle any kind of threat in London."

"Is that where Delia is? In London?" Sinclair had asked. "With *terrorists*!"

Gardiner had not been able to answer. They would have to wait. For more than a half hour they had been sitting, listening to a grandfather clock ticking, each audible second like a flail on the skin. It was pure agony, not knowing what had happened.

Holly looked around the room, conscious of trying not to stare at the two men. The Balmoral decor was very baronial, with Macbeth-esque dark-oak paneling and an enormous stone fireplace—which would have looked perfect in a medieval laird's privy-council chamber. The lead-paned casements were draped with scarlet-colored tartan. She had a view of the spires of Edinburgh Castle. The old fortress was a beautiful sight, with its massive stone battlements silhouetted against the stormy sky.

Suddenly they heard raised voices, the door opened, and an official strode in with great energy. He introduced himself as Peter Scripps, head of the Metropolitan Police.

Holly looked him over as he shook hands with Jim Gardiner. Scripps was a beefy man, medium height, powerfully built, with the physique of a former sportsman. In his mid-fifties, his girth told of a regular diet of meat pies and a pint or two in the evening. He carried black leather gloves and wore an abused-looking Burberry raincoat that he struggled out of and tossed onto the chair. As he shook hands all around, his grip was strong.

"Mr. VerPlanck," he said, clasping Ted's hand in both of his own. "May I say how sorry I am to hear of your loss."

VerPlanck nodded, speechless. Holly liked Scripps instantly for the kindness in his eyes.

"I'm afraid we must press on," Scripps said, turning to everyone else. "We have a kidnapping in progress, and we are also dealing with a serious national emergency."

Sinclair's attention was riveted on Scripps's face.

"What can you tell us?"

Scripps turned to the policemen guarding the door.

"If you don't mind."

The officers stepped outside, and Scripps immediately pulled out a chair and sat down.

"Please make yourselves comfortable."

"What can you tell us about Cordelia Stapleton?" Gardiner asked anxiously as he sat down and put his cane on the floor.

"We know Miss Stapleton and Mr. Charles Hannifin were abducted from the British Museum about two hours ago," Scripps said, and checked his watch. "Just before eleven o'clock this morning."

"*Charles Hannifin?*" VerPlanck exclaimed. "He's on the board at the Met!"

"Yes. He appears to be the primary target," Scripps said. "Cordelia Stapleton was taken along with him."

"How do we know that?" Sinclair asked.

"Witnesses. The director of the Egyptian collection was left unconscious, with several broken bones. On the way to hospital he came to and gave us his testimony."

"Did anyone else witness the abduction?" Gardiner asked.

"Yes. There were bystanders—a Japanese tour group. We have a translation, and so far the statements concur."

"All this happened in London two hours ago," Sinclair interrupted. "I don't understand the timing. We were already on our way *here*."

Scripps nodded briskly, as if he had anticipated the question.

"I contacted your associate Jim Gardiner to ask him to come to Edinburgh. I needed help locating a medical expert."

Scripps hesitated a moment before he spoke again.

"We were initially investigating an art-theft ring, but now, with this kidnapping, I'm afraid the situation is a lot more complicated than we first thought."

Somewhere in the English Channel

CORDELIA OPENED HER eyes. There was nothing but blackness. She blinked once to be sure. Yes, her eyes were open and she wasn't dreaming. She was awake and alive and somewhere in the pitch dark.

And it was bitter cold. She was lying on a block of ice. But it *couldn't* be ice. It was so frigid it made her body ache. She put her hand down, felt the hard surface, and discovered it was metal!

Trying to sit up, she found movement was difficult. As she shifted her position, pain shot through her head. Then there was a swift and disorienting spell of dizziness.

"*John*," she said.

Her mouth formed the word, but no sound came out. In the darkness, she saw Sinclair as clearly as if he were standing in front of her. He had a slightly worried expression. It was the same look he had when he was waiting for her to surface from an underwater dive. When she came up, she'd always signal to him—give him the thumbs-up. And then relief would wash over his face.

"*I'm here*," she said to him now.

The words rasped out and echoed around her. But he wasn't here. *Where was she?* Somewhere empty and dark. Cordelia tried to stand up, but it felt like weights were pinning her to the floor. Her head was throbbing.

Hold still. Wait a minute more and rest. Then try again. She sat there and experimentally wiggled her feet. Why was she barefoot? Her shoes must have fallen off. She *really* needed to get out of here.

One, two, three, go. Attempting to lift herself up, she felt her head spin again. It was strange to be dizzy in the pitch black. How could the room reel when she couldn't see anything?

But she could sure *smell* something—the overwhelming stench of fish. Not a fresh catch. Rotten, pungent. An irrepressible flash of nausea came over her and the bile rose in her mouth, and she knew she was about to be sick.

She propped herself up on one elbow and vomited onto the floor so violently her ribs hurt. Not quite done, she heaved again. Awful, acrid taste. The stinging liquid went up into her nose. Her eyes watered.

"Agghhhkkk . . ." she said, moving away from the odor of the bile. There was a faint chemical smell to it. She must have been drugged but had no real recollection of what had happened. The last memory she had was of climbing into the van behind Charlie Hannifin.

There was a faint glow near the floor and she looked down at the light on her wrist, her luminescent diving watch. She checked the time and discovered she had been unconscious for about twelve hours. Emptying her stomach seemed to have cleared her mind a bit. But her entire body ached, and she had no desire to move. So she stayed propped up on her elbow.

Staring at the compass function on the dial, she read her GPS position. The numbers swam before her eyes.

Right now, it was too difficult to calculate location in her fuzzy brain. She really should concentrate on the other signals around her.

Water! The scent of it came to her—the saline tang of the ocean.

Cordelia could always sense water. Some people say you cannot smell water, but she knew that was wrong. Wild animals are able to detect the presence of water in drinking holes.

The next thing Cordelia noticed was the floor. It wasn't a floor at all. It was the bottom of a ship! After her years of shipboard life, the clues added up quickly.

They were under way, moving rapidly. The rumble of diesel engines sounded about a steady 1,200 rpms. She could feel waves shifting the vessel. Judging from the way the craft was lightly pitching—bow to stern—the chop was not heavy.

Each dip of the deck revealed more information. She could tell by the way the craft was moving that her position was close to the bow. It was a midsize ship, not more than sixty feet long. That was an easy guess, because the research vessel she had worked on was about the same size. Larger ships moved differently—slower and with less of a seesaw motion.

Also, the boat was in open water. Ocean waves were different from those in an enclosed body of water. So, in terms of location, if they had started in London they must have moved down the Thames. Judging from the elapsed time, they were out past the English Channel.

All that gave her a lot of information. Not bad, for working in the dark.

Balmoral Hotel

PETER SCRIPPS OF the Metropolitan Police was explaining how Cordelia had been abducted. Sinclair, Ver-Planck, and Holly were sitting silently—appalled at what they were hearing.

"Let me make sure I am perfectly clear on this," Sinclair cut in. "You're saying that the people who abducted Cordelia are *terrorists*!"

"Yes," Scripps affirmed. "Their leader is an Egyptian named Moustaffa."

"An Egyptian?"

"Originally. But he has connections all over the Middle East and North Africa. He's spent time in Saudi Arabia, Yemen, Iraq, Syria, and Morocco."

"Does he have a nationalist or religious agenda?" Gardiner asked, taking up the thread of questioning.

"No."

"Then what's his purpose?"

"Moustaffa leads a community of radical activists—anarchists with a hatred of Western governments. They are out to destroy the industrial elite."

"How many of them are there?"

"The numbers are unclear. They are a loosely affiliated cyber-community. We have been tracking them through the Signals Intelligence Unit."

"That tells me nothing," Gardiner complained.

"We track their electronic communications, and believe there are two thousand members. They log on, log off . . . and disappear."

"What do you know about Moustaffa?" Gardiner asked.

"We have a team assembling a dossier on him right now. Another unit will debrief you when we finish up here."

"Why not now?" Sinclair demanded.

"I need to ask Mr. VerPlanck some questions about that night at the Met."

"The *Met*?" VerPlanck asked.

"Yes. The FBI has uncovered a terrorist cell that launched the attack at the gala."

"Is it Moustaffa's group?" Gardiner asked, putting two and two together.

"We believe so. And we think they are planning something even bigger."

"What does that have to do with *me*?" VerPlanck asked.

"The gunmen were hired as waiters by a catering company run by the Manucci family—being in the cargo-shipping business, you may have heard of them."

"I have," VerPlanck said. "The Port Authority has been watching the Manucci crime syndicate for years. They have infiltrated the dockworkers."

"Have you had any direct contact with the Manuccis that you think might be relevant?"

Suddenly, the conversation took on the tone of an interrogation. VerPlanck sat up straighter and looked Scripps directly in the eye.

"The Manuccis don't usually interact with legitimate businesses," he said starchily.

"Well, I ask you for a very good reason. They've been connected to the theft of your cup."

"What!"

"You lost me," Sinclair chimed in.

"Mr. VerPlanck, your property was stolen to fund terrorist operations. The Manucci family took a cut, but most of the proceeds went to Moustaffa's personal account in Gibraltar."

"So you think a *terror* organization stole the Sardonyx Cup?" VerPlanck asked.

"Yes."

"That doesn't make much sense. The cup would be too recognizable to sell outright. In terms of monetary gain, it wouldn't be easy to get rid of it. There were other, more lucrative things to steal in my apartment."

"For some reason they wanted only the cup," Scripps pointed out. "By the way, it was very foolish of you to try to recover it on your own."

"I was only protecting my wife," VerPlanck said.

"So you *knew* she helped them?" Scripps asked in surprise.

There was a shocked silence in the room. Sinclair, Gardiner, and Holly exchanged worried glances. Had they helped VerPlanck cover up a criminal act!

"That's not true! She had no connection to any of this!" His words rushed out in a torrent of denial.

Scripps looked grim and waited for VerPlanck to calm down. Ted pulled out his silk pocket square and mopped his forehead with it, then stuffed it back into his jacket.

"I was only protecting Tipper from bad publicity, nothing more," VerPlanck explained.

"Your wife was working with Charlie Hannifin," Scripps repeated.

"No! I assure you, she couldn't *stand* him! They never exchanged two words."

He stopped and looked thoughtful. "Well, that's not entirely true. I just realized they sat together the night of the gala. Not by *choice*. Tipper was livid that Hannifin was seated next to her."

Scripps shook his head sadly.

"We have traced a fifty-thousand-dollar check from the Manuccis to Mrs. VerPlanck."

VerPlanck stared at Scripps bleakly as he went on.

"She was helping him steal your Cézanne also."

VerPlanck sat shaking his head in disbelief.

"We found your Cézanne in the warehouse in Queens with Hannifin's signature on the paperwork. As a director of the Met, he was in the perfect position to ship it without raising comment."

"I'm sorry to interrupt," Sinclair cut in. "But I can't just sit here talking about art when Cordelia's *life* is in danger!"

"You will be debriefed on Ms. Stapleton in another meeting," Scripps replied.

Sinclair's temper suddenly flared.

"Damn your meetings! We're wasting time!"

"Mr. Sinclair, I understand your frustration. But this investigation is bigger than my section."

"What do you mean by that?" Gardiner asked.

"We are bringing in the Secret Intelligence Service, the Security Service—MI6 and MI5. They'll take you and

Mr. VerPlanck to a secure location just west of here for a debriefing session."

"My God, I can't believe this is happening!" Sinclair said, hurtling to his feet and pacing the room like a caged animal.

"Please, Mr. Sinclair, bear with us. In cases of this magnitude, we coordinate all our intelligence. I've arranged transportation."

On cue, the door opened and the two police guards stepped back inside.

"Gentlemen, if you would follow us."

The door closed behind them and only Holly and Gardiner remained. Sinclair, VerPlanck, and Peter Scripps were on their way to the next meeting. Gardiner was hurriedly gathering up his raincoat and briefcase.

"How can I help?" Holly asked as she watched him limp painfully about the room.

Gardiner turned to her with embarrassment.

"I could use your arm for support. My balance is not quite what it once was, and I need to locate Paul Oakley."

"I'd be happy to walk with you."

"I should warn you, this is not a pleasant place. Dr. Oakley is underneath the city at an urban archaeological site."

"Why does everyone want to talk to Dr. Oakley?"

"Paul often works for British Intelligence on terrorism issues."

"I see."

"He's my partner," Gardiner explained. "We've been

together for about a year. That's why the police called me. I'm here to find him."

"Oh, *now* I understand why we are in Edinburgh."

"I was here talking to Peter Scripps about locating Paul when we got word that Cordelia had been kidnapped."

"I feel *awful* about that," Holly commiserated.

"This is not really your problem. You were asked only to help find the cup, and here you are in the middle of a terrorist investigation."

"I know, but Sinclair is an old friend, and I promised to help Mr. VerPlanck. So count me in."

"Well, your presence is very much appreciated, my dear, even if everyone is too distracted to tell you so."

"There's no need to thank me. I'll do anything I can to help," Holly said, starting for the door.

Gardiner picked up his cane and turned to her with an apologetic smile.

"Holly, I hope you're not afraid of ghosts. They say it's haunted down there."

Ayrshire, Scotland

Sinclair and Ted VerPlanck sat in the back of the military helicopter. The *thwump, thwump, thwump* of the rotors cut off all conversation as they lifted off the compound and banked sharply to the left. VerPlanck sat immobile, lost in his own dark thoughts. Sinclair had two questions swirling around in his mind. Where was Cordelia? And where were they going?

The officer at the controls hadn't revealed their destination, but the compass on the flight panel indicated west-southwest. Sinclair also noticed the pilot's right sleeve was emblazoned with an embroidered SAS parachute patch. The Special Air Service was an elite counterterrorism force. That insignia was an indication of the level of meeting they were headed toward—this unit didn't play taxi driver for just anyone.

The aircraft gained altitude and skimmed over the Scottish countryside at 160 miles an hour. Below, the landscape looked like a large pasture dotted with cotton balls of sheep. They flew above the silver ribbons of country road for a while and then banked sharply over open terrain. The landscape became rougher, steeper, with fewer houses.

After twenty minutes of flying time, Sinclair suddenly got a glimpse of cliffs and the blue ocean. From the direction their flight had taken, he presumed it was the west coast, an area he knew well. Every year he drove through here to catch the ferry to the Isle of Man TT motorcycle races.

The pilot pointed down at a gray stone fortress with crenellated towers—just like a fairy-tale castle.

"That's Culzean," he shouted over the noise as he prepared to land.

The words meant nothing to Sinclair. He leaned toward the window to look out at the structure. They circled and swooped lower. A gorgeous estate was perched high on the cliffs, surrounded by acres of formal gardens and manicured grounds.

No activity, however. One car was parked in the oval drive and three Land Rovers were in the back. The chopper hovered over the vast lawn, then dropped slowly. The landing gear kissed the grass and settled.

With the rotor blades still whirring, a military officer yanked the door open and motioned for Sinclair and Ver-Planck to climb out.

"What *is* this place?" Sinclair shouted to VerPlanck over the sound of the chopper taking off again.

"Culzean Castle."

"So he said. But who lives here?"

"Nobody. But it once belonged to General Dwight D. Eisenhower. The people of Scotland gave it to him as a private residence."

"*Really*? I've never heard of it," Sinclair said as they sprinted across the lawn.

"Eisenhower saved the British Empire when he was Supreme Commander of the Allied forces during the Second World War. It was a thank-you present."

"Did he ever come here?" Sinclair asked, surveying the towers.

"Yes, often. He loved golf. Played here . . . after his presidential terms until his death in 1969."

"Interesting, but why are we here *now*?" Sinclair asked as they followed the officer toward the castle.

"MI5, MI6. That's shorthand for the Security Service and the Secret Intelligence Service. Rumor has it they hold high-level meetings here in times of national emergency."

"Sort of like the COBRA meetings in Downing Street?"

"Yes. Except these are a lot more clandestine. If the heads of security from the United States have to fly in, they take a private jet to the USAF base in Alconbury or Lakenheath and then fly here by helicopter. They're in and out without being officially in the United Kingdom."

"How do you know so much about all this? You're not a *spy*, are you?" Sinclair asked, nearly stopping in his tracks.

"Oh, goodness no!" VerPlanck assured him. "But I've crossed paths with intelligence services on both sides of the pond. In the shipping business, we often get access to information that might be valuable."

They had reached the wooden door of the castle, and two military officers carrying weapons came out to greet them. Sinclair and VerPlanck stepped through the door as another helicopter passed overhead.

"You may be right about this meeting," Sinclair said. "That's a military aircraft coming in right now."

Mary King's Close, Edinburgh

HOLLY AND JIM Gardiner walked down a dim tunnel that was lit by bare electric bulbs strung on a wire. Their footsteps echoed in the empty subterranean corridor. The passageway sloped sharply downhill and disappeared into the gloom. It was extremely cold, and Holly shivered in her light raincoat. What a sinister place! Despite her earlier bravado, she was beginning to regret she had agreed to come.

Gardiner had explained that this was the entrance to Underground Edinburgh—a rabbit warren of dark streets beneath the modern city. Until a few years ago, not many people knew the old neighborhoods still existed. The labyrinth of medieval passageways had been sealed and abandoned. City planners had simply built over the top, using the four-hundred-year-old structures as foundations for the new construction.

Archaeologists were now excavating the old boarded-up stone houses below the modern city. Paul Oakley was working with them.

"We'll have to walk all the way down," Gardiner apologized to Holly. "Paul's cell phone doesn't get a signal this far underground."

Holly was supporting Jim Gardiner with all her strength. His left leg dragged, deadened from nerve damage. Castle Rock, the city's original bedrock foundation, was directly underfoot and he was having trouble with the uneven surfaces.

"I apologize for having to lean on you like this. I'm not quite ready for this terrain."

"You're doing fine," Holly replied. "If you don't mind me asking—what happened to your leg? Was it an accident?"

"You wouldn't believe it if I told you."

"I've heard a lot of crazy things. Try me."

"A female Russian spy put poison in my coffee at Heathrow Airport. It was a powerful nerve agent, nearly killed me, and left me with a lot of damage. . . . And no, that's not a movie plot. It really happened."

"Oh, my God, that's *awful!*"

"I'm glad it was me. They were actually after Sinclair and Cordelia. It was a close call."

Holly wondered what Sinclair was doing with Russian spies but didn't inquire.

"What does your doctor say about recovery?" she asked instead.

"My doctor is Paul Oakley," Gardiner said with a laugh. "He thinks I might get back to normal, eventually."

They walked for a few moments in companionable silence as she looked around at the vaulted ceilings. It was eerily quiet in the old abandoned street, except for the faint rumbling of traffic overhead on the Royal Mile, the city's main thoroughfare.

"Tell me about this place. I've never heard of it before."

"This little lane is Mary King's Close. We are walking down the actual street that ran between the houses. A 'close' is short for 'enclosure'—or 'alley.' It was named after Mary

King, a textile merchant who had a shop here in the 1600s."

"Why was this neighborhood abandoned?"

"Sanitary considerations. This was a poor section of the city . . . a breeding ground for disease. So the city council voted to brick it off and build a more modern city on top. They only discovered that the old structures were still down there a few years ago."

"What is Dr. Oakley doing here?"

"Studying the plague. He's a virologist. This entire area was quarantined in 1644, and he's working with the archaeologists to find out more about the contagion."

"What could he possibly learn from the ruins?"

"The city of Edinburgh had a disease-control system— a quarantine that was both humane and effective. Because the street was sealed in 1753, urban archaeologists can still enter the homes where the victims lived. This is the only place in the world where they can still do that."

Holly looked at the gaping doorframes along the street. The hollowed-out shells of the houses were cavelike and frightening.

"And these are the actual houses where the victims lived? How interesting!"

"Actually, I find it a bit horrifying," Gardiner admitted. "This place is rumored to be filled with paranormal activity."

"*Really?*"

"Psychics come here from all around the world to speak to the dead. Some get so overloaded, they have to leave. Supposedly, there is a plague victim, a little girl named Annie, who communicates with people."

"How incredibly creepy!" Holly said nervously. "I can't imagine what it was like to live here."

"Paul told me that people were packed together in the cellars of the buildings, sleeping on lice-infested straw, freezing in winter, constantly breathing in smoke from the coal fires."

Holly nodded, horrified.

"People who had a little more money, merchants' families, lived on the upper floors. Only the rich could afford light and air in those days," Gardiner continued, indicating the upper floors of the old buildings.

The houses on each side of the passageway were seven stories high, covered with vaulted ceilings of stone.

"It must have been terrible."

"Ripe for plague, that's for sure. Rats everywhere."

Holly glanced down at their feet with apprehension, but Gardiner took no notice.

"This street we're walking on right now was slick with human refuse in the old days," he went on. "There was no sewage system. People would just throw their slops out the windows from above."

"They'd just empty their chamber pots out the *window*?" Holly asked, appalled.

"Yes. Apparently they'd yell '*Gardy-loo*' and then fling the contents of the chamber pot out the window. The expression was a corruption of the French *Gardez l'eau*—which means 'Watch out for the water.'"

"No *wonder* they boarded up the street. Did many die from the plague?"

"It was devastating for many families, but not as bad as in other places in Europe. That's why Paul is trying to find out how so many survived."

"Any idea?"

"Not yet, but there are clues. Paul is sifting through the physical evidence, going over old city plans, and reading public-health accounts from that time. He hopes to develop a quarantine system for our modern cities."

"Paul Oakley is trying to figure out how to deal with an outbreak of the plague *today*?" Holly asked. "Is that why we need him now?"

"Yes. They believe terrorists are going to attack a major city with bubonic plague."

"So *that's* what this is all about!" Holly gasped.

"MI6 is in the process of briefing Sinclair and Ver-Planck about it. We'll join them right after we collect Paul."

At the far end of the long passage, the harsh glare of LED lights illuminated a team of workers carefully removing a brick wall. Gardiner and Holly headed toward the activity.

The electric lanterns distorted the shadows of the workmen. Holly imagined ghostly human figures patrolling the parameters of the original tenement houses. She repressed a shudder. Who knew what horrors had occurred here. This was the most morbid place she had ever seen!

"There he is," Gardiner said, pointing toward a man working at a crude trestle table fashioned out of two sawhorses. He was seated on a wooden crate, writing on the makeshift desk. Oakley was not yet aware of their arrival, so Holly had time to study him. The virologist was thin, youthful, with sandy hair, seemingly in his mid-forties. The glow of the electric lantern picked up the angular shape of his face. From time to time, he blew on his hands to warm them. A white cloud of vapor rose as he did this.

"Paul!" Gardiner called.

The man looked up, startled.

"*Jim!* What are *you* doing down here?"

Oakley jumped up, knocking over the crate with a clatter that echoed in the empty tunnel. The workmen turned and froze in surprise.

Gardiner labored up to Oakley and spoke quietly.

"I've been contacted by New Scotland Yard. We need your expertise."

"What are you talking about . . . ?" Oakley replied.

"I hesitate to tell you here. But it has to do with what you have been working on at Porton Down," Gardiner said.

"*Oh, my God!* Let me get my things. I'm coming."

Culzean Castle, Ayrshire

SURVEYING THE EISENHOWER drawing room, Sinclair could easily picture the ex-president in his later years, reading a book or writing his memoirs. The grand salon was oval in shape, with a fireplace at each end. There was a stately elegance, but the room was also comfortable in the typical English country-house style: deep-seated armchairs surrounded the hearth and a cheerful blaze burned at the grate.

They had just been told that officials from the British Home Office would be arriving in a few minutes, along with the head of MI6. Sinclair knew that the inclusion of MI6 meant the terror threat was international—that organization supplied the British government with foreign intelligence.

But what did all this have to do with Cordelia? No one had said anything about her!

Sinclair walked over to the bay windows and looked out at the coastline. VerPlanck silently joined him. On either side of the castle's promontory, the rugged cliffs stretched away in both directions. The sea was bashing the rocks, sending up plumes of white spray.

"This is the Firth of Clyde," VerPlanck remarked. "On a clear day, you can see all the way across to Ireland."

Sinclair wasn't interested. He was scanning the sky for incoming helicopters. Above the water, he picked out a speck—an aircraft working its way toward them. Intelligence officials, no doubt.

Just then, he heard the door open behind him. Four uniformed military officers stepped into the room and took up guard positions. A dark-suited man entered, carrying a clipboard.

"Mr. Sinclair, Mr. VerPlanck, before we start you will need to sign the State Secrets Act. All information discussed in this room is considered classified."

"Fine," Sinclair said brusquely.

He held his hand out for the form, signed it, and passed the clipboard to VerPlanck.

"Sir James Nicholson of MI6 will join you momentarily," the official said, checking the signatures. "He will be accompanied by Dame Constance Muston, the security minister in the Home Office."

As if on cue, the door opened and a man and woman walked in. The head of MI6, Sir James Nicholson, was tall and thin, dressed in a beautiful dark gray silk suit. The scarlet handkerchief in his breast pocket added just the right amount of dash.

Dame Constance Muston of the Home Office was in her mid-sixties, with a figure as trim and erect as a steel blade. She was wearing a black trouser suit with sensible low-heeled shoes. Her only ornamentation was a deep purple amethyst pin on her lapel.

During the introductions her eyes were grave. She indicated for them all to take their seats. Sinclair chose the armchair nearest the fire. The warmth on his shins was welcome in the chilly castle.

In the center of the room a mahogany pedestal table

was being set with afternoon tea, sandwiches, and cakes. At the sight of the food, Sinclair realized he had not eaten anything since breakfast. Yet even now, eight hours later, he wasn't hungry.

Refreshments were served and people talked quietly among themselves. A waiter came over with a plate of sandwiches and Dundee cake. A second waiter poured from a silver teapot and passed cream and sugar.

Sinclair had always admired British sangfroid, but under these circumstances he found afternoon tea was more than he could bear. When a waiter approached, Sinclair refused the teacup with an abrupt wave.

"It's a damp day, sir," the waiter said, bending low to speak to him quietly. "You won't be having any tea?"

"No, thank you," Sinclair said morosely.

"Perhaps a drop of something stronger to warm up? I could find you some Eisenhower scotch; it was blended especially for your president. Perhaps you'd like to sample a wee dram?"

Sinclair looked up, surprised. What a wreck he must look to elicit that kind of sympathy! But a drink would be welcome.

"Yes. Thank you."

A decanter appeared. A good measure was splashed into a crystal glass. He took a sip and felt a little more settled.

The meeting was beginning. Security officers gathered around and began taking up the extra chairs. Within moments two dozen people were assembled, although no one was introduced by name.

"I suppose you are wondering why you've been asked

to come here," Dame Constance began. "The American officials are joining us shortly. And we are waiting for medical experts as well. We'll officially begin the meeting when everyone arrives, but first let me express condolences, Mr. VerPlanck. A terrible tragedy."

"Thank you," VerPlanck said numbly. He continued to stare into the fire. The silence was interrupted only by the sounds of spoons stirring tea.

"They never explained. How did she . . . die?" VerPlanck asked, almost as an afterthought.

"Her body was found in a cabin in the Grand Teton National Park in Wyoming," the Home Office minister replied. "The cause of death appears to be complications from exposure."

"Why was I never contacted by the kidnappers?" VerPlanck asked.

"It appears the demand for ransom was interrupted, and the kidnappers abandoned Mrs. VerPlanck."

Ted squeezed his eyes shut, apparently trying to control his feelings. He exhaled deeply and looked at the fire for a long moment. Then he got up slowly and walked over to the window. He stood there staring out, surreptitiously wiping his eyes.

"Mr. Sinclair," Dame Constance continued after a moment. "I'm afraid I don't have good news for you either. We have *not* found your companion, Cordelia Stapleton."

"Do you have any leads at all?" Sinclair asked, his mouth suddenly dry.

"Unfortunately, yes. We have found the man who was abducted with her—a Mr. Charles Hannifin. His body was recovered from the Thames River this afternoon. Drowned."

She spoke with perfect professional composure and no sign of emotion at all.

Sinclair's breath caught in his chest. *Charlie Hannifin was dead!*

He stared at her, sitting in her straight-backed chair, unruffled, her silver hair perfectly coiffed. She returned Sinclair's gaze, her eyes intelligent, grave. There were no soothing platitudes or expressions of false hope. Her tone of delivery implied that she believed Cordelia might have suffered the same fate.

Shattered, Sinclair looked away and stared at the fire. The word "drowned" reverberated in his mind. He could feel his lungs constrict and the beginnings of a familiar respiratory pinch of hyperventilation in his chest. *His darling girl, drowned!*

Sinclair was aware of a faint rattling sound. He looked down and saw that his hand was clutching the side table, where a teacup was vibrating against its saucer. He put his scotch down.

The faces before him blurred. Important men in dark suits were typing into portable notebooks. They didn't look up. He was flushed, hot. His shirt was buttoned too tightly against his neck. A black wave of claustrophobia hit him like a tsunami. Then the room began to swirl around.

"Mr. Sinclair! Are you all right?" Dame Constance asked, leaning toward him. She sounded like she was underwater.

"Just need some air," he gasped, and stood up unsteadily.

"Can we get you anything?" she asked.

"No. Please excuse me," he managed to say as he bolted toward the exit. "I'm sorry, I'll be right back."

Sinclair groped for the door handle and found his way out onto the hall landing. The military officers stood aside, allowing him to pass, then closed the door after him.

The corridor was quiet. He stood at the top of the main staircase. A quick glance over the banister made him dizzy again. Red-carpeted steps spiraled down three stories to the ground floor. He had a quick mental image of pitching over the railing, tumbling over and over until he crashed onto the black-and-white marble entrance hall below. The vision was so vivid that he backed away and flattened his back against the wall.

He stood still, eyes closed, trying to regain his equilibrium. If he could calm his breathing for a moment, the vertigo might pass. But a second wave of claustrophobia welled up in him. It was a full-scale attack! He had to get outdoors, and quickly!

He forced himself away from the wall and clutched his way down the three flights of stairs, his knees trembling with each step. He slammed through the door and rushed out into the freezing garden.

It was better outside. He bent over to get blood into his head, gulping down the cold air. Squatting, with his face inches from the turf, he tried to breathe slowly through his mouth, forcing oxygen into his lungs. He felt as if his chest was going to explode.

"*Delia!*" he cried.

It came out as a gasp. Foolish to call out her name like

that, but perhaps she would know he was trying to communicate. *Even if she were dead.*

Just then, on the verge of crushing despair, he saw a clear image of Cordelia's face in his mind. She was laughing, her hair swinging over her shoulder. He knew she was still alive. She hadn't drowned.

That was the turning point. His vision sharpened and the fresh air cleared his head. He managed to fight back the panic. Finally, carefully, he stood up and took his first deep breath. And then another.

As the air filled his lungs, he noticed his surroundings for the first time. He was in a large enclosed garden rimmed on all sides by a high stone wall. The vegetation was dormant and the flower beds had been pruned and mulched. There was an oblong carpet of grass—a croquet lawn with the iron hoops still in place from the summer season.

The sun had dropped and it was bitter cold. But he needed to stay a moment longer to give himself time to recover. Why did this claustrophobia keep happening? Every time he thought his condition was under control, he had another attack.

Sinclair had been cursed with this ever since his young wife had died on a snowy night, crushed to death in the wreckage of their car. For years now, his response to extreme stress was shortness of breath and claustrophobic hyperventilation.

It didn't take Sigmund Freud to tell him he was physically reliving the horror of his wife's death over and over. The attacks occurred whenever someone he loved was in danger. If he could deal with the situation, all was well. But if he was powerless to help, he usually fell victim to the debilitating symptoms.

He had tried many times to bring the attacks under control. There were breathing exercises and mental training. But it inevitably welled up again. He thought about the scene he had created upstairs with the British officials. Everyone had a weakness, but why did his have to be so *visible*?

Now that he was feeling better, it was time to think about helping Cordelia. He strode around the garden, breathing deeply, filling his nostrils with the damp Scottish air. He beat his arms for warmth as he walked.

The wooden side door to the castle opened and squealed on its hinges. Sinclair looked over to see who had followed him, and VerPlanck walked out. The man looked like hell. His face was gray and his eyes were red-rimmed. He walked across the croquet lawn, moving quickly toward Sinclair.

"Pardon me, John," VerPlanck said. "Forgive me for intruding . . ."

"*What?* I have to think. . . ."

"I'm sorry, but they need you back upstairs," VerPlanck told him. "The American officials have arrived."

Unknown Location, English Channel

THE SHIP WAS moving with a steady rhythmic motion. Cordelia could feel the deck sway under her as she sat there. It was pitch black. She figured that she was probably being held captive in the hold and there must be a door or a hatch somewhere.

She moved her legs and realized that there was nothing constraining her. No one had tied her up, probably because she had been unconscious.

Cordelia tried to stand up, but the pain in her head was excruciating, so she crouched down again. Better to take it in stages. Crawl before you walk.

Feeling along the filthy floor on her hands and knees, she touched debris that stuck to her palms. In the dark, her fingers encountered something sticky—probably a grease spot. She wiped the substance on her skirt and kept going. If there was a vertical wall, it might be possible to lean on it and stand up.

Suddenly, her fingers stubbed against a hard surface. It was the side of the ship. The metal was so cold it hurt, but she leaned on the wall and managed to pull herself erect. It took all her concentration to stay upright. Why was she so weak?

Cordelia knew she had to get out of there quickly. Her fingers brushed along the surface, blindly feeling for a door. She finally touched a light switch. The shape was instantly recognizable and she flipped it on. Bright light flooded the area.

There was nothing in the vast space except a generator and a pile of tarp in the corner. The shape of the hold—squat and wide—suggested some kind of trawler. The stench of rotten fish confirmed this. Her shoes, high-heeled pumps, were on their sides next to the tarp, abandoned like two orphans—a patch of vomit distressingly close to them.

She walked over, put them on, and suddenly felt more prepared for whatever came next.

Could she escape? Only one door was visible, toward the back of the hold. Cordelia walked over and turned the handle. It moved! But suddenly the door was wrenched open from the outside.

A tall, heavyset man stood there in a black rain slicker, hair plastered down on his forehead. A pistol was pointing at her.

"Where do you think you are going?"

Cordelia sat in the captain's wheelhouse wrapped in a blanket. The gunman had handed her a bowl of lukewarm soup and a hunk of bread, and she forced the food down, despite her lingering nausea and dizziness.

The fishing trawler was in the open ocean now and, by her estimate, traveling at about twelve knots. Even inside the pilothouse it was freezing cold. The scratchy gray blanket was not really thick enough to keep her warm and smelled of motor oil and fish.

The man steering the craft placed himself between Cordelia and the instrument panel, blocking her access to

the maritime radio. She couldn't see the electronic naviga-
tion system either. But she had some information—the
GPS on her watch showed that they were somewhere off
the English coast.

Her abductors were rough-looking guys in their
mid-thirties. There were only two of them. One was
the gunman from the museum; the other looked like a
genuine fishing captain. He was dressed in foul-weather
gear and a knitted cap and piloted the craft with considerable skill.

Neither man took much interest in her; they seemed
intent on getting to their destination quickly, and kept
checking their watches. She was only cargo to them.
Cordelia observed the men for a while and then drifted
off to sleep. There appeared to be no immediate danger
here.

Cordelia stood on the deck of the fishing vessel, shivering,
still feeling woozy. Whatever drug they had given her was
wearing off slowly. It had been more than sixteen hours
since the abduction.

Out on deck, it was absolutely *frigid*. She clutched the
dirty blanket closer to her, but the wind was cutting right
through the fabric. The pitch and roll of the boat was a
dead giveaway—they were far from land. No sign of a
coastline, a lighthouse, or even a maritime buoy.

The two men who had abducted her were peering out
into the night, waving a flashlight back and forth. In the
narrow beam, she could see the waves churning into sharp
peaks.

The men appeared to be searching for something.

Their backs were turned, so she took the opportunity to look around for a gun, a cell phone, anything at all. But all she saw were some messily coiled lines.

There was no way to escape. Swimming in this chop would be suicidal. The water temperature would sap her strength before she got ten feet. So she sat down on a stationary locker and hugged herself to control the shivering.

If she had to guess, judging from the amount of time they had been traveling and the speed of the boat, she'd say by now they were well out of the English Channel. Cordelia purposely crossed her arms over her chest to glimpse the dial of her watch. The digital GPS read latitude N 48°19', longitude W 5°18'.

After years of being on ships, figuring out a geographic location was second nature to Cordelia. She estimated they were off the coast of Brest, France—an area known for its fishing boats. But calculating her position gave her absolutely no idea where they were headed.

The ship could travel farther along the coastline to Spain's Cape Finisterre, the western edge of the European continent—named after the Latin *finis terrae*. After that, it could be North Africa or the Straits of Gibraltar to the Mediterranean.

"There she is!" one of the men shouted, pointing out over the railing. "Get the fenders in. Portside."

A white light was approaching. The orb got larger, until Cordelia realized she was looking at the cabin lights of a ship. Within moments a gigantic white yacht loomed up alongside the fishing vessel. It was a beauty—two hundred feet or more. Classical lines. A Feadship. Exquisite woodwork. Fabulously expensive.

"Ahoy, *Khamsin!*" the gunman shouted.

Khamsin? Wasn't that the name of a wind in the western Sahara? Sinclair had told her about it.

"Come on," her captor said, turning to Cordelia. "Time to meet the boss."

"Fine." Cordelia sounded a lot braver than she felt.

The two men grabbed her blanket and flung it aside. Then they seized her arms and hoisted her up on the lip of the fishing vessel. Apparently they were going to pass her from one boat to the other. In this kind of weather, a ship-to-ship transfer would be difficult. She would have to leap from one deck to the other in treacherously slippery leather shoes! The greatest risk was that she might fall overboard and be crushed between the hulls of the two boats.

She balanced her feet on the narrow rail as the huge yacht bucked in front of them like a horse in a rodeo. The two men held her arms as a crewman on *The Khamsin* reached down for her. When the two ships were level, the boat crew propelled her toward the other deck. The man on the yacht caught her and hauled her up.

She slid and fell against him, clinging to his sweaty neck. His strong arms gripped her and held fast. She was repulsed. The wet wool of his peacoat had the pungent smell of Turkish tobacco and beer.

"Where's the other one?" he called back to the crew on the fishing boat.

"He slipped."

"Slipped?"

"Yeah. Drowned. In the Thames."

"She isn't going to like that."

"Well, what the hell can I do about it?" the man replied. "The stupid bastard jumped overboard and tried to swim. He didn't get two meters."

"OK, mate, I'll tell her. Why don't you push off now?"

"You don't have to tell me. This weather's getting ugly."

Within seconds the fishing trawler disappeared into the darkness. Cordelia clung to the rail of *The Khamsin* and watched it disappear.

Culzean Castle

SINCLAIR NOTED THAT every seat in the Eisenhower sitting room was taken by both CIA and British intelligence officers. Dame Constance looked up when Sinclair returned and waved at an assistant to bring another chair. He was directed to take a place near the front of the room.

Sinclair hoped that now they would tell him more about Cordelia. He craned his neck, looking for the others. Dr. Paul Oakley stood by the door, almost as if he were waiting in the wings. Gardiner and Holly were perched nervously toward the back of the room with Ted VerPlanck.

It was a private meeting. *Very* private. All the civilians signed another sheaf of papers before they began—American documents this time, confidentiality agreements. They had to promise that they would never breathe a word of this meeting to anyone.

Dame Constance asked the Americans to begin the briefing. The attack in New York had given them the jump-start on intelligence. Paul Oakley would follow. There were also American doctors from the Centers for Disease Control and Prevention and the National Institutes of Health, but Oakley had rank. He was the world expert on infectious diseases and had full clearance at Porton Down—Britain's highly secret bioweapons research facility.

As the meeting settled down, a CIA officer signaled for the lights to dim. The first image on the screen was a man's face. Mid-fifties, unshaved, a touch of cruelty about the mouth. He could have played the role of any Third World dictator.

"Moustaffa Gemeyal, the ringleader of the terrorist group Common Dream. Born in Cairo in 1959, emigrated to the UK as a teenager," the CIA agent said. "He communicates with his followers via the Internet. He is what we call a 'charismatic radicalizer.' "

The next slide showed Moustaffa crossing a city street in Cairo.

"Moustaffa's home base is Egypt. We've been monitoring him for the last three years through his Internet communications. His message has always been antigovernment but has become increasingly violent. He was moved to our Terror Watch List about three months ago."

The next photo was of Moustaffa on the aft deck of a large yacht with a dark-haired woman. The woman's face was obscured by large sunglasses and a broad-brimmed hat. But from the neck down she was clearly visible. The only clothing she wore was a jade green thong.

Moustaffa was standing next to her, his hand resting lightly on her waist as they spoke. They looked like an intimate couple, with their heads together, deep in conversation.

"Lady Xandra Sommerset, British citizen," the CIA director said. "Worth about two billion dollars, mostly from her late father's business investments. Mother Egyptian. Moustaffa is her current paramour."

The next slide clicked. Moustaffa was poised on the

swimming platform of the yacht, clad in a scant black swimsuit. He had an impressive, buffed body. The bulge in his Speedo conveyed an obvious virility.

"Moustaffa is a textbook narcissist—an inflated sense of self-importance, a firm belief in his own superiority, and a pathological craving for adulation."

"It's hard to believe a woman like Lady Sommerset would put up with that," observed one of the MI6 officers.

"To the contrary, her psychology dovetails with his perfectly."

"How so?" the British official demanded.

"U.S. psychologists have analyzed her interviews in the media. They have concluded she has a deep-seated inferiority complex. Chronically low self-esteem."

"You mean *magazine* profiles. I'm sorry, but that sounds like American psychobabble to me," the British official snapped.

"You may dismiss it, but psychological profiles are very often accurate predictors of potential action," the CIA official countered.

"Like what?"

"Her insecurities would make her a perfect pawn for Moustaffa."

The CIA officer moved to change slides.

"How long have they been together?" the British official persisted.

"Six years. And recently they have been inseparable. For the past three months they have been meeting frequently on her yacht at various places around the world."

"And his organization?" asked Dame Constance, trying to move the conversation along.

"He has one point two million Internet followers globally who profess allegiance," the CIA official responded. "They are only loosely affiliated with his movement. There is no official way to join his organization; there is only an online forum for discussion. We monitor the participants."

"That is enormous reach!" Dame Constance remarked, taken aback.

"He presents himself as a messianic figure, a violent dreamer. But in reality he is a high-functioning sociopath."

"How many people are directly under his command?" Dame Constance asked.

"We really have no idea how many people he calls on to execute his *illegal* activities. But I think we can safely assume that, for security reasons, his true inner circle is relatively small."

The CIA official turned to his associate. He held out his hand for a file, took it, and riffled through it.

"Moustaffa makes most of his money in vector military weapons, small arms. But he is known to dabble in toxins—anthrax, microbial and other biological agents."

"His customers?"

"He sells to anyone with enough cash. The first time we came across his name was in 1995, when we investigated the sarin-gas attack on the Tokyo subway. He was rumored to be a potential supplier."

"Never proven," the head of MI6 interjected.

"True, but you might find *this* interesting," the CIA officer continued.

He punched the video button and a new image appeared—that of a brick mansion with a green roof. Two

Soviet-era Ladas were parked out front in the snow-covered driveway.

"This dacha outside of Moscow is the former home of the nineteenth-century vodka merchant Pyotr Smirnoff and now the offices of the Main Directorate of the Council of Ministers."

The image changed to an aerial shot.

"About twenty years ago, the same building was the headquarters of Biopreparat, the Kremlin's biological weapons program—what was then known as 'germ warfare.'"

"How is that related to Moustaffa?" the head of MI6 asked.

"Take a look," the CIA director said dramatically.

The next photo, a close-up, showed a much younger looking Moustaffa getting out of a car in front of the building. He had longer hair and was wearing a black leather jacket and jeans.

"*Great* photo!" the representative of MI6 said. "Thank God for the Cold War. You people were really on your game."

"Thank you," the CIA officer said proudly.

"So even then Moustaffa was involved. . . ." Dame Constance pressed forward.

"As a young entrepreneur, he helped procure clandestine substances for the Soviets," the CIA agent continued. "They had forty sites in Russia and Kazakhstan to develop various toxins, bacteria, and viruses. Everyone needed supplies, and Moustaffa was the point man."

"His motivation?" she asked.

"Money. Moustaffa's clients paid him huge sums. He was in it for the cash."

"And now?"

"Same. His art-theft scheme has generated hundreds of millions of dollars over the last five years."

"So why the political angle?" asked the head of MI6. "What is the messianic message all about?"

"We're not sure. Perhaps he believes his own antigovernment propaganda. People with a narcissistic personality disorder often start believing their own fantasies."

"Interesting point," said Dame Constance. "But forgive me for not being convinced. What are the goals of his organization?"

"Moustaffa has various rants. All predictable. He specializes in conspiracy theories about big government. His group—Common Dream—is dedicated to overthrowing Western governments."

"With an attack?" asked Dame Constance.

"Yes, we have been monitoring the web traffic and believe he will strike soon."

"How soon?" she asked quietly.

The CIA officer paused dramatically.

"At the Sharm el-Sheikh World Economic Forum next week."

There was absolute silence. Fingers stopped typing. The sound of pen on paper was suddenly arrested. Sinclair looked around at the faces in the room. For the first time since they began, expressions were bleak.

"As you are aware, the summit will host twelve heads of state, from European and Asian countries, as well as the U.S. president and the UK prime minister."

"How many people in total?" asked Dame Constance.

"We estimate fifteen hundred participants, maybe two

thousand. Not counting the media. Bankers, business figures, and government ministers—and also this," the CIA officer added as he clicked on an image.

It was a work of art—a highly detailed medieval triptych. The painting was entirely out of context, as if a random slide had been inserted in error. There was a murmur of confusion and shifting in the seats.

"This is not a mistake; take a closer look," the CIA officer urged.

Sinclair leaned forward to examine the image of a medieval apocalyptic painting. Every inch of the surface was covered with people. Some were writhing in agony, others fleeing an advancing army of skeletons. A scene of utter devastation, with cities burning and ships dashed on the shore. The sky was purple and black.

"I assure you this is relevant. You are looking at Pieter Bruegel the Elder's *Triumph of Death*. Oil painting on panel from 1562 depicting an outbreak of the bubonic plague."

"Significance?" Dame Constance spat out with irritation.

"Stolen from the Museo del Prado in Madrid last week."

"And . . . ?" she said impatiently.

"The work was shipped to the U.S. State Department—the *original*, I might add. The date of the Sharm el-Sheikh conference had been spray-painted on the front."

There was silence.

"Sent by Common Dream," the CIA officer concluded. "We can only assume it is some kind of warning from Moustaffa."

No one moved.

"This will be a *joint* operation," said Dame Constance. Everyone nodded.

"Gentlemen, please open a new case file. I propose the code name Operation Dream Catcher."

The shuffling of papers and clicking of keyboards went on for several minutes. The news had mobilized everyone. The CIA director stepped to the front of the room again and called everyone to order.

"Measures must be taken to counter this threat. But I think it advisable to know what's at stake if we do *not* succeed in thwarting the biological attack."

There was a murmur of apprehension, and everyone settled down immediately.

"Dr. Oakley, we can begin. You have five minutes," the CIA director said. "And, if you don't mind, keep this in layman's terms as much as possible."

"Understood."

Paul Oakley stepped up to address the group. He looked very young in his khakis and sweater. And, unlike the intelligence officer, his briefing didn't start with a fancy slide show. He simply stated the facts. The calmness of his voice made the information even more chilling.

"Bubonic plague is the most lethal disease known to man. It is highly virulent and killed a quarter of the population of Europe in the fourteenth century."

"Could we move directly on to weaponization of the plague?" Dame Constance asked impatiently. "We don't have much time."

"Certainly," Oakley agreed, unruffled. "The United

States worked with *Yersinia pestis* as a biowarfare agent in the 1950s and 1960s. It was never deployed and the program was terminated."

Sinclair tried to concentrate, but his mind kept going back to Cordelia. Where was she now, and what was she doing?

"The Soviets had more success," Oakley continued. "They developed a powdered form of the bacterium that could be sprinkled like talcum powder."

"Did they use it?"

"There are stories of the Soviets trying to assassinate Marshal Tito of Yugoslavia with the powder. Nothing was ever confirmed."

"Did they test it?"

"Yes, aerosols were tested on animals. It works. With an airborne exposure, an average person uses ten liters of air a minute, and a monkey a little less than half that. If a standard dose kills monkeys, it would also kill humans."

"Besides aerosols, are there any other methods of disseminating the disease?" asked Dame Constance.

"Fleas," Oakley said.

"You're *kidding*," the CIA agent burst out.

"No, I'm not. The Japanese army in World War Two reportedly dropped canisters of live fleas to spread the disease in Manchuria."

"That seems very crude," the official from MI6 said.

"But effective. Plague was transported primarily by fleas in fourteenth-century Europe. And fleas were also carriers during the Great London Plague of 1665. During that outbreak, each week, seven *thousand* people died."

"Surely all that is ancient history," the CIA officer said dismissively.

"Yes and no. The plague epidemic in China in 1894 eventually came to San Francisco via fleas on shipboard rats. As late as 1900, more than a hundred people died of flea-borne plague in California."

"But Moustaffa is not going to drop *fleas*," said the MI6 officer.

"Technologically we are beyond that. There are much better ways to spread the disease."

"Well, we can't sit here and talk about the theoretical. Of all the possibilities the attack could take, what is your best guess?" asked the CIA officer.

"An aerosol."

"Is that possible?"

"The only thing that has stopped terrorists from doing that up until now has been lack of technical know-how."

"And could Moustaffa have figured out how to release bubonic plague?"

"He'd probably opt for *pneumonic* plague. Not bubonic."

"What's the difference?"

Paul Oakley reached over and took a sheaf of papers from his briefcase.

"I thought we'd get to that sooner or later, so I prepared a handout."

They silently passed the papers from person to person. The photos were horrific. Patients covered with livid purple boils. Sinclair stared at the page, sick with horror. What a terrible way to die!

"If you look at photo A-1, these are classic symptoms

of bubonic plague. You will note the buboes that give bubonic plague its name. Those are swollen tender lymph nodes in the armpit or groin," Oakley instructed.

"So if this is bubonic, what is *pneumonic* plague?" the CIA officer asked.

"With pneumonic plague, there are no swellings. The disease is airborne, spread by droplet infection—transmitted when a person coughs. It spreads very quickly in a population."

Dame Constance tapped her watch significantly.

Oakley nodded and delivered the final line of his briefing with chilling precision.

"The most important point is that the pneumonic form of the disease is *much* deadlier."

"How deadly?" asked Dame Constance.

Oakley looked at her, his face taut with anxiety.

"Virtually no one survives."

The Khamsin Motoryacht

CORDELIA LOOKED IN the vanity mirror and gasped. What a fright! There were streaks of dirt on her forehead and chin, and her suit was a mass of grease stains. She looked around the elegant bathroom for something to help her clean up.

There were delicate linen guest towels with blue anchors embroidered on them. She soaked one in hot water and lathered up a tiny bar of perfumed soap. First her hands and face. Her legs were filthy, knees encrusted with motor oil from crawling on the floor. She swabbed at the heavy grease until most of it was gone and threw the stained towel in the trash. Time to face the enemy.

Cordelia opened the door to find a young crew member in a white steward's coat waiting for her. Not at all menacing.

"Your tea is in the salon, miss," he said in an Australian accent. "Lady Sommerset will see you now."

Lady Sommerset? That name was very familiar. Where had she heard it? Cordelia followed him through a narrow hallway to the aft salon of the boat, racking her brain for any shred of information.

A dark-haired woman looked up as they entered. Cordelia recognized her instantly. The famous Lady X! Lady Sommerset was the British socialite who was always in the tabloids. Still youthful in her mid-forties, she had enormous eyes the color of burnished gold. She wore a magenta silk caftan, and her bare feet were tanned and festooned with gold toe rings.

Seeing her beautifully dressed and lounging on the cream-colored banquette, Cordelia felt a flutter of hope. Clearly this elegant woman would release her immediately. It was all a mistake! Those two thugs didn't know what they were doing.

Lady Sommerset stood to greet her. Cordelia found herself thinking that pictures didn't do her justice. She was beautiful and moved with an elegant grace.

"My apologies for your uncomfortable transportation."

"I'd really like to know what's going on," Cordelia said.

"We needed Mr. Hannifin. You had the unfortunate luck to be in the wrong place," Lady Sommerset replied. "I'm afraid I cannot change what fate has delivered to you."

Her tone was charming, sympathetic, but the message was insane!

"Fate?" Cordelia gasped. "I was held at *gunpoint!*"

"Well, that's all over now," she soothed.

"You don't understand. I was *drugged.*"

"Well, you won't be treated like that on *The Khamsin*. The tradition of this ship is hospitality. So please, make yourself comfortable."

Lady X waved airily for Cordelia to take a seat.

"I insist on being put ashore immediately!"

"I'm afraid that won't be possible. We need to keep you on board for a while."

"Where are we headed?"

"Venice. I have a palazzo off the Grand Canal. When

we reach the city, I will make arrangements for you to be returned to London."

"I need to call someone, to let them know where I am."

Lady X did not answer.

"Please, come sit down," she invited. "I ordered some tea for you."

A white-coated steward appeared, and he poured a pale green herbal-smelling concoction into a delicate porcelain cup. Cordelia suddenly realized how terribly thirsty she was. She accepted the tea and put in a spoonful of sugar. The infusion smelled a bit like mowed grass, but it made her feel enormously better. Lady X watched with a polite smile.

"Don't try to pretend this is a social event," Cordelia said. "Abduction is a *criminal* act."

"This is not abduction. You are my guest. I assure you, I meant no harm."

"No. Of *course* not."

"Dr. Graham, I will keep this simple," Lady X replied. "If you do what I ask, I will return you to dry land, un-harmed."

Cordelia started in surprise. *Dr. Graham?* Did Lady X think she was talking to Holly Graham? Clearly this was a case of mistaken identity.

"You've got the wrong person, I am *not* Dr. Graham," Cordelia said, putting her cup down.

"These little games will not work, Dr. Graham. We know you were meeting with the British Museum about Artemidorus," Lady X pointed to the sarcophagus.

"I was *not* . . . I was meeting . . ." Cordelia broke off, noticing the large crimson cartouche strapped to the banquette. It was held in place with bungee cords to prevent it from toppling with the movement of the ship.

"You *stole* that?"

"Yes," Lady Sommerset said with a smile, unruffled. "I'm sure you recognize it. I'm returning it to where it belongs. You have tortured him enough with your medical tests."

Cordelia looked at the Egyptian coffin. It was clear Lady X was insane. She *stole* a *mummy*? How utterly bizarre!

"What happened to Mr. Hannifin?" Cordelia asked. "I want to know."

"He slipped. Drowned. So tragic."

"I see."

She kept silent and drank her tea. This was serious. *Slipped?* More likely was *pushed*. It was a big ocean. In seas like these, he wasn't *ever* going to be found. She'd better watch her step.

"The crew will find you some other clothes," Lady X said, surveying Cordelia's stained suit with disapproval.

"Thank you."

"Please, take your time to finish your tea. When you are ready, you can ring the call bell and someone will show you to your cabin below."

Cordelia nodded, still staring at the sarcophagus. Lady X noticed her gaze.

"I need you to help me with Artemidorus," she explained. "I'm sure you are delighted to be reunited with your—"

"You want me to help you steal a *mummy*?" Cordelia gasped. "*That's* why you abducted me?"

"It's deteriorating and I need your help. I'm sure your concern for the artifact is as great as mine," Lady X admonished.

"All I know is you'd better let me out of here when we put in to Venice, or there will be serious consequences."

"There is no reason why this voyage shouldn't conclude amicably. Now, I wish you a good night."

With that, Lady Sommerset drifted out of the salon in a sweep of magenta silk. Cordelia heard the door lock behind her.

Federal Plaza, New York

CARTER WALLACE WAS pacing around an empty office in the federal office tower in lower Manhattan. The furniture for the FBI Stolen Art Division was remarkably shabby, presumably the choice of government budget minders. Steel desks, mismatched chairs, a stained carpet, and an exhausted-looking ficus plant in the corner. The workspace made Carter's basement cubby at the museum seem luxurious.

If the FBI had to put up with this kind of decor, there was one feature to compensate—a million-dollar view. Standing on the twenty-third floor, Carter could see all of Wall Street and the expanse of New York Harbor beyond. The Statue of Liberty looked like a toy, perched on her little island in the middle of the blue water.

The door opened and the head of the Stolen Art Division walked in.

"Dr. Wallace, thanks for getting in touch with us. I'm Joe Viles, supervisory special agent on this case."

As he shook hands, Carter noted that the guy was classic FBI—close-cropped hair, a gunmetal gray suit—clearly impervious to any style trends.

"Pleased to meet you," Carter said, taking the seat he was offered. "I remembered something that might be of use. An art theft in London last year."

"And the significance?" Viles asked, reaching for the computer mouse on the desk.

"The objects were Egyptian, and Charles Hannifin was in London at the time they were stolen. I know, because our director at the Brooklyn Museum met with him over there."

"I *see*," Viles replied, pausing. "Which museum?"

"The Flinders Petrie Museum of Archaeology, London."

"Let's look for a notation on the database." Viles turned to the computer screen and scrolled through a few cases, clicking on image after image.

"Do you remember the time of year?"

"April."

"Here we are," the agent said. "April of last year. Globally, over a thousand art objects were stolen in that month alone."

"How many files are there in total?" Carter asked, shocked.

"Ninety thousand," Viles replied. "The files that have been stamped CLOSED are solved. The rest are ongoing operations."

Carter could see as Viles flipped through the images that most of the objects had *not* been recovered.

"I can't believe you have to sort through all this."

"You're lucky we have these records. Until a few years ago the FBI didn't follow transshipment of stolen art."

"Why'd you start? What changed?"

"Art thieves changed. Art theft has become a major criminal activity attracting drug traffickers, money launderers, organized crime."

"How'd *you* get involved?" asked Carter.

"Undergraduate degree in fine arts. That got me a job at Starbucks."

"So then what?" Carter asked.

"After 9/11, I went back for a master's degree in domestic security studies, and then a law degree."

"That seems pretty qualified. What'd you need me for?"

"I need your eyes. Look at the files and see what clicks."

"Sure, no problem," Carter said, pulling his chair up to the desk. The agent lounged nearby, surveying Carter in a friendly fashion.

"I hear you're the guy who tipped the police off about the Met."

"Yeah, well . . . It wasn't much," Carter mumbled. "And they haven't recovered a fraction of what was taken that night."

"Don't kid yourself," the agent replied. "This case is *huge*. If Hannifin is involved in this theft, my superiors will be very interested."

A few hours later, a beautiful scarab flashed on the computer screen in front of Carter. In the photo, the ancient gold object had the inimitable look of a genuine artifact.

"I think I found something!" Carter called out.

FBI agent Joe Viles appeared in the doorway.

"Really?"

"It was stolen last year in London."

"Are you sure?"

"The description matches perfectly. 'Egyptian funerary object, Heart Scarab of Hatnofer, ca. 1466 BCE; Western Thebes, Flinders Petrie Museum, London.' *That's it!*"

"Read me the case number. I'll find the paper file. Nice job."

"Thanks," Carter said, rubbing his temples.

"You know, you're pretty good at this kind of thing," Viles said, pausing in the doorway. "You should think about working at the bureau."

"*Me?* Join the FBI?" Carter said, incredulously.

"As a consultant—we need trained archaeologists and art experts to help us identify stolen objects."

"I had no idea."

"We're not just a bunch of guys looking for drug shipments, you know. Of course, you'd have to pass a security check. But since you've already found half the missing art from the Met, your clearance would be pretty quick."

"Thanks. But from the number of files I've had to look through today, there's a lot greater chance of finding something as an archaeologist digging in the sand," Carter joked.

"You may be right about that," Viles said with a laugh. "I'll be back in a minute."

Carter ambled out into an employee break room and fed his spare change into a hot-drinks machine. The vending dispenser whirred, dropped a paper cup, and then dribbled out coffee, powdered creamer, and an avalanche of sugar. After one sip, Carter spit it out and dumped the mess into the trash.

As he walked through the hallway his phone rang. The international area code was 44—London. Of course it was Holly; she was the only person he knew in that city.

"Uh . . . hello, Holly." He verbally stumbled, sounding like a clod.

"Carter, how are you?"

"I'm good, keeping busy."

"Listen, I'm calling because you left me a message warning about Charlie Hannifin."

"Yeah, he's really . . ."

"How did you know he was involved in something illegal?"

"His name is all over the paperwork," Carter answered. "You aren't anywhere near him, are you?"

"No, I'm not. He's been abducted."

"What! How?" Carter asked.

"The British Museum. I was scheduled to have a meeting there. But I canceled it. He was abducted about the time I was supposed to be there."

"Wow, I'm glad you're safe."

"Yes, thanks. Is there anything else you've found out about Hannifin?" Holly asked.

Carter considered telling her that he was helping the FBI. It would make him sound smart. But this meeting was probably confidential, and he didn't like bragging on the phone.

"No. Working on a few angles, but nothing concrete yet," he said casually.

"Please let me know if you find anything out. I mean *anything.*"

"Sure."

"Take care, I'll be in touch."

He stumbled through a good-bye, making as big a fool of himself as possible, and then hung up.

At least Holly was safe. Now to find the art. That would *really* impress her.

The FBI agent was back at the desk, rummaging through an accordion folio of documents.

"Where'd you go?"

"Saw the coffee machine and tried it."

"Yeah, I should have warned you about that."

"Too late," Carter said with a laugh. "Listen, I just heard Charlie Hannifin is missing in London."

"No surprise there. I'd go missing if *my* name was all over a shipment of stolen art."

"Yeah, well, my colleague just told me that Hannifin was kidnapped."

"*Kidnapped?* We'll check into it."

"Did you find the file?" Carter asked.

"Yeah, you were right about this scarab. It's from a case file with six other pieces."

He handed Carter the transparencies of Egyptian funerary objects. "Here they are. Recovered two months ago in Italy."

"Where were they shipped from?" Carter asked. "No, let me guess . . . the Freilager Zone in Zurich."

"That's right."

"And sent where . . . ?" Carter asked.

"We found them in a warehouse in the old quarter in Venice. Art, jewelry, watches. Oh, and a Maserati. We never caught the thieves."

"Well, I suggest you get on the phone to the Italian police," said Carter. "If Hannifin was involved in both robberies, maybe these are the same people who hit the Met."

"It's worth checking out."

"Let me know if you turn up a twelve-foot mummy cartouche. Bright red. Face painted on the outside. We're missing it at the Brooklyn Museum."

"Will do."

"Well, I guess that's it for me," Carter said, picking up his jacket. "Glad I could help."

"Wait. If we find another warehouse with stolen goods in Venice, we're going to need somebody to ID the art. The bureau chief in New York would like you to fill out the application to work with us as a consultant."

"You'd hire me? Just like that?" Carter asked, agog.

"We'd have to run a security clearance and give you a training course for a day or so. But if you went we'd pay your travel expenses and an hourly rate. It's pretty good money."

"You'd pay me to go to *Italy*?"

"If the art turns up, we really can't spare anyone from this office."

Carter thought about it for a moment. No use hanging around the Brooklyn Museum when Holly was in London.

"Sure! Why not? I'd have to clear it with my boss, but I've always wanted to go to Venice."

Grosvenor Street, London

JOHN SINCLAIR CLIMBED the steps of the town house and was greeted at the door by his assistant, Malik. The young man was now frantic with worry. Sinclair was not at liberty to tell him the full story—only that Cordelia had been kidnapped. But each time Sinclair received a call or came back to the house Malik questioned him. Today, he must have been waiting in the hall for Sinclair to come home.

"Anything yet?"

"I'm afraid not," Sinclair said, turning away so he wouldn't see Malik's features droop with disappointment. His assistant's dedication was a comfort. For the last decade, Malik had mastered every detail of Sinclair's life with seamless perfection, from chartering planes to keeping his schedule. It had taken a lot to tempt Malik away from the glorious sun of the archaeological dig in Turkey to a rainy English climate. It had been Cordelia who had convinced Malik to move to London. Malik was devoted to her.

"What's this?" Sinclair asked, taking a large envelope from the hall table.

"That package was delivered this afternoon."

"Thanks, Malik," Sinclair said, picking it up with disinterest and climbing with leaden tread up to his library.

He patted Kyrie on the head and poured himself a drink before he examined the large manila envelope. His

name had been printed in black felt-tip pen. There were
no other distinguishing markings.

He broke the metal clasp and slid the contents out. At
first glance it appeared to be a photo. He turned it over. A
Post-it, stuck to the back, had a phone number.

Sinclair examined the photo closely and saw it was the
print of a medical X-ray. Suddenly, he got a chill down his
neck. It was a CAT scan of a mummy!

Holly had been right about making an offer on Artemidorus; their little fishing expedition had worked!
Here was a response from a black market dealer. Sinclair
reached for the phone and dialed Holly's room at the Ritz.
She answered, sounding tired.

"Hols?" he said. "It's Sinclair. Can you come over to
the house right away? I think we may have found your
mummy."

At eight o'clock in the evening Holly Graham arrived. She
walked up the front steps of the town house thinking that
this was the last place she *ever* expected to be invited to.
With Cordelia missing, Holly felt like she was trespassing.

The houseman opened the door and beckoned her to
come with him. He was young and slight and spoke with a
Turkish accent.

"Mr. Sinclair is waiting for you in the library."

She followed Malik up two flights of stairs. Her feet
on the carpet made no sound. She passed by beautifully
appointed rooms filled with antique furniture. This was a
real Edwardian mansion!

Malik stopped in the doorway of a huge library that
was lined floor to ceiling with mahogany bookshelves.

There were leather chairs in front of the fireplace, and a dog lounged before the brass grate.

"Your visitor is here, sir," Malik said, stepping aside to let Holly pass.

Sinclair turned, gaunt with fatigue, a distinctive green volume of classical literature from the Loeb collection open in his hand. He tossed the book onto the library table and reached for an envelope.

"Hols, thanks for coming."

"No problem. It's the least I can do."

"Take a look at this, would you? It was delivered this afternoon."

Sinclair thrust the envelope at Holly. "It's a response to my offer to buy Artemidorus on the black market."

Holly slid the X-ray out, walked over to the map table, and twisted the gooseneck lamp to shine directly on the paper.

"What do you think? Is it genuine?"

She looked up at him. His appearance was awful—eyes pink-rimmed from lack of sleep and face drawn. Day-old stubble aged him by ten years.

"Give me a moment, John."

She sat down and studied the scan in the bright light. There were a myriad of details that suggested it was *not* Artemidorus.

"No luck, John. It's not him," she declared, putting the glossy photo back on the table.

Sinclair looked crushed. He slumped into the chair next to her.

"Sure?"

"Yes, I'm certain. I'm sorry."

"Wait," he urged desperately. "Please, take another look."

"I don't *need* to, John."

She understood his desperation—any progress on finding the art thieves might lead to Cordelia. But she wasn't going to lie to him.

"OK, just tell me how you know."

She picked it up again, very conscious of him sitting close to her. Their hands were almost touching as they held the paper.

"Artemidorus had very long femurs."

"Yes?"

"Normally, you measure the length of the femur in centimeters, multiply by 2.6, and then add 65, and that gives you how tall a person is in centimeters," she explained, pointing to the mummy's thighbones on the paper.

"And?"

"Artemidorus is well above six feet. But, just looking at this photo, I can tell you this mummy is barely five feet tall."

"I see."

She pointed to four white masses in the middle of the body. "Do you see these objects in the abdomen?"

"Yes?"

"They put the vital organs back in after they were mummified and wrapped in linen."

"What's the significance?"

"Artemidorus doesn't have his organs. He was rich and could pay for the alabaster canopic jars for his organs."

"Hmmm . . ." said Sinclair. "What else?"

"The brain. Embalmers would insert a long metal hook through the sinus cavity and pull the brain tissue out. They would have to break the front sinus bone to do it."

"I see."

"But this bone is not broken and the brain tissue is intact. Further evidence this person was poor. They skipped a few steps."

"I had no idea you could read so much into these things."

It was clear he was disappointed. She hated to continue, but it was better to go through the full litany of proof to dispel any doubt.

"See the skull? Artemidorus has a huge bash in the back of his skull. This mummy doesn't."

"Well, you don't have to go on. I'm convinced."

"But I haven't told you the clincher," Holly insisted. "If you notice, the mandible, or jawbone, is narrow and the pelvic inlet tells you everything."

"What am I looking for?"

"See, the pelvic bone is broad and round and the sacrum is wide. I don't even need radiography for the soft-tissue analysis. This is *not* Artemidorus."

"You're saying . . ."

"The hip bones are wide and there is no penis. This mummy is a *woman*."

LADY XANDRA SOMMERSET sat in the salon staring at the decaying sarcophagus. She had known that the mummy would deteriorate slightly in the salt air, but this was much worse than anything she had imagined. Half a dozen patches of green fungus had suddenly bloomed like little flowers all over the top of the coffin. Xandra started to wipe them off with a tissue but then stopped. What if she damaged the finish?

Artemidorus was also emitting a ripe odor that was becoming unbearable in the enclosed salon of the yacht. The beautiful artifact was being destroyed!

Venice was still a two-day sail away. Once she reached the palazzo, she could put the mummy in a room with regulated temperature and humidity. Her apartment—like many others in the submerged city—was climate-controlled to preserve the furniture and antiques. She'd keep Artemidorus there until it was time to travel to Egypt.

Xandra jumped up and paced the salon. It was inconceivable that her efforts to return the mummy to Cairo would be in vain. But if Artemidorus kept rotting like this they'd have to dispose of him at sea.

Something had to be done, and quickly! She *had* to persuade Dr. Graham to help! So far the woman had refused. Xandra hurried down to the portside forward cabin and rapped on the door.

"Dr. Graham, I have to talk to you."

There was a scuffling around and then Cordelia's right eye appeared.

"What do you want?"

"Please come with me."

Cordelia opened the door a few inches. She was dressed in a black tracksuit and sneakers.

"I need your professional advice," Xandra said.

"I already told you, I'm not a curator."

"Come with me, or I'll throw you off the ship."

"*What!*"

"Either help me or swim—your choice. But it's sixty meters deep."

Cordelia followed Xandra to the salon. Together they surveyed the sarcophagus.

The coffin was still bound to the banquette with padded ropes. Fungus had cast a grayish film over the cartouche, the glorious crimson color was dull, the portrait panel mottled with mold. It looked like Artemidorus had been afflicted with a disease.

"I'm afraid I can't help you with this," Cordelia said. "I don't know what to do."

"Why not?"

"I told you before. I am *not* Dr. Graham. My name is Cordelia Stapleton. You have kidnapped the wrong person."

"But you were at the British Museum," Xandra insisted.

"I was meeting Dr. Trentwell about a *marine archaeology* project in Alexandria, Egypt."

"Then where is Dr. Graham?" Xandra sputtered.

"I have absolutely no idea," Cordelia replied coldly. "But if you contact my partner in London I expect he will be able to tell you. His name is John Sinclair."

Lady Xandra Sommerset sat on the banquette and looked at Artemidorus. Tears formed in her eyes. She was destroying the mummy. After all her plans, Artemidorus would not survive the trip to Egypt. She needed professional help, and soon.

How could she have mistaken Cordelia Stapleton for the famous Egyptologist Dr. Hollis Graham? Now that she had done an Internet search, she could see they looked *nothing* alike. Cordelia was tall, lithe, with dark hair, while Holly was a petite voluptuous blonde. Why hadn't she bothered to check this before?

Now Cordelia had to go. She had witnessed too much and knew too much. There was no way she could walk free.

Moustaffa appeared in the doorway of the salon. He was wearing a windbreaker and his hair was ruffled after being out on deck.

"Xandra, are you still moping in here?" he asked. "It's a gorgeous day. Let's go outside for some lunch."

"I couldn't possibly eat," Xandra moaned. "Just *look* at him."

Moustaffa glanced over at the cartouche with amusement.

"We should just toss that thing overboard. It's disgusting, and the boat is starting to stink."

"*No!*" Xandra burst out. "I want to get this to Egypt. I

need a conservator to help me preserve Artemidorus until I can get him back to Cairo. Can't you think of *something*?"

"Let me work on that," Moustaffa said, scratching the stubble of his beard. "What about the girl? What are you planning to do with her?"

"She's up on the top deck. I told Sigge to push her off the stern once we are clear of any boat traffic."

"How about asking her boyfriend for ransom? We never got paid for the VerPlanck woman in Wyoming. Let's get something for this one."

"I am *not* in the kidnapping business," Xandra said crossly. "Art is one thing. People are quite another."

"Just this once. It would be silly to pass up the opportunity. I did some digging on Cordelia Stapleton. She just inherited a lot of money, and her boyfriend is loaded."

"I don't know. I'm too worried about this," Xandra said, gesturing toward the mummy's coffin.

"Don't fret about it, my love. Leave the details to me. I'll get you a curator *and* some money for the girl. You can count on it."

Cordelia stood on the top deck of *The Khamsin,* her wrists bound with plastic restraints. It appeared that her future was not good. They didn't need her. She probably should have lied and pretended to be Holly Graham. But, realistically, how long could she have kept that up? Lady X would have figured out pretty quickly that conservation was not her profession.

She sat on the gear locker and looked at the ocean. Definitely a bad day to be tossed into the Med. Very choppy. She checked her wrist GPS and it read N 37°32', E 8°36'—they were roughly off the coast of Tunisia. They'd probably push her off with the restraints on. She'd sink like a stone!

She twisted her bound hands. The plastic cords were unbreakable and cut into her skin. She looked around to find something to help release them.

Next to her was a rack of Indian clubs—the wooden bowling pin–shaped weights lined up neatly. It was perfect! Even though her hands were bound, she could still hold on to something. She would clobber people as they came up from below.

Cordelia seized the ten-pound club, awkwardly grasping it around the neck with both bound hands. She stood over the ladder. Sure enough, two minutes later a man's shaggy head appeared from down below. She swung hard and bashed the man with a thud. He fell, crashing down onto the deck below.

She stood there, still breathing hard. Adrenaline pulsed through her veins and helped clear her head. But a jolt of fear hit her brain. She was going to die!

With shaking hands, Cordelia raised the club over the opening again and waited. Nothing. There was only the sound of the bow wake alongside the ship. Why weren't others coming? Surely somebody must have heard the falling body.

She heard the unmistakable click of a pistol behind her and turned slowly. A tall, muscular man was smiling at her. His weapon was pointed at her heart.

"You shouldn't have done that. He's going to have a hell of a headache."

She kept her eyes on the pistol. Moustaffa gestured for her to sit on the gear locker. When she was seated, he put the gun in his belt and walked over to her, grabbing the Indian club. He swung it and made a feint, missing her head by a fraction. She flinched in terror.

He laughed, delighted at her fear.

"Look at me!" he snarled.

She looked into his eyes. There was not a shred of sanity in them. He was an animal. Her heart was hammering so hard she could hardly breathe.

"I admit I came up here to push you off the back of the boat. But it appears the tide has turned. I'm going to make some money off you."

"What do you mean?"

"Ransom," Moustaffa replied. "How much do you think you're worth?"

"Plenty. Call my partner John Sinclair in London. No, wait, call Jim Gardiner. He's my lawyer. They'll pay you whatever you want."

"How much?" Moustaffa asked, looking her up and down as if assessing her.

"I don't know. Just call them. They'll talk to you."

"I'll do that. In the meantime, stay in your room."

"I will."

"And let me make something perfectly clear," Moustaffa said. "Your friend John Sinclair had better come up with the money or *you* will pay."

Moustaffa reached for her chin and pulled her face up to his. He was vulgar-looking—thick lips, bad skin. Strong arms. She thought he could crush her neck with one hand.

She squirmed, but his mouth came down over hers, his tongue probing in a disgusting, dirty violation. She clamped her jaw shut and wrenched her head away, but his grip was like iron. After a minute, he finally let go of her, laughing.

"If your boyfriend doesn't come up with the money, you are going to pay me, *personally*."

"No, he will. I promise!"

"If he doesn't, I am going to take you down below and get my money's worth. You'll *beg* me to kill you by the time I'm done with you."

Secret Intelligence Service (MI6), London

THE HEADQUARTERS OF the British spy agency was a monolithic pile of modern architecture near Vauxhall Bridge in London. Many people in the intelligence community referred to the building as Legoland, because of its boxy appearance. But, once inside, Sinclair thought MI6 headquarters more closely resembled a Babylonian ziggurat. Only the high priests could enter the inner sanctums of those sacred ancient temples; they alone were the keepers of dark secrets.

It had been an agonizing forty-eight hours since the high-level meeting in Scotland. Intelligence agencies in Europe had been scouring the globe for Cordelia, with little success. Then, suddenly, Sinclair, Holly, Jim Gardiner, and Ted VerPlanck had been summoned—a clear indication that something new had been discovered.

As they took their seats around the conference table, Sinclair noticed that VerPlanck pulled out a chair for Holly, and they sat side by side. Gardiner, looking ashen and quite ill, struggled to the far side of the room, as if to avoid any unpleasant news. Sinclair sat solo, braced for the worst.

"I have called you here because of a breakthrough in the case," Sir James Nicholson began.

"What is it?" Sinclair blurted, unable to control his anxiety.

"Everything is starting to come together," the spy chief said, signaling for the lights to dim. He clicked onto two mug shots.

"First, from American Intelligence: the FBI made two arrests in Wyoming. We believe these are the men who abducted Mrs. VerPlanck."

"About time someone found them!" VerPlanck said bitterly. "I certainly hope they will be prosecuted to the full extent of the law!"

Nicholson didn't pause but clicked again. Another image filled the screen—a beautiful dark-haired woman in a red dress, running down the steps of the Metropolitan Museum.

"Lady Xandra Sommerset at the gala in New York," he explained.

"So she's involved?" Sinclair asked.

"Yes. She was the mastermind behind the art robberies in New York last week, including the theft of the Sardonyx Cup and the mummy case from the Brooklyn Museum."

"And how is that connected to Cordelia?" Sinclair asked. "Or is it?"

Another click displayed an incredible yacht of enormous proportions.

"This is *The Khamsin,* Lady Sommerset's yacht. Registration Valletta, Malta. Now assumed to be in the Mediterranean."

Sir James looked directly at Sinclair as he spoke. "We know Cordelia Stapleton is on board."

"*She is!*" Sinclair cried out. "Are you sure?"

"Yes. We apprehended the men who transported Ms. Stapleton to *The Khamsin.*"

"How did you find them?"

"After we learned that Charles Hannifin drowned in the Thames, our people went down to the dockyards and found the two men who operated the fishing boat that transported Ms. Stapleton to the yacht. Once they understood the serious charges against them, they told us everything."

"Could you verify their accounts?" Gardiner asked in his lawyerly way. "How do you *know* Cordelia was on that fishing boat?"

"We went over it carefully. DNA swabs reflect Ms. Stapleton's presence in the hold of the ship."

"DNA samples? You mean blood?"

"No, apparently she was sick."

"Are you sure it was she?" Sinclair asked.

"Yes, we're absolutely certain. We cross-referenced her medical records from her employer—Woods Hole Oceanographic Institution. The samples matched."

"So she was transferred from a fishing vessel to the yacht. Where is that boat now?" Sinclair asked tensely.

"Last port of call for *The Khamsin* was Alicante, Spain, where it took on a full load of fuel."

"How far could they go with that?" asked Gardiner.

"We are working up possible routes. In terms of range, I expect Mr. VerPlanck can answer that for us," Sir James said.

Ted VerPlanck looked up at the ceiling and thought about it for a moment.

"Based on the standard for that model, a full load of fuel would last about five thousand nautical miles. The yacht could go pretty much anywhere . . . the Med, Adriatic, Ionian. Even down the coast of Africa."

"So how do we find her?" Sinclair cut in.

"It won't be easy. *The Khamsin* is moving through international waters, flying a Maltese flag of convenience," Sir James explained.

"What about the authorities that border the Med?" asked Holly. "Can't *they* do something?"

"The yacht is skirting a half-dozen countries. Unfortunately, most of them couldn't organize a chase by sea."

"But this is a *kidnapping*!" Holly argued.

"Spain, France, Italy, Monaco, Croatia, Greece, and Turkey all working together—even if they cooperated, it would take too much time."

Sinclair stared at him, distraught. "We need to do *something*!"

"We are. Here is the plan. The vessel will turn up at a checkpoint very soon."

"What do you mean, a checkpoint?"

"A maritime 'big ship report' area. They keep strict records of boats that transit certain areas. The Strait of Gibraltar, for example. A boat the size of *The Khamsin* would be required to notify the authorities they are passing through."

"That's a start," said Gardiner.

"No. There's a problem with that," VerPlanck spoke up.

"What do you mean?"

"*The Khamsin* could wait until nighttime and sneak through the radar scan by staying close to another large vessel. The radar signature would read as only one boat, not two."

"True, but we have another lead," the MI6 chief went on to say. "We know that Lady Xandra usually takes her yacht to Venice this time of year."

"So you think she's heading there?"

"She had a standing reservation at the marina on the Giudecca Canal. If *The Khamsin* docks there, we will be notified immediately."

"You've spoken to the port authorities?"

"Yes."

"And if she makes an appearance, then what?" asked Sinclair.

"Then we'll make a deal, Mr. Sinclair. And that's where we will need your assistance. As government officials, we can't negotiate with terrorists."

Grand Canal, Venice, Italy

V ENICE WAS GLORIOUS! Carter let the breeze ruffle his hair as his water taxi traversed the Grand Canal. He hung out the back of the boat, enthralled with the beautiful maritime city. Instead of the snarl of modern traffic, there was a ballet of vaporetti, ferryboats, gondolas, and other small craft bobbing in the morning sun.

He had learned a lot about Venice from reading the guidebooks on the plane. The ancient city was called "La Serenissima," or "The Most Serene"—because its citizens had preferred trade to war. Now that he was here, Carter could see it *was* serene in the truest sense of the word.

The soft beauty was enchanting. As his boat passed by the old palaces, with their graceful balconies and sheltered terraces, Carter suddenly understood why Venice had inspired countless masterpieces. He couldn't resist trying to capture it himself, taking photos of the sea entrance, St. Mark's Square, and the iconic winged lion atop the tall granite pillar.

The water taxi turned into a smaller canal, and suddenly it was cool and dim. Old buildings flanked him on both sides, their walls coated with green moss at the waterline. Iron-grilled doorways appeared at intervals, where stone steps led into the palazzi and hotels.

They passed under a swan-necked bridge, and Carter conjured up a romantic tryst: two lovers, kissing in the night. Of course, his next thought was of Holly. He was willing to admit she was a fantasy. Fleeting rapidly. But he wasn't giving up entirely.

He slumped back in his seat and realized that Holly was the reason why he was here. Motivated by a desire to become her hero, he was desperately trying to find the stolen art. But whatever unrealistic expectation had driven him, this was the best thing that had happened to him in years!

Looking at a gondolier passing by, he was struck with one of those rare moments of crystalline clarity. *This* was a defining moment. He had spent too much time among the dusty artifacts of a dead civilization. But now, due to an unexpected turn of events, he had found his way again. Venice had unleashed a pent-up hunger that had *nothing* to do with Holly.

He wanted to live! Roam the globe. Travel. His future was *out there*! The shimmering beauty of the world lay before him, and until now he had been ignoring it.

Carter found his Venetian epiphany short-lived; his tour of the city had to be put on hold. Practicality intervened. An hour after his arrival, he received a message to go to the water entrance of the Hotel Bonvecchiati to meet the local customs police.

As he waited on the stone landing, he noticed the day had suddenly turned damp and chilly. In the space of an hour fog had rolled in, and the canals were now misted and mysterious. He could barely make out the shapes of the buildings on the far side.

He buttoned his trench coat and thrust his hands into

his pockets. Boat traffic had slackened. A lone gondola glided around the corner, appearing silently out of the fog. A man in a traditional striped shirt and straw boater maneuvered the craft with a long pole. The dark hull of the gondola passed by, ominous and ghostly. In the rear, a young couple were embracing on the red velvet settee, oblivious of all but each other. Then they were gone, swallowed up in the mist.

Somewhere nearby he could hear the *putt-putt* of a motor. Carter tried to see through the wall of white fog, but with the sound distorted, it was impossible to tell how close the boat was. Suddenly, a police vessel appeared directly in front of him. The pilot cut the engine and maneuvered the craft up to the stone landing.

"Dr. Carter Wallace?" the officer asked.

"Yes, that's me."

"Please get in."

"Sure," he said, looking at the bobbing boat.

He had no idea how to climb into the moving craft. Apparently water transportation was not for the fainthearted. Carter closed his eyes and leaped. He fell on the cushioned seat just as the engine kicked in. The officer tactfully ignored his clumsiness and turned into the canal.

London

IT WAS MIDNIGHT at the Grosvenor Street town house. John Sinclair flung down *Memoirs of Hadrian*. Reading was futile. It had been a long, difficult day. Sleep, or even shutting his eyes, was inconceivable! The town house reminded him of a tomb. All four stories were echoing with emptiness now that Cordelia was gone.

This was her home, even though they both lived here now. She had inherited the beautiful brick Mayfair mansion a year ago from a distant relative. It had originally belonged to Cordelia's great-great-grandfather Elliott Stapleton, a famous Victorian explorer. It was a handsome property. Most of the furniture was original, and the decor retained the elegant masculinity of the original owner.

Sinclair's whole life was nothing without Cordelia. Even this library, his favorite place on earth, seemed like a prison without her. He had never been so distraught in his life.

Tonight the fire crackled in the grate, mocking his gloom with its coziness and warmth. His dog, Kyrie, lay dozing before the brass fireplace fender. Restless, Sinclair walked over to the sound system and began mindlessly scrolling through the music.

He selected Brahms's *Ein Deutsches Requiem*—the spiritual tone seemed appropriate. The poignant composition roiled out of the speakers—a beautiful Mass sung in German. Sinclair's playlist didn't usually include religious works. Piety didn't come naturally. He always favored science over theology. But tonight he'd take all the prayers he could get.

This afternoon, surprisingly, *The Khamsin* had made contact with Jim Gardiner's office via satellite phone. A call had come, asking to speak to Sinclair, demanding ransom. As suspected, the yacht was headed to Venice, arriving the day after tomorrow.

Sinclair had negotiated for Cordelia's release with Jim Gardiner hovering behind him nervously. British Intelligence couldn't be involved because of the government's policy of not directly negotiating with terrorists. However, MI6 agents had gathered around him as he set the terms.

Everything was fine, Lady X had assured them. The "cargo" was on board. However, there would be a "fee" for transporting Cordelia to Venice. Sinclair had blanched at all the talk of Cordelia as an inanimate object. Fortunately, Lady X agreed to their figure—two million dollars. Safe delivery wouldn't be a problem, but she had one firm condition: that everyone on *The Khamsin* would be granted immunity from prosecution.

Sinclair looked around the room for affirmation. The agents nodded. Done, Sinclair had agreed.

Lady X had then turned the phone over to Moustaffa to make arrangements for the money drop. The terrorist had taken quite a different tone. He was much more aggressive, upping the price twice. Throughout the conversation, no one had been allowed to speak to Cordelia.

Sinclair had been sitting with British intelligence agents on both sides of him. Only he could negotiate, but they wrote out suggestions and tips for him on a computer notepad. They communicated wordlessly as the negotiations proceeded. At one point Jim Gardiner appropriated the tablet to type a question to the MI6 officers.

> Should we ask to speak to her?

The agent typed the instruction to Sinclair:

> Ask for proof of life.

Sinclair shot him a confused look.

> That is standard procedure in hostage negotiations.
> Do it.

Sinclair did as he was instructed. The reaction was violent.

"I'll give you proof of life!" Moustaffa had growled.

He had put the phone down and dragged Cordelia closer to the receiver. They had heard the sound of someone being slapped, hard—the unmistakable smack of an open hand hitting someone's face. She cried out. *It was Cordelia!*

Sinclair had stood powerless, staring at the intercom, clenching and unclenching his hands. By the second blow he had started to curse under his breath, threatening Moustaffa with all kinds of bodily harm. Tears rimmed Gardiner's eyes as he listened.

The call concluded with Moustaffa vowing to kill Cordelia if the money didn't turn up. Sinclair was to proceed to Venice, where he would be notified of when and where to make the drop. He should come alone. Then the line went dead.

Sinclair had gone wild with fury. The British intelligence officers assured him the slapping was staged and sounded worse than it actually was. Moustaffa would not harm Cordelia seriously. He needed her alive and undamaged if he wanted to walk away with four million dollars of British taxpayers' money. Leave it to the professionals, they said.

Then they had sent him home with clear instructions. He would be transported to Venice tomorrow. An entire MI6 team would be on the scene to help him—British Intelligence would set up operations in the Hotel Danieli. The success of the operation was dependent on him being patient, keeping his head. The only thing they required tonight was for him to go home and sleep.

As if he *could*!

Sinclair walked over to the sideboard, seized a cut-crystal tumbler, and shoveled in some ice and poured a double splash of Laphroaig. Just then, his assistant, Malik, walked in. He looked pale with worry as he put a tray on the library table.

"Margaret made you a fresh pot of coffee and some cheddar scones. She was concerned you didn't have any dinner."

"Thanks, very kind of her," Sinclair replied.

"You should try to rest."

"You should get some rest yourself."

"I know we'll get a break in the case soon," Malik said with a newfound authority that came from watching BBC detective shows.

Sinclair gave him a hint of a smile.

"I'm sure you are right. The British are very good at this sort of thing."

It was pitch dark when Sinclair woke up. For the briefest moment he reached across the bed for her. The sheet was cool and flat. Then he remembered Cordelia was gone. Today, he would fly to Venice to pay the ransom. As he swung his legs out of bed, he vowed that Cordelia would come home or he'd die trying.

At six a.m., Sinclair stood with Malik on the threshold of the town house and watched the traffic on Grosvenor Street. Car headlights were still glowing orange in the darkness. It was damp and cool and felt like it would rain.

A black sedan pulled up, driven by a British security agent. Jim Gardiner was the passenger in the front seat. Sinclair handed his coffee cup to Malik and clasped his hand good-bye.

"Good luck."

"I'll bring her back," Sinclair promised, his throat tight.

Malik nodded very quickly and looked away. Sinclair headed toward the car and opened the back door. *Holly Graham was in the rear seat!*

"*Hols!* I didn't know you were coming to Venice with us!"

"MI6 called me. There are some new developments," Holly explained, sounding almost apologetic.

"No, I didn't mean . . . I'm glad for your company. You've been terrific about all of this."

He slid into the car beside her. Gardiner turned around to address him.

"Apparently Moustaffa and Lady X want to return Artemidorus. They want Holly to come to Venice and verify it's the real mummy."

"They're giving it *back*? Why would they do that?" Sinclair exclaimed.

"Lady X says she had a change of heart and wants to return it to the Brooklyn Museum."

"That's so *strange!*"

"I know. It's almost as if the mummy is some kind of bonus," Gardiner said, shaking his head in bafflement. "Moustaffa says he will divulge the location of Artemidorus when we pay the ransom for Delia."

"How bizarre!" Sinclair exclaimed.

"You have no idea," Gardiner continued. "Lady X says the ancient spirits are telling her to return it."

Sinclair laughed mirthlessly.

"Well, that pretty much convinces me that *both* of them are out of their minds."

Venice

CARTER WALLACE LOOKED around at the piles of stolen art in the warehouse on the Giudecca Canal and tried to calculate the total market value. Tens of millions, easily. The space was stacked with crates of different colors. Along the far wall there was a row of tables with stolen objects, all tagged and numbered like items at a garage sale.

"We found this warehouse a few days ago, thanks to your information," the policeman told Carter.

The officer was a very trim-looking fellow with lots of stripes and insignia on his formfitting jacket. How did Italian policemen manage to look so dapper? Carter glanced down at his own rumpled khakis. Some FBI agent *he* would make! He hastily tucked in his oxford shirt.

"The curators have gone through only a few of the crates," the policeman explained.

"Why is it taking so long?"

"We need the insurance companies to sort out what belongs to whom. If we don't do this legally, things will be tied up in court for decades."

Carter shook his head, looking around the warehouse. What a terrible environment for art! The building was on the edge of the industrial district, along the main canal. Like everything in Venice, water vapor permeated the building, the air, even the floor. These objects were at serious risk if they didn't move them out soon. He was glad Holly wouldn't witness this kind of destruction. It would upset her terribly.

Carter walked over to the tables. There were five Fayoum mummy portraits among the artifacts. The wooden panels had been laid out so that the ancient faces stared blankly back at him.

Carter unconsciously reached for his cell phone. He should tell Holly about this. Any excuse to hear her voice. But he had no illusions. She wasn't exactly thinking of *him* day and night.

On second thought, he'd wait until he recovered Artemidorus. Then she would *have* to give him his due. That mummy was her baby. Carter put his cell phone back into his pocket. He'd wait. Besides, unrequited love was so damn pathetic.

"Signor Wallace, could you come here please?" The policeman gestured with both his hands, as if it were very urgent.

Carter walked over to see what was the matter.

"We have found a Venice address on one of the pieces," the policeman said.

Carter looked at the packing slip. It was printed in English.

X. SOMMERSET 34 CALLE MINELLI VENICE.

"Where is this?" asked Carter.

"It is in the Dorsoduro district, off the Grand Canal. Not far from your hotel."

Carter recalled his airplane reading. According to guidebooks, the Dorsoduro district had for centuries been favored by foreigners and the upper crust of the city. Even now, many apartments were still owned by wealthy expat British and Americans.

"Well, *that*'s a start," Carter said. "Why don't we go there and ask a couple of questions?"

"No, we cannot do that without official permission."

"So let's get permission."

"Today is Friday. And Monday is a holiday. No one will be able to do that until Tuesday," the policeman said.

"*Tuesday!*" said Carter.

"*Sì*. On Tuesday we will ask."

"OK, if you say so," said Carter, looking at the paper and memorizing the address. He handed back the packing slip.

There was nothing to stop him from going to Calle Minelli by himself. Maybe the police wanted three days off, but *he* didn't.

He'd go and stake out the place himself. Nobody would notice. If he loitered with a guidebook, he'd look like every other tourist lounging around this city soaking up atmosphere. Finally, he was getting somewhere!

Holly Graham walked along the side of the canal. It was her first visit to Venice, and she had never seen such a beautiful city. Sinclair and Jim Gardiner had gone off to their briefings about the money drop, but she wasn't needed. So she'd decided to take a stroll, and was immediately entranced by her discoveries.

The small stone passageways between the canals were a charming labyrinth, with their twists and turns. She kept finding new bridges that arched over the canals. From time to time she would duck into one of the mysterious churches that smelled of candle wax and incense. She was thrilled with the beautiful architecture, lovely religious paintings, and stained-glass windows.

But it wasn't just the historic objects that took her breath away—the shops were absolutely sumptuous. Store after store was filled with beautifully handcrafted items— elegant gloves, leather goods, blown glass, exquisitely milled paper, and beautifully designed jewelry and gold. She coveted almost everything she saw.

It was good that the weather was holding up for all this walking around. She had heard that Venice could be hot and muggy in the summer. During *acqua alta*—the high-water time of year—tourists had to wear high rubber boots. But today was cool and the pavement was dry.

She wandered for hours, losing all track of time. Finally, her legs aching and her stomach growling, she looked at her watch. Nearly one o'clock! It was time to get back to the hotel and check in with Sinclair and Jim Gardiner. With a guilty jolt she remembered just what kind of pressure they were under, and here she was playing tourist.

The Hotel Danieli was on a main thoroughfare, right next to the famous St. Mark's Square. The hotel faced the sparkling expanse of the Venetian Lagoon. There was no place more visible or more luxurious to stay. They had chosen the hotel for that exact reason—the Danieli gave them credibility. Anyone with the means to enjoy this hotel would certainly be able to come up with the multimillion-dollar ransom.

Holly stepped inside the palatial lobby and let her eyes adjust to the dim interior. It was the epitome of Venetian elegance, with thirty-foot ceilings and marble columns.

The beautiful reception area had a soaring staircase that wound its way up to banquet rooms above. There were enormous bouquets of ivory roses in elaborate urns at the check-in desk. Comfortable tapestried chairs and low tables were placed throughout the lobby, where coffee and drinks were served.

Holly looked around for Sinclair and Jim Gardiner. Instead, she found Ted VerPlanck sitting near the door, as if waiting for someone. She had no idea he was in Venice! He hadn't been invited by the intelligence people to help with the ransom operation. She wondered if he had come of his own volition.

VerPlanck looked up when he saw her, and for the first time in days he smiled. Holly was relieved. Perhaps some of his depression was lifting.

"Sorry to startle you," he said. "When I heard you'd left, I just *had* to come along. I booked a suite here."

"Sorry, I didn't have time to call you," Holly apologized. "It was a last-minute thing. The kidnappers asked that I meet with them to get Artemidorus back."

"I heard." VerPlanck smiled. "MI6 wasn't all that happy I showed up."

"Why not?"

"It seems I am too high-profile. I've been told to stay out of sight."

"And you're sitting in the *lobby?*" Holly laughed.

"I was waiting for you. The concierge said you went out for a stroll. I was hoping to waylay you for lunch. Have you eaten yet?"

"No, I haven't. That would be lovely. But maybe I should check and see if anyone needs me."

"Already did," VerPlanck said. "The Brits want only Sinclair and Gardiner. I'm odd man out and, according to them, you're still free to do what you like."

"So you talked to the intelligence team?"

"Yes. I asked if they wanted my assistance, and they promptly told me no. Too many cooks, they said. So I just checked into the hotel to wait it out."

"Wait for what?"

"I am anxious about Cordelia, of course, and I also want to see if my Sardonyx Cup turns up. I hear they found a warehouse of stolen art."

"Well, no matter what the reason, I'm glad you came."

"So am I. I nearly forgot how beautiful Venice is."

"This is my first time. I *love* it already."

"I'd like to take you to one of my favorite restaurants," VerPlanck said. "The food is absolutely authentic."

Holly had assumed Ted would take her to a fussy, over-priced restaurant with crisp linen and bowing waiters. Instead, Dalla Marisa in Cannaregio was a tiny place, tucked into a marble-paved side street. When they walked in from the damp street, it was informal, crowded, warm, and the scent of delicious food was overpowering. Exactly the kind of restaurant Holly might have picked herself.

"Marisa sets the menu," Ted explained. "It's an *osteria,* which means the owner is the host. So there's not a lot of choice. But everything she serves is delicious."

They took their seats at one of the small tables lined up against the wall. The place was crammed with local people. A teenage boy came over and poured some mineral water into two glasses and set them before them.

"Would you like some wine?" Ted asked her.

"No, I better stick to this." She indicated the sparkling water. "Considering what's planned for this evening, I'd better not be drinking wine at lunch."

"You're absolutely right," Ted agreed automatically, but then his eyes narrowed with concern.

"What's planned?" he whispered.

She leaned over toward him, as if speaking intimately. In the din of the restaurant, no one could hear.

"I have to go with Sinclair for the drop-off. It's tonight at La Fenice Opera House, during the intermission."

"How does it work?"

"We give the kidnappers the money, and they're going to turn over Cordelia and tell me where to pick up Artemidorus."

"Holly!" VerPlanck said. "That sounds—"

"Dangerous?" She smiled. "Don't worry, half the audience in the theater will be . . . well, you know."

VerPlanck nodded as the waiter approached. He spoke rapid Italian to the young man and they concluded quickly. Within minutes plates of antipasti were placed on the table.

"What *is* all this?" Holly asked.

VerPlanck leaned over and pointed to each dish and explained.

"It's all seafood. Local. Mussels coated with bread crumbs, cheese, and herbs. *Baccalà*—salted cod—with red peppers. This is marinated fish, *branzino*. And baby octopus in tomato sauce."

"That sounds pretty exotic to me," she said.

"Save room," he advised, pouring her some mineral water. "There's a lot more to come."

That was followed by a creamy pasta dish flavored with Parmesan cheese. Then a main course—*fritto misto* with shrimp, baby squid, and sole.

The waiter then put down two plates of what appeared to be vanilla pudding.

"What's this?"

"Dessert," he said.

"I can't eat another thing!" she said with a groan.

"You have to have just a bite," he offered, holding his plate toward her.

She took a spoonful and put it in her mouth. It was the creamiest, most delicate flavor she had ever tasted.

"What on *earth* is that?"

"Whipped mascarpone flavored with brandy and rum."

"That's it! I'm giving up my apartment in New York. I need to eat here every day," she joked.

Ted laughed delightedly.

"Very few women these days have an appetite. It's refreshing."

"That's not my problem." Holly laughed. "I love food."

"Would you do that . . . live outside the United States?"

"Sure," Holly said. "I used to do a lot more traveling when I worked on expeditions. But now funding for field-work has dried up. So I spend a lot of time at the conservation lab. Basically a desk job."

"Where would you travel?" VerPlanck asked, pouring her another glass of San Pellegrino.

"Anywhere. No, let me amend that. Anywhere near water."

"Why water?"

"I think I told you, I grew up on the ocean. My dad

was a ferryboat captain on a little island called Cutty-hunk."

"Right. I remember. Buzzards Bay, Massachusetts. I sail there often," VerPlanck said. "And your mom was a landscape painter. I saw her work at your apartment."

"Sometimes when she was busy I would keep my father company on the boat. We'd always have New England clam chowder in a thermos, with oyster crackers. If the day was foggy, I'd help pilot the ferry. I love the sea."

"Given your background, Egyptology seems an unusual career."

Holly smiled. "Yes, I know."

"You're smiling. How'd that happen?"

Holly looked down and shook her head.

"I feel silly telling you all these things."

His eyes were on her face. For the first time ever, she could see he had momentarily forgotten his troubles and was actually enjoying the day. That pleased her.

"My mother used to go to a private island called Naushon to paint," she explained. "It's owned by the Forbes family. And there are several large mansions on the island. My mother was commissioned to paint the owner of the house. I used to go with her."

"That must have been an adventure."

"We'd go over in the morning by boat. The gentleman was very elderly, close to ninety-five years old. His family wanted a portrait of their patriarch. As my mother worked, he used to show me his books. His collection."

"Was he an amateur Egyptologist?" VerPlanck guessed.

"More than that. He *knew* Flinders Petrie. *And* Harold Carter, who found King Tut's tomb in 1922."

"Fascinating!" VerPlanck exclaimed.

"I read every book in the library, and when he died, he left me many of his notes and manuscripts."

"So from then on . . ." VerPlanck prompted.

"Well, in undergraduate school I dabbled in Greek and Roman history. That's how I ended up specializing in Roman-era Egyptian artifacts."

"You are a *very interesting* woman," VerPlanck gushed. "I could talk to you all day."

Holly took a sip of her cappuccino.

"You flatter me, Mr. VerPlanck," she said, her smile fleeting. "But I'm afraid we haven't got all day. I have to get ready for the opera."

The Khamsin, Venice Yacht Club

Lady X sat cross-legged on the bed in the master cabin of *The Khamsin*.

"Turn around," she commanded.

Cordelia pivoted in front of her, moving woodenly. She was wearing a low-cut yellow satin evening dress.

"I don't think so," Lady X said, scrutinizing her critically. "I don't think it's quite your color."

Cordelia said nothing.

Lady X walked over to the closet and selected a red evening gown.

"The opera in Venice is very dressy. I think this would look better on you."

Hotel Danieli, Venice

THE FIVE-STAR HOTEL was filled with British and American security people. On the third floor, the sign on a banquet room door read PRIVATE EVENT. Inside, a half-dozen MI6 agents were setting up listening devices for tonight's operation.

CIA officers were posing as hotel guests in the lobby, although a sharp observer would have noticed that their level of physical fitness was superior to that of a typical tourist.

The plan was for Sinclair and Holly to exchange four million dollars for Cordelia during the second intermission of *Aida*. Sinclair had spent the day learning the ins and outs of hostage negotiation and transfer.

Moustaffa had requested Holly come along also so he could give her the details about returning the stolen mummy. It was dangerous, but there had been no choice. British Intelligence had reassured Sinclair they would watch out for Holly's safety. Her presence had an added benefit—she would be good cover for Sinclair during the money drop. A man alone at the opera would generate attention, whereas a couple would not.

Holly had left the Hotel Danieli on the arm of John Sinclair. She had looked as regal as a queen, wearing high heels, a beautiful fuchsia silk dress, and a black opera cloak.

VerPlanck had been instructed by MI6, in no uncertain terms, to stay *out* of the lobby. He was forced to watch the departure from the private balcony of his suite.

Holly and Sinclair crossed the plaza in front of the hotel to the gondola dock. Holly took Sinclair's hand for balance as she stepped into the waiting boat. From the knowing way Sinclair reached out for her, Ted could surmise a history between the two of them. She had smiled as they settled together on the settee. Sinclair said something and she nodded. They clearly had a past. If VerPlanck had to venture a guess, he'd say Sinclair hadn't lost interest.

The gondolier began to maneuver the craft out into the lagoon, and VerPlanck watched the long, dark silhouette of the boat bob slowly down the Grand Canal, then glide into a side passageway. Even though VerPlanck could no longer see them, he stood on his balcony and looked out at the sky.

It was just starting to turn to dusk, the air was getting cooler, and the typical evening mist was descending over the canals. The beautiful dreamy fog made Venice a romantic place for lovers and poets . . . and himself.

Holly was constantly in his thoughts. And that shocked him. How could he even *consider* another woman? It was indecent! After all, Tipper had been dead less than a week. The cremation had been yesterday, and a memorial service was scheduled for when he returned to New York.

But Ted found it hard to think about Tipper. He was angry, sad, and rather perplexed. After the years he stood by her, how could she have turned against him? He was grieving, of course, but truth be told, he couldn't forgive her. The shock of what she had done hurt him to the quick.

He turned and again looked in the direction of the Grand Canal. La Fenice Opera House was a short distance away. The moment lost its overtones of sad reminiscence and took on a stark reality. Moustaffa and his henchmen had murdered his wife, and now Holly was all dressed up and on her way to meet the killer.

A very dangerous operation had begun!

La Fenice Opera House, Venice

SINCLAIR GLANCED OVER and saw that Holly's face was frozen with apprehension. In all the years he had known her, she had never been this nervous. Rather the opposite—she had always been the quintessential cool blonde. But tonight she was trembling as she negotiated the stone steps of the opera house in her high heels. He gave her arm a squeeze and got a tight smile in return.

Of course, she *looked* fantastic. A dramatic opera cloak in black velvet, a bright fuchsia silk dress underneath. Her sandals were delicate, flimsy things. For some reason, the sight of her bare feet in the strappy shoes made Sinclair anxious. She looked so *vulnerable.*

He wished MI6 hadn't insisted on Holly coming with him. Supposedly, Moustaffa wanted to return the mummy. But Sinclair wasn't buying it. Something was wrong. But he had no choice. Moustaffa called the shots, and the deal for Cordelia *had* to go through.

They had taken precautions. Holly had been fitted with a tracking device in her left earring. Her right earring had a button that could be turned to activate a distress signal. A small natural gesture on her part—fiddling with her earring—would bring intelligence officers to her aid immediately.

The security people had warned Sinclair that anything could happen, even gunfire. He wasn't armed. Never liked weapons. And he certainly wasn't trained to use them. Sinclair figured this kind of operation usually called for a bulletproof vest. But that wasn't possible when wearing a formal suit. So he dressed normally and prepared himself for the worst.

But there *was* backup. Agents were scattered throughout the audience of the theater. He and Holly stood on the top step to make sure that anyone who needed to see them would get a good look. Sinclair carried the blue plastic bag from Libreria Toletta bookshop in Dorsoduro. Inside was an art volume on Renaissance architecture, with an expensive bookmark—a bearer bond for four million dollars. That was the preferred method of payment, it seemed, for those who collected filthy lucre.

Holly slipped off her cloak and folded it over her arm so the bright pink dress would be visible to everyone. She took a cigarette out of her evening clutch and held it to her lips. Sinclair lit it for her and then pocketed the lighter. The gesture telegraphed to the agents that they were "good to go."

Back in the hotel, when it came to deciding who would be the one to light up, Sinclair had asked Holly to do it. His notoriously bad lungs were already constricted from stress. Smoking would only make it worse, and he couldn't risk another panic-induced incident. So Holly stood next to him and smoked as they waited for the signal.

Once all the agents were in place, he and Holly could proceed inside. Six backup agents were supposed to be stationed in the plaza. Sinclair noted the Italian man sitting in the café across the street. A middle-aged gentleman was walking his dog, puffing on a cigar. A scruffy college student with a backpack sat on the steps. He wasn't sure, but any of them could be MI6 operatives.

Sinclair could hear water lapping nearby in the canal, but the heavy fog muffled all other sound. They waited on the steps until other theatergoers started to arrive, laughing and chatting about the evening's performance.

Sinclair could just make out the primary agent, whom he had met earlier in the day. He was smoking a cigarette, leaning on the stone parapet of a bridge. That man would shadow them all night, staying close by during the performance. As if on cue, the man dropped the smoldering butt into the canal, looked over at Sinclair, then walked up the steps past them into the opera house. That was the signal.

"Shall we?" he suggested to Holly. She threw the cigarette away and gave him a tense little nod. As an afterthought, she remembered to smile.

"Don't worry, Hols," he said to her in a low voice. "It's going to be fine."

He took her hand to give her courage and noticed her fingers were ice-cold.

Ristorante al Teatro, Venice

CARTER WALLACE KEPT his eyes glued to the couple standing on the top step of the opera house. From where he was in the outdoor café, the woman was clearly visible. Even from here she looked fabulous!

Funny how he hadn't noticed her when she walked by earlier. His eye had been drawn to Sinclair. He kept thinking, "Hey, I know that guy from somewhere." Then the vision of Sinclair dancing with Holly at the Temple of Dendur came back to him. After he realized it really *was* Sinclair, he looked back at the woman to check her out. Pretty blonde. It figured—Sinclair seemed to favor the type. But he hadn't recognized her—her back was turned to him, her face hidden.

Carter kept staring at her. The pretty satin sandals clacked on the stone of the opera steps as she climbed up. Something resonated when she moved. It was the way she lifted her hand to check her hair. He realized it was *Holly*! He lurched out of his chair, about to call out. Then he shrank back.

What could he say? His brain was forming a hundred questions: *Holly and Sinclair together in Venice? What on earth were they doing here?*

Of course, he didn't have the right to ask questions. She owed him nothing and could date whomever she chose. So he sat in the damp café feeling cheated and wondering all kinds of crazy things.

Holly and Sinclair stood on the top step, apparently getting some air before the opera performance. Her pink dress was vibrant. You could see her a mile away. A beautiful figure glowing against the dreary night.

The color irritated him. Why was she done up like a fashion model? And she was *smoking*! Now, *that* really galled him. She had given him such a hard time in New York when *he* had a cigarette! He still remembered the disapproving look on her face. What a little hypocrite!

His mind tried to make sense of what he was seeing. Was she seriously involved with Sinclair? For how long? Was it a chance encounter when they met at the gala in New York, or had they planned the meeting all along?

Carter needed to get the full story. But his brain kept focusing on all the irrelevant details: her dress, her smoking.

Finally, he had to face the truth. It was obvious. *Holly and Sinclair were involved in the art-theft ring!*

Once the suspicion formed, the shock of it was intense. Why the hell else would they be in Venice? This was where the stolen art was being shipped. And most of the objects were Egyptian, Holly's specialty. She would know what to steal and where to sell everything for the best profit. *She was a thief!* Nothing else made any sense.

Carter looked back at the theater steps, and she was gone. Latecomers were rushing into the opera house. He had missed the opportunity to confront her.

Well, that was probably for the best. What would he say? Should he call the authorities? Did he have the guts?

He drained his café espresso to the dregs. The unmelted sugar on the bottom of the cup dripped onto his tongue. He placed the cup in the saucer and thought about it some more. It wouldn't be fair to blow the whistle on Holly. Not yet. He had to be sure before he accused her of anything. And there was only one way to find out the truth.

Carter threw a ten-euro note on the café table and got up, his chair scraping the pavement. A man walking by gave him a hard stare. Carter ignored him. He was going to go to the palazzo in the Dorsoduro district—Calle Minelli, the address that was listed on the packing slip. If Holly showed up there, he would know the truth.

La Fenice Opera House

THE CROWD WAS milling around the pink marble entrance hall with excitement. Crystal chandeliers glowed, programs were handed out, and everyone was beautifully dressed in their evening clothes. Couples were greeting one another with air kisses and exclamations of delight. There were very few tourists in the off-season and everyone was speaking Italian.

Sinclair found himself thinking that under other circumstances this performance would have been great fun. He loved opera. But tonight the cacophony of social interaction was getting on his nerves.

He and Holly should probably loiter in the lobby until they saw Lady X. But time was dragging and she wasn't there yet.

He steered Holly over to read the huge poster—*Aida*, by Giuseppe Verdi. Leave it to Lady Xandra Sommerset for the dramatic gesture—an opera with a storyline that involved ancient Egypt. *Aida* originally opened in Cairo in 1871, to great acclaim. But it was right here, at La Fenice, that it made an *official* debut a few years later—and became an international hit.

He looked over at Holly. She was staring blankly at the performance announcement, her eyes fixed. To most people, she would appear calm, but he knew better.

"Let's get rid of our coats, shall we?" he asked.

They joined a line of people. Sinclair handed his top-coat and Holly's cape to the coat check woman; then, with great trepidation, he passed over the blue plastic shopping bag containing the book and the ransom money.

"Would you please put this bag on a separate claim ticket?" he asked.

The coat attendant took the bag from him and put it in the rack above. His eyes involuntarily followed the plastic bag. It was a four-million-dollar package. She handed him the red plastic disk. Number 27.

It went into his right-hand pocket. The plan was simple. All he had to do was slip the claim ticket to Lady X. At the end of the first act, Lady X would collect the book from the coat check and leave the building. At a nearby location, she and Moustaffa would make sure that the money was the agreed-upon amount and in the proper form.

Then, during the second intermission, Moustaffa would bring Cordelia to the opera house. He would rendezvous with Sinclair and Holly in the upstairs supper salon. If all went well, Cordelia would be released.

Sinclair took Holly's hand and noticed that her fingers were warmer. He bent over and whispered in her ear.

"Wish me luck."

Her blue eyes looked up into his. They were frightened.

"Good luck, John," she said. She couldn't even manage a smile.

"Come on, Hols, we can't stand here all night. Let's go face the music."

He gave her a wink and drew her up the red-carpeted

steps to the main floor of the theater. The seats were beginning to fill up. He looked down at the tickets in his
hand. Orchestra level, as Lady X had instructed. Programs
in hand, he looked around at the famous opera hall.

La Fenice was a legend. Its name translated as "The
Phoenix"—a mythical bird that rose up from the ashes.
Twice in the theater's long, glorious history, the building
had burned to the ground. Each time, it had been rebuilt
to the original design, most recently in 2003. Standing
here tonight, he observed that the opera house was as
splendid as ever.

Tier after tier of boxes rose all the way to the ceiling—
gold and pastel rococo ornamentation on the walls and
rose velvet chairs. It was a noble setting in every sense.
One could imagine aristocratic Venetian ladies, dressed in
silks and satins, gossiping behind their lace fans.

Sinclair took his eyes off the architecture and scanned
the sea of empty orchestra seats.

"No sign of her."

"She'll come," Holly replied. "I know she will."

Hotel Danieli

A HALF-MOON HAD risen above the lagoon, creating a shimmering magic. The fog had dissipated along the quay. Gondolas, secured for the night, were bowing and dipping in the dark water.

No one in the third-floor banquet room was looking out the window. Inside, three MI6 officers were hunkered over a video monitor. They were able to see the interior of the opera house through a pin camera in their agent's lapel. As he walked around, they could see who was entering the theater. Sinclair and Holly were visible on the left-hand side of the screen.

"I see them, but where's Cordelia?" Jim Gardiner asked, crowding in behind the intelligence agents. "Shouldn't she be there by now?"

"No, sir," an agent replied politely. "Ms. Stapleton is supposed to arrive after the second act, during intermission. So I'd say you have about an hour and twenty minutes to wait."

Gardiner started to walk up and down the room nervously. He was well aware that pacing drew attention to his limp, but he needed to keep his nerves in check. From time to time, he glanced over at VerPlanck and gave him a forced smile.

The American tycoon sat on the far side of the room, hands on his knees, looking wan and nervous. Finally,

Gardiner went over to him and sat down on a cut-velvet settee.

"This is killing me," Gardiner groused. "I wish they'd get on with it."

His irritated tone hid the emotion that was churning inside. He often used gruffness to counter his tender heart. As a business lawyer, it wouldn't do to let people know he was the biggest softie in the world. Especially VerPlanck, who was a client.

"You and Cordelia are very close, aren't you?" VerPlanck asked.

"Yes." Gardiner nodded. "I was the family estate lawyer."

"Orphaned, was she?"

"Yes, that poor kid lost both parents when she was twelve. She had nothing but a bank account. And even *that* wasn't really very much."

"So you were her guardian?" VerPlanck ascertained.

"Oh, more than that," Gardiner said with a sigh. "Cordelia and I, well, we've been through thick and thin together."

"I'm sure you made quite a difference in her life."

"I would have adopted her, if they had allowed it. But laws were different back then. Same-sex couples were not even allowed to think about it."

"Pity," VerPlanck said.

"Nah." Gardiner shook his head. "Didn't matter. I loved her. What do I care what they call it on paper."

"She's a lucky girl," VerPlanck said. "To have someone like you."

"Well, now she's a lucky girl to have found someone

like *Sinclair*," Gardiner amended. "That man would lay down his *life* for her."

"Then she is twice blessed," VerPlanck said, and continued to stare at the monitor. A bright pink dress glowed on the screen. Holly was walking through the lobby and into the theater.

La Fenice Opera House

SINCLAIR STOOD IN the aisle, next to row number E, seat 1. The seats were filling up, people stepping around him, as he lingered.

"John?" Holly asked, her blue eyes questioning. "What next?"

"We may as well sit down," he decided. "If you don't mind, I'll take the outside seat."

They settled in and started looking through the program. It was a pointless exercise. The words on the page were not registering in his brain, and all his senses were hyper-aware, waiting for something to happen. He could tell that Holly was strung as taut as a violin string. *Where was Lady X?*

Four people approached his row. They had seats in the middle. He stepped out to let the couples by, glancing at each of the women as they brushed past him. Neither of them even remotely resembled Lady X.

The theater was almost full. Five minutes until the curtain. His nerves were so raw that sitting still was an effort. He fought with himself not to check his watch again.

Then he heard a commotion from behind. Cries of *"Xandra darling!"* rang out. He turned quickly to look. Lady X had just arrived and was greeting her friends in Italian at the back of the theater.

Of course! How could he be so dim? She was an

international celebrity; there would be no low-key arrival for *her*. Dressed in a silver fox cape over a jade green dress, she was flamboyantly elegant. Absolutely *stealing* the show. People in the parterre boxes were pointing at her and observing her through their opera glasses.

Her progress was slow as she made her way down the aisle to the front section. Sinclair turned his eyes back to his program, but he could hear her coming up behind him. Then she stopped right next to his seat. He continued to read, wondering what was required next. Surely *she* would be the one to make the overture to him.

As he kept his eyes lowered, he could smell her heavy perfume, and out of the corner of his eye he saw her pointed black stilettos in the aisle right next to him. So he casually looked up, as if just noticing her standing there. She was staring straight at him.

"Oh, is this my row?" she asked. "I'm not sure . . . If it is, I believe you are in my seat."

"I'm . . . excuse me," Sinclair said, getting to his feet and going along with the charade. He pulled his stub out of his pocket and showed it to her.

She made a scene over searching for her ticket. Lady X wore snug gray leather gloves to her elbow, which made her fingers clumsy as she searched through the contents of her minuscule evening bag. An usher rushed over to intervene.

"Madame, may I assist?"

"Here it is. I'm afraid I forgot my reading glasses. Is this my row?" she said, handing her ticket to the usher

"Madame, you are in row F, seat 1," the man explained, pointing to the seat directly behind Sinclair.

"Oh, how *silly* of me," Lady X apologized. "I couldn't read it properly. I don't ever seem to be able to remember my glasses. . . ."

"Perfectly all right," Sinclair said. He was trying to figure out what was required of him. He needed to slip the plastic coat check disk to her. But he couldn't just hand it to her, could he?

He needn't have worried about the mechanics. Lady X was well ahead of him. She put the opera ticket stub into her satin bag and let the tiny purse slip out of her hands. It hit the floor and spilled the contents into the aisle.

"Oh, dear . . . how *clumsy* of me," she said, smiling at Sinclair. He looked down. A lipstick, lace handkerchief, pocket mirror, and small leather billfold were scattered on the red carpet. She didn't move to pick any of it up. He understood immediately.

"Allow me," he said, bending down and gathering up her articles and restoring her bag to her with a slight bow. Now inside her satin clutch was disk 27 from the coat check.

They both took their seats, Lady X sitting directly behind him. He didn't turn around again but stared straight ahead.

Was that all there was to it? His heart was beating so hard he could almost hear it. He kept his eyes on the red velvet curtain.

"Did she get it?" Holly asked under her breath.

He gave her a silent nod as the lights dimmed and the orchestra struck up the familiar overture.

An hour later, Sinclair was still worrying and the opera was dragging on. He had barely registered a note. After the first act, Lady X had left. Now, during the second act, her seat had remained empty. All was going as planned. Lady X had presumably picked up the book with the ransom and was long gone.

During the next intermission, Moustaffa was supposed to meet them and return Cordelia. Intermissions for opera and ballet in Europe were slightly longer than in the States, much more of a social event. There was enough time for people to eat small plates of food and drink champagne between acts. La Fenice had several elaborate supper rooms on the upper floor.

Act 2 was almost over. Onstage, a stream of elaborately costumed people were parading through the Great Gate of Thebes in the Triumphal March. The famous melody was lovely—so much so, Sinclair often found himself humming it in the shower when he was in a particularly good mood. Now he barely heard a note. Finally, the velvet curtain dropped. The lights came up and the conversation started to buzz.

He couldn't help but turn around. The seat where Lady X had been sitting was empty.

The pink marble supper rooms of La Fenice were packed. There were four separate large salons, with tall cocktail tables scattered throughout, where people could eat standing up. When Sinclair and Holly got to the second floor, customers were lined up ten deep at the service counter to buy the small sandwiches and pastries, champagne and espresso.

"Would you like something to drink?" Sinclair asked Holly.

"No. Let's just circulate."

They began a slow amble through the rooms, trying to make themselves visible. The noise was deafening as people chatted and laughed. It was almost impossible to see anyone who wasn't immediately in front of you.

The instructions from Moustaffa were to come here and wait. Cordelia would be returned. But now that Sinclair saw the layout, he didn't know *which* of the rooms they were supposed to stand in. He and Holly walked through once and then returned to pass through again.

"I don't see her," she said. "Did they tell you what Cordelia would be wearing?"

"No," Sinclair said.

His answer was brusque, but unintentionally so. Pressure was building. Security agents had briefed him extensively on the exact moment of exchange. They had drilled him on proper technique. Countless lives had been lost when a hostage exchange was botched. Above all, they said, be firm and businesslike. No heroics. There would be law-enforcement people nearby, but it was up to Sinclair to make sure Cordelia was returned in a calm and orderly manner.

Suddenly, he got a quick glimpse of a slim woman on the other side of the archway in the next salon. Holly saw her at the same time and silently touched his arm to alert him.

The woman's build was the same as Cordelia's. She was wearing red. She turned toward him. His heart stopped. *It was Cordelia!*

Their eyes connected. He could detect no sign of relief in her face; it was a mask of terror. Then she started walking toward him slowly, as if in a dream.

Something was wrong! She was moving woodenly, with no expression. A dark, powerfully built man was walking with her. It appeared she was being propelled along through the crowd. As they drew nearer, Sinclair could see the captor's arm encircling her waist with a grip of control.

A chill went down Sinclair's spine. The man was Moustaffa! Older than the pictures. More dangerous-looking. Intelligent and cunning eyes.

Sinclair took a moment to assess him. The man's Italian clothes were elegant, but his features had been coarsened by drugs and alcohol.

Sinclair was shocked to see the expression on his face was one of elation, amusement. There was an awful realization that, to Moustaffa, this was all a game—a power contest. Human life meant nothing.

When they met in the middle of the room, the four of them stood in a small closed circle—tense, hostile, but pretending to be socially engaged. A conversation between acts of an opera. To the outside world, everything would have looked friendly. It was anything but.

Cordelia's eyes locked onto Sinclair's and stayed there. She was silently pleading for help.

"Delia," he asked quietly. "Are you all right?"

"Yes," she said.

The halting way she spoke told him everything. She was terrified. *What had they done?*

"Would you please get your hands off her," he said with superhuman restraint.

He was starting to sweat. The roaring in his ears was his blood pressure climbing. He forced himself to stay calm, but it took every ounce of willpower.

"Don't worry. You can have her back," Moustaffa said, not moving. "This is an exchange."

"We have complied with the terms perfectly," Sinclair countered. "You have your money. Now let her go."

"We just raised the price a little."

Moustaffa smiled nastily; his teeth were artificially bonded and white against his dark tan. At his jawline there were a few pockmarks from adolescent acne.

Sinclair's eyes were drawn to something in his hand. The object glinted in the light as Moustaffa turned it in his fingers. *It was a hypodermic needle, held loosely against the fabric of Cordelia's dress!*

"Your pretty friend might begin to feel very unwell by the end of the evening if you don't listen carefully."

Sinclair was frozen by the sight of the needle. The tip was centimeters from Delia's body. A mere slip would be all it would take. His lungs constricted in fear.

"What do you want?" he asked quietly.

"You can have her, but only in exchange for Dr. Graham," Moustaffa said.

Holly, standing right next to him, inhaled sharply. Although she didn't move, her fear was palpable. Holly had been told to let Sinclair lead the discussion and was clearly waiting for him to respond.

"Out of the question!"

"Well, then, Ms. Stapleton is going to die. I'm afraid there is no antidote to this virus."

"No!"

This was monstrous! He couldn't decide between Cordelia and Holly!

"It takes about twenty-four hours," Moustaffa was

explaining. "Plenty of time for you to say good-bye. But it won't be a pleasant parting."

Sinclair couldn't take his eyes off the uncapped needle, inches from Cordelia's side. A quick jab and it would be over. He considered using brute force, simply trying to overpower Moustaffa. But the man looked capable of fending him off long enough to do his dirty work. The needle was much too close to risk anything at all. The moment lengthened as Sinclair struggled for an option.

In his peripheral vision Sinclair could see that an agent was hovering behind their group. The man looked over for an indication of what was happening. Sinclair shook his head. *Stay back*, he telegraphed with his eyes. The agent nodded and stepped to the side, pretending to read a program.

"Make your choice, Mr. Sinclair. You have ten seconds," Moustaffa repeated. "And your security people over there will not do you any good. Once she's infected, it's over."

"*Wait! Just wait!*" Sinclair demanded. "What on earth do you need Holly for?"

"Am I to take that as your answer?" Moustaffa said, putting his index finger on the plunger of the syringe.

"It's *inhuman*!" Sinclair exclaimed. "To make me decide . . . I can't . . ."

Sinclair felt Holly brush by him and stand directly in front of Moustaffa. She looked the killer in the eye.

"There is no need to ask Mr. Sinclair for permission for me to accompany you," she said coolly. "I can speak for myself. I accept your proposition. *Now, please release Miss Stapleton!*"

Venice

CARTER LURKED IN the alcove of a church in Calle del Cristo, a small stone alleyway in the quiet part of the city. He was hidden in shadow, squatting down with his back against the damp stone wall. It was a good place to hide. No one would discover him there, and the view was perfect. The old palazzo was across the canal, clearly visible. The windows were dark, framed by red velvet. It appeared no one was home.

He settled on his haunches. The evening had turned cool, bordering on cold, but he wasn't uncomfortable so far. He stayed immobile, shifting when necessary to keep his legs from cramping. There was only the sound of lapping water and the acrid scent of pigeon droppings.

He didn't mind being here for a while; there was a lot to think about. Foremost, the idea that Holly was involved in the art-theft ring! Holly had certainly fallen off her pedestal if she was involved in this!

Carter crouched in the alcove nursing his disappointment for what seemed like hours. Just as he was beginning to think his vigil was futile, there was the distant purr of an engine. A gleaming wooden motorboat emerged from the broader canal. The pilot pulled the craft up to the stone landing and cut the motor. It bobbed silently as the passengers stood up.

In the gloom, Carter saw two people and a driver. A

man and a woman balanced on the rocking boat as they prepared to make the leap to the stone landing. The man went first. Carter caught a glimpse of him, dark-haired, powerfully built. He held his hand out for the woman.

She was wearing a dark cape, the hood up, her face not visible. She refused his help and managed to descend expertly, her high heels clattering onto the stone as she recovered her footing. They ascended the steps of the water landing and went through the heavy iron gate of the palazzo. The boat idled in the canal, sending a drift of gasoline fumes in his direction.

On impulse, Carter advanced out of his hiding place with no plan other than to get closer. He started toward the nearest bridge to cross over to the house.

Suddenly, someone hit him with a swift punch to the lung! The blow took him totally by surprise, and hurt a *lot*! His arms were grabbed from behind and twisted until he thought his shoulders would dislocate out of their sockets. Then he was wrestled to the ground. The knee in his back nearly broke his spine. A hand grabbed his hair and pressed his cheek to the ground. As he opened his mouth to gasp in pain, he could smell pigeon droppings on the flagstones.

"Who are you?" he asked. The man's accent was British.

"American, Brooklyn Museum," he wheezed.

"Get up," another man said, toeing him in the ribs with his boot. "And keep quiet."

"Hey, what's the idea?" Carter whispered as he scrambled up.

"We're British Security, watching the house," the man said. "What's your story?"

"I'm a curator from the Brooklyn Museum, hired by

the FBI to recover the art," Carter gasped. "I was waiting for Dr. Hollis Graham."

Just then the rev of a motor caught their attention. The wooden speedboat pulled away from the water landing and turned into the canal. The fan of the wake grew wider as the boat moved away. In the back were the same two figures, the man and the woman.

His heart sank with disappointment. They were getting away! He strained to get a better look at the woman. As the boat picked up speed, her dark cape wafted open and the hood blew back. Carter caught sight of blond hair and the bright pink dress.

"*That's Holly!*" he cried out.

"Are you sure?" they asked.

"Of *course* I'm sure. We've worked together every day for five years. It's her."

"We'll radio ahead and let the others know," the agents assured him. "They'll intercept them out in the lagoon."

"I can't *believe* you beat me up and let *them* get away!"

"Don't worry," one of them replied. "We have people following the boat."

"*Hey!*" the other agent called out from the bridge. "There's something on the boat landing. I'll go get it."

Carter walked over to take a look. The agent negotiated his way down the moss-covered steps. He picked up the blue plastic bag from the stone and carried it back up, dripping.

"That's the bag Sinclair was carrying when they went to the opera!" Carter burst out.

"You don't miss much, do you?" the agent said. Together the two men opened the bag and pulled out an art book.

"Is it still there?" one agent said.

One of them shook the volume upside down. Nothing fell out. He paged through, just to be sure.

"They took it," he declared.

"What are you looking for?" Carter asked.

"The money," the second agent said, flipping through the book quickly.

"What's this?" Carter asked, pointing to an inscription on the flyleaf, written in black felt-tip pen.

"I don't know."

"Did you put it there?" Carter asked.

"No, it was a brand-new book," the agent replied.

They all looked at the inscription. The ink was starting to run on the wet page.

"Holly wrote it!" Carter exclaimed. "It's a message in ancient hieroglyphics."

"And I suppose you can read it," the agent said with a smirk.

"Actually, I can."

They fell silent as Carter examined the book closely, holding it toward the streetlight.

"So what does it say?" the agent asked, his tone considerably chastened.

"Sinai. These are the symbols for the Sinai Peninsula in Egypt."

Hotel Danieli

JOHN SINCLAIR'S SUITE at the Hotel Danieli was the perfection of Venetian splendor—a large wood-carved canopied bed draped with burgundy velvet, and across the room mullioned-glass doors, slightly open to the balcony, with a view of the shimmering lagoon beyond.

Cordelia lay on the bed dazed. None of it had any impact on her. She was still living the nightmare of a hypodermic pressed to her body. She could see the gleaming needle against the fabric of her dress. Death had been so close, merely a half inch away.

"Delia, *please*! Don't think about it anymore," Sinclair pleaded. "You're safe now."

She turned to Sinclair and wound her arms around him, trying to focus on what was real. His body was warm and strong. She ran her hands over his face and chest, pressing her palms to his heart. She could feel it beating. He was here. The horror was over.

"I *knew* you would find me," Cordelia said.

"I would never give up, you must know that."

"Hold me, I'm cold," she said, pressing into him. He threw a leg over hers and pulled her even tighter. They fit together perfectly, breathing in and out in tandem.

"Delia, tell me what happened. I want to know."

"He's a *monster*," she whispered. "John, you have no idea. He's *really* evil."

The horror of Moustaffa's kiss filled her mind. She involuntarily shuddered in revulsion. Sinclair felt it and sat up, taking her face between his two hands. He searched her eyes.

"Did he hurt you . . . in any way?" Sinclair asked, white-lipped with anger. "*Tell* me."

"No, John. He tried . . ." Cordelia started and tears formed in her eyes. She ducked her head and brushed them away.

"*Delia, don't cry!* I'll kill the son of a—"

"I'm sorry . . . it's just the stress . . . the relief of being safe now. I'm fine. Really."

Sinclair sat up and let out a stream of vehement curses in what sounded like Turkish. There was no need for translation.

"He didn't *do* anything, John," she assured him. "He threatened to, but he had Lady X on board the whole time. She walks around practically naked. That must have been enough."

Sinclair was quiet, gazing toward the doors of the terrace, the moonlight illuminating his expression.

"John, what is it?"

"I'm wondering about Holly. Now *she's* on that boat."

Sharm el-Sheikh, Egypt

WHEN MOUSTAFFA WALKED into the Four Seasons Hotel, it was delightfully cool. A fountain burbled in the center of the lobby. The tiled floor, whitewashed walls, and rattan furniture created an atmosphere of luxurious informality.

He strode over to the front desk, flung down his bag, and played the part of a spoiled tourist, arrogantly demanding his room be upgraded. Then he booked a masseuse, a private car, a personal dive guide, and reservations for every evening. The hotel staff was in a full-blown tizzy by the time he finished with them.

He strolled out to the terrace restaurant, with its gorgeous vista of the Red Sea. A handful of guests were enjoying lunch, admiring the view. A canopy protected them from the scorching sun, and potted palms surrounded each table. There was a slight breeze and the palm fronds stirred, making a clacking-rustling sound.

Moustaffa sat down and ordered a freshly squeezed orange juice and a salad with grilled shrimp. He hoped to stay here for the next week, posing as a wealthy scuba enthusiast with a full dive schedule every day at the RAS Mohammed National Marine Park. It would be an amusing pastime, and would also serve as a good diversion until Lady Xandra Sommerset arrived.

Xandra was making the voyage by sea. He'd left her

with the understanding that she'd join him here in Sharm el-Sheikh the day before the attack. He could not understand why the woman was obsessed with bringing the cartouche of Artemidorus back to Egypt, and it was irritating that she had been sidetracked from the original plan.

But then, that was Xandra. She had her enthusiasms, some of them wacky. But her bank account was partially funding Moustaffa's operation, and her boat was the perfect cover, so he indulged her.

The logistics of moving the coffin were a nightmare. Their only option was to smuggle it into the country on her private yacht. The stolen mummy was too large to conceal. And the smell was now so overpowering that it had been an absolute necessity for Moustaffa to disembark *The Khamsin*. Xandra seemed able to bear the stench, and the crew was paid handsomely to ignore it.

Dr. Holly Graham remained on board, helping to keep the remains from deteriorating further. The Egyptologist would have to be dealt with later. But Moustaffa didn't have time for that kind of detail right now. There were other things to attend to.

The plan was going well. Computer disks with the data for re-creating the plague had been delivered to the lab in Cairo. His men were formulating the biological agent right now, and there were eight days until the start of the international economic conference.

That was plenty of time to get the canisters primed and ready. Installing them would be done the day of the attack. And then his vision would be fulfilled. He would single-handedly destroy the industrial powers of the world.

The Khamsin Motoryacht

HOLLY GRAHAM STARED at the crimson sarcophagus in disgust as Lady X hovered behind her. What had this woman done? It was *abominable*! The British Museum would be devastated to see what had happened to its precious mummy.

Holly put her head in her hands. A wave of nausea passed over her. Of course it was because she was so upset. First the abduction. Now with the stench coming off the coffin and the movement of *The Khamsin*. Her stomach was feeling very unstable. She sat on the couch, staring at the carpet, trying to get hold of herself.

"What do you think?" the British aristocrat asked, standing in front of her. Lady X looked very anxious and unsure of herself.

"You have single-handedly destroyed one of the most valuable artifacts in the entire world!" Holly snapped.

"Can you help me preserve it until we get to Egypt?"

"Why Egypt? I don't understand," Holly exclaimed.

"I want to bring Artemidorus back to his homeland. Surely you can understand that."

"But this is a *horrible* way to do it. By letting the mummy decompose!"

"I didn't mean to. You have to help me," Xandra pleaded. "Let me explain."

She abruptly sat down in a chair across from Holly,

leaned forward, and put her elbows on her knees in an attitude of friendly confidentiality. Holly couldn't help noticing at once how beautiful Xandra was—her long, silken hair, the long, flowing caftan. Her eyes were amazing—topaz in color, tilted up at the corners like a lion's. How could this elegant woman have perpetrated such a horror?

"Dr. Graham, taking Artemidorus was not my choice. It was *his*. I remember standing at the British Museum looking into his eyes on that portrait panel, and he *spoke* to me! I heard his voice clearly. He called me his 'Queen.'"

"You can't be serious."

"No, I assure you. He said we should sail *The Khamsin* to his kingdom, where he would make me his queen. We are going back to Egypt *together*."

Holly stared at the woman. It was clear that Xandra was mentally disturbed. But who would know? The British aristocrat was so polished, her symptoms of insanity were masked by her sophisticated social skills.

"So if it was *his* idea to do this," Holly asked sarcastically, "what's he saying now?"

"I'm afraid I killed him. He has stopped speaking to me."

Holly looked at her in bafflement. This mummy had been dead for two thousand years, and Xandra thought she had killed him.

"I had no idea he would deteriorate this fast!" Lady X was saying. "But I had to do it. He told me to!"

Holly couldn't help making one more bitter retort.

"Well, that makes *two* corrupt men who are telling you to carry out their personal agendas—Artemidorus *and* Moustaffa."

"No, please. Don't blame Moustaffa. This was my decision."

"I'll help you with this because Artemidorus was *my* responsibility. No other reason. It's going to require some supplies."

Lady X opened her mouth to give a gushing response and then stopped herself. Her manner turned cold again.

"Thank you, Dr. Graham. I'll get you anything you require."

Sharm el-Sheikh

CARTER WALLACE WAS on the forward deck of Ted Ver-
Planck's gorgeous sailing yacht, the 125-foot *Moon-
Sonnet*. Even at this early hour he could tell the day was
going to be hot. The boat was anchored off the coast of the
Sinai Peninsula. If he squinted his eyes and looked across
the shimmering water, he could make out a strip of land—
Sharm el-Sheikh.

The famous resort—sometimes referred to as the
Riviera of the Red Sea—was less than an hour's plane ride
away from Cairo. Beaches lined with luxurious hotels ca-
tered to a clientele from the Middle East as well as Europe.

Carter shifted on the cushioned seat of the yacht and
looked at the sliver of land. It was irrational, but he felt
that if he kept it in sight nothing bad would happen to
Holly.

A lot had happened in the last few days. After that
fateful night at the opera, Holly had been spirited out of
Venice aboard Lady X's yacht. *The Khamsin* had motored
away like a ghost into the fog. But as it left the Venetian
Lagoon British Intelligence had quietly trailed it.

MI6 chief of operation thought the best thing to do
was to track Moustaffa by sea. The British agency had
rented a racy-looking fifty-meter Benetti and installed
some paid actors to pose as the owners of the vessel.
Carter was agog. Leave it to the Brits! The CIA could never

get away with chartering a yacht! They'd be up on Capitol Hill within a week, explaining their extravagance to the American taxpayers.

Carter's biggest surprise had been when MI6 had asked him to come along. Clearly, the trick of reading hieroglyphics had impressed them, along with his newly issued FBI credentials.

The spy ship was a marvel. Belowdecks there were nine Royal Navy antiterrorist specialists, and the hold was equipped with more listening capacity than a cave full of bats. They stealthily trailed *The Khamsin* through the Adriatic and the Mediterranean. From time to time, their surveillance equipment had picked up Holly's voice, especially if she were near the windows of the salon.

For the first few days, Carter would hover over the audio specialist, begging him for a chance to listen in. After a while, whenever he showed up the technician would simply hand over the earphones.

Just listening to Holly made him sleep better at night. There was no apparent danger. She seemed to be speaking in normal tones—the conversation was mundane, her American accent easily distinguishable from Lady X's rounded English vowels.

The spy ship had to keep its distance from *The Khamsin*, but whenever he could Carter trained his binoculars on the yacht. Occasionally, he got a glimpse of Holly on deck, standing at the railing, looking out over the water.

Moustaffa was no longer on board. That much they knew. He had disembarked onto a fishing boat at Dumyat, thirty miles west of Port Said. British Intelligence was disappointed to have lost him momentarily, but Carter was relieved. Moustaffa's departure removed the only real threat to Holly's safety. Now she was alone on the ship with her mummy, Artemidorus, and the crazy English-woman who stole it.

Lady X was a real piece of work. Not bad-looking, but a certifiable nut job. By now Carter had realized that Xandra was the woman in the *kalasiris* tunic he had observed that night of the New York gala—the lady who forgot her panties.

It seemed that buck naked was her usual M.O. The British aristocrat was frequently spotted sunning on deck completely starkers! Carter noticed that the British sur-veillance team was on special alert whenever there was no cloud cover and Lady X was catching some rays.

Holly had plenty of people following her besides Carter. After the botched hostage exchange in Venice, all of Holly's other friends—Ted VerPlanck, Jim Gar-diner, Cordelia, and Sinclair had decided to track her also, boarding Ted VerPlanck's boat *The MoonSonnet* in Piraeus, Greece, where it had been docked for the winter season.

The two ships leapfrogged each other through the Ionian and Mediterranean seas all the way to the Suez Canal, heading to the same place—the Red Sea. It had been no surprise to anyone when Lady X's gleaming white superyacht put in to the marina in Sharm el-Sheikh.

The MoonSonnet didn't follow. VerPlanck anchored well out of sight. At the suggestion of British Intelligence, Carter had switched from the MI6 boat to VerPlanck's yacht. The luxurious vessel could sleep twelve people, and was now a base of operations for the civilians.

And there was the added advantage of VerPlanck's private security team. He always had three or four ex-military men on board, ever vigilant against Somali pirate attacks and other predators around the world.

Carter came out of his reverie when he heard footsteps behind him on the deck. He turned to find Cordelia Stapleton looking toward land. She appeared as worried as he was. Both of them were in the same boat, so to speak, because her boyfriend, Sinclair, was also in Sharm el-Sheikh helping with the operation.

"Good morning," he stammered. "Did you sleep well? Are you feeling better?"

"Actually, no." She smiled ruefully. "Not with John on shore."

Her hair had been freshly washed and hung in damp strands, creating a wet mark on the shoulders of her cotton shirt. She was dressed in white jeans and was barefoot. In the glare of the sun, she looked pale and still a little shaky.

Carter leaped to his feet and offered her a seat.

"They just brought me breakfast—homemade granola. Although I guess that's an oxymoron. How do you 'home make' something when you are on a yacht? Unless, of course, it's *home,* which I guess for VerPlanck it is."

He realized he was babbling. Pretty women did that to him.

"I'm a little too nervous to eat right now," Cordelia said with a smile.

"Let's just hope if Moustaffa makes his move they can

get that biological weapon," Carter said, trying to sound a little more serious.

"I can't quite believe we *want* him to try something."

"I guess if he doesn't we'll never find the damn thing," Carter pointed out.

"By the way," Cordelia asked, turning to Carter, "what's this I hear about you nearly catching Moustaffa back in Venice?"

"Oh, what an exaggeration!" He grinned, delighted. "Who told you that?"

"The British agent who was on board last night. They're all very impressed. They want to recruit you."

"Listen," Carter said. "I'll stick to mummies and museum curators—only the dead and the passive-aggressive. You can keep the homicidal maniacs."

Cordelia laughed, but the smile faded quickly.

"Do you think Sinclair and Holly will be OK?"

"Yes." He nodded. "If there is anyone I would put my money on, it's John Sinclair."

"What about Holly? I'm sure you're worried."

"Yeah, it's been rough."

"She saved me that night at the opera. I'm so grateful to her. You have no idea."

"Yeah, I heard," Carter said. "I'm not surprised."

"Have you known her long?" Cordelia asked.

"About five years. Not that she pays much attention to me."

"I'm sure she cares for you."

"Not really. I've stopped kidding myself. She's way out of my league."

Carter glanced over. Cordelia was really very lovely,

sitting there in the morning sun, her feet tucked up on the cushions beside her. He couldn't help but think that Sinclair was insane to cheat on her the way he did. Cordelia was too good for him.

"Actually, I hate to mention it, but Sinclair still seems to have feelings for Holly. I understand they have some history together."

"Oh Carter, no," she assured him, her eyes wide with earnestness. "That was *years* ago. John has made it perfectly clear. They're just friends now."

When John Sinclair walked into the Sharm el-Sheikh Conference Center, he looked very much the part of a corporate CEO, carrying a file folder emblazoned with the logo of a major U.S. oil company.

"Name?" the security guard asked. "And may I see some government-issued ID?"

"Bob Anderson," Sinclair said. "Comanche Oil."

He slid a Texas driver's license across the desk.

"Thank you, sir," the guard said, waving him through the turnstile.

Sinclair walked inside to the hallway. It was going to be a long day—the first day of the World Economic Forum. Most of the conference would take place indoors, in the modern air-conditioned complex, away from the Egyptian heat. Today was the main event. There would be an opening address, a full day of meetings, and a formal dinner. The second day was for the working sessions, where participants hoped to make deals and hammer out future business relationships.

With the Middle East in the throes of a seismic power shift, attendance was going to be unusually high. Twelve heads of state would make an appearance tonight, including the presidents of France, China, and the United States; the prime ministers of Britain, India, Japan, Israel, Russia, and Spain; the chancellor of Germany; the king of Jordan; and the ruling prince of Saudi Arabia. There were business executives from 250 of the world's largest multinationals and delegates from 70 countries.

It was eight a.m. The motorcades from the hotels would be arriving soon. Sinclair needed to be briefed at the security command center before the activity started. As he stood at the elevators, several traditionally garbed Arabs stepped out. Sinclair entered the elevator along with a large Chinese delegation and punched the button for the third floor, the security center.

Sinclair had never been to Sharm el-Sheikh and was astounded at the size of the complex. Many high-level meetings took place here: peace conferences, corporate gatherings. He had been told that press attendance at the World Economic Forum was much larger than in previous years. This morning reporters stood outside, four deep behind a cordon, thirty feet back from the door. Security personnel had been doubled, tripled even. Armor-clad SWAT teams now patrolled the conference site. Their shiny helmets gave them the appearance of a swarm of black flies.

Lady Xandra Sommerset scanned her clearance badge at the electronic door of the conference center and passed through the security checkpoint. She had been prescreened under her false identity—that of a Belgian banker. As she walked through the room, no one even looked up.

In her current guise, even the most avid tabloid reader would not recognize her as an international celebrity. The flat shoes, serious navy blue suit, and ugly horn-rimmed glasses were perfect camouflage. Her brown hair was tied back into a messy ponytail, the earmark of an overworked female executive with little time for personal grooming.

But the most effective transformation was her body shape. Xandra was now middle-aged and frumpy—underneath her clothes, she had padded her midsection, expanding her waistline to very matronly proportions. In a stroke of genius, Lady X had achieved the impossible: she had managed to look plain.

Holly Graham was standing in the kitchen of the Sharm el-Sheikh Conference Center slicing carrots. She had been conscripted into the kitchen staff for the duration of the conference. Moustaffa had alerted his Egyptian henchmen, and there had been no problem getting her hired by the catering company. It was clear his underworld contacts were global. He now stood next to her, arranging salad and shrimp on individual plates for the luncheon.

Holly wished that *somebody* would recognize her. Moustaffa, however, was hoping for the exact opposite. He had radically altered his appearance, shaving off most of his eyebrows and plucking his hairline. There were two foam tablets in his cheeks to change the shape of his face. Dressed in baggy trousers and a huge white cook's jacket, he looked much heavier than he was in real life. No one stopped him as he entered the kitchen.

He warned Holly that she was his insurance policy—a human shield. If anything untoward happened, she'd be the first to die.

John Sinclair scanned the monitors of the third-floor security post. There were high-resolution cameras in every hall and conference room. Face-recognition technology was sweeping the participants at ten-second intervals, running them through a central database of international underworld criminals. The sophisticated programs had been fine-tuned to identify the distinctive features of one man: Moustaffa.

So far, the hundreds of scans and checks had turned up nothing. Once or twice a monitor would beep, but closer examination of the person on the screen would reveal it was not the terrorist they were seeking. Nevertheless, Sinclair felt in his bones that Moustaffa was there.

The chief of security leaned over and pointed at the screen.

"That's him," he said.

"Really?" Sinclair asked in disbelief.

"Positive. Look next to him."

Sinclair leaned forward and examined the grainy monitor to see a woman standing nearby.

"That's Holly!" he said.

"Correct. We spotted her the moment she came in."

"Get her out of there!"

"I'm afraid that is not possible, sir," the intelligence chief said. "We don't want Moustaffa to know we're onto him. For now, she's staying exactly where she is."

Paul Oakley sat in on the session entitled "Public Health in the Middle East." It was interesting. He would have liked to concentrate on the discussion. But that was not what he was there for.

The intelligence experts were convinced that Moustaffa was going to target the conference with a biological attack. Oakley had been told to keep his eyes open and not draw attention. He was to report anything he saw. Personally, he was praying that his professional expertise would *not* be needed.

The grand ballroom was as cool as a refrigerator. The morning sessions had ended, and hundreds of people were swarming in for the midday meal. There were no assigned tables. That was the whole point. People could sit together and continue the discussions with whomever they liked.

John Sinclair selected a table right in the middle of the vast ballroom. Several French oil executives were already seated, discussing the Arab Spring and the current political climate in Egypt.

Two Chinese participants took places next to him. The first course had already been served, so they all began to eat their salad and shrimp. Sinclair picked at the lettuce and looked around.

Large trolleys were being rolled out for the hot

entrée—baked chicken in a phyllo pastry. The waitress came from behind and placed a plate down over his right shoulder. Sinclair looked at the food and noticed that he was hungry; it smelled delicious.

"Here you are, John," she said.

It was Holly's voice!

Sinclair started to turn toward her.

"*Don't!* He's at the next table."

"*Moustaffa's here in the dining room?*" he whispered.

"Yes. Keep your face turned to the left and he won't recognize you," she said, and served the Chinese executive next to Sinclair. The man from Shanghai began to eat and paid no attention to the conversation between the American businessman and the waitress.

"Is he going to strike?" Sinclair asked, moving his napkin up to cover his mouth as he spoke.

"Yes. He says it's tonight," she added under her breath, and started to move to the next guest.

"Wait, Holly. *Why* would he tell you?"

"He loves to brag," Holly said with a sigh and rolled her eyes. "About everything."

She continued passing plates to the guests, working her way around the table. In a moment she approached Sinclair from the other direction.

"The team has been watching you since Venice," Sinclair informed her. "So you haven't been alone."

"I was hoping that was the case. Anyway, I had my earring," she said, reaching up and fingering the hidden alarm.

"Will he try to put anything in the food?" Sinclair asked, looking down at his plate.

"I don't know," Holly said.

"Holly, do as I tell you. There are a hundred security men in the hall. Just walk up to them and get some protection."

"No, John."

"*Don't argue, do it!*"

"*No!* When this is over, he'll let me go. He says he'll disappear and leave me free."

"And you're going to *believe* him? Why did he bring you here to the conference in the first place?"

"I guess because it was too dangerous to keep me on the yacht—too many people on the dock. He says he *will* kill me if I try anything."

"Holly, *please*! Walk out now. Don't be so stubborn!" Sinclair said.

"No, I'll stay," she said, collecting his salad plate. "I'm in the perfect position to learn more about the attack. Keep me in sight. I'll try to get a message to you."

She turned to serve the adjacent table and then moved away, passing out the lunch plates to two more groups.

Sinclair watched, anxious and frustrated. That was typical; she wasn't going to listen. Holly turned and gave him a quick glance, then pushed the empty catering trolley back to the kitchen.

Incredible! Holly Graham had just turned herself from a hostage into the best asset they had.

The sessions beginning at two o'clock were filled to capacity. In one room, the Japanese prime minister talked about alternate energy sources for the Asia Pacific region. In Conference Room Two, participants grappled with the topic of how new technologies would help Middle East economic development.

On the third floor, intelligence officers were glued to the screen, watching Moustaffa in the kitchen. They had redirected all their surveillance to him and hung on his every move.

Sinclair's attention was focused on a grainy, live image of Holly Graham. She was taking luncheon plates off a trolley and stacking them near the industrial dishwasher.

"I want to get her out of there!" Sinclair demanded.

"No, it might spook him," the chief of operations said. "We need him to stick to plan."

"He's right under your *nose*," Sinclair said, pointing to the monitor. *"You're just going to let him do this?"*

"Of course not, but we need to find out where he put the bioweapon. We can't have bubonic plague floating around out there."

"What if he doesn't make a move?" Sinclair asked.

"We need to find the weapon, regardless. The canisters could be on an automatic trigger. A timer. We need him to lead us to them."

"But what if he doesn't and we don't stop him in time?"

"Short of shutting down this conference and evacuating the building, we have no other option but to watch and wait. There are Egyptian relations to consider. Things are at a delicate stage, politically."

"To *hell* with that!" Sinclair burst out. *"People are going to die!"*

"We couldn't convince the world governments to

cancel the event. All the high-level participants were informed of the threat, and they opted to stay."

Sinclair sighed resignedly. "I assume you went over the ventilation systems and that sort of thing, to make sure he can't put anything through the air ducts," Sinclair said.

"We have been here since two a.m. Air-conditioning ducts, heating units, ventilation systems, the works."

"Do we know what the substance looks like?"

"Most bioweapons are aerosols. It's probably in a canister. We searched the building top to bottom and removed anything that could possibly contain a bioagent. We even replaced the fire extinguishers. So far, nothing."

"Something could be brought in later," Sinclair suggested. "By someone on a second shift."

"No. There's only one shift. Twelve hours straight. They come in at luncheon prep and stay through the dinner."

"Why's that?"

"The hotel didn't want to have to deal with double the number of kitchen staff."

"What about a delivery?" Sinclair asked.

"We are screening all incoming packages. And the workers are not allowed outside, not even for a cigarette."

The room fell silent as they considered the options. A panel of forty camera monitors flickered; the screens reflected the normal activity of a conference. People stood, walked around, and talked together.

Sinclair's eyes were drawn again to the camera that recorded Holly's workstation. The kitchen was active. She turned and picked up a stack of plates. As she went by the security camera, Holly suddenly looked up at the lens. It seemed to Sinclair that she was staring right at him.

Then deliberately and slowly, she winked at the camera! He simply couldn't believe the nerve of the woman. Holly Graham was a *very* cool operator.

It was late afternoon on *The MoonSonnet,* and about eighty degrees, but it felt comfortable with the breeze blowing across the aft deck, the perfect combination of hot and cool. Beyond the railing was the gorgeous turquoise sea. The Sinai Peninsula formed an unbroken line of land on the horizon.

Carter Wallace sat with Ted VerPlanck, saying very little. They were both drinking gin and tonics, and with each sip the ice tinkled in the glasses enticingly. Carter marveled at how the rich do everything to absolute perfection—the heft of a crystal glass, just the right squeeze of lime.

He glanced across the deck at his host. VerPlanck appeared to be waiting for events to unfold with dispassionate equanimity. He certainly *looked* as if he hadn't a care. Lounging in the wicker chair, impeccable in his Nantucket red pants, white oxford shirt, and blue linen blazer, he was every inch the gentleman.

Of course, that kind of sangfroid came with the turf. VerPlanck had been trained to hide his feelings from birth. He was the bluest of the bluebloods, and that blood ran cold. The old joke was that the only things these people showed any emotion about were their dogs and their horses . . . and their boats, apparently.

Ted clearly loved his. And, Carter had to admit, Ver-Planck's yacht was the most beautiful thing he had ever seen—very old school. This was no vulgar gleaming superyacht. The billionaire had explained it was a 125-foot, three-masted schooner that had been built in the Netherlands. The lines were extraordinarily elegant. The hull was painted a deep navy blue, which offset the beautiful teak deck and woodwork. The masts were thick, each fashioned out of a single Douglas fir.

He had learned that *The MoonSonnet* was a type of boat known as a motorsailor, because it had both sails *and* engines. Six-hundred-twenty-four-horsepower Caterpillars for a cruising speed of twelve knots, VerPlanck said.

The sails were mesmerizing. Sitting under the expanse of white, the sound of the taut fabric straining and snapping in the breeze made his blood stir. With sails up, *The MoonSonnet* skimmed over the blue water as smoothly and swiftly as a magic carpet.

The romance of the seafaring lifestyle was growing on Carter. Waking up to the gentle sound of the waves and the fresh breeze. All this was a luxury he had never experienced.

The staff treated him with incredible courtesy. But they really won him over when he went down to the galley late one night and asked for a beer and some potato chips. They had offered him a choice of sixteen varieties.

Despite the luxury and comfort, Carter was nervous. It was hard not to get impatient, especially when he learned that Holly was in the conference center. And here he was, stuck with the old guys—VerPlanck, Gardiner. And, of course, Cordelia, who was still recovering from her ordeal and spent a considerable amount of time resting belowdecks.

MI6 had asked Carter to keep an eye on everyone aboard *The MoonSonnet*. It was a big job, they assured him. So *insulting*! Now that the operation was under way, they were treating him like a kid.

"You've worked with her a long time, haven't you?" VerPlanck asked, breaking into his thoughts.

The older man was attempting to sound casual, but his voice had a certain tension. It was clear he was talking about Holly again.

Carter had begun to notice the early symptoms of infatuation. Day and night, VerPlanck spoke of no one else but Holly.

"Yes, we've known each other quite a few years," Carter admitted. "She's the reason I wanted to help catch the art thieves."

"Then how could you possibly think she was involved in the thefts?" VerPlanck queried.

Carter blushed. That had been a gross miscalculation on his part, one that he was ashamed of, in hindsight.

"When she turned up with Sinclair, I distrusted her on every level."

"Why?"

"She was smoking," Carter said.

Ted looked perplexed.

"So?"

"The Holly I knew didn't smoke. She even gave me crap about smoking myself. So she was either a liar or someone who had a lot to hide."

"I see."

"Then she suddenly turns up with Sinclair. And, just a few weeks before, she pretended they hadn't met for years."

"So you were . . . suspicious?"

"No. Jealous," Carter admitted.

"You were jealous?" VerPlanck asked, surprised.

"Yes, she's a beautiful woman," Carter said, giving him the knowing eye. "I'm sure you noticed."

"Yes, so I have come to realize," VerPlanck said smoothly. "You care for her?"

"Yes, I do. And, unfortunately for me, the rest of the world does too."

"Has lots of admirers, does she?" VerPlanck asked.

"You could say that," Carter affirmed.

"Are you and Holly . . ." VerPlanck asked, fading off for loss of words.

"No," Carter admitted, standing up. He put his glass down on the side table. He turned back to VerPlanck.

"Thanks for the drink. I need to go below to check on something."

"I hope I haven't offended you," VerPlanck returned.

"No, it's fine," Carter assured him. "I'm feeling a bit useless all of a sudden."

"Certainly not. You've done so much."

"The truth of it is, right now in Holly's life I'm just a bystander."

Cordelia walked out onto the top deck of *The MoonSonnet* and looked at her watch. The day had dragged and it was seven o'clock at night. A picture-postcard sunset was beginning to form. She intended to watch the sliver of land until it faded from view. Sinclair was out there, and at great risk.

"No news is good news," VerPlanck remarked, standing behind her.

"Hello," she replied, turning to him. "I can't help but wonder what's going on."

"Let me get you a glass of wine," he offered. "We can keep each other company, and you can tell me about your work in Alexandria, exploring the underwater ruins."

Cordelia sat down on the cushioned banquette.

"Thank you. I'm sure all this waiting is hard for you too," she said.

Ted handed her the glass of wine, chilled to perfection.

"There's a blanket behind you if you are cold," he said. "It might get cool as the sun goes down."

"I was terribly sorry to hear about your wife," Cordelia said, reaching for the cashmere throw.

VerPlanck turned and looked out to sea, away from the shoreline.

"I'm still very depressed about what happened," he said. "I can't pretend to understand it. I truly loved her. In the end, she ended up hurting herself."

"I'm very sorry," Cordelia said.

"To be honest, it's been years since we had any real

connection. In a strange way, I feel like she has been gone for a long time."

"I'm sure that has been lonely for you," Cordelia said. "I know how that can be. I'm familiar with solitude. I was orphaned at the age of twelve."

VerPlanck smiled at her.

"John Sinclair is a lucky man," he said. "And you, young lady, have the whole world in your hand."

"Let's hope so," Cordelia said. "I can't help but feel that we should have heard something by now."

Sharm el-Sheikh

TEN CARS IDLED in the dusk of the Egyptian night. The U.S. president's motorcade was ready to leave the Four Seasons Hotel. President Thomas Walker was a punctual man, ex-military, and a person who many people felt had the qualities of a historic predecessor—President Eisenhower.

To many conservative voters, Walker had all the requirements of the modern age—top honors from West Point and tours in both theaters of war, Iraq and Afghanistan. After a stint as CEO for a major tech firm, he had swept into office as the new hope for the country.

True to his habits, Walker emerged from the hotel with brisk strides and a bounce in his step. After the daylong conferences he had hit the gym and was on his second wind.

Right on the dot of seven, the motorcade pulled away from the portico of the hotel and headed toward the conference center. President Walker had never been late for a high-level dinner since the day he was elected. A terrorist threat was not going to delay him tonight.

As Holly stood in the dining room of the conference center and looked across the sea of vacant tables, she had a sudden flashback of the Metropolitan gala. Had that been only a little more than a few weeks ago? How things had changed!

Here she was, at another formal dinner a world away. No beautiful white evening gown this time. In a waitress uniform, waiting for a terrorist to strike. How had all *that* happened?

The afternoon had passed quietly. She actually found the mindless kitchen work soothing, and all the people around her were reassuring. Anything to protect her from that fiend Moustaffa.

She shuddered to think of him. The evening she had been taken hostage, as she had boarded *The Khamsin,* he had groped her obscenely. The crew had been helping her climb up on the boat and had pretended not to see. The whole time he was on the yacht, Moustaffa leered at her constantly and made obscene gestures whenever Lady X turned away. Holly had locked her door every night and lain awake in fear of a midnight visit.

Suddenly, she longed for home—the little sunlit apartment in Brooklyn. She wanted her life back and missed working at the museum, gossiping with her colleagues. Where had Carter Wallace been all this time? The last she heard from him was when he called her to warn about Charlie Hannifin.

Funny, Carter was such a lumbering bear of a guy, she never realized how clever he was. Half the breakthroughs in this case had been because Carter had noticed the van on the night of the gala. He helped find the stolen art in Queens, always one step ahead of the professional investigators.

Of course, Carter had been right. Hannifin *was* a crook and had been involved in art thefts for a long time. She would thank him when she saw him again, and hoped this would be over soon. They would apprehend Moustaffa tonight. And then they could all get on with their lives.

She picked up an embossed card next to a plate and looked at the menu. The food had been carefully chosen with an eye to dietary restrictions, factoring in the tastes and cultural diversity of all the participants.

The first course was spinach and goat cheese salad, followed by lamb—a common dish in the Middle East. Then there was an intermediary vegetarian course—a timbale of eggplant and other vegetables—then fruit, cheeses, and a sweet dessert of cherries jubilee.

Not that *she'd* be getting any of it. The kitchen help had already been fed. Earlier this afternoon, she had sat at a long table with the rest of the staff, eating without any apprehension, figuring the lamb stew was safe. After all, Moustaffa was wolfing down exactly the same thing only a few yards away from her.

But this dinner was another matter. They'd keep their eyes on Moustaffa to make sure the food wasn't tampered with. Intelligence officers had replaced half of the catering staff, switching them with trained operatives.

Moustaffa seemed to realize that special agents were positioned all around him. He had looked at the new waiters with amusement and didn't seem to care. But Holly was glad a British special service officer was stationed next to her, clad in a white waiter's jacket. And there were at least two dozen more just like him, moving about the room.

Her nerves made her giddy. Holly found herself thinking that on a culinary level this event had the potential to turn into an absolute farce. Some of these officers were not very handy with the plates. She imagined there'd be plenty of spilled wine and dropped entrées.

They still hadn't found the WMD canisters. Paul

Oakley had said that weaponized plague, while possibly a powder, would most likely be in the form of an aerosol. Every likely hiding place had been searched and investigated. But nothing had been found.

Precautions had been taken and the top dignitaries were informed of the threat. There was a contingency plan—to remove VIPs to a so-called safe room in the basement of the hotel if an alarm was raised. Only twelve people would fit inside—just enough space for the heads of state.

Although the room was small, it was very secure. The belowground bunker even had its own air supply and communications lines. Until now, it had never been used. Hopefully, tonight that wouldn't change.

Most of the dignitaries had risen to the occasion. When informed of the threat, everyone had agreed to stay. They dealt with this all the time and refused to cave in to terrorist threats.

The surveillance apparatus was state-of-the-art. Every eye would be on the dining room. There were pinpoint microphones among the flower arrangements. Agents would listen in on the conversations from one floor above.

The world leaders would dine facing the ballroom, sitting on a raised dais. Moustaffa would be serving the tables at the back as they waited for him to make his move. But even at that distance, the security teams were jumpy. He had said that he would strike tonight.

Paul Oakley looked at the monitors and wondered where in *hell* the canisters could be. Every inch of the hotel had been searched. Every box in the kitchen had been examined. The cocktail hour was over and the luminaries were taking their places. If he had to bet, an attack would come this evening. After all, twelve of the most powerful men in the world were all here. When would Moustaffa ever get an opportunity like this again?

Oakley closed his eyes to shut out the men sitting on the platform. It was almost inconceivable to envision them contracting plague. They were all so powerful. Yet they could be felled with one single aerosol spray.

Paul couldn't help but think about plague. The swelling of the armpits and buboes in the groin, the crushing fatigue, labored breathing, coughing fits, searing pain in the lungs. Then, after a few days, the epidermis would begin decomposing, the body putrefying even while the victims were still alive. The burning, needlelike pains all over the body would turn into the characteristic dark patches of the Black Death.

They had to avert the disaster! There *was* a vaccine. But it had never been tested. And inoculating the heads of state like guinea pigs had not been an option. So there they sat, eating their spinach salad, tempting fate.

President Walker was making his way to the microphone to give opening remarks about peace and prosperity in the region. John Sinclair kept one eye on the U.S. president and another on the audience. They never found the canisters. Oakley estimated there had to be up to a dozen to contaminate a room of this size. They had to be *somewhere*. But so far, nothing.

Moustaffa told Holly he was planning the attack tonight. As an additional taunt, he had even revealed the timing. It would happen just as the dinner was ending, he had said. So confident! He was so sure of success. And they couldn't seem to stop him.

Sinclair looked across the ballroom and gritted his teeth. Moustaffa was standing twenty yards away. If Sinclair had his way, he'd just kill him now and be done with it. But if the plague canister was an automatic trigger, they'd all die. So there was no choice but to watch and wait.

Sinclair gave Holly an encouraging glance as she passed by. She smiled back. Funny how fate had thrown them together again. No question, Hols was a wonderful woman. And, truth be told, part of him still had great affection for her. But she couldn't hold a candle to Cordelia.

He closed his eyes and thanked all the powers of the universe that Cordelia was safe. As bad as this was, it was nothing compared to the agony he had been going through while she was missing. VerPlanck had been such a godsend. To have Cordelia secure and guarded on *The MoonSonnet* was all he could ask for.

The *MoonSonnet* Motorsailer, Sharm el-Sheikh

IN THE DINING room of *The MoonSonnet,* Cordelia picked at her grilled fish and periodically looked at her watch. She could barely swallow.

Everyone on VerPlanck's ship was aware of what was happening. The bridge of the boat had been set up with state-of-the-art communications equipment. From there they could speak with the security control room on shore. Cordelia had even talked to Sinclair a few times during the day, but all the conversations had been brief. There had been too much to do.

Tonight, Ted VerPlanck was tactfully ignoring everyone's emotional state. Conversation was forced but determinedly cheerful, avoiding any mention of what was going on at the conference center.

Carter was telling VerPlanck about a new find in the Valley of the Kings. Jim Gardiner was eating heartily, his usual response to stress. But Cordelia was inconsolable, tears shimmering in her eyes.

"Don't worry, Delia," Gardiner said, putting down his fork. "It's going to be OK. This will be over and you'll never have to worry about him again."

Cordelia laughed and wiped her eyes.

"Sinclair is never going to change," she said, smiling.

"He will most *certainly* find another way to get into trouble. I'm sure of it."

"Well, honey, I'll have a talk with him," Gardiner replied. "I'll tell him he needs to find a hobby or something else to keep him out of harm's way."

"What do you think he should do?"

"I think it's time he took up something safe . . . like golf."

"Not *golf*!" VerPlanck said, looking over at Gardiner in mock horror. "Surely we haven't come to *that*."

Sharm el-Sheikh Conference Center

AFTER-DINNER SPEECHES WERE about to begin. The fruit plates were being cleared. The chief organizer of the conference was extolling Egypt for its gracious hospitality. Participants were profusely thanked—individually, collectively, and nationally. Sinclair listened with half an ear and shifted in his seat. Nothing had happened.

Suddenly, the kitchen doors opened and there was a commotion at the back of the room. He immediately thought of the attack at the Met. Was *this* the moment?

He scanned the room. Nothing amiss. Moustaffa was standing in the middle of the tables, watching the parade of dessert trolleys being pushed into the ballroom.

The pièce de résistance of the dinner was to be cherries jubilee. A bit of culinary theater. Standing at each table, a waiter would ignite the cherries, brown sugar, and liqueur and sauté it over an open flame on a flambé cart. The juices and brandy would blend, and then the succulent sauce would be spooned over a scoop of vanilla ice cream. Certainly it could all have been prepared in the kitchen. But this kind of tableside flourish made the dinner special.

Holly had been assigned to help pass the plates at Table 4. She stood directly behind Sinclair. He turned and spoke to her, as everyone watched the waiters enter the room.

"Still nothing?" he asked.

"I can't imagine when . . ." she started and then her eyes widened. A thought occurred to her.

"John, do you happen to know if they checked the flambé equipment on the dessert trolleys?"

"No, why?" he asked, puzzled.

"There are twenty-five trolleys, one for every two tables," she explained.

"Yes?"

"John, inside each cart there is an eight-ounce canister of butane—"

"Oh, my God!" Sinclair said, turning to her with panic in his eyes. *"Do you think . . . ?"*

"Yes," she said. "I do."

He looked over at Moustaffa. The bastard was looking at him and laughing. All around him the waiters were rolling their carts into place. The look on Moustaffa's face was triumphant. Slowly, the terrorist turned and walked back to the kitchen. *He left the room!* Sinclair took Holly's hand.

"You're right. This is it! Holly, come with me right now!"

The waiters were now in place, and everyone watched them expectantly. The flaming cherries would be spectacular—a lovely touch of elegance to the dinner. Each waiter stood next to his dessert trolley holding a long-necked lighter, ready to fire up the butane burners to flambé the cherries.

The president of the United States leaned over to speak to the Japanese prime minister.

"I can't remember the last time I had this dessert, but it's really special," he remarked. "I do hope you like cherries."

"I certainly do. And I understand that your first president, George Washington, also liked cherries very much."

Sinclair raced out into the hallway. Four security men were standing around the empty corridor, waiting for the dinner to end.

"*You have to clear the room! . . .*" Sinclair shouted, his lapel mike transmitting to the security center. "*It's the butane canisters. The weapon is in the dessert carts! Moustaffa just left through the kitchen!*"

The security men in the corridor all raced toward the door of the ballroom. One turned back.

"*Sinclair, go to the safe room! Make sure they are ready and the hallway is clear!*"

Every single officer in the third-floor control room leaped to his feet. They were looking at one another in confusion.

"*No! He's wrong!*" the head of operations shouted. "We checked the dessert carts. The canisters were *fine*!"

"Clear the room! That *has* to be it!" his second in command snapped. "Moustaffa said the attack would come at the end of dinner."

"I don't . . . *no*! Keep everyone in place," the head of operations insisted.

"*If we don't clear that ballroom, they could die!*"

The two men stared at each other in horror. They had directly conflicting opinions. A wrong decision would be fatal. The head of operations caved in.

"You're right," he said. "Let's get everyone below. We'll err on the side of caution."

The chief of operations turned to the security officers.

"Evacuate the dais! Do it now!"

Moustaffa sat at the industrial table in the kitchen with four pistols pointed at his head. Security teams had forced him into a secure position and were keeping him pinned there until further orders. Despite his capture, Moustaffa was smiling.

This plan was proceeding perfectly. In about three minutes the security team would evacuate the dais and move the dignitaries via elevator to the underground passage. All twelve of them would go inside the safe room and shut the door.

Inside, the room would be airtight, sealed, with ventilation only through a closed circulatory system. The lock would be set for a predetermined thirty-minute period. No one inside or outside the vault could override the mandatory seal. They'd be trapped. *There, in that bunker, the weapon would be triggered, with all twelve of the world leaders inside!*

Paul Oakley heard Sinclair's voice on the speakers in the command center. *How could this be?* They had searched the entire kitchen. And the butane canisters had *not* been overlooked. All the cylinders were attached *underneath* the burners of the flambé carts. The security team had disassembled the apparatus and had examined each one extensively.

But Sinclair had to be right. It must be some other system in the trolley. Something they hadn't noticed.

Another device, perhaps on automatic detonate, related to the butane burner? Once it had been lit, some kind of seal would melt and the bioweapon would be released. The mechanics of it eluded him, but the thought of it was *awful*.

The commanding officer got on the IFB microphone and spoke directly into the earpieces of the agents in the dining room.

"Do not light the butane lighters. Wheel the carts back into the kitchen immediately!"

The phalanx of waiters extinguished their lighters in unison and began pushing their trolleys back toward the kitchen.

An announcement came over the loudspeaker in a calm but authoritative voice.

"Ladies and gentlemen, unfortunately we have run late for the dinner program. Please excuse the interruption, but photos of the guests of honor must be taken at this time."

A murmur of disappointment swept through the room.

"The gala dinner has concluded. Would everyone please exit the building in an orderly manner."

The guests collected their belongings and began to move toward the exits. It would probably take at least twenty minutes for everyone to pass down the corridors and go out the front entrance. If an attack was imminent, it would be too late! Security personnel swarmed the dais and began to move the dignitaries quickly to the rear door.

Sinclair and Holly stood in the steel elevator on the way down to the subbasement.

"I hope to *hell* we're right," Sinclair worried. "We may have just caused an international incident for no reason."

"John, that *has* to be it," Holly assured him. "You saw his face. He was laughing. He was happy to be pulling it off."

"It just seems somehow . . ." Sinclair wavered.

Just then the door opened onto the subterranean corridor. The passage toward the safe room was lined with security personnel. Sinclair walked out of the elevator, suddenly mobilized.

"They're evacuating the dais!" he announced.

Each man stood at the ready, facing the steel elevator. There were at least ten male agents and one female, all dressed in blue blazers.

Sinclair moved rapidly down the corridor toward the safe room, Holly following behind.

"Hols, I just want to check inside one more time," Sinclair said. "Come with me. I don't want to leave you."

Holly nodded tensely. The security personnel let them pass.

As they approached the door, Holly glanced at the lone female security agent. Nondescript in her somber suit, she was an ordinary-looking woman with a thick waist, pulled-back hair.

Then Holly saw the topaz eyes. They were open wide in anticipation. The eyes of a tiger. The color was unforgettable. *It was Lady X!*

"John, it's her!" Holly said.

Sinclair grabbed Xandra by the arm in a lightning move, his reflexes honed by years of fencing. He spun her around. The agents turned and leveled their weapons at her.

"This woman is Moustaffa's accomplice!" Sinclair shouted. *"Get her out of here!"*

Xandra stepped back against the wall with her hands up. Sinclair hesitated. There was something in her expression—a hint of smugness in the look. The expression didn't seem right. He glanced at her eyes. They were triumphant. This was not a woman who had just been caught. *Something was wrong.*

Sinclair turned and looked inside the safe room. It was empty. There was only a conference table and twelve chairs. Silent. Ready. Yet he could feel a sinister vibe.

Sinclair stepped into the room and walked around to the other side of the table. There, taped to the leg of a chair, was what looked like a shiny silver fire extinguisher! Attached to the canister was a pressure gauge, a dial like those on Cordelia's diving gear.

Holly came into the room and walked up behind him.

"John, what is it?"

Wordlessly, he pointed down at it.

"Please move out of the room," a security agent called to them. "The elevator is coming down."

"Oh, my God!" Holly said to Sinclair. "He's put the weapon in here!"

Out in the corridor the elevator pinged, the steel doors opened, and twelve world leaders stood inside. The security team surged toward the elevator to flank the officials along the hallway. The drill had been practiced in advance. The dignitaries would move en masse down the passage, surrounded by armed guards.

Sinclair turned to Holly in horror.

"We have to do something!"

"Just tell them!" Holly urged.

The group of dignitaries and security men were coming toward them at a fast trot. The cadre of security men had their weapons drawn. They would reach the safe room in a matter of seconds!

Sinclair reacted fast, moving toward the door. There wouldn't be time to explain! No one would listen. *They didn't realize they were rushing to their deaths!*

Sinclair gripped the handle of the heavy steel door and pulled it. It was very cumbersome but started to swing toward him slowly.

"John, what are you doing!" Holly shouted behind him.

The door was nearly shut when the first security officer fired at him. The shot the door with a ping.

"You're going to lock them out!" Holly yelled.

The door slammed with a heavy clang. The last thing he saw was the shocked faces of the world leaders out in the corridor. Sinclair turned the swivel handle and punched the green button on the automatic lock. *He and Holly were now sealed inside!*

The chief of operations looked at the screen. The subterranean passage was cluttered with people milling about. It wasn't supposed to work like this. By now, they should be in the safe room!

Agents had formed a ring around the world leaders, but some of the dignitaries were very agitated and started banging on the safe room door. It was locked. Nobody could open it! At least not for a half hour.

The security officer glanced at the monitor that revealed the interior of the vault. John Sinclair and Dr. Graham were inside, apparently having a heated argument. Just beyond he could see the outline of a cylinder, taped to a chair.

He picked up the mouse and zoomed the interior camera in on the object. Yes, it was a canister! Sinclair had closed the door to protect the others. *Bravo!* That was very fast thinking.

But right now the top priority was to get all the officials out of the corridor and into their motorcades. Sinclair was on his own.

"Oh, my God, John, you've just locked everyone out!"

Holly was shouting at him.

He squared off to face her, taking her by the shoulders.

"Holly, I've never been more sure of anything in my entire life."

"But they won't understand, John. They'll think we are the terrorists. They just *shot* at you!"

"I don't care what they think. We can't let them in here. They will die!"

Sweat was pouring down his face. He couldn't believe it had come to this.

"So we're locked in?" she asked.

He looked over at the canister and didn't reply.

"With that?" she asked, white-lipped.

"Yes."

"Can they get in?" she asked.

"No, once the door locks, it can't be opened for at least thirty minutes. And even then, only by the people inside the room. That's how it's designed."

"We can't get out!" Holly said.

"No," he said.

"Can anyone help?"

"There's a hotline. I'll call upstairs."

"But that canister could be on an automatic trigger," Holly said, pointing to it. "It will kill us."

"If it goes off, it will. And the timer is probably set to go off relatively quickly," he added.

Holly shrank back against the door. Sinclair turned and approached the canister. The phone was on the table, the canister right below it, taped to the chair leg.

"John, please don't go near it!"

"I have to. It's our only chance."

Paul Oakley looked at the monitor of the safe room camera. Sinclair and Holly were inside. Another camera in the hall showed a cluster of men on the other side of the door. The U.S. president and the prime minister of Japan were trying to open the door. Others were pounding on it. Shouting. Security teams surrounded the group with drawn weapons. But there was nothing they could do. The room had been sealed.

What had Sinclair done? He knew about the lock. There had to be a reason.

The phone on the console buzzed next to him. Oakley stared at it. It was the hotline to the safe room.

Everyone else had left the command center. He was alone.

"Oakley here."

"Paul, it's Sinclair."

"What's going on?" Oakley asked, breathless.

"Are you near a monitor? Look at the chair in the corner," Sinclair replied. *"The canister is here."*

The MoonSonnet Motorsailer

CORDELIA, JIM GARDINER, Carter Wallace, and Ted VerPlanck were all standing around the wheelhouse of *The MoonSonnet* listening to the commotion. The ship-to-shore radio was squawking and breaking up into jumbled noise. From the sound of it, the command center at the conference hall was filled with shouting.

"It's happening!" Carter blurted.

"They just said they're evacuating the ballroom!" Ver-Planck said with a gasp.

Cordelia sat down on the captain's bench.

"I feel sick," she said.

Ted VerPlanck came over and put his arm around her.

"Don't worry, they have it under control," he lied.

Sharm el-Sheikh Conference Center

S INCLAIR, DON'T TOUCH it!" Oakley said into the phone. "What should I do?"

"Move away and stay near the ventilating shaft. If it goes off, at least the incoming air will blow the aerosol away from you."

"OK, Paul, will do," Sinclair's voice came back. "There's only one canister. Weren't we expecting more?"

"Yes. We thought the attack would take place in the ballroom, but this room is much smaller."

"Understood," Sinclair said grimly. "I guess you are telling me one is enough."

Oakley didn't answer. He put his head in his hands. There was no way they would survive if the weapon had an automatic trigger. They were as good as dead.

"Paul, get the security team down here," Sinclair was saying. "There has to be a way to override this door lock!"

"They're on their way," Oakley assured him.

With the twelve top leaders standing in a basement hallway, every security officer was already there.

Oakley saw the situation clearly. Sinclair was asking for help to open the door. That wouldn't happen.

If there were any chance that the canister would fire off, the security team would not risk it. Nor would they listen to any pleas of desperation. Sinclair and Holly would be insignificant casualties. That door would stay *closed*.

"Holly," Sinclair was saying, "get over into the corner. And stand directly under the air shaft!"

She moved quickly across the room and stood where the ventilation system blew fresh, cool air down on her. In the draft, wisps of hair stirred around her face.

Sinclair hung up the phone and went to join her. She looked absolutely white with fear. On impulse he leaned over and kissed the top of her head.

"We'll be OK, Hols," he said quietly.

"We will?" she asked, glancing up at him. Her eyes were enormous.

"Yes, Oakley says to stay here under the . . ." Sinclair stopped. His head snapped up to look at the wall next to the ceiling.

"What is it, John?"

He stared up at the grating of the ventilation shaft. The opening to the air duct was less than three feet wide, covered by a slatted aluminum grille.

"Do you think you could fit through that space?" he asked, pointing at it.

Holly's eyes followed the direction of his finger. She considered.

"It looks big enough," she concluded.

"Stay here," he ordered.

He dragged a chair over from the conference table to the wall and jumped up on it. He could just reach the bottom of the vent. It was lucky he was so tall. He could probably yank the cover off. But how was it attached?

There was a quarter-inch gap between the grating and the surface of the wall. It was screwed on. And the construction was a solid concrete block. This was not going to be easy to remove.

He tried prying it off. His fingernails just fit under the lip of the metal. He pulled, nearly wrenching his nails out in the process. It hurt like the dickens, but he tried again.

"I can't get it." He grunted, trying one more time.

"Try this," she said.

He looked down and she was handing him a large knife.

"*Where in hell did you get that!*" he gasped, staring at it in disbelief.

"I stole it from the kitchen. It was in my pocket, under my apron. I thought it might come in handy."

Sinclair grinned down at her.

"Hols, you're a *fantastic* woman!" he said.

"*John!* Don't *talk!* Just get us out of here!"

The knife was strong, used for cutting raw meat. He slid it in between the metal and the concrete and torqued it. He did it several times until the knife bent under the pressure of trying to pry off the grid. He got enough space between the grate and the wall to slide his fingers in and gave a tremendous pull.

Finally, with the sound of the screws tearing out of the cement block, the grate came loose. A shower of dust fell onto Holly's hair. Sinclair handed down first the knife and then the metal frame.

"Get another chair and put it next to the one I am standing on."

She dragged a chair over and positioned it.

"Climb up here, I'll push you through the opening."

"Are you sure?" she asked, craning her neck to look up at the gaping hole in the wall.

"It's the only way. I don't know where it goes, but keep sliding along that air shaft as far as you can. Don't stop. Hopefully the ventilation flow will keep the aerosol spray away from you if this thing goes off."

"I am not sure . . ."

"Just *do it*! Keep going. Maybe there is an exit. Now come here, I am going to boost you up."

Sinclair reached down for her. Holly took his hands to balance and then stepped up on the seat of the adjacent chair. It was going to be tough to get her up there. The opening to the air shaft was at least four feet above her head.

Sinclair stooped down and linked his hands to form a stirrup.

"Kick off your shoes and put your foot here. Let me give you a lift."

"Oh, my God, I can't! It's too high!"

"We can do it! I'll count to three, then up you go. Just grab for the opening."

"OK, I'll try," she said, wobbling on the chair.

"One, two . . . three!"

He pushed her up with all of his strength. She struggled against him to pull herself higher, and suddenly he felt her get a grip on the opening to the shaft. He locked his arms around her legs to lift her higher. Her elbows were in the air shaft now; he could feel her moving her upper body. Sinclair squatted down and placed her feet on his shoulders.

"Hols, push against me, harder! I've got you."

He strained to stand up as her feet bore down on his shoulders. Finally, the pressure eased. She had managed to pull herself in. Her bare feet disappeared into the tunnel. There was considerable banging and thumping as she tried to advance forward.

"Come on, John," she called back. "There's room for you now!"

"Keep going," he yelled.

"Aren't you coming?" she shouted.

Her voice echoed out of the empty hole near the ceiling.

He looked back at the canister taped to the leg of the chair.

"I can't," he called to her. "I won't fit."

The MoonSonnet Motorsailer

T HE SPEEDBOAT COULD be heard approaching in the darkness. Ted VerPlanck signaled with a flashlight, making long, deliberate swoops. Finally the craft came in sight, with two men wearing police armor and helmets.

"Delia, can you get those fenders in?" VerPlanck shouted to her.

She flipped the bulky cylindrical cushions over the rail to hang down the side of the boat. The two crafts would tie together, and the fenders would prevent the hulls from scraping against each other. Cordelia readied herself to catch the lines as the security team tossed them.

"What's going on?" Jim Gardiner called as they got within hailing distance. "The radio went silent."

"We turned it off," the officer said as they pulled alongside and cut the engine.

"Why? What's going on?" Carter asked.

"We had an emergency. They've evacuated the entire hall. Hang on, we'll explain."

Sharm el-Sheikh Conference Center

SINCLAIR WALKED OVER to the hotline and picked it up.

"Paul?"

"Yes, John, I'm here."

"I got Holly up into the ventilation shaft. See if someone can pull her out of there from the other end, will you?"

"Oh, that's *brilliant*! I'll get on it right away." The relief in Oakley's voice was heartening. Sinclair hated to burst his bubble.

"Paul, you still there?" Sinclair said.

"Yes, John?"

"The bad news is I can't fit. My shoulders are too big. Is there anything else I can do?"

There was a long, agonized silence. Finally, Oakley replied.

"Take your shirt off and tie it over your nose and mouth. If the canister goes off, shut your eyes and keep them shut."

His tone was flat. Sinclair listened to him and his heart sank. Oakley clearly had no hope that anything would help.

"We'll get you out, John," Oakley said with false cheer. "Cover your nose and mouth and sit under the ventilation shaft."

"OK, will do," Sinclair said. He hung up the phone and started unbuttoning his shirt.

Holly found she couldn't really crawl. She was worming her way along, using her forearms to push herself forward. There was not much elbow room in the tight space, so she also had to use her feet to push along inch by inch. She was able to get some grip on the metal surface with the tips of her bare toes. It was slow, but she could shimmy herself along.

It was hard work. And hot! Her skin stuck to the steel walls of the ventilation shaft, rubbing painfully as she tried to move. She could feel abrasion burns on her elbows and knees.

She remembered how, as a child, the hot metal of the playground slide would grab and tear at her skin exactly like this. Funny, how childhood recollections pop up so suddenly. The memory made her sad. How short life is! And how *precious*.

Every inch she crawled, she moved farther away from Sinclair. He was trapped. It wasn't fair.

Tears streamed down her face as she struggled forward. An awful dull ache filled her chest. Surely this was what a broken heart felt like.

She pictured Sinclair's face. He would be urging her to keep going if he were here. Her heart swelled with affection for him. He wanted her to live. He wanted her to stay alive and tried so hard to save her, even though he was doomed. It was up to her to honor his final wish.

And for some reason that was enough to make her

keep going. The crying stopped. She found the strength to crawl forward again.

Holly heard voices and saw a light. It wasn't the blinding light of a near-dying experience. It was the beam of a flashlight playing off the wall of the shaft about thirty feet ahead.

She started to sob. There were people calling to her. She was absolutely weeping.

"Dr. Graham," a male voice called to her. "Can you hear us?"

Dr. Graham? How *formal*. When she got out of here, she would certainly tell them to please call her Holly. She started to crawl forward.

"I'm here," she gasped as she moved faster. They sounded quite close.

"Dr. Graham, are you there?" they asked again.

"Yes!" she shouted. *"Yes, I'm here!"*

"We're going to toss a rope into the shaft and snake it down to you. Wrap it around your chest under your arms and we'll pull you out!"

"OK." She started to cry again with relief.

Sinclair sat directly under the ventilation shaft and looked at the metal canister taped to the chair. It wasn't very big. Hard to believe it was deadly. There was a pressure gauge and some other contraption on top.

Oakley had said to stay away from the canister. The device could have an automatic trigger and might detonate if it was tampered with.

No use trying to disarm it. All he had was a bent

kitchen knife. And he had no idea what to do. Fixing his motorcycle was about as mechanical as he got. The only thing to do was move away and hope for the best.

The sounds from the shaft overhead were getting faint. He had heard the crying. Holly must be at the end of her rope. He had never known her to break down before.

He had hollered for her to keep going. He hoped she heard. Suddenly, the sobbing stopped and he could hear her crawling again. Hols was a tough woman. She would make it.

Himself, he was not so sure. Someone damn well better get this door open soon. He closed his eyes and waited. Pointless, really. He was kidding himself. They weren't coming for him. They were probably evacuating the building, making sure everyone else was safe. Heads of state outrank mere archaeologists. Anyone could tell you that.

He couldn't help but recall the medical pictures Oakley had passed around in the Eisenhower Apartment at Culzean Castle. The swelling under the armpits and the groin. A litany of horrific symptoms. What really bothered him was that the skin would actually start to decompose while the person was alive! Turn black, start to putrefy. Without a doubt, the Black Death was one of the most evil diseases in the world.

Sitting there, he made up his mind. If he got the plague, he wouldn't let anyone see him like that. Not even Cordelia. He wanted her to remember him in the prime of life. Not a half-rotted corpse, dying in a hospital bed. He made that promise to himself as he sat in the corner. Then he tightened his shirt around his nose and mouth, pulling the arms snugly.

The MoonSonnet Motorsailer

CORDELIA COULDN'T STOP crying. Her face was buried in the bulk of Jim Gardiner's shoulder. Others sat around *The MoonSonnet* cabin with glum faces.

"There are two teams in Hazmat suits trying to pull Dr. Graham out of the air shaft," the agent was telling them.

"What are the obstacles?" Gardiner asked.

"There is an intersection of two shafts about two hundred feet in front of her. There is egress about thirty feet beyond that. If she can get to that junction, we can get a rope to her and pull her out."

They took this information in and digested it. Ver-Planck was ashen. His eyes had the glassy stare of shock. He looked at everyone in turn as they spoke but seemed to have no urge to respond.

Carter had the opposite reaction. He was wild. He stood and paced the salon in frustration and anger.

"I can't *believe* Sinclair would lock her in!" he ranted. "When he *knew* there was a canister in there."

Cordelia raised her head from Gardiner's shoulder and glared at him.

"How *dare* you! Of *course* he would. He wanted to save everyone else," she snapped. "He's not *selfish*, like other people."

"But he wasn't making that decision on his own. Holly was in there with him!"

"He had no choice," she replied, her voice rising in anger.

"I'm sorry, Cordelia, but I don't see it like that. It was a thoughtless thing to do," Carter answered. "Heroic, but unthinking. He should have let the professionals take charge. That's what I would have done."

"He's twice the man you are!"

Her face was red and there were tears coursing down.

"Delia, *don't*!" Gardiner shushed her. "No one is at fault."

VerPlanck rose from his chair and walked to the aft door.

"We're all upset," he admonished. "We are all saying things we will regret. Carter, why don't you step outside on deck with me? I believe we both need some air."

Carter Wallace stood on the deck of *The MoonSonnet*, breathing hard.

"Thanks," Carter mumbled. "I didn't mean to . . ."

"Everything will be forgotten tomorrow. It was only the heat of the moment," VerPlanck assured him.

"But I still can't believe Cordelia would take me apart like that!"

"From what I understand, she has been an orphan for most of her life. Sinclair is pretty much the only thing she has in the world," VerPlanck explained.

"Do you think they'll get Sinclair out?" Carter asked.

"I'm sure of it. There has to be an override system on the door," VerPlanck assured him.

"That's a relief. I hadn't thought of that," Carter admitted. "And it sounds like Holly is going to be OK."

"Yes, you heard the security officials. They'll pull her out of the air shaft and she'll be fine."

Carter closed his eyes and gripped the railing of the boat. Relief washed over him. She was going to make it. When he opened his eyes, VerPlanck was looking at him.

"If you'll forgive me, it seems you are pretty emotionally involved with Holly," VerPlanck ventured. "Is there something you would like to talk about?"

Carter turned to him with abject honesty.

"I was pretty infatuated for a while."

"Was?"

"I'm getting over it. Slowly. Listen, I know what's going on," he said to VerPlanck.

"Going on?" VerPlanck repeated.

"You're crazy about her too."

"No, not at all," VerPlanck denied.

"Bullshit."

VerPlanck looked at Carter in astonishment as a variety of emotions played over his face. At first he appeared to be offended, then embarrassed; finally he crumpled.

"Is it that obvious?"

"To me it is," Carter said. "But then I know all the signs."

"I see."

"And when this is over . . . this terrorism stuff. When it comes to Holly, I won't stand in your way."

"That's very *noble* of you," VerPlanck said.

"No, it's not. It's realistic. She doesn't care for me at all."

"Well, thank you, Carter, but I can't really act on my

feelings right now," VerPlanck said. "It wouldn't be decent. My wife just died, you know."

"Yeah, I heard. I'm sorry."

"Yes, so am I," VerPlanck said.

They both looked out at the dark water for a moment.

"Listen," Carter spoke up. "You'll probably punch me in the nose or throw me overboard for saying this, but you shouldn't worry so much about being *decent*. Other people weren't all that decent to you. In fact, it sounds to me like you were the only *decent* person involved in all of this."

VerPlanck turned to Carter with troubled eyes, but he didn't reply.

"So don't let your decency get in the way with Holly," Carter urged him. "Women like that don't come along very often."

Ted nodded slowly.

"I see your point, Carter. Well, I may take my chances on catching her interest. If you don't mind."

"Go for it," Carter said. "Don't wait too long."

"Thank you," VerPlanck said.

"By the way, while we're being so honest and open and everything . . . You know she was once in love with Sinclair," Carter offered.

"Probably still is," observed VerPlanck.

"Nah. Not after he exposed her to bubonic plague. That would pretty much finish it for most women."

"One would *hope* so," VerPlanck said, smiling. "But in *my* experience women are funny."

Cordelia and Gardiner sat alone in the salon of *The Moon-Sonnet*. She was still fuming.

"I can't believe Carter had the nerve to criticize John like that!"

"Give him a break, Delia," Gardiner soothed her. "Can't you see he's half out of his mind over Holly?"

"Yeah, but *she's* going to live," Cordelia cried. "And John is going to . . ."

She couldn't finish the sentence and sat there, defeated.

"No!" Gardiner said firmly. "No, he's *not*. You just wait and see."

Sharm el-Sheikh Conference Center

SINCLAIR LOOKED AT his watch. He couldn't help but calculate his odds. It was a quarter after ten. The formal dinner was supposed to be over at ten sharp.

How clever of Moustaffa to have outwitted them all. The master manipulator had cranked up their nerves to the breaking point and then had herded them to their deaths like cattle to a slaughter.

Sinclair thanked his stars that the attack had been stopped in the end. Or maybe not. Here he was sitting on the floor, waiting to be doused with a spray of weaponized plague. How smart was that?

The phone began to ring. Sinclair stayed where he was and listened to it. The phone was on the table right above the canister. Too close. He shouldn't go over to pick it up. Twenty minutes had gone by since they shut the door. An automatic trigger would activate pretty soon.

The phone kept ringing shrilly in the enclosed space. It sounded urgent. He second-guessed himself and considered the possibilities.

What if they had figured out a way to dismantle the canister? Or wanted to tell him how to open the door? It could be any number of things.

He looked over at the canister again. The timing was too close. He shouldn't approach it. Surely it had been set to go off any minute now.

The phone kept on ringing, shattering his nerves. He wanted to answer it, just to stop it. And if they were trying to reach him, there might be a way out. He made a decision. He walked over to the phone and picked up the receiver.

"Hello?" he said.

Just below him he heard a hiss. He looked down at the canister. It was spraying a fine mist of particles into the air, like a can of hairspray with the button permanently depressed.

"Agghhh . . ." he gasped as he threw the phone down and headed to the corner. He didn't rush. There was no need. He was a dead man already.

Paul Oakley hung up the phone and turned to the chief of security.

"I didn't get a chance to tell him the door code," he said in a leaden tone. "It was too late."

"The canister?"

"Yes, it detonated," Oakley confirmed. "Just now."

"Oh, hell!" the man said. "We're going to Plan B. Send in the guys with Hazmat suits. Seal the building."

"What about Sinclair?" Oakley asked.

"Get Sinclair out of there and into a biocontainment unit. We're taking him to Cairo—the U.S. Naval Medical Research Unit, NAMRU-3. It's the only place we can take him, unless you want to airlift him to Europe. NAMRU-3 is equipped for the highest bio-security level, BSL-4, to handle the deadliest diseases."

"We're talking about weaponized plague. Are they any good at that sort of thing?" Oakley asked worriedly.

"They're the *best*. If U.S. troops are hit with bioweapons during battle, the NAMRU team has the expertise to diagnose what pathogen was used, right in the field. They have been investigating outbreaks of disease in this part of the world since World War Two. The Centers for Disease Control and Prevention also has doctors at the lab in Cairo working with them. This is where you get the real hard-core stuff—Ebola, Lassa fever, SARS, avian flu. We couldn't do better, if you want to save him."

"NAMRU-3 sounds perfect. But Sinclair doesn't have much time," Oakley said. "I'd like to go along with him to fill them in on what happened."

"You're already cleared. I have a helicopter standing by."

"How did you get that kind of transportation so quickly?"

"It's been on standby all night. In the worst-case scenario, it was supposed to be used by the president of the United States."

Sinclair sat in the corner and yanked the shirt away from his face. This was ridiculous. The spray had hit him four-square in the eyes and he had been lethally contaminated. Leaving his shirt tied over his nose and mouth now wouldn't accomplish much. He put the white oxford shirt back on and buttoned it up. Might as well meet his fate fully clothed.

That aerosol was clearly a death sentence. He knew that from Oakley's lecture. And if there was any doubt, it really struck home when the door to the safe room opened. Six medics walked in wearing biocontainment suits with their own air supply. They clomped over to him with the slow gait of astronauts. And when they talked their voices sounded robotic, transmitted through the microphones in their headgear.

"Hey, buddy," one of the spacemen said to him. "Hang on. We'll get you fixed up."

The condescending cheerfulness of the medical worker told Sinclair the whole story. They were speaking to him the way people spoke to terminally ill patients in the hospital.

"Let's get you into this." The medic indicated the gurney with a biocontainment tent. Clear plastic and stiff, it lay in jumbled folds, ready to be assembled. They pulled the tent off and Sinclair climbed onto the rolling stretcher. He lay there feeling foolish. After all, he still felt fine.

They began setting up the struts to support the plastic tent. He watched them struggle awkwardly with gloved fingers, then closed his eyes, trying to make it all go away.

How had this happened? In his mind he was transported back to the room at the Mark Hotel, the night of the gala in New York. He had been lying there just like this, a little lethargic from jet lag, anticipating a lovely evening. Cordelia had been moving about the room, and he was vaguely conscious of her fiddling with things as he dozed on the bed.

She had looked gorgeous that day, glowing with excitement about being in Manhattan. Sinclair remembered that he had entertained the thought of a seduction before the party, just to get the evening off to a jolly start. Cordelia was not in the mood at first—she was all fluttery about getting ready and concerned about the creases in her dress. As he dozed on the bed that evening, she had tried to quietly unzip the suitcase, but it had made a tearing sound and he had woken up.

The same sound occurred now. Sinclair opened his eyes and they were zipping him into the tent and closing the Velcro flaps over the teeth of the closure. A hiss of air was pumped in near his head and puffed up the tent. Cold air blew over his face.

He was fully sealed in, and he fought his claustrophobia for a moment, taking deeper breaths. Through the clear plastic, the figures were moving around the room.

"All set?" they asked him, and without waiting for an answer started to push him to the door.

Here we go, Sinclair thought. This is not the way he had pictured his end. But there really wasn't any choice. It was time to go.

Paul Oakley looked across the tarmac at Sharm el-Sheikh Airport and saw the waiting military helicopter. The rotors were already churning, and evacuation medics were standing, waiting for Sinclair. The airport was often used by the Egyptian military, and this operation had all the appearance of any other government flight, except the medics were pushing along what looked like a plastic coffin.

Sinclair was zippered into a negative-air-pressure biocontainment module, complete with oxygen and a microphone for speaking to the outside world. He was completely sealed in, rolling on a collapsible ambulance gurney, being pushed along by medics dressed in bulky suits and bubble helmets. As they got closer, Paul could see Sinclair's face through the plastic.

"Paul, how much time do I have?" Sinclair asked. His

voice sounded tinny on the microphone. Oakley looked at Sinclair's eyes. They were calm, resigned.

"Don't think like that, John. We are going to do all we can."

Sinclair blinked slowly and sighed.

"I know you will. But promise me one thing. Don't let Delia anywhere near me. If I'm going to die like this, I want to die alone."

Moustaffa was sitting in a private plane, heading back to the United States. He looked at his watch and laughed.

"It's done. Everyone is dead," Moustaffa declared.

"Think again, asshole," the military guard said to him. "They didn't fall for it."

Moustaffa's head jerked up, surprised.

"Your buddy John Sinclair tipped them off. They evacuated the building. Everyone got out safely. The press never knew."

"I demand a lawyer. I'm a British citizen," Moustaffa said. "You can't charge me with anything. I had nothing to do with any of this."

"Save it for the guys at Guantánamo. It's an act of terrorism," the guard replied. "Haven't you heard? We have a special place for people like you."

NAMRU-3, Cairo

THE MEDICAL UNIT officer at the front desk had been stonewalling Cordelia for several hours, saying that there was no record of any such patient. When she mentioned the word "plague," his eyes had widened, but he denied any knowledge of a case being admitted.

She became more and more infuriated, demanding to be let into the isolation unit to verify it herself. With each exchange he was icily polite, calling her "ma'am."

The desk officer was young, but he had the firm demeanor that comes with military training. Besides, she wasn't the first person to be denied admittance. This hospital—NAMRU-3—had been studying infectious diseases in the Middle East since the end of World War Two. They dealt with contagion every day.

"What do you mean, I can't go in!" Cordelia demanded, flailing her arms.

"Take it easy, Delia," Gardiner calmed her, putting a hand on her shoulder.

"I can't let anyone onto the sixth floor. Doctor's orders," the medical officer explained to Gardiner, as if to reason with someone sane.

"Doctor? *What* doctor?" Cordelia snapped. "*Who* is this so-called *doctor*!"

"Dr. Paul Oakley," he announced. "He's the head physician on this case."

Delia whirled around to face Gardiner.
"Jim! Do something!"

Paul Oakley came out looking weary. His white coat gave
him gravitas. Now he looked older, more beaten down.

Gardiner rose from the couch in the waiting room.

"Paul?"

Oakley didn't speak until he sat down next to Cordelia. All the steam had gone out of her. Now she was just
scared.

"Paul, what's going on?" she asked. Tears were trembling in her eyes.

"Sweetie, I wish I had better news," Paul Oakley said.
"He's . . ." He stopped and took a breath. "Well, we just
have to hope for the best."

"Do you mean he could . . . ?" Gardiner asked.

"It is a possibility."

"Ohhhhh God!" Cordelia howled, bending over, holding her stomach, and rocking back and forth. *"Oh God,
no! Please please please . . ."*

Gardiner stood in the hall with Paul Oakley.

"What's happening, Paul?" Gardiner asked.

"I don't think he's going to pull through, Jim," Oakley
said. "I'm sorry."

"Isn't there anything you can give him?"

"Yes, not to be too technical, but antibiotics can work
if the disease hasn't overwhelmed the body's defenses. I
gave him oral antibiotics on the way here and set up an
IV drip as soon as we got him into the isolation unit. So
far nothing has had any effect. I'm afraid it's the strain.

It's bubonic, luckily. If it were pneumonic, he'd be dead by now."

"You just sequenced the genome for the Black Death. Doesn't that kind of research help?"

"Not exactly. There were three major plagues, historically. The Black Death in medieval Europe, the Justinian plague in the sixth century, and then another in China in 1894. I have cross-referenced everything we know about those outbreaks."

"And?"

"This is different. We haven't seen anything like this. It's an enhanced pathogen. We ran it through a poly-merase-chain-reaction analysis . . ."

"No, wait! Don't start with the jargon," Gardiner said, holding up his hand. "You're going to have to slow down on this or I won't understand."

"Come have a look," Oakley said, walking over to a machine. It looked like a normal laptop with a huge computer attached. On the screen was a graph of multicolored lines fanning out into a wide spectrum.

"This is a PCR machine, one of the fanciest diagnostic tools in the world. It helps us analyze the DNA of the toxin Sinclair was exposed to," Oakley explained. "Within three hours of Sinclair's arrival here, we were able to sequence the DNA and confirm he had plague. The good news is it's bubonic and *not* pneumonic."

Oakley then reached over to the lab sink and picked up a sealed plastic container.

"This is a Mueller-Hinton agar—in other words, a type of petri dish for growing bacteria. This sample is only common flu. We are keeping the disk with Sinclair's plague in the negative-pressure lab. It's too contagious to handle like this. But I can show you how we run antibiotic susceptibility testing on this one. That would determine which drugs would help Sinclair."

Oakley held the plastic disk up to the light. It was cloudy with yellow film. White dots were scattered across its surface.

"Imagine that this petri dish has been coated with a sample of the disease that Sinclair is fighting. Each of these dots is an antibiotic," Oakley said, pointing to the dozen pinprick dots scattered across the surface.

"And what are you looking for?" Gardiner asked, squinting at it with interest.

"If a certain drug would be effective in treating the disease, there would be a clear ring around the dot, like a doughnut."

"I see a few circles that look like doughnuts," Gardiner observed.

"Which tells us that those antibiotics work on this strain of flu. Sinclair's plague needs twenty-four hours before we have results."

"And if there is no change the dish stays the same?" Gardiner asked.

"That would mean that the antibiotics are not effective for treating the strain of plague that Sinclair has," Oakley said dispiritedly.

"So it could be a lot stronger?"

"It may be a so-called designer disease, created to be antibiotic-resistant or evade immune responses. Even with the normal strains of plague, there is a high mortality rate. About fourteen percent of people who contract the disease die of it."

"I had no idea!" Gardiner gasped.

"There are about twenty cases a year in the United States. That jumps to about three thousand people globally."

"And vaccines . . . ?" Gardiner asked.

"Those have to be administered in advance. There aren't any commercially available vaccines."

"Why not?" Gardiner asked.

"Vaccines are hard to produce. They have to be made from heat-killed and chemically treated strains of bacteria cells. And there really is no demand for them, so it's not profitable to make a vaccine."

"So a city would be totally vulnerable if this contagion were released?"

"Pretty much. The U.S. government put in biodefense stockpiles of antitoxins and chemical antidotes after 9/11. But when it comes to vaccines they inoculate only researchers who are working with the plague."

"Which is why the terrorists chose this," Gardiner said.

"I'm afraid so. We've been working on plague at Porton Down for a few years now. Planning defensive measures in case of an attack. Sinclair is the first victim."

Oakley looked worn out. His white coat was sagging off his shoulders, and his face was drawn. It was clear he had not had any rest. Gardiner put a hand on his arm and spoke to him urgently.

"Paul, I'm going to ask you a favor," Gardiner said.

Oakley looked at him, resigned.

"What, Jim?"

"I need to see Sinclair. To ask him to please let Cordelia in. It's killing her, being shut out like this. If he dies without talking to her . . ."

Paul Oakley sighed.

"I promised I wouldn't let anyone in. Especially Cordelia. He was clear about it."

"He won't mind if it's me," Gardiner said. "After my accident, I came back from the *dead*. And he watched me do it."

Oakley looked off down the corridor, trying to decide.

"All right," he agreed. "Just for a few minutes."

"Thank you."

"You'll have to suit up, of course," Oakley added. "Come with me."

He turned and walked into the negative-pressure unit. Gardiner followed him in, limping heavily.

The room was silent, with the occasional beep of a machine taking an automatic reading—not the usual cramped hospital room, more like an operating theater. Plenty of space on either side of the bed to allow people to move around and work. No windows. The strong overhead light hurt the eyes.

The bed had all the appearance of a bier, and Sinclair was in a plastic tent, sealed like a glass coffin. Gardiner got a quick mental flash of an Egyptian king in his cartouche. The tent had the same dignity and finality. The body inside was pale, eyes closed. A shadow of the handsome man Gardiner knew.

Paul approached and checked the readings.

"Well, at least he's stable," the doctor remarked.

"Can he hear me?" Gardiner asked.

Just then, Sinclair's eyes opened. Then widened.

"Jim," he said weakly.

"How are you doing?" Gardiner asked.

The corner of Sinclair's mouth inched up as if he were trying to smile.

"Hurts like hell," he said. "I don't recommend it."

"Delia needs to see you," Gardiner said.

"Can't," Sinclair said, shutting his eyes wearily.

"Can't, or won't?" Gardiner pressed.

Oakley made a quick chop with his hand. A motion for Gardiner to lay off.

There was no answer. Sinclair's eyes were still closed. For a moment it seemed he had drifted off. Then his mouth slowly moved. He opened his eyes again.

"Can't see her. Not like this, Jim. Not like this," he said.

Sinclair's eyes dropped lower and then shut. He lapsed into a deep sleep.

Paul Oakley motioned for Gardiner to follow him out into the decontamination area.

"I told you. Stubborn as hell," Oakley said.

"God, I hate to see him like this," Gardiner said, pulling off his N95 mask, overcome with emotion.

"Don't give up yet," Oakley said. "That kind of mental toughness might be exactly what he needs to pull him through."

Cordelia sat up, feeling her head spin. She could be anywhere in the world—New York, London, Chicago. Hospital waiting rooms were all the same—the identical furniture, the same sorrow, and the lurking presence of death. Doctors had come and gone in a never-ending stream from the U.S. Navy, and some had flown in from the Centers for Disease Control and Prevention in the United States.

It had been two days. Gardiner had brought her food, a change of clothes. He had begged her to take a rest. To go to the hotel, grab a quick shower, take a nap. She would have none of it.

"I'm staying here, Jim," she had insisted.

Finally, Gardiner had left, limping painfully, shaking his head, promising he'd be back in a while. He needed to lie down.

Ted VerPlanck had come and gone several times, always solicitous, always deeply aware of the strain she was under. He'd comforted her as best he could. She could see that it took considerable effort for him to express his feelings. He was not a man who acknowledged his emotions easily.

VerPlanck was better at tangible things: bringing her a paper cup of tea and the cashmere throw he had first offered to her on the deck of *The MoonSonnet*. She was glad to have it. A security blanket. Cream-colored, soft. She had draped its folds around her as she waited.

They had cleared the unit when Sinclair came in. Only the specialists stayed. He was untouchable in a plastic tent. All she wanted to do was put her arms around him.

Down the hall the elevator dinged, and there was the *clack, clack, clack* of footsteps coming. Unfamiliar pace, rapid, determined. Cordelia looked up and her eyes widened in surprise as Holly Graham whipped around the corner. *What was she doing here?*

Holly was dressed in a coral-colored V-neck sweater, a blue jacket, and buff-colored slacks. Her figure was elegantly curvaceous. She walked with purpose. And she looked very worried.

"Hello, Cordelia," she said quite naturally, as if they spoke often. "I thought you might need something to eat."

She proffered a plastic bag.

"Oh, thank you."

"It's Egyptian beef and rice. Quite good."

Cordelia accepted it politely.

"What time is it?"

"Three o'clock," Holly told her.

"Three o'clock?"

Cordelia tried without success to understand that information. She had no idea if it was day or night.

"Three in the afternoon," Holly supplied, aware of her confusion. "Why don't you try to eat?"

Cordelia opened the bag and the rich scents wafted up.

"This smells really delicious!" she said.

"It's one of my favorites. The rice has almonds, golden raisins, cardamom, cinnamon. And beef with spices."

Cordelia took the lid off the container and found a plastic fork at the bottom of the bag.

"Is there anything to drink?" Cordelia inquired.

"There's a container of orange juice in there also."

"Thank you," Cordelia said, fishing for it. "I realize I never thanked you for that night, at the opera. It was very brave, what you did."

Cordelia found her words came with ease, and she meant them. Holly waved her hand, brushing away the gratitude, and quickly changed the subject.

"Hey, I meant to tell you," she said brightly. "The British have Artemidorus now. They say the damage can be repaired."

"That's great! What about the cup?"

"They just found it in a secret compartment of *The Khamsin.*"

"Ted VerPlanck must be pleased to recover it," Cordelia replied.

"Ted really believes the cup has special powers. He's determined to share it, for the benefit of others."

"Oh, that's nice of him," Cordelia replied.

"He is planning to donate the cup to the National Gallery in Washington so that the public can see it."

"That's wonderful," Cordelia said. "After all the trouble he went to recovering it."

"He's quite a generous man," Holly said, and Cordelia could see a glimmer of feeling behind the words.

Cordelia thought that Holly and VerPlanck would end up together. Not right now, but someday. They were so perfectly matched—elegant, understated.

"Have they let you in to see Sinclair yet?" Holly asked.

"No," Cordelia admitted.

"Well, he's a tough guy," Holly said. "Likes to fight his battles on his own."

"Really?" Cordelia asked. "Was he like that when you knew him?"

"Oh, *please,*" she said with a laugh, ignoring the nuances of the question. "He was always on his own, aloof."

"You think he still is?"

"Well, he *was,* until he found you. It's wonderful, Cordelia."

"We've been together in London for a few months now. But when I met him he was living in a really remote part of Ephesus. I think he communicated regularly only with his dog."

"He's a lone wolf. That's for sure."

Cordelia put her fork down and moved the aluminum-foil container to the side table. Her appetite had vanished.

Lone wolf. The image was so strong. Didn't they always go off on their own to die? Is that what was happening?

Holly leaned over and put her hand on Cordelia's arm.

"It's OK," she said. "Sinclair's the strongest man I have ever met. I think he'll pull through, and so does Ted."

Out on the street, it was warm. Holly peeled off her jacket and slung it over her shoulder. The military hospital had been freezing.

VerPlanck had urged Holly to visit the hospital, saying that Sinclair was hanging by a thread. By his account, Cordelia was having a very rough time, so Holly had gone to see her.

Everyone seemed to think Cordelia was perfect for Sinclair. It was time to clear the air. Wasn't that the phrase Sinclair had used that night when they had drinks?

Of course Cordelia had been surprised, but she was gracious and thanked Holly for her bravery the night of the opera. Silly girl. Holly had done it for Sinclair. Oh well, let Cordelia have her illusions.

Everyone was predicting Sinclair's imminent death. But there was no doubt in her mind that he would make it. He could not be felled by something so ancient as the Black Death. Sinclair was too strong. His spirit was indomitable.

Ted VerPlanck's dark car was idling across the street. With the smoked windows, it was hard to tell if Ted could see her or not. He had promised to take her to the Kom el-Shoqafa catacombs in the Karmouz district of Alexandria. It was a fourth-century royal mausoleum styled in the same pattern as the Christian catacombs in Rome.

Ted had been doing everything he could to cheer her up, convinced she must have PTSD from her experience. Of course, that was partially true. But Ted VerPlanck had already helped with the recovery.

VerPlanck opened the car door and stepped out.

"How's Cordelia?"

"Not great," Holly said.

"Wait here for me for a moment," Ted said. "I'll be right back."

The MoonSonnet Motorsailer,
N 40°03', E 26°17'

CARTER WALLACE STOOD on the deck of *The Moon-Sonnet* and felt the wind in his face. They were in the Dardanelles, heading to the Sea of Marmara and into the Bosphorus. First they'd stop off in Turkey, and then in a few days they'd be in the *Black Sea*!

VerPlanck had been very appreciative of Carter bowing out of Holly's life, and the billionaire made sure the consolation prize was sweet. *The MoonSonnet* was Carter's to use as he liked for a whole month!

The crew got him anything he wanted: club sandwiches, beer, even steak. And the freedom of it! He charted the course every day with the captain as they sat in the wheelhouse drinking their morning coffee. This was more fun than he had ever had in his entire life. Right now, they were planning on docking for a few days in Istanbul.

But lending the boat wasn't the end of the man's generosity. VerPlanck was going to fund a dig for Carter in the Valley of the Kings. And when Carter returned to New York they'd talk about his heading a new VerPlanck Center for Ancient Civilizations.

What an amazing guy! He really had turned out to be a prince. But the best part was Holly had found her match.

Carter laughed to himself. It had been silly of him to think he could ever capture the attention of a woman like Holly. She was like an Egyptian queen. Regal, unapproachable. Not in his league. It was a good thing schoolboy crushes were not fatal. No use mooning over things he couldn't have. He had a lot of life to live!

NAMRU-3

T ED VerPlanck walked through the silent corridors of NAMRU-3 carrying a wooden box with a brass handle. He held it as gingerly as if it were the most precious object on earth. To him, it was.

The Egyptian authorities had recovered the chalice in the hold of *The Khamsin* that morning. The moment the security guard placed the crate in his hands, VerPlanck knew what he was going to do. Since medieval times, the Sardonyx Cup was thought to have miraculous healing powers. Now he would put those powers to the test.

It wouldn't be easy. VerPlanck knew that he would have a hard time convincing some of the world's best doctors that an ancient cup could be used for a cure. He would ask that the cup be placed next to Sinclair's hospital bed. Medical science was failing; it was time for a higher power.

Ted firmly believed in the legend of the Sardonyx Cup's miraculous healings. Many evenings, as he had sat on his living room couch, he had felt a special aura around the pedestal—he could feel a benign force every time he came within a few feet of the cup.

VerPlanck moved through the hospital corridor with a sense of purpose, praying he wasn't too late. The only person he encountered was Cordelia, stretched out full length on a waiting room couch—fast asleep. She lay with one arm flung over her head, her face pale. VerPlanck lightened his tread so he would not wake her.

Around the next corner, the hallway was empty. This was the sixth floor, where severe contagion was treated. Only people with special clearance were allowed. By rights, he really shouldn't be here. On the left was the heavy glass window of the ICU, and through it he could see nurses and doctors standing around a large plastic tent.

Although the room was soundproof, VerPlanck had little doubt about what they were saying. Their postures were defeated, their gestures hopeless.

VerPlanck rapped on the outer pane of glass and six pairs of startled eyes looked at the unannounced visitor above their respirator masks. Oakley gestured for Ver-Planck to wait.

Ted took a few steps away and rested the crate on a counter.

Oakley came out of a negative-pressure air-lock door, drying his hands with a paper towel.

"Mr. VerPlanck, what are you doing here? And what's that?"

"The Sardonyx Cup."

There was a shocked pause, and Oakley's eyes hardened.

"Absolutely *not*! I certainly don't have your faith in miracles, and I don't think Sinclair buys into that sort of thing either."

"I'm not suggesting he does."

"Then *why* did you bring it?" Oakley replied, exasperated.

"I hired Sinclair to get this back for me. I want him to know he succeeded."

"He's not conscious."

"Even so, he might wake up."

Oakley's eyes flicked to the crate and back to Ver-Planck's face. His expression softened.

"Sinclair always says that he's a 'man of science.' He really wouldn't like any kind of mumbo-jumbo. Especially now."

"Please. I want to do *something*."

Oakley sighed and looked down at the ugly linoleum floor as he thought about it.

"OK. You win. I'm pretty much at the end of my options."

"Put it anywhere he can see it," VerPlanck advised.

"For the record, I think you're wasting your time. He's getting weaker."

"How long does he have?"

Oakley was silent.

"Surely you have some idea?" VerPlanck insisted.

Oakley's lips were pressed into a firm, professional line. He spoke with clinical detachment.

"If I had to guess, I'd say the odds are he'll be dead within the hour."

Sinclair opened his eyes. The room was empty. There was only the *shuussss shussss shusss* of compressed air pumping into the plastic biocontainment unit. His eyes focused on random things in the room, his gaze drifting aimlessly until it fell on something that didn't quite fit.

The Sardonyx Cup!

The patina of the beautiful object glowed in stark contrast to the modern steel instrument cabinets. Sinclair blinked, clearing his vision. No, it was not a drug-induced mirage—the richness of the amber-colored stone, the muted gleam of ancient gold were real!

His next thought was of Cordelia. She was safe! He had managed to keep her safe, and that's all that mattered. Where was she? When could he see her?

Suddenly, he realized he felt much better. The pain was no longer with him. His skin no longer felt like it was on fire. There were only petty annoyances now: a dry throat, the ache where the IV needle had punctured a vein. He could catalog a list of minor discomforts, but the grinding agony was gone.

Sinclair looked over at the door, but there was no one in sight. The machines kept up their deathly rhythm, thumping and wheezing, each computer-driven instrument tasked with keeping him alive. But suddenly he wanted the thing off, this goddamn plastic coffin. He wanted to sit up.

He tried to knock the tent away, but nothing happened. He was too weak. It was all he could do to slide his finger onto the bell. He felt for the oblong square and depressed the buzzer.

As he called the nurse, he realized he was going to make it. Life had stopped draining out of him and was filling him up again. He could feel his limbs and feet. His hands felt a twinge of energy. His lungs could draw air without effort.

He was going to live!

Jim Gardiner heard the phone ringing as he lay on the bed in the darkened hotel room. As he woke, his first thought was of Cordelia. She needed him.

Sinclair had died and he must go and hold her, as he had done so many times in the past—after the death of her parents and when he had come to see her at school. During graduations, weddings, funerals, every other event of her young life, he had been there. Wiping her tears, telling her to keep going, it would all be fine. Now it was time to do it again.

He sighed. He was so tired, so weak from this cursed illness. But he sat up, reaching for the ringing phone. Every joint creaked. He figured he could get dressed and get down there in about a half hour. It wouldn't take long. He lifted the receiver to his ear.

"Hello," he said.

"Jim, it's Paul!" Oakley was shouting. "He made it!"

"What?" Gardiner asked, still befuddled by sleep.

"Sinclair!" Oakley said. "He's awake and talking. Cordelia is with him now. They're together."

"*Oh, thank God,*" Gardiner said. "*Thank God!*"

Acknowledgments

I WOULD LIKE to express appreciation to all who have supported me in writing this novel. My deepest love and gratitude goes to Maurice Tempelsman for all the advice, direction, insight, and encouragement, as well as unflagging enthusiasm for my new career.

Much love to my wonderful sons, William and Beau Croxton, for all their help on this and every other project I undertake.

Many thanks to my family—Campion, Susan, Nan, and Ted Overbagh—for their advice and encouragement.

I feel privileged to be associated with the excellent team at Scribner. Many thanks for superb professionalism on every aspect of publication: Roz Lippel, for great insight in the editing and shaping of this book; Brian Belfiglio and Lauren Lavelle, for publicity; Kara Watson and Greg Mortimer, for online advice; the art team of Rex Bonomelli; and copy editor Katie Rizzo.

I would like to express deep gratitude to my agent, Mort Janklow, for encouragement and excellent advice along my new path as a fiction writer—and for mentoring me in such a thrilling new career. Much appreciation to the firm of Nancy Seltzer & Associates: Nancy Seltzer, Aron Gerson, Kim Correro, Tamara Trione, and Minda Gowen, for expert help with the difficult job of publicity.

I am deeply grateful for the help and guidance of the

visual team for this series—they are beyond compare. Photographer Carol Seitz and stylist Kim Wayman always can be counted on for exceptional talent in producing and styling author and online photos. My heartfelt thanks also to photographer William Croxton, who put in grueling hours on still photography and video production while on location in Egypt and Scotland, as well as the oversight and production of edited documentary videos. Much appreciation to Buttons editing company in New York for their professional help in producing videos for the book: Rich Macar and Paul Levin.

In terms of research, many people have been generous with their time and have allowed me access to wonderful new places of interest for my readers.

I would like to express deep appreciation to the Naval Medical Research Unit—NAMRU-3—for their help and hospitality while I was visiting Cairo to research infectious disease treatment: Captain Robin Wilkening, Dr. David Rockabrand, and Captain Joseph Surette.

I would like to thank the Brooklyn Museum curators in researching this book: Dr. Edward Bleiberg, curator of Egyptian, Classical, and Ancient Near Eastern Art, and Lisa Bruno, conservator of objects, for all their excellent information on ancient mummies and for allowing me to accompany their team for a CT mummy scan.

Many thanks to Paul Pomfret, property manager of Culzean Castle, and all the curators and staff for their hospitality during my multiple visits to Scotland to research the history of the Eisenhower Apartment.

Thanks to the National Gallery of Art in Washington,

D.C., for research and information about the real Sardonyx Cup.

Heartfelt thanks for the nautical and navigational help of Captain Joe Russell and Captain Ben Batsch. If *The Khamsin* is off course, the fault is entirely mine.

And last, special thanks to my wonderful supportive friends and colleagues who have cheered me on.